IN THE GRIEVING OF HER DAYS

Francis
with best wishes
Lucy

September 2020

Other books by Lucy Beckett

Novels

The Time before You Die

A Postcard from the Volcano

The Leaves are Falling

The Year of Thamar's Book

Non-fiction

Wallace Stevens

Richard Wagner's Parsifal

York Minster

In the Light of Christ: Writings in the Western Tradition

Poems

The Returning Wave

In the Grieving of her Days

Lucy Beckett

GRACEWING

First published in England in 2020
by
Gracewing
2 Southern Avenue
Leominster
Herefordshire HR6 0QF
United Kingdom

www.gracewing.co.uk

ISBN 978 085244 902 8

Typeset by Word and Page, Chester, UK

Cover design by Bernardita Peña Hurtado

*For my son Ben Warrack, once a soldier
and his wife Charlotte Manisty, a doctor*

Nunc vero anni mei in gemitibus, et tu solacium meum, domine, pater meus aeternus es. at ego in tempora dissilui quorum ordinem nescio, et tumultuosis varietatibus dilaniantur cogitationes meae, intima viscera animae meae, donec in te confluam purgatus et liquidus igne amoris tui.

Et stabo et solidabor in te, in forma mea, veritate tua.

Truly now in the grieving of my days, you Lord, my eternal Father, are my consolation. For I have fallen apart in times whose coherence I cannot grasp, and my thoughts, the innermost guts of my soul, are torn to pieces by upheavals of every kind, until in you I shall flow together, cleansed and melted in the fire of your love.

Then I shall stand and be whole in you, in your truth, which gives me form.

Saint Augustine
Confessions 11.29–30

Part 1

27–30 September 2019

When she had rattled the lift gate shut with a final clang, Clare Wilson, seventy-seven years old and carrying a shopping basket, heard her telephone ringing inside the flat. It went on ringing, persistent, annoying, while she got her bag out of the basket and her key out of the bag, opened her front door and reached the kitchen.

"Mum! Where've you been? I've been trying to find you for hours."

"Darling, I'm sorry. I've been out."

"Out where?"

"Just out. I went to Mass, actually, and then—"

"Mass? But it's Friday."

"There's no law against going to Mass on a Friday."

"O, honestly, Mum! Why don't you have your mobile switched on like everyone else in the universe?"

"And have it go off in the middle of Mass? Certainly not. Anyway, I didn't take it with me. It's on the table."

"Well, there you are. Pointless having it, as I've said before. And why don't you leave the message turned on for the landline?"

"Penny, please don't be so cross. I'm old, don't forget. I don't have to like answering machines and mobile telephones. I see people crashing into each other in the street because they're gazing at a telephone instead of looking where they're going. Anyway, what were you trying to find me for?"

"Can't you imagine? When I couldn't find you, I wanted to make sure you were OK."

"Of course I'm OK."

"You never know. Accidents happen. But in the first place I was ringing to see if you had any ideas about this boy I ran into—well, I didn't exactly meet him, but he put this note in my hand when I was in the petrol station."

"What boy? What note?"

"Sorry. I'll start again. I was filling up the car in that huge place on the South Circular. Rows of petrol pumps, you know the one. I went to the shop bit to pay and when I came back there was this boy washing the windscreen with one of those long mops. He didn't stop when I wanted to open the car door, so I said "Thanks" and hoped he'd go, but he leant over me as I got in and before I could shut the door he produced this piece of paper, out of his pocket I suppose. He was still holding the mop in his other hand. I had to take the piece of paper and I put it on the seat beside me and drove off. When I got home I looked at it. Capital letters. Just three words. FROM LIBYA HELP."

"Libya? O darling, how awful. What did you do?"

"I haven't done anything, except try to find you. At first I thought I'd just tear up the note and forget it. I did tear it up and put the bits in the bin. But then it seemed—I don't know—wrong to do absolutely nothing. I thought you—well, perhaps not you but your friend, what's his name, Hakim, might know what to do. If this boy is really from Libya."

Penny knew perfectly well what Hakim's name was.

"What about Charles?" Clare said. "Have you told him?"

"Absolutely not. You know Charles. He'd say tell the police—it's their business, this sort of thing. He'd say 'this young man's probably an illegal immigrant'—can't you hear him?—'God knows how he got here. They all say they're from countries they can't be sent back to, where they might be tortured and all that, when most of them aren't and no one can check. Libya's a very good example.' That's what Charles would say. He says it when there are boats on the news, being picked up with people arriving from France. He thinks there are far too many immigrants already, half of them only pretending to be refugees. You know he does. Boris told them, just the other day, these people in boats, 'We'll send you back', didn't he?"

Clare thought for a moment or two. Penny was right, about Charles at least. Clare had heard him, several times, use the dismissive phrase "economic migrants", as if that description dissolved people's existence as desperate human beings.

"Mum? Are you still there?"

"I'm still here. How old do you think he is, this boy?"

"Sixteen, maybe. He could be older. Or even younger. Very thin."

"Is he black?"

"Black as your hat. That's why he can't be from Libya, can he? Libya is Arabs isn't it? Maybe Charles is right. Maybe I should ring the police."

Doesn't she read the papers?

"No. Please don't. What if he has no ID, no passport? They'd arrest him and put him God knows where. Better to do nothing than tell the police. And anyway, Penny, it's Friday afternoon. Aren't you going to Leckenby?"

"Not today. Chaos in parliament. You must have noticed. We have to be here in case there's a vote. And we're going to Manchester tomorrow. Party Conference. It starts on Sunday."

"Of course."

Clare, who had noticed, because she did read a paper and always listened to the middle hour of the Today programme, hesitated, and then said, "What does Charles think is going to happen next?"

"He doesn't say. Probably he has no idea. I don't think any of them know what's going to happen except maybe the little group in Downing Street. But Charles thinks Boris is wonderful and we'll win the election whenever it happens. That's all he cares about, really."

"And you, what do you think?"

"I don't think. MPs' wives aren't paid to think. Boris makes a nice change from boring old Mrs May, I must say. But I do wish it was all over. Brexit this, Brexit that, Brexit the next thing. I'm sick to death of the whole business. Aren't you, Mum, sick of it, I mean?"

"Not exactly."

3

In sixty years of adult life, she had never cared so much about any public issue.

"So, look", Penny was still talking. "Can I leave it with you? What to do about the boy. If anything. It's rather your sort of thing, isn't it?"

"Yes, leave it with me. Poor boy, in any case. I'll think. I'm very glad you told me."

"Thanks, Mum. 'Bye."

"Goodbye, darling. 'Bye. Have a nice time in Manchester."

She got up from the kitchen table, took off her mac, and hung it on its hook in the hall of the flat, really only a passage with a small table, big enough for the post and a hairbrush, and a mirror and a row of hooks. She had lived here for so many years, for thirty years with Simon, for ten more by herself, hardly moving anything, that the mechanics of everyday life were more or less automatic. Home, in other words. Back to the kitchen. Kettle. Mug. Teabag. She put away the shopping, milk, a Camembert and two slices of ham in the fridge, two expensive fishcakes in the freezer, spinach and tomatoes in the veg rack, a couple of brown rolls, good with honey, in the bread bin, and reached out to turn on the radio for the five o'clock news programme, changed her mind, and didn't.

She sat down with her mug of tea, to think.

If she still had a car, would she drive off, now, to the South Circular in the middle of the Friday evening rush hour to see if she could find first the right garage and then Penny's thin black sixteen-year-old asking for help?

Well, would she? Probably she wouldn't. She had heard on the radio a couple of programmes about modern slavery. Suppose this boy were being kept as a slave by sinister Albanians, or whoever? Trying to find him, asking about him in the garage, might be dangerous. Or might make Charles so furious, if he found out what she'd done, that life would be difficult for Penny. "Your mother is unbelievable. Why can't she just be a nice old lady minding her own business?"

She had gone on an anti-Brexit march and he was angry when her photograph was in the Evening Standard, though no one identified her or made anything of it. She had also gone on the great Stop the War march in 2003. Charles was all for the war, and therefore embarrassed by the scale of the march, but only said wasn't she too old for demos? In 2003 he hadn't yet become a politician.

All the same, she was glad Penny had told her about the boy. She might not have. She was, mostly, too much under Charles's thumb, perhaps too admiring of him—no doubt a good thing in its way—to do anything he might not approve of. In nearly thirty years as his mother-in-law, Clare had never seen the point of Charles, beyond his being, so long ago when he married Penny, quite good-looking, with an attractive voice. He had always seemed stupid as well as ambitious and competent, unaware of what other people might feel, guaranteed to miss anything beyond or beneath the immediately obvious,

Simon, never quite a Marxist but all his life a socialist, or at any rate a committed member of the Labour party, had disliked Charles from the beginning. He had treated him, for Penny's sake, with politeness, but a politeness that had never rung true. She often wondered whether Penny, who didn't notice much more than Charles did, had heard the slight falseness in her father's voice, talking to Charles, talking to Penny about Charles. Simon did at least love, and spoil, Penny's two girls when they were small children.

When Penny, obviously proud of him as a presentable, well-set-up boyfriend with a good salary and a flat in Pimlico, first brought Charles home, he was a boring, confident young man, working in the City doing something neither Penny nor Clare had even tried to understand. Simon, who was an economist, did understand Charles's work, didn't bother to explain beyond "It's all about moving money that isn't actually money from one notional place to another for rich people who have no idea of how the process works. It's very profitable." He clearly didn't approve. Now Charles was a boring, confident middle-aged MP, who had spent, Clare suspected, some of the fortune he seemed to have earned in the City in donations to the Conservative party, which, in collusion with the dozen local Tories who actually chose the safe-seat MP, had given him an unlosable constituency for his second effort to get into the House of Commons. (His regulation first attempt had been in a safe Labour seat in south London where he and Penny had dutifully canvassed without any expectation of winning.) That the constituency was in Yorkshire, and that Clare's mother's family house, where her cousin's son now lived, was in the constituency, had no doubt helped the selection of Charles as the candidate, and made it possible for Charles to give Penny the joy of spending half her life in Yorkshire which she much preferred to London. She also, her mother knew, ever since she was a small child staying with her Yorkshire cousins in the school holidays, had always much preferred horses to people.

Charles and Penny had a smallish house, once a vicarage, not far from her cousin's, where they spent most weekends. Penny's two horses were looked after by a girl in the village in return for riding them when Penny was in London, and Penny hunted on Saturdays in the winter. On Saturday evenings they often held or attended fund-raising efforts of various kinds for the Tory party or the hunt. This life, with the assumptions that supported it, had seemed old-fashioned to Clare when she was growing up; that the web of associations, kept going by the same families two generations later, had survived another sixty years was difficult to believe but an evident fact.

Charles on most Friday afternoons held a constituency surgery in one of the market towns he represented. Clare had often wondered about these unscheduled, unrecorded meetings with random local people turning up to ask for help. Charles was probably quite effective when he could see there was something he could do, banging heads together with a couple of telephone calls to County Hall, or writing, or getting his secretary to write, a firm letter to the local hospital trust. But if there were nothing he could do because the person opposite him across the table was only unhappy or mad or needed someone, anyone, to talk to, or all three, Charles would be unlikely to have the faintest idea how to help. Tough, he was. Tough can be successful in front of an audience—she had seen Charles at hustings meetings in town halls—but is very much less successful with one other person. No wonder his daughters, Penny's daughters too, of course, so pretty and bright when they were little, were now, grown-up, as far away as they could get, or that was how it seemed to Clare. One had taken a degree in social sciences at Royal Holloway; this was an enterprise her grandfather would have approved of as left-wing but her father scorned for the same reason. She was rebuilding an earthquake-damaged village with an NGO in Nepal. The younger girl was in Vancouver where she had chosen to go to university. They emailed their grandmother very occasionally, to thank her for money she had sent for their birthdays, or to say, when they remembered her, that they were fine. Penny seemed not to miss them at all.

Clare missed them, particularly Carrie who was in Nepal, and whose company she had now and then enjoyed when Carrie was a student in London. They had gone to the theatre together and to one or two Proms concerts: Clare's flat was a quarter of an hour's walk from the Albert Hall. Carrie noticed things, found Clare's spectacles before she realized she was looking for them, had always registered the one thing in that day's *Guardian*, which naturally she read on line, that Clare had also thought particularly important (Charles read the *Daily Telegraph*; Penny seemed not to read anything), and before Nepal had for years given Clare for Christmas or her birthday one new paperback that she hadn't heard of and always found properly interesting. "I knew you'd like him. We men of the left must stick together."

She finished her tea and put the kettle on again. More tea might help. This boy of Penny's at the petrol station. What should she do? What could she do? Carrie would have thought of a plan. Actually Carrie, who was fearless, would probably have set off for the South Circular on the bike she rode everywhere in London and found and rescued the boy.

"Your friend Hakim might know what to do", Penny had said. Well, perhaps.

Penny had met Hakim once, five years ago when he had not long been in London and was staying in Clare's flat. Hakim was flawlessly polite to Penny, as he always was to everyone, and after a few minutes of awkwardness from Penny, had left for the Museum.

"Really, Mum. Is this sensible? Collecting this Arab out of nowhere just because he took something out of your eye on that cruise. Remember how fragile you were then, only a few months after Dad died, and not that long after Matt as well. Particularly Matt. You probably over-reacted. Quite understandable if you did."

"Don't patronize me, Penny. I was sad about Dad. I still am. But I hadn't become an idiot just because I was a widow. As for Matt - Matt had nothing to do with it."

This was probably not true, she admitted to herself but not to Penny.

"I'm not saying you'd become an idiot", Penny had said. "Far from it. You've always been cleverer than any of us except Dad. Just that you were vulnerable then. And a Libyan, of all people! Libya's a terrible country, Charles says. Always has been. This chap might seem OK to you. He obviously seemed OK when you met him over there, being a guide or whatever he was being. But how much do you really know about him? How do you know he isn't a terrorist? Charles is horrified that you got him over here and even more horrified that he's living in the flat. Charles says, 'Tell your mother to remember Lockerbie.'"

"So like Charles, to make such a fuss. He really needn't worry. Lockerbie was more than twenty years ago, and was all to do with Colonel Gaddafi. Hakim's family suffered terribly from things the Gaddafi regime did, and would never have got mixed up with terrorists. In any case, Hakim's a scholar. I told you. He's a classical archaeologist. He was trained in Beirut and Palmyra and he knows a great deal about the Greek and Roman cities of Libya and the Middle East. His Greek and Latin are both excellent. Also his English, as you've just seen. He learnt English off the Internet and in the year he spent studying in Beirut, because in Gaddafi's Libya English was completely forbidden."

"That doesn't mean he mightn't be dangerous."

"Dangerous to me? I don't think so. Or perhaps you mean dangerous to Charles? Even if I'm wrong to trust him, and I'm sure I'm not, you might tell Charles that what MPs' mothers-in-law get up to doesn't usually do much damage to MPs' reputations."

"Mum! Charles is worrying about you, not about his reputation. Well, hardly at all. And I suppose he's a keen Muslim? Charles thinks after 9/11 we shouldn't trust any Muslims. Your chap could easily be a terrorist as well as an archaeologist, don't you see? Some of the bombers here have been doctors. And another thing. You need to be careful he doesn't want money off you. I can see he's a plausible sort of character."

"Penny! If everyone were to expect the worst of everyone else, where would we all be?"

"Safer, probably", Penny said.

Clare had tried to bring up Penny and Matt as Catholics, but she had failed, or perhaps the Church had failed, to keep either of them alongside her. She had taken them to Sunday Mass until they were too old and too bored for her to make them come with her. She had had no support from Simon. In fact, the opposite. "Why should they go? It's your thing. It may well not be theirs." She knew she should have been strong enough to persuade Simon to let her send them to Catholic schools, but it was no good: he was adamant that, after his own privileged education, in an Anglican public school where daily prayers and Sunday church had, he said, convinced him at fourteen and for good that God did not exist, his children were definitely going to state schools, and definitely not to Catholic state schools. He thought Catholic schools even worse than Anglican schools because, according to him, their only reason for existing was the indoctrination of the young who should be free to make up their own minds about everything.

Penny, growing up, had never shown the slightest interest in the Church or anything to do with religion. She had been married in the village church, Anglican, at home, Clare's mother's home, in Yorkshire, more because she liked the oldness of the church and wanted to please Charles's parents than for any religious reason. (Clare herself, at the time a recent Catholic convert, had also been married in Yorkshire, though in the nearest, dowdy, Victorian, Catholic church. Simon had, without enthusiasm, gone along with this; Clare's mother had been mortified. "Such a shame, darling, not to have a proper wedding. People won't understand.")

Matt, particularly after he joined the army, had at least once or twice asked her questions about what she really believed. Looking back now, as she often had in the years, twelve years already, since his death, she remembered, not for the first time, one conversation in particular. It had taken place late at night when Simon had gone to bed and long after Penny had married and left the flat, and it had begun because Matt was staying for a few days' leave before he was to go to Iraq with his regiment. It must have been in the winter of 2005.

She had asked him if he was afraid, setting off for a war.

"Well, a bit, I suppose. But actually in an odd way more interested than afraid. A war, you know, an actual war. It's what soldiers are trained for. A war rather than a mess we're sent into to make it marginally less horrible, like Northern Ireland or Republika Serbska." He had served in both, for several months. "People hating each other for no reason except who they are. At least Saddam Hussein was a proper enemy to fight. Though it does sound as if it's changed, or changing, from a war into a mess."

Alas, Clare thought, on this ordinary day in September 2019: how much more of a mess Iraq is now than it was then, even though then there was officially a war. When there was any news from Iraq, now way down the list of priorities because of Syria and Yemen and wretched Afghanistan, though not as far down as Libya, it was always bad. ISIS was supposed to be over, but there went on being stories of suicide attacks and fights between different kinds of Muslim, some Iraqi, some not. And there were still plenty of refugees who couldn't get out, and others who couldn't get back. And the government was weak enough, and hated by enough of its own people, to make Baghdad a place where people were still killed all the time.

Matt—she could see him in her mind's eye on that long-ago evening—got up from the corner of the sofa where he had been sitting, poured himself a weak whisky and soda from the drinks tray on the chest of drawers, and sat down in his father's armchair.

"Did you know", he said, "when they're sending you to a war zone they make you write a letter to your parents in case you're killed. I did one before we went to Bosnia. Last week I thought I'd better have another go. I'm supposed to be more grown-up than I was then. But I found it really difficult to decide what to put. I kept starting and stopping and thinking 'Dad would think that soppy'." He laughed. "Dad's such a one for seeing through things. He'd think I'd written stuff only to please you, not really meaning it. He'd be wrong, but that's what he'd think."

"That's a bit hard, darling. Poor old Dad. You mustn't think he'd be cynical about something like that. He wouldn't."

"I don't know. He might. Me and Dad—it hasn't been great, has it? I've always felt he was disappointed I wasn't cleverer. When I was at school I think he thought I didn't bother enough. I expect he was right. But if I'd bothered more, I still wouldn't have done as well as he hoped. I nearly put something about all that in the letter. Then I thought if I was dead I didn't want Dad to be remembering my school reports, so I didn't."

"Quite right. To leave all that out, I mean. Water under the bridge. After all, you did perfectly OK at university and you've done so well in the army."

"Respectably, I suppose you could say. And after making such a fuss to start with, Dad's actually been pretty good about the army. Better than I expected. He's even sometimes sounded quite interested in what I'm doing."

"He's proud of you."

This was true. Simon had been proud of what Matt had done as a soldier so far, particularly in Bosnia, where it had been possible to do some solid work rebuilding broken villages and broken communities. Since 2003 Simon had been convinced, as she was, that the war in Iraq was a hideous mistake and wished Matt didn't have to go there. Both of them had tried never to let Matt see that this was what they thought.

"Is he? Well, perhaps. If he really is, I'm glad. Though I still don't understand why was he so negative when I decided to be a soldier."

"He was negative about the army, not about you. You know why it was: he didn't think much of the army when he'd had to do National Service all those years ago. He was mostly in Germany, ruined Germany, not very long after the war, and he thought a lot of what the National Servicemen had to do was fairly pointless. Years later he was still grumbling about sergeant majors yelling furiously at homesick boys about nothing much. And for some time after that what wars we had were nasty colonial affairs, Malaya, Cyprus, Kenya, of the kind he hated and felt ashamed of, long before it was fashionable to be ashamed of the empire."

Remembering Simon vividly for a moment, she recognized all over again how often he was right, because he used his intelligence, and because his moral sense was acute even though he believed in no God to back his idea of what was right.

"But I think really he just felt he was wasting time. He'd got a scholarship to Cambridge. He wanted to get on with his life. But that was the 1950s, another world. He knows that now. He's been impressed by what you've told him, and by how obviously you think much of what you've done hasn't been a waste of time."

Matt picked up his glass. Clare was holding a mug of camomile tea in both hands.

Looking back now, she remembered the hot mug.

"Mum - "

"What?"

"If I'm killed in Iraq, what would Dad think?"

She put the mug down to give herself a few seconds.

"What would he think? He wouldn't think. He'd be shattered. In pieces. As I would be. Just as much as I would be. You know that, don't you?"

"I didn't mean would he care. I meant would he think it worth it? Is what's going on in the Middle East worth fighting for? Worth dying for? Is Mr Blair tagging along with President Bush worth dying for? Specially now that Saddam Hussein's in prison and can't do any more harm. And there weren't any WMD after all."

"Soldiers have to do what they're ordered to do by a government that honestly thinks it's doing its best for the peace of the world."

"Mum! That sounds like a speech you've made to Dad when he was saying we should never have gone into Iraq. He hasn't said it to me but it's perfectly obvious what he feels. Millions of people feel the same of course. I'm sure plenty of soldiers do, but we can't say so. It's a bit like barristers. They have to do their best for a criminal, even if they're quite sure he's guilty, only neither the criminal nor the barrister must actually say so."

She couldn't answer this.

Matt didn't know that two years before she had walked up to Hyde Park to join the march against the war. She had asked Penny to come with her. "Mum! It'll be horrible! Far too many people. I couldn't bring the pushchair. Anyway, Charles thinks we've got to deal with the weapons of mass destruction. And I've got to fetch Carrie from school."

Stop the War. If only. Simon had sympathized but thought demonstrating a waste of time. Rightly, as it turned out.

So she went back a bit.

"Dad knows you'll always do what you have to do, because that's what you signed up for when you joined the army."

"That's how we have to think, how I have to think, isn't it? It's what you're trained to think. And the bottom line is that a few people have got to be soldiers, haven't they? And once they've decided to be soldiers, they have to do what they're told. Do their best, like barristers have to, whatever they think. Anyhow—"

He leant forward in Simon's armchair.

"When I was trying to write this letter, it was easy to imagine you and Dad reading it. You'd be crying. Dad would be trying not to cry. Here in the flat. You sitting there. Him sitting here. After what? A telephone call? A soldier on the doorstep? It used to be a telegram, didn't it? In the First World War, those telegrams you read about, so many of them. You and Dad would be here. Facing each other. Like this. Where would I be? Dead. What does that mean, really?"

Remembering now him saying this, she knew it had been exactly as he described it when there was, two years later, the soldier on the doorstep with the news that he had been killed in Afghanistan, in Helmand province, by an IED. "What's an IED?" she had said. "A bomb, Clare", Simon had said. "An amateur bomb." And when the soldier had gone, they had sat facing each other in misery, with Matt dead, an absence between them, always until Simon's death, and now an absence in her because she was by herself. But also a presence. Every night before she went to sleep she prayed for a list, lengthening now that she was old and more and more people were dying, of those she loved who were dead. Matt and Simon were at the top of the list, and then her father, and her mother whom she found more difficult to remember clearly. Safe with God.

But all those years ago, on that evening before he went to Iraq, she had said, "O darling. Such an enormous question."

She had picked up her still hot tea, taken a sip and then put the mug down again, on the straw mat, still there, on the table beside her chair.

"I wish I knew how to answer it", she said. "I'm not sure anyone knows how to answer it."

"Come on, Mum, you're a Catholic. A proper Catholic. Probably the only one I know apart from the odd priest one comes across. There was a good padre with the regiment in Bosnia. He used to say Mass at the back of a jeep with a few soldiers gathered round. They turned up whether they were Catholics or not. Perhaps he would have known the answer. But you should, if anyone does. All those years and years of going to Mass."

She thought of her father, her much-loved father, who had died at home in his flat in Hampstead, where he had lived alone for ten years after her mother's death. He had moved there because he had always liked Hampstead, where he had lived as a refugee when he first came to London, and because, by himself, he needed only a small flat. He died so quietly, in his sleep, in the early hours of the morning, that though she and the nurse who had helped her through those last weeks were watching him, the moment of his death was not perceptible, at least not to her. Yet when the nurse said, "He's gone", that was exactly how it seemed. He'd gone. The body lying in his bed looked exactly as it had looked a few moments ago when he was, just, breathing. But the body was no longer him. He had gone. Away. Where to? The life, the breath, the spirit, the soul: what had gone? Where to? She had leant over the bed and, with her thumb, drawn the sign of the cross on his forehead, smiling a little as she thought how he, who had regarded the Catholic Church as a malign organization, both anti-Semitic and un-English, would have said, indulgently, "Well, if you must, you must." Then she sat beside his bed for perhaps twenty minutes, while the nurse went down to the kitchen and made them both cups of tea, in what was the deepest, quietest silence she had ever known. God bless him, she had thought, and nothing else.

"I don't know the answer, darling. If anyone said they were certain of the answer, I wouldn't believe them. But I do know that there is an answer."

"I don't understand."

"I don't know what happens when someone dies. I know that a dead person isn't here, with us, in the world of time and change, where his body or her body is, left behind. But I also know that the person isn't nowhere, no longer anything, like a candle-flame that has been blown out. If there were only emptiness and the black wick of the candle, then the life of that person wouldn't, in the end, have meant anything at all. You know, like Macbeth said, a tale told by an idiot, full of sound and fury, signifying nothing. But that isn't how it is. A life has meaning. When someone dies, we consign the person to God, send them to the safekeeping of God who gave them the spark of life. God is the guarantee of the meaning of each person's life, beyond time and place, in his eternity."

"But what if you don't believe in God? I don't. Dad doesn't. Most people don't."

"It makes no difference."

"Really? No difference? How can you say that, Mum?"

She thought. She longed for him to understand.

"If there is no God, what I'm saying is nonsense, wishful thinking, superstitious rubbish, whatever you like to call it. But if there is God, in whom all our lives begin and end and mean what they mean, then whether or not people believe that this is so makes no difference."

Matt looked at her and frowned. When he frowned he looked more than usual like Simon.

"That can't be right, can it? How can it make no difference? It's no good, Mum. I don't understand."

She wasn't going to give up. She thought some more.

"Have you seen *Casablanca*?"

"You know I have. You took me and Penny to see it years and years ago when I was about twelve. And there's a video of it here somewhere. I must have seen it three or four times at least. "

"Well then. You remember at the very end, when Humphrey Bogart lets her go away with her good, boring husband, he says, 'It doesn't take much to see that the problems of three little people don't amount to a hill of beans in this crazy world.'"

She nearly cried, saying the words, because Matt, in a few days, was going away to fight in a war.

"Of course I remember. No one ever forgets the end, like no one forgets the *Marseillaise* in the bar. But I don't see what it's got to do with God."

"What it's got to do with God is that either the problems of three little people really don't amount to a hill of beans, because people come and go, live and die, in a meaningless universe. Or people's love and courage and self-sacrifice for a noble end mean a very great deal. Which of those do people feel at the end of the film?"

"The second, of course."

"Well, there you are."

Matt looked at her as if she were slightly mad.

"Am I? Where?" he said.

She laughed.

"Never mind. Let's try something easier."

She drank the rest of her camomile tea and put down her mug.

16

"Imagine a ghastly prison camp, in Siberia, say. It's the middle of winter. There's typhus. A young man is dying, with a high temperature, a rash all over him, shivering, hallucinating. An old prisoner knows it would be sensible to leave the boy to die without touching him. Instead, he wraps him in his own worn-out blanket, his own padded coat which is falling to pieces, hugs him for a bit more warmth, comforts him with old prayers which the boy probably doesn't even hear and wouldn't recognize if he did. When he dies the old prisoner takes back his coat and his blanket, wraps himself up against the cold, and a week later is feverish himself. After a few days he dies. Both of them are buried in shallow graves hacked out of the frozen ground by other prisoners. No names to mark the graves. Only numbers in the camp records. Is the last kindness of the old man to the young prisoner without meaning, without value, because not known about in the camp among all the misery, not known about anywhere, and useless in ordinary terms since both will sooner or later die? Or is it good because it is known, recognized as good, somewhere else?"

"How do you mean, somewhere else?"

"In what the Russians call 'eternal memory'. The eternal memory of God."

"But Mum, how do you know there is such a thing?"

"I don't know. I believe."

"It's beyond me, the whole thing's completely beyond me."

"That's fine. All of it's beyond all of us, and always will be. But there, beyond time, to eternal memory, is where, through death, we travel. Or so I believe. Never mind, for now. Just— when you're out there, and it's scary, and maybe there will be deaths, injuries, whatever—remember that everything means something. It does help."

"I suppose. Perhaps I vaguely see what you mean."

"One question, one short question, to bear in mind. It was asked in some book, I can't remember which, by a Polish poet, one of my heroes, who died last year, very old. Here's the question: 'Where is the truth of unremembered things?'"

Matt was silent. For a minute or two she let him think, and then said, "You see?"

"You mean", eventually he said, "that if God doesn't remember unremembered things they are lost for ever. Is that right?"

"Yes. It may not be right but it is what I mean. And it's a very comforting thought if one has to look at the possibility of death—which isn't just a possibility after all, but a certainty that each of us is going to have to face one day."

Another long silence. Then Matt said, "It is. A comforting thought, I mean. As well as death being a certainty. I wouldn't have expected to think so, but I do. At least for now. Thank you, Mum."

Then she said, "O darling, come back safely. Please."

He laughed.

"I'll try."

She swiftly regained her grip on herself.

"Succeed. As I used to say to schoolboys late with essays, 'Can you get it to me by Tuesday?' 'I'll try.' 'Succeed.'"

He laughed again.

She stood up and said, "Now we must both go to bed. It's late."

"Mum", he said, as he also stood up, and leant over to switch out the light on the table beside his father's chair. "Have you ever said all that to Dad?"

"No. I haven't even tried. It wouldn't be any good. You know Dad. He would classify the whole subject under 'religion' and stop listening at once because, according to him, religion is nothing but nonsense people console themselves with because they're not brave enough to face the truth. Actually what we've been talking about isn't exactly religion. Religion is much more about what you do than about what you think."

"Is it? Is it really? I didn't know that. So the boys gathered round the padre saying Mass in a field in Bosnia were doing religion whatever they believed or didn't believe?"

"Yes. They were."

"And if talking about death and God isn't talking about religion, what is it?"

"I don't know. Unclassifiable. Basic philosophy, perhaps."

"No wonder I didn't understand it."

"But you did. Enough. Bedtime, Matt."

As she got into bed beside Simon, who was too fast asleep to stir, she wondered whether she had meant that Matt had understood enough, to help him, perhaps, through whatever lay ahead, or just that that was enough talk for one evening.

How much had he understood? She never discovered, because they never had another conversation about death, let alone about God. He was six months in Iraq and when he came back, brown and thin and seeming much more than six months older, he told them very little about what he had been through. He went to Staff College and wrote essays and surprised himself by how well he did. And then he went to Afghanistan.

Back in the present, with her second cup of tea on the kitchen table, and mulling over the question of what, if anything, to do about Penny's boy from Libya, she looked at her watch. Nearly half past five.

Hakim. It was Friday. She knew that since he had moved, four years ago now, to a flat of his own, rented of course, in north London, he had started going regularly to the local mosque for Friday prayers, not having been to a mosque while he was living in her flat, or, for years before he left, in Libya. When he told her that he had started going to the mosque, and was glad that he had, she had said, "Why, suddenly?" And, thinking of Catholics she knew who had started going to Mass after years and years of lapsed absence, she added, "Did your family, when you were a child, take you to the mosque for prayers?"

"No", he said. "In Libya it was complicated. It was complicated by politics, like everything else in Libya then. Gaddafi was devoted to Islam, or said he was, and saw himself as a great Muslim leader. Maybe he was genuinely pious. I don't know and it seems unlikely. His Islam was all about power. His own power. All Arabs should be his kind of Muslim—which many are not, and also many Arabs are Christian, which was a fact he couldn't deal with, and many are not religious at all—and all should be his followers. So educated Libyans, like my parents, who were Muslim, yes, but only with the vague ancestral loyalty that most English so-called Christians seem to have, avoided mosques and imams because so many of them were under Gaddafi's horrible control."

By this time, Hakim's English was practically perfect.

"But now, in London, I see the difficulties for Muslims, the way that people suspect all of them because of what a very few of them have said, and because of what even fewer of them have done. Murders and bombs in the name of Islam, and the victims anyone in the bus, the tube, the street, including Muslims of course because there are many of them here. This is terrible, and in some ways the people for whom it is most terrible are the innocent Muslims, who are almost all the Muslims in England. So they need solidarity. There is very little I can do to support them, but another professional person to join the doctors and lawyers who come to the mosque for Friday prayers is one more sign that the poor, the people who work in shops or look after the old and the sick in their homes or drive buses or clean offices at five o'clock in the morning have the support, have the faith in common. It has done me good to remember that God is God, and it does me good to remember, even for a moment, five times a day as a Muslim should, though sometimes I forget."

What time did Friday prayers happen? Late afternoon? Early evening? Better not to bother him for an hour or two.

Should she bother him at all? Might she get him into some kind of trouble if he tried to help? He was here in London perfectly legally, but with Brexit looming over everything, and the Home Office, according to the *Guardian*, making life difficult for any immigrant of any kind who ran into officialdom for any reason, she didn't want to entangle him with the police. Or worse. If the Libyan boy, or the boy from Libya, supposing Hakim were able to find him, were some kind of slave, might the criminals employing, or not employing but using him, be violent? If harm came to Hakim because of something she had done—

She admitted to herself, as she sat at her old kitchen table with her cooling cup of tea and her reading glasses in their case on the William Morris tablecloth beside the *Guardian*, open at the crossword puzzle, as she had admitted to herself many times before, that she loved Hakim more than was sensible. Not, as Clare had thought at once and probably ever since, though she had not said so again, because he was a substitute for Matt, a replacement for her beloved boy who seemed to her a boy, though he was thirty-six when he died, because he hadn't married or had a child—girlfriends had come and gone, two of them serious, but marriage had never come of these relationships—and would never grow old. Perhaps at the very beginning, when Hakim, another mother's son with his life in danger, had needed rescuing, he had been to her a kind of reparation delivered by fate or chance, or at least a partial consolation, for the loss of Matt.

But as soon as he was part of her life, and that was very soon since it seemed at once obvious that he should stay in the flat, at least to begin with, almost the opposite turned out to be the case. Hakim was as different from Matt as a young man could be who was not far off the age Matt had reached when he died. She wondered often whether they would have made friends if Matt had been still alive. Impossible to tell.

He had written to her in 2013, a totally unexpected voice out of what had become the terrifying shambles of eastern Libya. His letter was sent on from the British Museum where she still gave occasional talks to school groups on Roman history. She remembered being puzzled by the envelope, the stamps, the Arabic postmark making the date indecipherable. She didn't know anyone in an Arabic-speaking country. There was no address on the back of the envelope, but at the top of the letter a post office box number in Benghazi.

To Doctor Clare Wilson
The British Museum
London WC1B 3DG
UK

Dear Doctor,
Perhaps you will remember me. In 2009, October, I was the guide at Cyrene among the temples. I helped you because an

insect had flown into your eye. Do you remember? The accident was in the wind on the hill of the Temple of Zeus. You thanked me when you went back to the buses and said I had done well as a guide. I found your name because you were a lecturer for your group. I listened to your talk the next day on the Greek churches at Apollonia. It was a very good description.

I wish to leave Libya, where is now very dangerous for me. My home is in the city of Derna. Your ship stayed there one night for your visit to Apollonia. My father, from Derna, was killed in the fighting in Benghazi last year. He was a doctor with a white flag to help the wounded but he was shot. My brother went to Tripoli to join the fight against the President and I hear nothing from him in one year and a half. I think he is dead. There are now Islam fighters from outside Libya coming, from Syria, from Iraq, I don't know where, and they are killing educated people they think not Muslim because Western education is not Muslim.

If this letter does reach you, please may it be possible for you to find me a visa to come to UK. I have a postgraduate degree, MA Classical Archaeology, from American University in Beirut. I can teach as you know. UK is nearer than US and I think UK is more open to Muslims than US after 9/11.

Please, dear Doctor, save me if there is any chance you may discover. I believe I am in serious danger.

  With hope and deepest respect,
   Hakim Husain

She read the letter, twice, and then, with her eyes closed, sat at the kitchen table, holding the letter in both hands.

She remembered him. Vividly, as if she were watching a brilliantly-shot film in vibrant colour, she remembered him, talking with expressive hands to a group of twelve or fifteen mostly elderly British tourists, all earnestly listening to him, on the grassy plateau with cypresses here and there and two or three ancient Mediterranean oak trees, in front of the tremendous Doric columns of Zeus's temple above the complicated ruins of the city of Cyrene. He told them of the wealth and prosperity of the Greek city, so ancient, from the seventh century BC, of the school of philosophy founded by a pupil of Socrates, of Cyrene in the Greek Mediterranean and the Ptolemaic empire and the Roman empire, and how it had always remained a Greek city, through rebellions and wars, and was still Greek when it was a Christian city in the late Roman empire. Clare knew all this already, but she was entranced by his account, in very good English, of what was his own, his history, his Cyrene.

As he was speaking, she noticed, thirty or forty yards away, standing in the shade of an oak, holding a walkie-talkie or a mobile telephone to his ear, a figure, dressed, as the guide was dressed, in a white shirt and black trousers, but with dark glasses and a belt that could have a had a hand-gun attached to it. She couldn't see clearly enough to be sure about the gun, but she could tell that this man was keeping an eye on the guide and was in touch with someone else, perhaps some superior policeman or official giving orders.

When she pulled her attention back to the guide, whose last few sentences she had missed, he was, to her horror, comparing the past to the present. "We in Cyrenaica have had our kings and our own republic. We have been ruled by Alexander and Ptolemy and Cleopatra, by Hadrian and Marcus Aurelius, and now we are ruled by the wisdom of the Brotherly Leader which he has written in his Green Book with his Green Pen to go with his Green Car and his Green Flags." He paused, to assess the reaction of his audience. No one laughed. Clare sensed the embarrassment of polite English tourists looking at each other for a lead. No one gave a lead. So he said: "We shall continue." No reaction to this either. "The walk down the hill to the next part of the city is steep and some steps are broken. Be very careful, please."

She was looking across at the minder under the tree, near enough to have heard everything the guide had said: he had been speaking in a loud, clear voice for those whose hearing was imperfect. She hoped the minder, the policeman, the government spy or whatever he was, didn't know English or couldn't understand irony. As she turned to follow the rest of her group, something flew into her eye, sharp, alive, frightening, stuck. She gasped and put both hands up to her eye but didn't rub it so as not to force whatever it was further in. The guide must have looked back to make sure all his flock were following him, and seen that she'd stopped, bent forward with her hands covering her eye. He came back to her.

"Allow me, ma'am", he said, putting a hand under her chin and tilting her head up. Her eye was shut tight, and painful, with whatever had flown into it still there. "Stay still, ma'am", he said, still holding her chin, and pulled a very clean, ironed white handkerchief from his pocket. Then he moved his other hand from her chin to her eye, held it open between his thumb and his index finger, and very gently took the insect out of her eye with the corner of his handkerchief.

"There", he said. "It has flown."

"Thank you. Thank you so much", she said, dabbing the tears running from her sore eye with a tissue from her bag. "I'm most grateful."

"It is my pleasure", he said, and hurried off to rescue with his leadership the group now scattered to look at the expanse of Cyrene's remains from the temple's high terrace.

The next morning, at Apollonia, a few miles away, once Cyrene's port and now a more confined collection of ruins between hills and the sea, Clare, her eye red and still a little painful, talked to half the group from the cruise about the Byzantine churches. Once there were five. Now, because much of the Greek port had gradually, through two millennia, disappeared under the sea, only three churches could still be seen, but one of them had very fine marble columns, some still upright, probably re-used from an ancient temple.

To Clare this was a magical place. Bishops of Apollonia had appeared in her long-ago unfinished thesis about Christian North Africa. She felt she had known all her life about these churches and the half-drowned port and the Greek theatre built into a hill above the town and the otherwise deserted African shore. She had never seen them before and found it difficult to keep what she was feeling out of her voice as she spoke to the group. She saw, hovering behind them, the young man who had taken the insect out of her eye. He had done the first talk of the morning, explaining Apollonia's history. She meant to thank him again, but, by the time she had explained to an earnest questioner that the cipollino marble for the columns, much valued by the Romans, with its green patterns in waves like the sea, had been brought across the Mediterranean from one of the quarries in the island of Euboea because it was found nowhere else, he had disappeared. Apollonia was the site of the cruise's last visit in Africa; that night the ship sailed from Derna for Crete. Looking back, she felt now, although she knew the feeling was ridiculous, that the prosperous, ageing tourists from England were abandoning Apollonia, Cyrenaica, all of Libya, to the horrors and dangers of war. There was no reason, then, to suppose that Colonel Gaddafi, who had already ruled Libya for forty years, would be defeated and later horribly killed, almost exactly two years after the end of the cruise, or that his death would lead so soon to the confused war that was still being fought between Tripolitania and Cyrenaica.

So, yes, she remembered him. She had thought of him several times since the Arab Spring, which had begun so promisingly, had in Libya turned into a disaster. Because of the minder at Cyrene with his dark glasses and his gun—she might have imagined she saw the gun but she knew it was there, in the background if not on the minder's belt—she thought the young guide, with his black smiling eyes behind spectacles and his clean white handkerchief, was probably dead. Could so reckless a scoffer, brave enough to mock Colonel Gaddafi under the eyes of a policeman, have survived another two years taking the kind of risk she had heard him take that day at the temple? If he had, could he have survived the battles in Cyrenaica, which had provoked the intervention of Britain and France to save lives in Benghazi? Not that the good effects of their bombs and sanctions had lasted very long.

But here he was, writing a letter. Not dead, or not yet dead, though his father, a doctor, was dead and his brother was probably also dead. He must have found her name on some website, or on the cruise information he had no doubt been given before the group first connected with him at Cyrene. And he had a master's degree from the American University in Beirut, a highly respected institution. Should she check? Probably. She knew she would have to check, although she was sure he was telling the truth. And his "Ma'am" as he dealt with the insect in her eye was surely learnt from well-mannered American students in Beirut.

She did check. He was telling the truth. A professor of archaeology in Beirut, whose name she knew, replied to her email with confirmation that Hakim Husain, from the University of Benghazi, had been awarded an MA in 2007 and that his record as a student had been exceptionally good. The professor told her that there was even a note in the file saying that anyone wishing to make a study of some aspect of ancient Cyrenaica should be put in touch with him.

She made a good case for him at the Museum, where a few graduate students were employed as assistants, and where the curators were always on the lookout for Arabic speakers from countries where antiquities were under threat as, certainly, they now were in Libya. There was never a shortage of the kind of work for which he was obviously qualified, and in 2013, when his letter arrived, it was still possible to persuade the Home Office to grant a visa to a scholar with a definite job promised, even—though it should have been particularly— from a country as administrationless as Libya had become.

So he came. He had enough money to find his way to Cairo, where the British Consulate, after weeks of investigation, stamped his passport with a visa, and then to get himself a ticket to London on an ordinary holiday plane. Clare met him at the airport, on a cold afternoon in February 2014, four and a half years since the temple of Zeus. She recognized him at once as he appeared out of Arrivals, looking about for her. He was conspicuous in a suit among the tourists, and he was carrying only an old canvas case without wheels. He saw her, came towards her and put down the case. She held out a hand, to shake his, but instead he laid his hand on his heart and bowed.

When Hakim had been in England a few months and was still living in her flat, where he was a most obliging and un-irritating lodger, an old friend had asked her a question that made her think carefully before she answered.

"What is it about this young man, Clare? You seem very attached to him although he's so young and so foreign, and I imagine a Muslim as well. And you such a Catholic."

She had had lunch today, this very day, after she had been to Mass and before she did a bit of shopping on the way home, with this same old friend. She hadn't got as far as telling Penny about this on the telephone—Penny was rushing her with her news about the boy—and she was glad she hadn't. Penny had never understood why she was fond of David Rose and wouldn't have approved.

They had been having lunch then, too, in the café of the Victoria and Albert Museum, which they both liked and could walk to from where they lived. She had said at once, she wasn't sure why, "I don't think he's much of a Muslim, though he's got it in him." And then, after a minute or two of silence because David deserved an attempt to sort out an accurate answer to his question, she had said something like: "I'm not sure. In the first place, he's an extraordinarily nice person. But so are lots of people one doesn't—"

She started again.

"Really I think it's the strangeness, the mysteriousness, of this Arab boy from such a difficult background, such a frightening past, and yet at the same time what he cares about, what he has worked so hard to understand—well, that's not strange at all, at least not to me. You could say that he and I have nothing in common, except everything, everything that isn't family and friends and everyday shared assumptions."

"You mean work?"

"Work, yes. Except that, as you know quite well, work isn't the right word. Work suggests what you do for a living, because you have to do something, saving the time when you're not working for what you really want to do. And it's true I worked for years when I was a teacher. I did enjoy it, but a good deal of what one had to do was definitely only work. I'm sure the same is true of medicine. And Hakim works, sorting, classifying, dating, identifying stuff in the Museum that's been waiting, sometimes for decades, for someone like him to be paid, though he's not paid much, to get down to it. All that's work, and it's fine. But I meant something else. Consuming interest, perhaps. Passion. That's it. Passion. For the vanished world of Rome, of early Christianity in North Africa, of the Greek temples in Cyrenaica that became Christian churches. He grew up not far from the ancient sites, the ruins, the fallen columns, the blue sea behind the stones, and all he wanted to do was to learn and understand. I just had the languages and the books, but from childhood, from when I was, I suppose, about ten, all I wanted to do was to learn and understand—the same things, the same world, as him. His world more than mine, but my world also. You see?"

David looked at her and smiled.

"Of course I see", he said, and then, "I suppose all this was always something Simon didn't share?"

She laughed.

"Absolutely not. That was OK. At least, it was fair. I knew nothing about economics. I always found it impossible to retain beyond about twenty minutes the simplest explanation of the most basic topic which Simon tried to get into my head. And he knew nothing about the classics. He'd hated Latin, along with God, at school, and wasn't at all interested in the distant past. Early capitalism was about as far back in history as he was prepared to go."

"The children?"

"Not a glimmer. No Latin at their school, and beyond stories from the *Odyssey* and the *Iliad* which I read them when they were little, they knew nothing. I called Penny Penelope in honour of Homer and faithful waiting, but she's never asked me why she has her name. I might as well have called her Kylie."

"No, Clare, not Kylie. In any case, Kylie wasn't invented when Penny was born."

"You're quite right, as usual."

She laughed as she spoke.

"Did I ever tell you about the most hopeless of my domestic efforts in classical education? We all went to Hadrian's Wall, camping, when the children were about ten and twelve. Simon had taken a good deal of persuading anyway, and the whole thing was a complete fiasco. It rained all the time and sheep ate the butter. The glamour of soldiers from Spain and Africa living and dying—there are some very moving gravestones - in Northumberland two thousand years ago had no appeal whatsoever. 'Poor them', was about as far as we got."

David smiled. "I can imagine."

He ate some more of whatever they were having for lunch, and said, "Did Simon read your book? Or the children?"

"The children certainly not. Simon very kindly read the proofs. The more sets of eyes the better, for proofs, he always said, and I read the proofs of both his books for him. I could spot basic mistakes though I didn't understand a word. He couldn't bring himself to say much about it, my book I mean. I think he said something like, 'You've done an awful lot of work, and I must say it's decently written.' I wasn't surprised, or got down, by his reaction. A book about Augustine combined the despised topics of God and Latin, so he wasn't likely to be enthusiastic, though I don't suppose Augustine was ever mentioned in the whole course of his education. People in England don't realize about Augustine, even Catholics half the time. That's why I wrote the book I suppose."

"Well, you converted me. Not to Christianity, I'm afraid, but to Augustine as a truly extraordinary, a truly brilliant man, and a fellow human being from so very long ago. Quite remarkable."

"You are kind."

"Not kind at all. You know I think that."

"Simon couldn't, or wouldn't, see Augustine's point. I didn't mind, much, that he wasn't interested in what I was doing, but I did mind, just occasionally, that, even when the children had grown up and gone, he wouldn't go on a holiday to see classical sites. Except in France. We did go to Roman France, Arles and Nîmes and Orange and the Pont du Gard, but only because he liked the food, and the wine. I so much wanted to go to Turkey, and even more to Syria, ten, fifteen years ago, when it was still one of the most civilized countries in the Middle East. Now it's too late. The dreadful civil war. I shall never see the Roman cities of Syria, even what'll be left of them when the war is over. But Hakim knows them well, knew them well, alas, one has to say. And when I went, all by myself, on that cruise, which Penny thought was a good idea, after Simon's death, and Matt's, and Penny and Charles paid for it, which was extremely generous of them, it was to see the Roman cities of Africa. And there, in Cyrene, was Hakim. And next day in Apollonia, when he bothered to listen to me talking—and then remembered me when he was desperate. And now he's here. So unlikely."

"I understand", her old friend had said.

"I know you do."

"It's not something that has to be defined." He looked at her over the café table and smiled.

"There are things", he said, "for which the exact words don't exist, and we can easily distort them by describing them in words that are slightly wrong."

Of course that's right, she thought, as she often thought about things he said.

"Do you remember asking me", he said, "if I'd like to come with you on the cruise? Something for us to do together, and you even hoped I might enjoy the Roman stuff too."

"And you said no."

"I said no. Partly because I thought Penny wouldn't like it. She might have seen it as the hijacking, by someone she's always suspected of being in some way up to no good, of a gift to you that she wanted to be pleased with as her idea."

He was probably right about this.

"And partly because I thought you should be able to enjoy the expedition and the Roman sites, and giving your talks about Augustine and the churches, without worrying about me being a bit old and arthritic for the walking, from buses to ruins and back, and getting about among all that stone. The cruise did warn that people no longer very good at walking might find it difficult, and might slow down everyone else. Perish the thought. I think I was right not to go with you. Though I should have much enjoyed seeing you enjoying your Greeks and Romans."

Once more he smiled.

"If I'd been there I'd have been able to get the insect out of your eye, and Hakim wouldn't now be in London. It's an ill wind."

Wonderful David.

David Rose was a doctor who, decades ago, when Penny and Matt were born and then were small children, had been her GP. He had actually delivered Matt, at home, in her bedroom here, in the days when GPs still did home births. He had always lived nearby, in South Kensington, in the small house where his surgery, now a flat where someone else lived, had been in the basement. He had been her friend ever since she had telephoned him in the middle of the night when Penny was nine months old because she thought the baby's terrifying cough and rasping breaths were going to kill her. "Croup", he said. "Don't panic. It's not as bad as it sounds. This is what you must do." And his kindness then and later had coloured those exhausting years of babies and toddlers and no help whatever from Simon. And, down the decades, there had been a good deal they had talked about that she could never have discussed with Simon.

She had much admired Simon when he was a young economics don—"they say at King's he's absolutely brilliant"—in Cambridge in the early '60s. Everyone she knew seemed to admire him, because he was clever and very attractive and he had a white Lotus Elite sports car. She was never the girl in a headscarf sitting beside him as the car whizzed along King's Parade, turning heads as was no doubt intended by both Simon and whoever the girl happened to be. But three years or so later, when she was still in Cambridge, struggling with the work, on African bishops of the fourth century, then an extremely unfashionable subject, for the Ph.D. she never finished, they met, properly, at an otherwise very dull dinner party given by the Professor of Ancient History, and six months after that meeting they married. They lived for another couple of years in Cambridge and then moved to London, where Simon had got a very good job at the London School of Economics, and soon Penny, and then Matt, were born. It took at least until Matt was a baby for her to realize that there were whole areas of her life that Simon found entirely incomprehensible and wouldn't have understood even if she had tried to give him a rational account of them. Religion and the classics mattered a great deal to her and would never matter in the least to him.

He did at least approve of her teaching, which she had begun in Cambridge, but wished she taught a useful subject.

She had all along been resolute enough, and sure enough of the real value of what, after Simon and the children, she cared for most, to pay no attention to this cloud of unconcern. As soon as Matt was at school she went back to work in a good London day school that believed in teaching classics, and she had always, as well, done everything for Simon and the children that needed doing. Which was quite a lot. Years later, writing her book on Augustine in early mornings and when Simon was at the university, she found the work such a delight that it was easy not to mind Simon's dim view of the enterprise. And when, with some difficulty, she managed to find a publisher, and there were even two or three friendly reviews, she felt vindicated.

And through all those years David Rose, though she didn't see him often, had been a friend closer to her than any of the four or five women she knew well and certainly liked. Why? How? She had no idea, and, as he had suggested when talking about Hakim, neither he nor she rated highly analysis of what needed no description.

He was, very quietly, gay. Six years older than Clare, he belonged to a generation in which a discreet bachelor would seldom discuss his personal life, and certainly not with a patient even when she became a friend. He was not a Catholic but had a couple of times said he wished he hadn't got such a deep Jewish suspicion of the Church. She felt that this, like the children's disconnection from the Church, had been another failure of hers. "Would you like to come to Mass with me one Sunday, just to see how unthreatening it is?" she had asked him once, not long after Simon's death. "O, I don't think so, thank you, Clare. I might see a patient there." Which was such a feeble reason that she saw she shouldn't have asked the question.

"So you're fond of this young man because you have been moved and inspired by the same things?"

"That's right. Perhaps it sounds rather silly."

"Not at all silly. A little, what? Un-English, is how one might put it. But then—"

She laughed. "But then I'm only half English, so that's hardly surprising. Is that what you were going to say? You're the only friend I have, you know, who always remembers that I'm only half English."

"One can easily tell. Or perhaps I can because I'm not in the least English myself."

"Of course. It's all this time been one of the things I like best in you."

David Rose was born in England, but only just: his mother had been pregnant with him when his parents arrived from Hamburg with his two-year-old sister in 1936. He never told Clare how they had managed to escape to England, though he had said that for a while his mother, who in Germany was a qualified and experienced nurse, had had to work as a cook for a family who thought themselves very noble for employing a Jewish refugee with one and then two small children. Later, during the war, she had worked in a big London hospital, dealing with casualties from bombing raids and from accidents in the blackout. David's father, in Germany a doctor, had died soon after the war—he had been interned as an enemy alien in the Isle of Man and then drafted into the Pioneer Corps—of the tuberculosis he had probably already contracted when he arrived in England. David remembered him as frail and coughing and speaking very German English.

Clare's father, who so surprisingly married the Yorkshire girl from a county family who became Clare's mother, was also a refugee and a Jew, and, like David's parents, spoke German and was not in the least religious. He was born and brought up not in Germany but in Prague, and he reached England—exactly how he had got out of Czechoslovakia, alone, and made the journey to England Clare had never discovered—as a fully-trained printer in 1938. He wasn't interned because he was a Czech, and the Czechs were known to be victims not friends of Hitler, and shortly after the beginning of the war he got a job printing propaganda at the Ministry of Information. It was there, in the ugly Senate House of London University, the home of the wartime Ministry, that in 1941 he met Clare's mother who was working in the typing pool. She had left school in

1940. The London Season, of dances and cocktail parties and presentation at Court of society seventeen-year-olds, had been cancelled because of the war. So she did a secretarial course in York because her parents didn't want her to join the services, where they thought she might be killed. When she got a war-work job in the Ministry of Information they had to let her go to London, which was certainly more dangerous. At eighteen, she was thrilled to go: she hadn't lived in London before and thought, rightly, that she would see more of the war there than if she were at some airfield or naval base, hemmed in by military discipline and with men doing everything interesting.

Clare had never been told whether her mother's parents had been horrified when their daughter wanted to marry a foreigner, a real foreigner with a strong German accent, and, what was more, a Jew. But the war was the war and by the time Clare was old enough to begin to notice what the grown-ups in her family felt about each other she could see that her grandparents were very fond of her father, who was warm, intelligent and funny, and quite unlike anyone else they knew. His own parents had disappeared in the war, first to the concentration camp at Theresienstadt and then, as far as he had been able to discover, on a cattle-truck train to one of the death camps in Poland. After the war he had been unable to trace a single relation alive in Prague or on any of the Red Cross lists of displaced people. So the Yorkshire family into which he had married became all the family he had. In time he became fond of Yorkshire, and London he always loved.

When, as now, sitting at her kitchen table dazed into remembering bits and pieces from the past because she didn't know what to do about Penny's boy, she thought of her father's lost parents, uncles, aunts and cousins, and of David's equally lost grandparents, uncles, aunts and cousins, among the hundreds of thousands, the millions, of the untraceable dead, she felt a familiar, deep sadness, beyond tears. And then she was suddenly furious as, lately, she had been quite often, about the unbelievable folly, stupidity, ungratefulness, arrogance and blindness of Brexit, which was in the process of wrecking the best efforts of so many people, in the countries that Hitler and

Stalin had crushed and ruined, to make a Europe where such things would be impossible ever again. It wasn't just in England that the long achievement of the European Union was being threatened: in Hungary, in Poland, in Italy, in Spain, even in Germany, right-wing nationalist politicians raising horrible echoes of the 1930s were becoming more and more popular. But that England should, by the reckless example of actually deciding to leave the European Union, be contributing to this danger, this blind, nostalgic drive towards heartless wrecking, was very hard to bear.

The people who voted for Brexit couldn't and shouldn't be blamed: they had been lied to for years, partly as a joke which made the lying worse, by Boris Johnson and his friends, partly as some kind of Machiavellian exercise of manipulative power by Michael Gove and his. They had been promised impossible improvements to lives that years of cuts in the most ordinary everyday support, for old people, for prisoners, for kids out of school, for families with nothing, had made miserable and frightening. They had been led to believe that somehow or other Europe and immigrants and Muslims, not usually distinguished from each other, were to blame for all their problems, and they had followed where they were led. But the politicians who cynically encouraged people to vote for Brexit, for short-term advantage or simply to destroy, deserved the execration of history. As did the politicians who had delivered the referendum to a public that then didn't care much about Europe, also for short-term advantage. That David Cameron was afraid of Nigel Farage was the underlying reason that the referendum ever happened. What made her most angry was the contempt for ordinary people that had achieved the result in 2016. "The proud man's contumely", she thought. Shakespeare knew. Shakespeare always knew.

What were they doing now, this evening, in Downing Street, to avoid disaster, those same contemptuous proud men? What could the sensible members of parliament do to stop disaster actually happening in three weeks' time, less, in twenty days? They were certainly trying, doing their best to prevent Brexit actually happening. Perhaps they would succeed. She prayed for their success—just, she knew, a translation of hope into prayer, probably itself to be ashamed of.

At lunch in the Victoria and Albert, only today, though her paralysis at the kitchen table after Penny's telephone call made it seem longer ago than today, she and David had begun by deciding not to talk about Brexit because it made them equally angry and equally sad. They had managed, through their soup and sandwiches, to talk about the new exhibition in the Science Museum, an exhibition about art and science in the nineteenth and twentieth centuries, which David had seen and Clare hadn't. "It's no good. I can't do science. You're a doctor so you're used to it." But he did make the exhibition sound interesting enough for Clare to promise to go, soon. "The Romantics, you know, specially Coleridge, one of your heroes, were as interested in science as they were in poetry. Those were the days."

Because of where they both lived, each of them near enough to the South Kensington museums to walk to them, though David was finding his shorter walk more and more difficult, they looked out for anything new they might enjoy. Clare was actually fondest of some old favourites in the Victoria and Albert, particularly, for some reason she couldn't remember, the lifelike bust of Henry VII, a Machiavellian power-manipulator if ever there was one, but a compelling presence and surrounded by Tudor household odds and ends in quiet, little-visited upstairs rooms, and the Raphael cartoons which she knew by heart and thought of almost as real records of the scenes they showed. She often thought how lucky she was to have, almost on her doorstep, so many beautiful things that might have been somewhere else, a tube-ride away, Henry VII in the National Portrait Gallery, the Raphaels in the National Gallery.

She had brought them back coffee from the counter and sat down again at their table when she said, "David, you're so good at politics, what do you think is going to happen to Brexit in the next ten days? The next month? There's a month and three days before Boris Johnson swears we're going to leave the EU."

"I have no idea. Truly, no idea. They've gone rather quiet in the last twenty-four hours. That could mean that Johnson and the crew round him really think they're on to the possibility of a deal that the House of Commons will pass, and they don't want to mess it up by saying anything much about it too soon. Or it could mean they're in too bad a fix to see any way out of the swamp before the end of next month and don't want to admit it. My hunch is that Johnson will miss his deadline and try to pretend there wasn't one. Who knows? A last-ditch deal like Mrs May's won't be the end of the world. But if there's another referendum on it I really think, and obviously hope, that the country might have come to its senses enough to choose Remain instead. The fact that Johnson and co are so against another referendum suggests they think the same. Meanwhile even the possibility of some kind of deal getting through the House of Commons will probably depend on the appalling DUP, who seem to get away with totally disregarding the fact that there was a proper majority for Remain in Northern Ireland. The DUP are, and always have been, a nightmare."

He sipped his coffee.

"Not bad, this coffee, considering", he said. She could see he was going to go on.

"I've said this to you before", he went on. "But it becomes more and more evident the worse everything gets. Partition is always a mistake, worse than a mistake, a disaster, with consequences down the decades in hatred and resentment that every outrage makes worse and screws deeper into people's souls. Ireland should never have been partitioned. The Catholics weren't going to murder the Protestants in a free and independent Ireland. In a single country they would all have shaken down and made the best of it generations ago. Who would have guessed that after forty years in Europe Ireland would have become one of the most liberal, one of the gentlest, societies anywhere? With a prime minister who is Indian and gay. Almost unbelievable. The DUP and their friends, allowed the odd ridiculous march, would have faded into obscurity by now if they had just been Irish.

"On a much greater scale, look at India and Pakistan, where Hindus and Muslims and Christians lived side by side in reasonable amity for centuries. Partition itself killed millions of people. And now India, where religion certainly hasn't disappeared under the tide of western progress, as people like Nehru, educated in faithless England, expected it to, has become a place where Hindu nationalists permit, even encourage, the bullying of Muslims as never before. And the treatment of Christians in Pakistan is even worse."

"I know." She did know, because of Hakim and the girl he wanted to marry. But she didn't want to stop David by interrupting.

Another sip of coffee. "And to me the most upsetting of all, Israel and Palestine, where bad policies, bad decisions and bad faith on both sides have made possible the compounding of partition with oppression in a way that is truly dreadful."

He put his hand on hers, on the table.

"I'm sorry, Clare. Getting carried away, again. It's old age, you know, and watching the consequences of politicians caring more about what happens to them in the next election than about what happens to the people they are supposed to be responsible for. This is true everywhere that's more or less democratic. Brexit is a perfect case in point. "

"Sometimes I think we'll both be dead before Brexit's sorted out", Clare said. "Perhaps just as well."

He laughed. "O Clare, no. Both of us are good for a few years yet, certainly you are, that much younger than I am, and in any case, you know, it's possible that people like us, old Europeans who have always seen the best in the European enterprise, have taken it all too hard. Perhaps it won't be as bad as we fear. Although—"

"Although?"

"I suspect, because the whole saga has made me profoundly cynical, that Boris Johnson has made the prospect of a no-deal Brexit so bad that anything at all that he manages to fix will seem a relief. Even if it's considerably worse, for business, for the economy, than Mrs May's deal."

She wasn't listening. She couldn't remember properly what had been in Mrs May's deal, if she had ever understood it.

"No David. We haven't taken it too hard. What Brexit's done is already so bad. People are frightened and don't understand what's happening or what they should do about it. You see anxiety, even fear, in people's eyes, as never before. In the Polish delicatessen, in the Pakistani corner shop—London has been so good at all this. Bad to start with, when the West Indians came after the war, much better since. Now I'm afraid nothing will ever be the same again. I knew how awful it was as soon as the result was clear on that dreadful day, and I was only glad that Simon, and particularly my father, hadn't lived to see it. And Penny and blasted Charles were actually pleased with the result, which didn't help."

"Yes, Clare", he said. "I will never forget that day. I left it till nine o'clock in the morning to telephone you. I thought you might have stayed up for the result and might be asleep. And there you were, crying at the kitchen table, sounding as if you had been crying for hours."

"It was the shock. I never thought it would happen. You were quite calm, I remember."

"Only because I wasn't surprised. I thought Cameron was taking the most terrifying risk from the start. And I felt for weeks before the vote that the over-confidence, the hubris, of the risk was heading for nemesis, a comeuppance that would do for Cameron himself, though by then that would hardly matter. What was tragic was that the defence of Europe was so half-hearted, so reluctant to raise the ghosts of the past, which should have been crowding round people in the polling stations as they voted. The ghosts that you and I have lived among all our lives. Instead the Boris Johnson lot were trying to use the war as a reason for getting us out, Britain proud to stand alone and all that, when real memories of the war should have led in the opposite direction."

He stopped for a moment, and then went on.

"You're right, of course", he said, looking down at his old hands on the table and then, his eyes sad, across the table at her. "We are not taking it too hard, not exaggerating. That this country should be tearing up so much that is good when it doesn't have to, and when no outside power has forced this on us, and that the consequences will be losses for generations to come that they won't even understand—the seriousness can't be exaggerated."

After a minute or two she said, "Have you thought any more about applying for German citizenship?"

"Not really. Not seriously. If I were twenty years younger, I'd certainly try. So that I could still be a European, free to travel, even live, anywhere in the EU. But it was already too late for me when the referendum happened and it's certainly too late now. There's no point in getting tangled up in a lot of bureaucracy, though I think I've got all the documents I would need, just as a gesture. An expensive gesture, what's more. What about you?"

"Me? O, Czech citizenship. I don't think so. I've thought about it once or twice, if only not to be British, but no. I've never been to Prague. I can't speak a word of Czech. It's too late for me too. We're old. Just as well, I often think."

"But you're not getting used to it? The idea of Brexit?"

"Absolutely not. I hate it more and more, the more likely it seems to be getting."

She looked across the table at him. He was still a doctor, still her doctor, though there were very nice GPs at the local practice off the Cromwell Road, three girls who all seemed about twenty years old.

"You know", she said, "I have bad dreams nearly every night. I never used to. Not even after Matt's death. I wake up with a sense of unavoidable disaster. I have nightmares about floods and lost children and boats that set off and have nowhere to land. It's because of Brexit, and also because of global warming. But in these nightmares, too, are the wretched Afghans, Iraqis, Syrians, Africans, who have left their countries because life there is impossible to bear. They struggle, who knows how, as far as Calais or Dunkirk and then somehow or other get themselves on a leaky boat or into the back of a lorry, and have nowhere to land, nowhere to go, because no one wants them, anywhere. And if Brexit is our own fault, and it is, so is the fact that life in half the countries people are desperate to get out of is impossible to bear. Afghanistan and Iraq: people die in both of them all the time. Bombs, shootings, drones. Poor Matt died in Afghanistan, in what one can now see was an ignorant and clumsy attempt by us to make life there better for ordinary people, and their life is far worse now than it was before we interfered in our old, patronizing, colonial way. "

"You're right, Clare. Good, brave Matt, like hundreds of thousands of others, almost all of them not British, was a victim of stupid, badly informed policies. We seem, down the generations, to have learnt so little. People are mostly entirely oblivious to the fact that a good deal of the mess in the world, in the Middle East and Africa, is our fault, the fault of Britain, with France, before it was the fault of America. And you're also right about these thousands of wretched people on the move. Put them in camps. Bribe the Libyans, with guns no doubt, to keep them. No one wants them anywhere. Like the Jews in Europe in the 1930s. Your father. My parents. And if this country hadn't taken them in, we wouldn't exist, you and I. Of course, plenty of people would say that that wouldn't have made any difference to anything—insignificant human beings, one by one, are infinitely interchangeable. A few hundred, a few thousand, more or less, so what? Why do we have a sense that we are worth something?"

"Because God wanted us to exist or we wouldn't have existed?"

He looked at her with the recognition of decades of friendship, and smiled. "Well, maybe. But it follows, in any case, that if you and I, one by one, are worth something—to God, if you like, but surely to each other—then so are the people who are dying in refugee camps or drowning in the sea. Worth something to someone, worth something, you would say, to God."

Remembering this, three hours later, she thought, there you are, as she had said to Matt all those years ago about the hill of beans.

That was lunchtime today. And now she knew about Penny's African boy washing windscreens at the petrol station and pleading for help in the only way he could think of. A boy from Libya. That meant that he had already managed to cross the Mediterranean, perhaps from one of the camps David was talking about, the camps in Libya where the authorities, who barely existed in any coherent form, had been paid by the European Union to hold captive people struggling to get to Italy. Keep them out. Build the wall. The only difference between Trump's detention camps for Mexicans and Libya's detention camps for whoever had managed to reach its coast—and coast was all there was in Libya—was that people noticed the American border more. There had been dreadful photographs of families, old women, children, in one of the Libyan camps only a week or two ago in the *Guardian*. Some of the men and women in those camps, having given money they had saved for years to the criminals organizing the journey, had travelled perhaps a thousand miles, some of them with teenagers, toddlers, babies, in rickety trucks from countries south or east of the Sahara. And then they had to face the sea. The blue and shining sea she had seen, the backdrop to Hakim's whole life, at Apollonia, at Leptis Magna, at Sabratha. But also a stormy, dangerous sea, the sea of Odysseus and Aeneas and the rage of Juno. So many unfit boats. So many people drowned, several hundred this year, and many hundreds more in the last three or four years.

Once Penny's boy had made it to Italy, where people had been so good but were now being less good, understandably, but also because they were being worked up by fascist politicians, and in Italy the label was exact, he had so far still to go. He had to travel up the rest of Italy, over or round the edge of the Alps, all the way through France, and then across the Channel. How had he done that? If not in a leaky boat, then perhaps clinging to the underneath of a lorry, or in a freezing container, or, more terrifying still, walking the tracks of the Eurotunnel with the trains roaring through the dark.

Every boy is a mother's son. Where had she read that? She thought of Matt in his inadequately armoured jeep on a mountain road in Afghanistan. She thought of Hakim, whose education had endangered but then saved him.

When, as now, she felt the world had become too complicated and too cruel for someone who was old and alone to cope with, she knew she needed the up-to-date understanding and the directness of the young to help her. That meant

Carrie. She wished again, acutely, that Carrie were in London, to tell her what to do. She had Carrie's email address. But she couldn't email Carrie in her crumpled village in the Himalayas to ask her advice about a boy working in a petrol station on the South Circular. So she tried to imagine what Carrie would say if, at this moment, she were to erupt into the flat, untidy and puppyish as she always was, scattering her coat, scarves, papers, bags, as she came to kiss her. Carrie had had a key for the last two years of her life as a student in London, in case it was easier to flop down in Matt's room in the middle of the night than to struggle back to deepest Camberwell where she shared a house with four other students. "It's an old-fashioned slum street, Gran. Don't come. You'd have a fit if you saw it. And the boys are hopelessly untidy. Socks in the bath." Pots and kettles, Clare thought.

From time to time Carrie would arrive without warning, often at this time of day when she had got to the end of whatever work she was doing, and felt like visiting Clare to chat about her life, perhaps the latest boyfriend, and, often, her parents, who according to her, although she was fond of them, were quite impossible. "Mum never does anything, does she? Because she's an MP's wife she has to go about looking as if she understands single mothers and food banks and universal credit and actually she hasn't a clue." "Well, she has to look after your father doesn't she? And I suppose politicians' wives—" "It's not good enough, Gran. What about a job? Can you imagine Mum doing a job? Plenty of politicians' wives actually work."

Then Carrie would cook supper for them both with whatever exotic ingredients had taken her fancy in Waitrose in the Gloucester Road. She was a good cook, but never washed up anything.

So as not to think about the boy in the petrol station, Clare remembered, with both amusement and some satisfaction, engineering, a couple of years ago, a date for Carrie and Hakim. Carrie must have been a second-year student, and Hakim had moved to his tiny flat in Wood Green. "Hakim! Where on earth is Wood Green?" "Not your kind of London, Clare. But it is cheap and it is on the Piccadilly Line, so it is perfect for the Museum." It had taken her months to persuade Hakim to call her by her first name. "Mrs Wilson"—he had found it difficult to believe that she had no doctorate—sounded too like school.

Clare had bought tickets for her and Carrie to go to *Waiting for Godot* at the Arts Theatre in Covent Garden. She loved the play, and she had taken Carrie at about twelve, really much too young, to see Ian McKellen and Patrick Stewart enjoying themselves no end as Vladimir and Estragon. She had been impressed by Carrie's reactions: she had laughed as much as anyone in the whole audience, and she had said at the end, "What had happened to poor Lucky?" That must have been ten years ago because it was shortly after Simon's death and Carrie had come, by herself, for the weekend instead of going to Yorkshire with her parents, to cheer her grandmother, which she always did.

So Clare, with a cold on the day of the performance, which she knew anyway was going to be a less good one, said she thought she had flu and shouldn't go to the theatre. Perhaps Carrie would like to take Hakim instead?

"Well, OK. He's nice. But will he make head or tail of *Godot*? A bit of a tall order, I'd have thought. But it's probably worth a try, if you think he might."

They had met two or three times in Clare's flat. Once, for example, she had had them both to supper, when David had also been there. Carrie had done most of the talking. David was fond of her and egged her on to describe a fierce row that had just taken place at her university about no-platforming. Carrie explained to a puzzled Hakim what no-platforming meant and, once he had grasped the concept, puzzled him further by telling him about a famous old feminist who was now being no-platformed for a disparaging remark she had made about transgender women.

David said, "For heaven's sake, Carrie, what's the matter with your generation? The young should learn not to be touchy, particularly on behalf of others, whom I don't imagine they have consulted, about every conceivable slight." But then, because, as Clare saw, he had noticed, as she had, Hakim looking as if he could scarcely believe the waste of outrage revealed by Carrie's account, he had added, "Especially when the world is full of real horrors".

"O, I know", Carrie said. "First world problem. But it's caused a huge hoo-ha."

Next time Clare saw David, he apologized for encouraging Carrie to embroider a story which was bound to be incomprehensible to Hakim. "I know you would like them to get on, those two. I'm so sorry."

"Never mind. Chalk and cheese anyway, I suspect."

"Probably. Carrie's a very splendid girl but she's entirely modern, entirely western, entirely secular, even though she's so committed to improving the lot of man. She thinks, as so many people do, that all sorts of things are obvious which aren't."

"David, you always understand."

Carrie and Hakim went to *Waiting for Godot*. The next evening, Carrie telephoned.

"Well, darling, how was *Godot*?"

"*Godot* was great. Thanks so much for getting the tickets. I don't think it wasn't quite as good as the one we saw all those years ago, but it was better than the student production I saw last year, and the Pozzo was brilliant, really scary."

"And Hakim? What did he make of it?"

"Difficult to tell. I think he enjoyed it. He certainly listened and watched really carefully. At the end he just said, 'Are there more plays like this one?' So I said no, there aren't. It's quite different from anything else. And he said, 'I can imagine it is different from all other plays.'"

"And?"

"And nothing, Gran. He's so polite. I don't think I've ever met such a polite bloke. We had a pizza after the play and he asked me about my course and what I might do next, and when I said, 'What about you?' he just said how lucky he is to be working at the British Museum and how kind to him you have been. I couldn't get anything else out of him. I thought he might tell me about Libya but he obviously didn't want to."

"Remember that he hardly knows you, and he's been brought up in a Muslim country."

"Well, of course. But I've no idea what that really means. Anyway, maybe he's gay? What do you think?"

"Carrie, for goodness' sake! You go to a play with a young man who's a foreigner and practically a stranger and because he doesn't make a pass at you, you think he's gay."

"That's not fair, Gran. I just wondered."

"I'm sorry, darling. I thought perhaps you were jumping to conclusions. I don't know whether he's gay. I think not, though that's just instinct. Obviously I have no evidence one way or the other."

"Ask David."

The young are very different from us, Clare thought. She couldn't possibly ask David any such thing.

A few days later Hakim came to borrow a book about Roman inscriptions. "I know everything is told to be on the Internet. But really not everything is, and a book is a book." After she had produced the book and they had discussed some damaged second-century inscriptions which had reached the Museum on stones from a building site in Lincoln, she said, "What did you think of *Waiting for Godot*?"

He closed the inscriptions book, put it on the low table in front of the fireplace (which held two electric bars and some glowing electric coals which Clare much disliked but was used to) and sat back in the chair, Simon's chair, which Hakim used to sit in when he was living in the flat. He clasped his hands and raised them, almost to his chin, a gesture Clare knew well. It signified intensity

"You are a wonder-worker, Clare", he said. "How did you know I would be so much interested in such a strange play?"

"A lucky guess."

"No. An inspiration."

"Is there a difference?"

"Ah."

She looked at him. His clasped hands were now in his lap.

He smiled. "Inspiration. A breath breathed in. Latin. No? The breath of God, perhaps. We have this idea in Islam."

She couldn't question him about this. It would be like questioning David about whether he thought Hakim was gay.

46

"So, the play. You enjoyed it?"

"'Enjoy' is not quite right, it was more than 'enjoy'. The play is brave and funny and sad. These old men are on a desert road in a war, perhaps after a war. They are afraid. They make jokes. They are friends but they annoy each other. They don't have enough to eat. A carrot is not enough. I have seen this. And then, with his slave, the dictator comes. He has an Italian name. He is Mussolini. A mad dictator who feels sorry for himself while people all around him are killed. He wants to show how great he is. He makes speeches. People have to tell him how great he is. But all is hollow. Mussolini came to Libya before the world war. My father told me he came. Libya then was supposed to be part of Italy, Italy's fourth shore, they said. It was not part of Italy. You have seen it. Even the most European towns, by the sea, they are not Italy. But Mussolini wanted Libyans to love him, like the dictator in the play. They had to fight for the Italian army. My grandfather, my father's father, was killed in that war. In 1940 the Italian army invaded Egypt. My grandfather was killed fighting against the British in the desert."

"Oh, Hakim. I had no idea."

"How could you know, Clare? It has been forgotten, even in Libya, which in 1940 did not yet exist. It was a long time ago. It was not the fault of any person now alive. But dictators do not change. The Italian in the play with his slave and his rope was also Colonel Gaddafi our Great Leader, mad, making speeches, always speeches, and wanting to be loved. While he was killing people around him. It is remarkable, this play, and remarkable to have been written by an Englishman when England has never known a dictator."

"Actually written by an Irishman."

"Not an Englishman?"

"No. Samuel Beckett was Irish He lived almost all his life in France. He was in France all through the war and the German occupation so he knew about dictators. He was nearly captured by the Gestapo in Paris where he was working for the Resistance. He wrote the play first in French. Not long after the end of the war."

Astonishment on Hakim's face.

"This is remarkable, even more remarkable. And so it is a play about a war, as I thought, about what is left after a war. I understood that it was. The two old men have been left, waiting—for what? For something, someone, better?"

"Well, yes. And don't you think it strikes people so strongly because all of us everywhere are waiting, for something better, perhaps for what we have been promised. Mr Godot will come."

"Jews wait for the Messiah. Christians wait for Jesus to come again. Muslims wait for the Mahdi. Nobody comes. Or there are mistakes, which is worse. The Mahdi who is not the Mahdi. The Messiah who is not the Messiah."

"I didn't know—"

"You didn't know I thought about these things? I did not ever think of them in my life until I came to London. London is marvellous for books. Because of my work at the Museum I have a reader's pass at the British Library. It is a walk away from the Museum, only fifteen minutes. I can learn anything. So I have learnt really about Islam, my own life for God, which I did not know."

He looked at her as if expecting something. Not wanting to disappoint him, she said nothing.

"Clare. May I ask you two things?"

"Of course, Hakim."

"Who is the boy?"

"Which boy? O, the boy in the play. I think if you'd asked Beckett, he'd probably have said, 'he's the boy in the play'. He didn't like explaining his work."

"I see", Hakim said, but looked a little downcast.

"I suppose the boy's just a messenger", Clare said.

"He could be an angel? Don't you think so? In Islam the messengers of God are angels. The second time he comes he says he is not the same boy who came the first time. But he is. That is like an angel, I think."

Again, the quality of Hakim's attention.

"I'm so pleased you made so much of the play" was all she said.

After a moment, he said, "My second question is, have you a copy of the play which I may borrow?"

"I'm sure I have, somewhere. Make us some coffee while I find it."

She knew where her old Faber paperback was, and that she also had the play in *The Complete Dramatic Works* so that if Hakim left the paperback on the tube she would still have the text, but she wanted a moment alone to disguise, a little, her delight at his response.

When she came into the kitchen with the paperback, Hakim was pouring water, just off the boil, into her old French cafetière.

"Here", she said. There were several pieces of paper tucked into the book. She tipped them out onto the table. One was a National Portrait Gallery postcard, a photograph of Beckett in a roll-neck sweater and an old mackintosh standing in front of two overflowing dustbins and a dirty brick wall.

"Look", she gave the card to Hakim. "This is Beckett".

He studied it for a minute or two.

"It is a wonderful face", he said, "among the rubbish."

He gave her the card. She turned over the other odds and ends she had left in the book.

"Listen to this", she said. She changed her spectacles for the ones she could read with, and read a few lines from a small piece of paper:

Prisoners dragged themselves along the empty country road.
"They'll shoot us if they see us getting away."
"You don't know, they may be waiting somewhere to see what we are up to; that would give them an excuse."
"Even if they've gone, where can we go?"
"Better to stay together."

She put the piece of paper down and looked at Hakim, who was pouring coffee into cups. He put the cafetière on the table, and then her cup and saucer in front of her.

"Please", he said. "Will you read it again?"

She did.

"It's not in the play", he said. "Not quite those words I think. It is a part he left out?"

"No. It's from the autobiography of a Czech Jew who made it to England at the end of the war, still only a boy. He wrote in Czech. He couldn't possibly have known the play. Someone not long ago translated his book. So it shows—".

She didn't know how to put into words what it showed. Hakim, in his imperfect English, did.

"It shows that the play is not unreal, as one thinks, but real, exactly real."

"That's right. It was all real."

David had lent her the autobiography, *The Survivor's Path* it was called, brief, simple, haunted by loss. "You should read this because your father was a Czech Jew, older than this man of course, and luckier." She had written out the short passage before returning the book, put it in her old copy of *Godot*, and forgotten all about it.

She gathered up the photograph and pieces of paper, tapped them on the table to keep them together, and put them behind a jug on the dresser.

"Here you are." Sitting again at the table, she gave Hakim the old paperback, and picked up her coffee cup. "Bring it back. I've had it a long time. Look." She put down the cup and took the book out of his hand. She opened it and showed him the title page. At the top, in small writing, was her name, then, Clare Feldmann, and, under her name, Cambridge 1961. She had bought it when she first saw the play, in a not very good undergraduate production.

Hakim took back the book, and saw, lower on the same page, a couple of quotations she had copied out. He read aloud the first one.

Silence is pouring into this play like water into a sinking ship.

He looked up at her, questioning.

"Beckett himself", she said. "He means the two old men help each other to survive with words." Keep talking, she thought, be brave and keep talking. How blessed she was to have David in her life.

"I don't understand the other lines you have written", Hakim said. "German, I think?"

He handed over the book, still open at the title page.

Wo keine Götter sind, walten Gespenster.

She laughed. "Goodness, how serious-minded I was in

those days", she said. "It means: 'Where there are no Gods, ghosts rule.' It was long ago I wrote that down, but I think it's a line from Novalis, a young German writer at the end of the eighteenth century. Very gifted and very sad. He was about your age when he died. Ghosts: that's what I used to think about the play. That there are only ghosts left. When I was very young, younger than Novalis, younger than you, I thought the play was about a world God had abandoned. I don't think that any more. And I can tell you didn't think that, when you saw the play."

He looked at her intently, to be sure he had understood this.

"No", he said after a while. "I did not think that, because I do not think that." Another pause, while he turned the paperback over and over in his hands. Then he looked at her again.

"God has not abandoned, even Libya."

She saw he was going to say something else.

"But the great sadness of the world is that so many people have abandoned God. Many many Christians have abandoned God and do much harm. Not so many Muslims. But the Muslims who have abandoned God and tell that they are the only true followers of the Prophet do the most harm of any people in the world."

That was two years ago. After the evening at the play, Carrie and Hakim, so far as Clare knew, had never seen each other again. Chalk and cheese indeed.

Since then, Carrie had got her degree. Clare had gone with Penny and Charles to the degree ceremony, Charles still churlish about Carrie's university and Carrie's upper second in social sciences.

After the ceremony, and after Charles, because he was an MP, had shaken hands with a professor or two who were supposed to feel honoured by his presence, they had all gone back to Charles and Penny's house in Barnes for lunch.

"So, young lady", Charles said to Carrie, over the strawberries and cream, "Have you made up your mind about my offer?"

Clare hadn't seen Carrie for weeks: she had been toiling for her final exams and, when they were over, away with friends on a round of what she called festivals, which Clare knew were not Edinburgh or Aldeburgh but weekends of tents, pop music and drugs in muddy fields.

"I thought", Charles explained to Clare, "that since she says she's so keen on improving the world, she might as well learn something about politics. There's a colleague of mine who's got an internship going in his office in the Commons. Well, in Portcullis House, actually. Same difference. Quite an opportunity for her. These jobs are hard to come by. He usually takes boys but he said he'd keep it open for her for a week or two."

"Dad", Carrie said, putting down her spoon and planting her elbows on the table. "If you think I'm going to work for the Tory party, for nothing, you haven't noticed anything at all about me for the last three years. In any case, I've had it up to here with this country, at least for the time being. Maybe when it's come to its senses I might come back. I don't think you realize how furious we all are at what you've done."

"Who's furious? And what am I supposed to have done?"

Clare could see that Charles wasn't far from losing his temper.

"Everyone I know is furious. Everyone under thirty, anyway. And what you've done is Brexit, which is wrecking so much for so many people. Have you really no idea how it looks to us? "

"You're exaggerating, Carrie. The trouble with your generation is that you didn't learn any history in school. It was all 'imagine you're a peasant in Anglo-Saxon Wessex'. Useless for understanding our past. When was the battle of Waterloo? I don't suppose you have a clue, or know why it mattered."

Charles could be quite eloquent when he got going.

"The battle of Waterloo's got nothing to do with it."

"That's where you're wrong. We saw off the French then and a hundred years later we saw off the Germans. Twice. There's no need, and never has been, for us to belong to any outfit run by the Germans and the French."

"Dad, how can you say that? You sound just like Nigel Farage. Dreadful man. If it hadn't been for him, and the Tories being terrified of him, none of this would ever have happened."

"You're talking nonsense, Carrie. I'm sorry, but you're simply wrong. Half the Conservative party has been deeply suspicious of Brussels for thirty years. Long before Nigel Farage was thought of. In this country we just don't like being bossed about by foreigners, specially not—"

"Dad! If you're going to say 'faceless bureaucrats', I despair. I really do."

"They want to turn us into citizens of a federal Europe, all exactly the same."

"That's not true, Dad, and you know it. After seventy years or whatever it is, are the Germans and the Spanish, the Poles and the Portuguese any more alike than they ever were? Absolutely not. Go to Germany and Spain and Poland and Portugal and look. And it's partly because they're so different that people of my generation want to go to university, to work, even to live, in different countries in the EU, and Brexit will mean we can't."

"Did you vote in the referendum, Carrie?" said Penny.

Clare, who knew she hadn't, thought that if Penny wanted to cool this conversation almost any question would have been better than that one.

"No. I didn't, actually."

"Well then", said Charles. "Who are you to complain now? If it was all so desperately important to you and your friends, why didn't you bother to vote? You were old enough, weren't you?"

"I was old enough, yes. But I didn't realize, I didn't understand—no one did. We didn't know because no one bothered to explain how miserable the whole thing would turn out to be. Also I assumed that the Leave people would lose. Masses of us did. I think half the people who voted Leave assumed they would lose too. They just wanted to give the politicians a fright. Which doesn't seem to have worked, by the way."

Charles let this go, and Clare had to admit to herself that Penny, by wrong-footing Carrie, had prevented Charles from losing his temper.

"All right, then", he now said. "If you're too hoity-toity about Brexit to take this opportunity to learn something about politics from the inside—which plenty of your contemporaries

53

would give their eye teeth for, I may tell you—what are you going to do with yourself now you're supposed to be an adult?"

"I'm going to teach English in Nepal."

Silence.

Clare, who knew about the Nepal plan, wanted to clear the pudding plates, put the kettle on for coffee, do something ordinary, but didn't move.

"But darling", eventually Penny said, "so very far away. Must you go so far away? And Nepal is probably very dangerous."

"A good deal safer than Barnes Common", Carrie said.

"O, let her go", said Charles, crumpling his paper napkin and chucking it on his plate, literally and metaphorically throwing in the towel. "If she's so fed up with this country, she might as well go and do something useful in the third world. Nepal was more or less part of the empire, the Gurkhas and all that. I expect they're still quite keen on Brits."

Carrie looked furiously at Charles across the table, but had also given up the fight.

She went to Nepal, came back for a few weeks in the summer last year, after teaching English for nine months, and was now rebuilding her village. She had an American boyfriend, a VSO volunteer who had graduated from a liberal arts college in Vermont. "You would like him, Gran. He's very serious and very sweet." Clare gathered that he had followed in Carrie's wake, moving from school classroom to damaged village after his summer holiday in New England; this didn't surprise her.

And Hakim? Often during the two years since the conversation they had had about *Waiting for Godot* she had wondered how he was. How, really, was he finding life in England?

Although she had seen him from time to time, over lunch in the café at the Museum or in the British Library, or when she asked him to supper, usually with David who found him interesting and sympathetic, for almost all of those two years she didn't know the answer to the question. She didn't know whether he had made enough, or any, friends in London. She didn't know whether he had a girlfriend. She didn't know whether or not he was reasonably happy in his life, though every time she saw him she thought he looked and sounded calmer and more cheerful than the time before and his English had become nearly flawless. He liked to talk about his work, and about the work of his colleagues in the Museum, so that was what they stuck to. He never gossiped, and asked Clare only, with his usual politeness, how she was, sounding as if he cared, and she always said she was well, which she was. Happy was another thing, and neither of them, as they talked, went near the possibility that there was unhappiness in either of their lives. Or loneliness, though Clare knew she was often lonely, and suspected Hakim was too.

A couple of weeks ago, however, she had invited him, and David, to supper because Charles had given her two brace of grouse, plucked and gutted and ready to roast, and she thought both of them might think a grouse on a plate with bread sauce and crisps and breadcrumbs—the sort of thing her mother loved to cook—would be an exotic treat. And perhaps spicy red cabbage, which she enjoyed making. No bacon because of Hakim. Four grouse. Three people. She considered various women, widows of course by now, who might like either David or Hakim or both, and decided against each one because there would be too much talk either about Brexit—her women friends were not wholly reliable about Brexit—or about children and grandchildren, dull for Hakim and David. So, the day before, she took three grouse out of her little freezer to thaw in the fridge, and made, because David loved it, a real trifle with real custard and syllabub on top.

In the morning David telephoned and said he had a streaming cold and couldn't come.

"Of course you mustn't come. Stay warm and drink lots of orange juice. Tea's good too. Lemon and honey in your tea. Would you like me to do any shopping for you?"

"Certainly not. I don't want you to catch this, and I'm not ill. Just not presentable."

She telephoned Hakim, who answered as he was walking from the tube station to the Museum.

"David's got a cold and isn't coming. Would you like to bring someone?"

Silence.

"I am sorry, Clare. I don't understand."

Idiot, she told herself.

"No, Hakim. It's me who should be sorry. I didn't explain. I thought perhaps you might like to come with a friend, someone who would be happy to meet an old person like me."

More silence. She heard something loud, a motorbike perhaps, pass him in the street. Then a distant police siren.

"I'm sorry", she said. "I'm afraid that wasn't a good idea."

"No, Clare, do not be sorry. The idea was very kind. But I should like to see you by myself, if that is acceptable."

"It's always acceptable, Hakim. I look forward to seeing you."

Over the grouse and the trifle, both of which she could see he much enjoyed, they talked agreeably about an old archaeologist in the Museum whom they both knew and who was about to retire, and the discovery, a couple of years ago, of a Roman settlement in the north of Yorkshire, unknown until glass and pottery and coins and stonework and jewellery had been found during excavations for a new stretch of motorway to be part of the A1, which was always mostly a Roman road. The more interesting finds had reached the Museum for analysis and dating. Hakim was very excited about this Roman town, which had as yet no name, and had twice been to Yorkshire to help with a survey attempting to establish an outline of its history. "Probably, from the coins, Agricola founded this town. The emperor was Vespasian. This is very early for Britain, quite late for Africa. It is most interesting. The foundations of a serious town probably show that the Romans were already intending to stay. Roman Britain was a success, like Roman Africa. It is so strange, for me to visit a frontier town in England, when I have worked in a frontier town on the edge of the Sahara desert. I have visited Hadrian's Wall, last year for my holiday, you remember, but that is later, of course."

She remembered the dripping anoraks at Hadrian's Wall, the children nagging for ice creams, and struggling with Simon to fold up wet tents while he was just managing not to say, "I told you so". She wished she had been able to walk those northern hills, and read those gravestones of soldiers from all over the empire, with Hakim.

After supper, Hakim helped her clear the table and she made coffee. They took it into the sitting room and Hakim settled himself in Simon's chair.

"Clare. I would like your good advice, please."

"I'll do my best, but—"

She paused because she wanted to say that the great gap between them, of age but much more of background and instinct made it unlikely that her advice would be helpful, but she didn't want to stop him before he'd started.

He helped her.

"But you are not responsible for me?" he said.

"No, Hakim. I'm not exactly responsible for you, but that isn't what I was going to say. I was only going to say that I'm so old that I'm afraid the world, or perhaps only this wretched country that I love, has overtaken me, left me behind. I think there are difficulties people of your age face that I don't begin to understand."

"I think you understand very much. And I do not belong to this country. That is one of my problems."

He picked up his coffee, drank a little, put the cup and saucer back on the fireside table.

"There is a girl", he said. "I think she would prefer me to call her a young woman. She is very serious, and very sweet."

Clare smiled, thinking of Carrie and her American, and how different from each other, nevertheless, Hakim and Carrie remained.

"She is not British. She is not from an Arab country. But she is Muslim."

"Is she Pakistani?"

"No. It might be easier for her, for her family, to be Pakistani. They are Indians. Their home is in Assam."

"I'm afraid I know very little about India. I've never been there."

"Assam is far to the north east, mountains and tea, tea plantations, that is to say. It is very beautiful, she says. But there are problems. Because Assam is next to Bangladesh, which is always very poor, people cross the frontier very easily into Assam, for better jobs and more money, and then there are too many and the Indian people dislike them because there is not enough work."

"This is happening in so many places in the world", Clare said. "Poor people resenting even poorer people."

"The result is that all Muslims in Assam are told they are Bangladeshi and must go back to Bangladesh, even if they are Indian since many generations. The government now in India, the government of Mr Modi, and the BJP party—I have forgotten what BJP means—have made things worse for Muslims everywhere in India but specially in Assam. Ayesha's father will probably not be persecuted because he is a doctor, but he has been in difficulties with the authorities because he has defended Muslims who have been beaten in the villages. Ayesha's father studied in America, thirty years ago. But now America is not a good place for Muslims. So Ayesha is here, studying medicine to be like her father—she has already five years' study in Assam and this is her final student year, her second year in London—and she is finding that England also is not a good place for Muslims."

"O dear, Hakim. I'm so sorry. I'm ashamed of this country now. Not long ago I was proud of London, proud of how cheerfully so many different kinds of people had been accepted. But since the dreadful referendum I read in the paper about hate crimes—what a phrase, unheard of until very recently—about how Muslims and Jews are being bullied, much more than they were before the referendum, and I'm ashamed."

Hakim finished his coffee.

Clare said: "Tell me about her, your friend. For instance, what does she wear?"

He understood what she meant.

"A headscarf, because she always has, otherwise very correct trousers and a tunic like so many Muslim women. And she is very beautiful which I think is part of the problem. Mostly things are OK. In the hospital she is welcome, except by a few of the patients, very few, she says. But in the street, specially at night if she has a late shift, she has a number of times been shouted at, and told to go home. Twice, people have spat at her. She is now afraid, going home alone, in the dark. Also she is now afraid to go to the mosque, the place where she should feel most safe, because two weeks ago her mosque was attacked at night, the door smashed down, windows broken, messages of hate painted on the walls."

"That's terrible, so upsetting."

"She is, for me, all the Muslims everywhere, and specially in Britain, who are hated because of what so few Muslims have said and done, and because British people know nothing, completely nothing, about Islam. She is the reason that I have been learning, myself, about Islam. Not in the mosque, where we have prayers and a good imam who recommends us to be gentle and faithful and not to drink alcohol so that we stay close to God—it is not so easy to stay close to God—but in books, the kind of books that did not exist in Libya when I was young. There were very few bookshops and they sold only books about Islam from Saudi Arabia."

"Is Ayesha a good Muslim?"

"I think she is in her nature good, a good person, and since she is in England, a year and a half already, she has, like me, become more interested in learning Islam properly. At home in Assam, her father went to the mosque and the family fasted at Ramadan but I don't think—how can I say this?—I don't think God was real in her soul until she came here and found that Muslims in Britain are feared. In Assam Muslims are despised because they are not Hindu and because they are thought to be pretending to be Indian when truly they are Bangladeshi. That is bad. But here they are feared, which is worse. So yes, in solidarity she is a good Muslim because she wants to show everyone that there is no need to be afraid of Muslims."

"She sounds like a very nice, sensible girl", Clare said, and realized how hopelessly English this sounded, hopelessly English and hopelessly bland. To move both of them on, she had to ask him a question.

"So, Hakim, why do you need my advice? Surely it's good luck that you've met Ayesha? You should be very happy that she's appeared in your life, and so should she."

Hakim got up from his armchair and walked about the room, as if there were something he wanted to say and didn't dare, or didn't know how, to put into words. Clare watched him for a few moments, and then got up herself and picked up the cafetière.

"I'm going to make some more coffee. Try and relax."

When she came back, ten minutes later, with fresh coffee and a new box of after dinner mints she had bought because David loved them, Hakim was standing with his back to the fire and his hands clasped in front of his chest. She put the tray on the table and peeled the cellophane off the box of chocolates.

"Sit down, Hakim. Have some more coffee. And a chocolate."

He sat down, took the coffee she handed him, shook his head at the box of mints.

He sipped his coffee, put the cup and saucer back on the table. He was looking away from her, at the annoying electric fire.

"Shall I marry her, Clare?"

It was not the question she was expecting. Clare felt a pang of protectiveness of her own, almost of jealousy, that she instantly recognized as wholly ridiculous.

"O, I see", she said.

"No, Clare. I think it is impossible for you to understand how—how complicated this would be."

"You mean, because she is Indian?"

"Indian? No. This is not itself a problem. But her family is not in Britain. I cannot meet her family. And my family—"

This was easier.

"Tell me about your family, Hakim. You have said nothing about your family since you came to London. Have you heard anything of your brother in all this time?"

"I have heard of my brother no certainty, no information. But he is dead, I am sure. If he was alive he would have telephoned or texted or emailed me. I have left contact numbers in Tripoli and in Benghazi where he would find them if he was alive. He is dead."

"You have never spoken of your mother?"

"No. I am sorry. My mother died when I was nine years old

and my brother was seven years old. She had cancer and was dying for some months in the house. My father said there was nothing that could be done. It was a rare kind of leukaemia. But my father also said actually she died because her heart was broken. Her father disappeared into prison where he died. His death was not known so my mother hoped he was alive. After she died her sister and my father and my brother and I hoped he was alive. Before the revolution the Leader released many prisoners. My grandfather was not released. In the revolution the prisons were opened. He did not come out. So he had died, but when he died, we do not know. This was what happened to the critics of the Leader. They disappeared and then, some time or another time, they died." He stopped for a moment.

"This was not rare", he said.

She thought of the Jews in Europe. She waited for the silence to pay some kind of tribute to all these victims of Gaddafi, and then said, "Your poor family. I'm so very sorry." Inadequate words. Better to go back to his question.

"But, as you are alone, or almost alone, Hakim, who is there to object if you were to marry Ayesha?"

"No, Clare. You do not understand. It is not objections that I would worry about. It is that I have no family to become Ayesha's family, no house, no town, no country for her. I think you do not know that in Muslim families it is expected, it is normal, for a daughter to leave her parents' house when she marries, and to live with her husband in the house, in the family, of her husband, or at least close to her husband's family. There she will be supported, taken care of. How can I give her what she should have?"

"But if you married her, you would support her and take care of her, wouldn't you?"

"Where could I do this? How could I do this? I could not go to Assam with her and marry her there: as a foreigner, an Arab, from a country of civil war famous for terrorists, how could I go there and not make problems for her father? Also I must work and there would be no work that I am trained for in Assam."

Clare thought, in what she knew to be deep ignorance.

"Is Ayesha planning to stay here, in England, when she has qualified? Does she hope to work here as a doctor?"

"She expects, next spring when she has passed her last examination, to go back to India and work as a doctor there, specially with the poor people, specially with poor women. She wants to help the girls not to be made to marry too young, so they can learn more. She wants to help the women who are dishonoured because their babies are girls not boys. Sometimes even now the girl babies are killed. And women still stay poor because they have too many children. She wants to help the women who are raped. Rape is like an epidemic in India."

Clare heard Ayesha talking behind his words.

"You speak English to each other, you and Ayesha?"

"Of course."

Clare could easily imagine these earnest conversations, over lunch in the British Library café.

"You know, Hakim", she said, "there is plenty of work here for Indian doctors. They've been very popular, very much respected, for a long time, in spite of the prejudices of a few patients. Perhaps you and Ayesha could get married and stay in England?"

"But that would be to separate her, to cut her, from her family and her future. How can I ask her to choose between me and everything she has loved, everything she has worked for? I think she lives much of her life to please her father. I, my life, my existence, could not please her father. I am a Libyan. This is the problem."

He sounded so forlorn that she wanted to hug him, but knew better.

"But surely things will improve in Libya? Nothing lasts for ever. One day, surely, it will it be possible for you to go home, with Ayesha as your wife? Doctors are valuable, valued, everywhere, always."

"Clare." Hakim leant forward in his chair, and raised his clasped hands to under his chin. "What is not possible is that you, in South Kensington, might be able to imagine how terrible is what is happening in Libya. I follow the news online, mostly from Aljazeera because there is never much news in

England from Libya. It is not a country that interests people here.

"I will try to tell you, now, for Ayesha and the decision I have to make, things I have not tried to tell you until today."

He stood up. She thought he was going to make a formal speech. But he said, "May I please find a glass of water from the kitchen?"

"Of course, Hakim, of course. Perhaps you could bring me one too."

She heard him go to the cloakroom, flush the toilet, then go into the kitchen, open and close the fridge. He came back with a glass of water in each hand, with ice in each glass, and put both glasses on the table. Clare said nothing.

"It is such a terrible story, the story of my country which is not a country now and, to tell the real truth, has not been a country ever."

He stopped.

She said, "But Libya. It's such an ancient name. The Romans—"

"It is an ancient name. It is not an ancient country. The name was for the desert. Or sometimes for a small part of the coast between Egypt—always there has been Egypt—and Cyrenaica, where is my home. Cyrenaica is an ancient country, and so is Tripolitania. But they are not the same country. I know when you visited on your cruise the country that is called Libya—", he looked directly at her and smiled. "Blessed be the day when you decided to take the cruise."

"Amen", she said, so quietly that he probably didn't hear.

"You saw how different Cyrenaica is, by no means the same as Tripolitania. That is so?"

"Yes, I did see. I knew that the history, the ancient history, was different. But I had no idea that two thousand years later the difference, the difference between Greece and Rome, even the difference between Greece and Carthage would still be so clear, so evident, to someone who was just a tourist."

"Clare, you are not a tourist. You are a person at home among the Greeks and the Romans, perhaps more at home among them than you are at home in South Kensington in 2019."

She smiled again, and saw he didn't notice.

"So you recognized the sadness of the conquered Carthaginians and their burning city, because you remembered Scipio Aemilianus grieving over Carthage and quoting Homer. 'Holy Troy will perish also, and Priam and the people of Priam.'" Hakim said the line in Greek. "And you knew Scipio's remorse was a hundred years before Virgil had written the destruction of Troy and Aeneas seeing Dido's pyre burning in the night as he sailed away for ever."

"I did, Hakim, I did. So when, on the same day the cruise took us in our buses to Carthage, I came round a corner in the wonderful museum in Tunis and saw Virgil there in a mosaic on the wall, it seemed as if time folded—" She stopped, on the edge of tears. All her life, since she was an earnest schoolgirl, the tears in Virgil had undercut her knowledge, as they had undercut Virgil's praise, of the ruthless imperialist Romans who had built on the charred ruins of Carthage the city Augustine knew.

Hakim swept on. "So Tripolitania is Carthaginian and Roman, and its history goes back to when there was no frontier at Tunisia and Algeria had not been invented. And Cyrenaica is Greek. Even the Romans connected Cyrenaica not to Tripolitania, but to Crete in a single province. And Greek it remains. More Greek by far than anything in Egypt except Alexandria itself."

Clare had heard him talk like this before, but never with such passion.

"What you do not know, Clare, and saw so little of because the Leader wished for tourists only to visit museums and ruins and spend money, is Arab North Africa."

"Yes. You're quite right. When I was doing my research a thousand years ago into all those bishops in North Africa, my work stopped, as if at a wall I couldn't cross, at the arrival of the Arabs. I knew nothing about Islam, I knew no Arabic. The church so quickly vanished, although there had been peaceful Christianity for so many centuries, and even after Belisarius— look at the lovely churches in Apollonia. Why the collapse? I had no idea."

Hakim drank half of his glass of water, put the glass on the table, and stayed leaning forwards in his chair, his elbows on his knees and his hands earnestly clasped.

"The history of Islam in North Africa is very long and also it is very confused. There were different rulers and empires and wars and fighting, over all the years from the seventh century to now. But the beginning was not confused. The Arabs came out of the desert of Arabia, united for the first time by the life and the teaching of one man."

"That", Clare said as he paused, "sounds almost like Christ, his teaching and his life."

"Like, yes, in some ways. The teaching is not so different—if people, Muslim and Christian people, lived actually by the teaching of the Prophet or the teaching of Jesus, the world would be a kind and peaceful world. Do they? Have they ever? Not ever. Not much."

Not much. Hakim's occasionally eccentric English struck her sometimes as unimprovable.

"In any case, all Muslims agree on the things that are needed to live as a good Muslim. The reason that they do not disagree is that what is needed is simple. You should believe there is only one God and that Muhammad is his prophet; you should pray five times a day, so five times a day you should remember God; you should fast in Ramadan, give to the poor, and travel once to Mecca if you can. That's all. You see, compared to Christianity, how simple. How easy to believe and how easy to be good."

He sat back in his chair, looking pleased with how he had put this.

"But, Hakim, that can't be right. It can't be as simple as you say. How about the sharia law we hear so much about?"

He leant towards her again, now frowning.

"What I hear is said in England about sharia law is almost altogether wrong. The idea of sharia here is that it is barbarous and cruel. This is not true and that this wrong idea is thought is the fault of Muslims themselves, few not many, who have forgotten that sharia is long and various and wide and full of books and scholars and opinions over hundreds of years.

Muslim scholars, not ordinary Muslim people, are like Jewish scholars. They go on and on disagreeing for ever. If a person made sharia as simple as possible he would say that sharia—I read this in one of the old books—is about 'justice, mercy, wisdom and goodness'. The word 'sharia', you know, means 'path to water'. Imagine how good, the path to water, if you live in the desert. Also, and this is more exact, sharia is to look after, for the people, five things: life, faith, family, property and the intellect. You see, Clare, that if this is all true, and I promise to you it is true, a free country with laws that are just, and with free judges, is already within sharia, specially if Muslims in the country are free to be Muslims, even if the country is not Muslim but called Christian."

"Like England, you mean?"

Hakim smiled.

"I speak of England, your good country."

"You make it all sound simple and full of hope. But it's not, is it? Not simple, not full of hope?"

"No, it is not simple, as it should be."

"I don't understand why you said it's simpler to be a Muslim than to be a Christian?"

He drank the rest of the water in his glass. She saw he was, among other things, enjoying this conversation.

"To begin with", he said, when he had put the empty glass back on the table, "the life of the Prophet was not like the life of Jesus. The Prophet was a man, only a man, and when he died, he died as all men die. I do not know Christianity well. There were not many Christians in Libya when I was a boy, some poor Egyptians who came for labouring work. Some Egyptians have been Christians always. But Egyptians are not Arabs, you know, though Arabic is their language. The idea of an Arab Christian was to me then entirely strange. But when I was a student in Beirut I met many Arab Christians from Lebanon, from Syria, and even two or three from Palestine, and I learnt a little. I learnt that Christianity is very complicated. Only to explain how Jesus, a man, was also Christ, a god who did not die, took hundreds of years of arguments. Is this correct?"

Clare laughed. "I'm afraid it is correct. You must have chosen a good historian of Christianity to tell you that."

"The man who told me said that the Christians in Egypt and Lebanon and Syria and Europe still, now, do not agree the explanation. Is this also correct?"

"Alas. Yes, it is."

"Perhaps, if these things are so, you may understand how good Islam would seem to the people when the Arabs came, because it is simple, not complicated at all. The Arabs were fighters. So people were afraid. But also, soon, people liked how easy it is to be a Muslim."

"Is that really true, Hakim? Don't Muslims disagree about all sorts of things, as Christians do? What about Sunnis and Shi'as? And—what are they called in Syria?—Alawites?"

"You are correct. And there are many more kinds of Muslim. They disagreed immediately, as soon as the Prophet was dead, about who should succeed him. And they have disagreed ever since, though for many years in many places different Muslims with different ideas and different histories have lived side by side with no fighting, no killing. Now there is very bad, very dangerous disagreement, partly because of the Iranian ayatollahs, who are extreme, fundamentalist, Shi'as, and even more because of the Wahhabis, the Salafis, who are extreme, fundamentalist Sunnis—have you heard of them?"

"I've heard the names. I don't know who they are."

"They are from Saudi Arabia, which is the great enemy of Iran. The Wahhabis say they are the only true Muslims. But their Islam is a small fraction, a sect I think in English. Wahhabism came out of the desert in the eighteenth century, very orthodox, very passionate, very narrow."

Another reaction to Enlightenment complication and subtlety? Like Methodism, and the Great Awakening, and Hasidism? But out of the desert? Clare said nothing while Hakim was explaining.

"Women must disappear into black clothes. To own women is normal. To own slaves is good. Murder is good in the name of this small sect. Suicide bombers are martyrs. Everything western is bad. Western education is worst of all. This is why

I was in danger." He pushed his glasses up his nose. "I look educated. I am educated, in a western profession. According to the Wahhabi ISIS fighters I deserve to die. But this is not the Islam of civilization, of the long past, of Tunis and Fez and Cordoba, and Baghdad and Damascus, and even Tripoli and Benghazi once. Of Timbuktu in the middle of the Sahara long ago, trashed now by Wahhabists. Of the Mughal emperors in India also, Ayesha would say."

"I don't understand. Again. How can Saudi Arabia, which is still mostly desert—isn't it?—make so many other Muslims, or any other Muslims, believe this horrible version of Islam?"

"Oil."

"What?"

"Oil. I will tell you."

She saw him think for a moment.

"The question might be: what has brought the Middle East and North Africa, the Arab countries but not only the Arab countries, Egypt as well, Iran as well, Afghanistan as well, to the terrible present? One part of the answer is the colonial policy of western countries, England, France, Italy, in the past, and now America, and even Russia, with the contempt and the ignorant interference which are the remains, the echoes, of colonial policy. And Turkey recently, with this President Erdoğan trying to restore the Ottoman Empire which is too long dead. "

She suddenly remembered Matt telling her in one of his letters that an Afghan colonel had said to him, "The Americans pretend to respect us. Really they despise us. To them we are black, like Africans, like slaves. An American would never shake my hand." At least he had said this to an Englishman.

She waited for Hakim to go on. After thinking a little more, he did.

"The other part of the answer to the question is oil. Oil has changed Iran, and has entirely changed the emirates in the Persian Gulf. Also it has changed Iraq. And Libya. In Saudi Arabia, most of all, and under the hands of a single family, oil has made everything happen that has happened."

"A single family? That can't be possible."

"Yes, it is possible, in the desert. A hundred years ago Saudi Arabia didn't exist."

"What? Surely there has always been Arabia?"

"Yes. There has always been Arabia. But—you will know this, Clare—Roman Arabia was two small provinces, possible to live in, possible to trade with. Arabia Petraea was part of Jordan, where wonderful Petra already was made. Arabia Felix was the fertile coast of the Red Sea. All the rest was Arabia Deserta, sand and stone and blazing heat, and only travelling Bedouin were there, and a few oases. In Arabia was Mecca, the centre, the heart, the holiest city of Islam. The rulers of Mecca for nine hundred years were the Hashemites, descendants of the Prophet."

He drank some more water.

"Then, very recently, early in the twentieth century, Abdulaziz—"

"Who was Abdulaziz?"

"I am sorry. He is known to all Arabs as Abdulaziz. In England he is Ibn Saud, two more of his names. Have you heard of him?"

"I think so. Didn't he have something to do with Lawrence of Arabia, in the First World War?"

"Exactly. He did. I don't know very much about Lawrence but I know that he was one of the Englishmen who made promises to Arabs, different promises to different Arabs, which were not kept. After that war, and the end of the Ottoman Empire, the Arabs had to fight for what they had been promised. Some lost, some won. The Hashemites mostly lost. Abdulaziz Ibn Saud won. He was a giant, a great fighter, also a clever man, the kind of man who is now in England called a warlord. Soon he ruled over all of Arabia, and captured Mecca where the Hashemites had ruled. The British could have stopped him but they did not. Abdulaziz favoured the Wahhabis and it was in Saudi Arabia that the black clothes for women, the slavery and the beheadings were called sharia in the 1930s. This was when the separation and bullying began of Shia Muslims, even the bullying of Shia pilgrims making the Hajj, even in Mecca itself, where almost all the ancient city the Saudis destroyed.

And they destroyed Shi'a shrines in other places and killed thousands of Shi'a. From this comes the hatred between Saudi Arabia and Iran."

"And the single family?"

"Ah, so difficult to imagine, in London. Abdulaziz was the father of forty-five sons."

"No! Good heavens! How many wives did he have? Poor them, in any case."

"Who knows? Wives, widows whose husbands had died in battles, slaves. Who knows? But every king of Saudi Arabia since he died has been his son. There have been six of these kings. The sixth king since Abdulaziz is the king who is now. King Salman. He is again the son of Abdulaziz, the son of Ibn Saud who knew Lawrence of Arabia."

"Hakim! How extraordinary! I don't think many people in England know all this—what a story!"

He opened his hands and held them out towards her as if to say, "There you are. Arabia is another world."

She got up, picked up the empty glasses, and said, "I do want you to go on. But I thought perhaps—some mint tea?"

"Some mint tea would be very good."

She put on the kettle, made two mugs of peppermint tea and took them into the sitting room.

"There. Tea."

She offered him the chocolates again.

"Yes, now a chocolate. Thank you, Clare."

"I still don't see how this one family, this warlord and his sons, in Arabia Deserta, could have made their horrible version of Islam spread so far."

"That has been the consequence of oil. Some American engineers found oil in the desert in the 1930s. Not just oil but huge, huge"—wide spread of Hakim's hands—"amounts of oil. So because the Saud family is the country and the country is the Saud family, the huge, huge amounts of money that oil has brought to them can be used for anything the family wants, and they want Wahhabi Islam to spread. So they spend billions—truly, Clare, billions—of dollars on educating Wahhabi imams and getting Wahhabi books written, and sending them out from Saudi Arabia all over the world, to countries with Muslim governments, all the Middle East countries, and to Morocco, Algeria, Tunisia—where I must tell you the people haven't liked Salafism much—also to the Muslim countries of central Africa, with terrible results, and, we know very well, to Afghanistan and Pakistan. And to Libya.

"But at the same time, making all this worse, more bloody, there is the story of Iran, since 1979 and Ayatollah Khomeini's revolution. The religious fanatics in Iran have been as cruel as the Saudis, with many more people in their own country to imprison and torture and kill. They are bitter enemies of the Saudis. They call them "camel-grazers". Iran is Persia and Persia is an ancient country, older than Athens and Rome, a country of deep civilization. This is a great contrast with Saudi Arabia. The Persians despise desert Arabs as barbarians who have no right to be guardians of Mecca and Medina. By the way, it is most painful to a Libyan to know that Khomeini might never have ruled Iran if our Leader hadn't killed Musr Sadr in Libya in 1978."

"What? Who was Musr Sadr?"

"I'm sorry, Clare, for how complicated is the story. Musr Sadr was a good Iranian imam, admired by many people. He was even a friend of the Shah. There would have been a quite different, a gentler, revolution if he had been alive. Gaddafi killed him. Who asked him to? Who knows?"

Hakim drank some of his tea.

"I'm sorry I interrupted you, Hakim. I didn't know any of this. No one explains, in England."

"You want me to tell more? It is all a bad story, a long story about bad Muslims, when most Muslims are not bad."

"Please go on."

"I will try." He took a deep breath.

"Everyone knows that America is the hated enemy of Iran but since Khomeini Saudi Arabia has been also the hated enemy of Iran. Always in wars they are on opposite sides, always they make things worse. In the war between Iran and Iraq, which lasted for eight years, with hundreds of thousands of dead, Saudi Arabia, as well as America, was on the side of Saddam Hussein. The Americans gave billions of dollars to support Saddam Hussein, to arm Saddam Hussein—so that he could invade Kuwait and fight America. How ridiculous is this?

"At the same time as the war between Iran and Iraq there was the war in Afghanistan, the Russians trying to conquer Afghanistan. Who armed the mujahideen with more billions of dollars? America and Saudi Arabia. What did the mujahideen become? The Taliban and Al Qaeda, the bombers of 9/11, who were all Saudi, by the way, and much later ISIS."

He paused. Clare was amazed at how little of this story she had ever known, though she thought she always tried to follow and understand the news.

"The Americans should be clever enough to tell the difference between Iran and Saudi Arabia. Iran is a country of long history, with many possibilities in its society and even some democracy, and Saudi Arabia is not. President Obama maybe understood this. President Trump has torn up President Obama's treaty with Iran.

"And the story is even more complicated. Iran arms and pays for Hezbollah and Hamas, so the Israelis make friends with the Saudis. And in civil wars, in Yemen, in Syria, the Iranians and the Saudis fight on opposite sides, pay much money to opposite sides, while the wretched people kill each other, lose their homes and starve.

"And all the time extreme Iranian and extreme Wahhabi teaching go on, and does encourage terrorists, even in England. So few of them, there have ever been, but since 9/11 cruel governments in the whole world have been able to use President Bush's 'War on Terror' to pretend that all Muslims are terrorists, so Muslims may be persecuted, imprisoned, killed. Putin organized terrorist attacks in Russia to justify the war against Muslims in Chechnya. Putin makes a great telling of how Christian he is, by the way. A boy of nineteen, an ordinary Russian conscripted soldier, was killed in Chechnya. He may never have been in a church. But now he is chosen to be a martyr. Killed, you see, by Muslims. Probably he will be called a saint.

"China, which is not Christian at all, is using the same trick, to call the Uighur wicked and dangerous: hundreds of thousands of Muslims, who have lived in China always, they have put in internment camps. This is called 'the people's war on terror', though the Uighur are a most harmless people. Also in Burma, the same again: the Rohingya are also harmless Muslim people who are killed and chased out of the country. They are also said to be terrorists. Really it is ethnic cleansing, as invented by Hitler and Stalin.

"All is very horrible, very cruel and very unjust. Nearly all Muslims love peace not violence. Do you believe me when I say this, Clare?"

"Hakim, yes, of course I believe you. Living in London, as I have for most of my life, I can see that there is no possible reason for being afraid of the vast majority of Muslims. Just one example: some of the people who were kindest to my old father when he was living alone in London were the Pakistani family in the newsagents where he walked, slowly, every day to get his paper and most of his simple shopping. And the Indian restaurant on his corner—perhaps they were Hindu, I've no idea, but they could well have been Muslims—kept a table for him on Sundays and gave him his favourite Indian lunch every week. They sent flowers when he died. I don't suppose the Pakistanis or the Indians knew he was a Jew but I don't think they'd have been less kind if they'd known."

"I am not surprised by this kindness. It is very good but it is not surprising. There is a respect for the old, an affection for the old, which is traditional in Muslim families, also I have no doubt in Hindu families. So from where comes the scorn for Muslims, the insults, the defence of Salman Rushdie for his book that shocked Muslims everywhere— this book and how it was defended was famous even in Libya - or the mocking treatment of Muslims in the French comic paper? I know very well that to be offended is no excuse for murder. The murders in Paris did only harm to all Muslims. But from where come the insults and the mockery that provoke and humiliate people? Do you know the answers, Clare?"

"O dear. How difficult and sad it all is. I don't know the answers. I'm not sure anyone does."

"What about the Crusades? Are the Crusades the answer? Do people still think Muslims are to be despised because they are unbelievers, even pagans? In some of the books I have read here—"

"No. I don't think so. In fact, I'm sure not. I doubt if most people in England have the faintest idea of what the Crusades were, how long ago they were, how brutal the Crusaders were. The first time most people heard the word 'Crusade' in relation to Muslims was probably when President Bush used it the day after 9/11 to give the impression that his 'war on terror' was actually a war on Muslims. Plenty of countries, as you say, have cashed in on that since."

He wasn't listening.

"So, if not the Crusades, what?" he said.

Clare thought, ate a second chocolate, finished her tea.

"The idea that Islam teaches and recommends violence is part of the problem, I suppose. I know it's not true, but there are plenty of people who think it is true."

She thought of something that hadn't struck her before.

"But maybe deeper than that is contempt for all religion. Religion does nothing but harm. Religion is dangerous nonsense, founded on lies, and responsible for practically all the awful things that happen in the world. That's a common view nowadays, among educated people as well as among the uneducated. It's certainly very common in France, where the idea was invented, in the eighteenth century. The Enlightenment."

Hakim looked baffled.

"No. You wouldn't have heard of the Enlightenment. Never mind. It was meant to be the light of reason banishing the darkness of religion, in France, also in Germany, England, and Scotland. It was good in some ways. It freed science. It freed the Jews from ghettos. But in other ways it just led to destructive cynicism. For instance, the comic paper you mentioned, *Charlie Hebdo*, where the journalists were murdered, attacks every religion, probably Christianity most of all, in the name of the Enlightenment, or what the French call *laicité*."

Another questioning look from Hakim.

"I always forget you don't know French. You know so much. *Laicité*. The French are passionate about it. It was in the name of *laicité* that they destroyed so much of their Christian past, and now they make a law banning even the hijab in the street. *Laicité* means 'secularism', 'secularity'—impossible words to understand, even in English. Let's think of some examples—"

Hearing herself, she realized she was in classroom mode. "Come on, Mum, tell us", Penny and Matt as children used to say, a quarter wanting to know whatever it was, three-quarters mocking. "She will anyway." Never mind. She would try to explain to Hakim.

"Israel, for instance, is supposed to be a secular state, not a religious state. The same is true of Turkey, founded to be secular after the Ottomans. Even more important, the same is true of America. And extreme Judaism, settler Judaism with all its cruel injustice which they say is justified by the Bible, and President Erdoğan's Islamism, and American fundamentalists, supporting settler Judaism and looking forward to the end of the world with only Americans being saved, are going against what is meant to be the secularism of their countries. They're also not doing the reputation of religion any good. Another example, now I come to think of it, is India, founded after the end of British rule to be a secular state because there were many different religions, and now look at what Ayesha has told you about the BJP."

"Yes. But religion doing harm, or religion being used so that harm is done—that's not the same."

"You're right, of course. Secularism, *laicité*, means separating religion from anything to do with the state, which sounds sensible. But it has always also meant, though this isn't usually said, hoping that religion will wither away."

"Really? Was the dying of religion to be hoped for? Could that be good?"

"It would be good if you think that all religion is an illusion based on lies, if you think that God doesn't exist and therefore has never existed. Perhaps in England where Christianity really is withering away, even though this isn't officially a secular state, you get scorn for Islam partly because people who hate religion haven't got much Christianity left to despise."

Hakim looked more puzzled than ever.

She smiled at him. "I'm sorry", she said. "I've only confused you. Forget all that. Stick to the root meaning of the secular, which is 'of this time'. Which means that secularists assume there is nothing else, no eternal horizon, no God. And that's becoming, for more and more people, at least in this country, how they see their lives. And because the idea of a real and eternal meaning to their lives remains frightening although they've rejected it, they're scornful of all believers in God and in meaning. They resent the very idea of such belief: they know it threatens their security, their complacency. So they turn on it when they can, with mockery, provocation, the desire to humiliate."

"This I do understand", Hakim said, and added, after a pause, "If only they knew that God accompanies us, consoles us, they would not feel afraid. This I did not know in Libya. I did not know it until I became sure, reading of Islam in old wise books in the British Library, that I am most lucky to be after all a Muslim. You, Clare, you know this because you are a real Christian, not just described to be a Christian because you are British."

"Well, yes, though it isn't always easy to hold on to this knowledge, to hold on to God."

He didn't hear, or didn't notice, what she had just said, but talked on, because he was thinking as he talked.

"I think it is not understood that this calling people Christian when they are not in fact Christians does very much harm. The so-called Christian empires, of the British, the French, the Italians, they were not Christian. They built huge churches, but these churches say, 'we are powerful and you are not'. They are not churches now."

"Yes, Hakim. I know. I saw the church in Carthage, on top of the hill. It seemed all wrong. "

On the cruise visit to Carthage, with her head full of Dido and Augustine, she had been shocked by this grand French nineteenth-century church, a white, assertive building on the false-medieval lines of the horrible white, assertive Sacré-Coeur in Paris. At its feet were Roman ruins and below them a maze of low, dark, burnt walls, the little that was left of Carthaginian Carthage. "Holy Troy will perish also." The church was shut. Reading later about Tunis she discovered that in 1930 the French, then 'protecting' Tunisia, had held a huge Eucharistic Congress at Carthage and colonial settlers had marched to the church dressed as crusaders.

"Is there a church like that in Tripoli too?" she said. In Tripoli the cruise buses had visited the national museum, with some good Roman mosaics and sculpture but also a whole room dedicated to Colonel Gaddafi's green car—his actual car was suspended from the ceiling—green flags, photographs, parades, speeches, the great revolution, forty years old in 2009 when she saw this hideous room. Their guide in the museum, without saying a word, ushered his group of cruise passengers into the Gaddafi revolutionary collection with a look somewhere between deadpan and irony. In Tripoli she hadn't seen a church.

"There is, but it is Italian, a Mussolini cathedral, of the 1920s. Now it is a mosque."

"I had no idea."

"No. How would you, Clare? This is recent, not ancient, history. These churches were for the colonists who were taking the land and making the people poor. Later they were killing the people, perhaps not in Tunisia, but certainly in Libya, and certainly in Algeria. These empires which were called Christian and were not Christian, but were only set for power and money, made 'Christian' become a word of hatred for Muslims. It had not been, or it had not always been, that Muslims hated Christians. The Prophet said that Jews and Christians were to be treated well. There have been many times and places where Muslims and Christians, and also Jews, all lived together, and where there was not hatred but kindness. They all believe in, they all love, also they should all fear, one God. But because of these empires, in Arab lands and North Africa, 'the West' and 'European' and 'Christian' began to mean the same thing, the same enemy. A couple of years ago twenty Egyptians, Coptic peasants from the remote countryside, hundreds of miles south of the Mediterranean, were beheaded by ISIS on a beach in Libya because they were called 'crusaders'. This was Islamic vengeance against Christianity. How much do you think these simple Egyptian Christians knew about the Crusades?

"I don't think people here understand how the attacks of the west, of Britain and France and now of America, on Arab countries look like attacks of Christians on Muslims. A friend I had in the university in Beirut was Iraqi, a scholar of antiquities in Baghdad who, like me, was studying for his doctorate. His museum lost almost everything in 2003. He told me that his family could not forget—how could they forget?—that his great-grandparents and his grandfather's sisters had been killed when the British bombed Baghdad in 1920. There was a rising of the people in Iraq against the British. But these were the first bombings of any city anywhere done to kill ordinary people, not soldiers. Now it happens every day somewhere, but this was the first time."

"No! Is this really true, Hakim? But why?"

"Why the rising of the people? Or why the bombing?"

"Both, I suppose."

"The rising was because of humiliation. This was the time of Abdulaziz who I was telling about just now. The Arabs were told during the war that they would be given their freedom, their independence, if they helped the British to defeat the Ottoman Empire. Your Lawrence of Arabia was making these promises. So the Arabs helped the British. But when the Ottoman empire had gone, the British empire, instead of giving the Arabs the independence they had fought for, got for itself this thing called mandate over Iraq, which was bad, and over Palestine, which in the end was worse. And this mandate made the Arabs understand that the British did not think them capable to rule over themselves. They felt humiliated in a way that the Ottomans had never made them feel. In Iraq the professional soldiers of the Ottoman Empire were dismissed by the British, as, by the way, the Americans dismissed the professional soldiers of Saddam Hussein in 2003. All this is why there was a rebellion. If you humiliate people they will hate you, and try to make you leave their country. If you dismiss soldiers and leave them with their guns, they will fight you. Many of Saddam Hussein's soldiers have been fighters for ISIS. Many of Gaddafi's soldiers are fighting now in the civil war in Libya. And in 1920 the rebellion was why the British bombed Baghdad, to punish Arabs. They could have fought the actual rebels but they bombed ordinary people, not because it was fair or right or likely to make peace, but because they could. Bombing from aeroplanes was new and clever. The Americans did the same, cruel killing of the Iraqis, not only in 2003 but before, in 1991, when they bombed an army that was running away and was no more a danger to them, and killed hundreds of soldiers, from the air. In war you should not kill soldiers who have given up the fight. But the Americans did, because they could. My Iraqi friend in Beirut said, 'The British and the Americans have been killing us for eighty years.'"

"Hakim. Please, no more. This is all dreadful, and I'm so ashamed, not only that the things you describe happened but that I didn't know about them. I do know about the Palestine mandate and, roughly, the history of Israel, but I knew almost nothing about Iraq before 2003. How could America have helped Saddam Hussein against Iran?"

"America can think only one thing at a time. Iran was an enemy so Iraq was a friend. In Afghanistan Russia was an enemy so the mujahideen were friends. Simple."

"And then the Americans were fighting the Taliban, and so were we. I remember Matt saying he met a Russian officer somewhere who said, 'Why did you British ever think you could win a war in Afghanistan? No one ever has.' O, what a terrible mess it has all been."

"Yes. And what is most terrible is that there is no sign of the mess coming to an end. In Syria hundreds of thousands of people have been killed, more ancient, ancient cities have been destroyed—the books of the ages were burnt in Mosul— and millions of people have left their homes. In Afghanistan where your son was killed doing his duty, peace be upon him, more and more people are killed every year since 2001. And in Libya no one is counting the people who are dying in detention camps, dying in fighting, dying from bombs. There is a civil war now for eight years, and the people who are dying are people, one by one, each a person with a family, a friend, even a—"

Suddenly Hakim broke off, covered his face with his hands and began to sob.

"Hakim! What is it? O—I'm so sorry".

She stood facing his hunched figure as he sobbed. She longed to go to him, at least to put an arm round his shoulders, but, having known for five years how careful he always was to avoid physical contact, she stayed still. Perhaps best to leave him alone for a few minutes.

She left the sitting room without a sound, and walked to her bedroom along the passage, left her bedroom door open and sat on her bed, shaky and with her heart beating too fast.

Had she upset him? She reviewed the last few minutes of their conversation. No. She couldn't see how she could have upset him. There was something she didn't know about that had risen up in him and broken his self-control, his manners, that grip and detachment which she loved in him.

Once before, she had seen him cry. It was on the day, not long after Hakim had moved out of the flat, when she heard on the Today programme the news of the death of Khaled al-Asaad, the old curator of the museum in Palmyra. She knew that Hakim had spent three months in Palmyra, sent by the university in Beirut to learn from Khaled al-Asaad whose entire life had been spent caring for the ruins and artefacts of Greek, Roman, Christian and Arab Palmyra. Now the teacher Hakim had revered had been tortured by ISIS because he had taken antiquities from the museum and hidden them to keep them safe. When he refused to say where they were, ISIS fighters beheaded him, and sent the film of the beheading round the Internet, round the world. He was eighty-five years old. Clare went to the Museum in the middle of that day to find Hakim. He was sitting at his desk staring at a picture of Palmyra on his computer screen. Everyone else who worked in the same studio was out at lunch. She sat down opposite Hakim. "I'm so, so sorry, Hakim", she said. He looked across his desk with tears in his eyes. He quickly sniffed and shook his head. "Thank you", he said. No sobs.

Now, she heard him go into the cloakroom by the front door, lock the door, noisily blow his nose, twice. He emerged, put things on the tray in the sitting room and took it to the kitchen, and then went back to the sitting room. She gave him another minute or two before she joined him.

He was standing in front of Simon's chair. She sat down and gestured gently towards him with one hand.

"Sit down, Hakim. Tell me, if you want to. But of course only if you want to."

He sat down and looked straight at her, his hands on the arms of the chair.

"I am sorry, Clare", he said. "I don't know what—I don't know what it was that—"

After a moment, she said, "I think you do." He didn't react, so she added, "I think you know what it was that suddenly upset you."

He nodded, still looking directly at her.

"Yes", she said. "Perhaps it might be good to talk about it? Only if you think it might help?"

He looked down at his lap. She watched him making up his mind.

"You have so much helped me", eventually he said. "I would not wish—"

I'm pretty tough, she wanted to say. Whatever it is, I can cope, after all these years.

"Perhaps I can help again, Hakim", she said, "with whatever it is."

"There is no one who is able to help", he said. But she could see that he had decided to tell her.

He sat up straight in the armchair and, with resolution, clasped his hands between his knees.

"OK", he began. She almost smiled at the breaking of tension but managed not to.

"I will try to tell."

He breathed in deeply.

'When I met you in Cyrene at the Temple of Zeus I was

twenty-five years old. I had completed my master's degree in Beirut, and then I was at home in Derna with my father and my brother. I did some guiding work for the visitors who came on cruise ships like yours and I was preparing to teach a course in archaeology at the university in Benghazi. I was also teaching some school students Greek. This, the Greek, was not official, but I would not be arrested for teaching Greek while the children's parents quietly paid me a little and the school pretended not to know about the lessons."

He took another deep breath.

"There was a nurse in the school. She helped the children who were not well or were afraid or sad when there were difficulties at home. Some fathers of children in the school were arrested, taken away by security police. Their families were not told why. There would sometimes be a trial. More often there would be no trial. The wives of such prisoners would tell the children everything would be fine, their fathers would come back one day soon. The nurse in the school would comfort these children, and sometimes their mothers also. She was very kind. She was the most kind person I have known."

He stopped because, Clare could see, he had to get himself together before going on.

"She was my friend. After school was closed—I was there only two afternoons each week—we walked to a café and had some coffee and baklava and talked. In the school holiday I took her to Cyrene and Apollonia and Ptolemais in my father's car—my father liked her very much—and told her the ancient cities and the Greeks, which she had not learnt before. At Apollonia we swam in the sea. This was 2010. The last year—"

As he talked, Clare could see the beach and and the marble columns, green and white in the sun, and the blue of the waveless Mediterranean. She willed him not to break down again.

A pause. Another deep breath.

"When the revolution began we were so happy, so delighted. After the example in Tunisia we thought at last, at last, the end of the dictator Gaddafi, after more than forty years. He was by now a mad old man—perhaps he had always been mad, I don't know—but he had been clever enough, after 9/11, to convince the powerful people in the West that he had changed, that he was no longer dangerous but was part of their war on terror. It was a trick. It was like Vladimir Putin's trick. The dictator Gaddafi pretended to fight in Libya so-called Islamist terrorists, and because of this pretence he would help the Americans to torture the prisoners they sent him, from Afghanistan and from Iraq, because he was suddenly good. He was not good. He was not ever good."

He stopped. He couldn't keep the politics going.

"Hakim", Clare said, to help him, "your friend the nurse?"

"Yes", he said, looking at his clasped hands.

"Straight away", he managed to go on. "When the revolution began, my brother went to Tripoli to fight. I could have gone with him. I did not go. For many reasons—"

He broke off again.

"I am sorry, Clare. I need to drink some water."

He got up, went to the kitchen, fetched another glass of water, without ice, and brought it back, already half empty.

"My father did not want both his sons to fight. Also I did not want to leave my father and—"

"And your friend? What is her name?"

"Samira. And Samira. I could not bear to leave her, in case I was killed in the fighting. Also—now it sounds foolish, probably not important enough—I could not bear to leave Cyrene and Apollonia and Ptolomais. I had to protect the cities in case bombs and fighters came. I was afraid there would be looting."

"Of course. I understand."

A long pause while he drank the rest of his glass of water.

"When serious fighting began in Benghazi my father went there, to help the wounded. Samira went also. She told the school she had to work for the revolution. She was killed on the third day she was there. She was shot by a fighter, even possibly it was a mistake, possibly it was a fighter on the side of the revolution who shot her. My father drove back to Derna to tell me. The road is long, more than a hundred and fifty miles, and was then very dangerous. He told me it was at once she died. There was no time for her to feel pain. He returned to Benghazi. Six weeks later he also was dead."

A long silence. She wanted to congratulate him for managing, calmly and coherently after all, to reach Samira's death.

"Thank you, Hakim."

He shook his head.

"I think", she had to go on, "you haven't told anyone in England about Samira. Is that right?"

He nodded.

"I understand. Some things are too sad, for other people. So thank you. For telling me."

Now he looked directly into her eyes.

"For a long time", he said, "for many years, I did not believe I could find another person, another girl, instead of Samira. Now, there is Ayesha, and you have understood that I have not told her about Samira. I am afraid—"

He couldn't go on.

"Are you afraid that she will find it difficult—perhaps that she will think she will never be the same to you as Samira was, as she still is?"

"No. No, not that at all. I am afraid to make her sad. I do not wish her to feel sorry for me. That is not necessary." He paused. "Also I am afraid that if I am too close to her, that if we have by chance beautiful times like swimming in the sea at Apollonia, she also will die. I was bad luck for Samira. She followed my father to Benghazi. She knew my father because of me. I will be bad luck also for Ayesha. I know. I wish her to be safe. Safe from me."

"O, Hakim. You're not a danger to her, or to anyone. You mustn't feel that you are. I think—"

How much should she try to explain to him? Well, he had told her the story. He was strong enough not to have told her, for more than five years.

"I think you are worrying too much about the harm you may bring to Ayesha because you have survived, to live and work in London, to be reasonably safe, in a reasonably stable country with at least no fighting and no bombs, while your family has been destroyed and Samira died. Is it that you feel you don't deserve all this—good fortune? Because that's what it is, isn't it? Good fortune, good luck—and no one deserves either good luck or bad luck. I'm sure that lots of nurses, and lots of doctors, have survived the fighting and the bombing. With better luck Samira might be still alive, and your father too. It wasn't their connection with you that caused their deaths. Of course it wasn't. You can see that, really, can't you, Hakim?"

Not looking at her, he shook his head.

She tried again. "You blame yourself because you were close to them, and because you're still in this world and they're not. But it's good, not bad, that you're alive, here, and now, and living your life as they would wish you to. And it's good for them as well as for you: you are here to remember them before God. A bridge between life and death."

A bridge as Clare knew herself to be, or at least believed herself to be, when she remembered before God every night people she loved who had died. But should she have said to Hakim what she had said about God? Perhaps remembering the dead wasn't a Muslim thing?

But he looked up and smiled, at last.

"You are right, Clare", he said. "You are always right. I remember them every day. And I do know that neither Samira nor my father would think me responsible for their death. So I should not think that I might put Ayesha in danger of dying?"

"Certainly not." She hesitated. "But perhaps there is really something else—something else that's holding you back?"

He sighed deeply but then smiled again.

"Why is it all so complicated now", he said, "with Ayesha, when with Samira it was so simple?"

"Because you are older, and wiser, and have lived through a lot. Also because you aren't at home, where, whatever the horrors and the problems, home was home, a place you loved, a place you still love, a place where you could judge without thinking other people's reactions, other people's idea of you and your life. Whereas now you live in a foreign country full of strangers whose reactions you can't predict, and where every day you have to speak a language that, however well you know it, isn't your own. And then Ayesha is also a foreigner, who also has to speak a language that isn't her own. She's a Muslim, like you I know, but India and Libya are as different as could be—"

"Yes! It is all these differences that make the complications. India and Libya are as different as Libya and England are different. I knew nothing about India. I have read a little, in some books and on the Internet, since I began to talk to Ayesha. Assam is very beautiful and I know she is homesick for the mountains and the tea plantations, as I am homesick for the fallen stones and the sea. But still I know almost nothing about India, this huge and ancient country."

He had brightened, and was talking almost as if he had forgotten, at least for the moment, Samira and those sobs.

"Even after five years I think I know very little about England, Britain—why are there two names? Also it is the United Kingdom. Three names. Why? I don't know even that, about this small and ancient country." He smiled, pleased with his echo. Clare saw how much better he was feeling.

He talked on.

"At least England and Libya have in common the Romans. And you could possibly say that India and Libya have in common Alexander. Though he never reached Assam. And no one is sure how far he came from Egypt into Cyrenaica."

He laughed, at himself.

"You see. Ancient history is good. Always it helps me. But my ancient history, your ancient history, Clare, is Mediterranean history. Ayesha does not share it."

"Never mind. You must get her to tell you about the history of Assam. Everywhere has its history, after all."

"No."

"No? But—"

"Yes. I am sorry. Yes. Ayesha has told me a little. Assam does have its history, a long history before the East India Company came and started to sell its tea to the world. The Indian workers were poor; the English company was rich. This is the usual arrangement in empires. The East India Company was like the American oil companies in Libya."

He stopped, and then started again.

"You wanted me to tell you Libya. I started but I haven't told you all the story. Do you want me to tell more?"

"Yes, Hakim, please do."

"I shall try. Libya after the Arabs came has almost no history at all. There were the cities by the sea. There were Arab rulers, different dynasties, most of them far away. Otherwise there is desert, where are camels and Bedouin and Tuareg, and fighting, sometimes. No wonder Libya was the last piece of North Africa to be wanted by a European country."

He broke off.

"I am sorry, Clare. Perhaps you know this?"

"No, Hakim. I don't. After the Romans, after the Christian bishops, I know practically nothing. What about Barbary pirates?"

"When the Arabs were not fighting each other, yes, there were pirates, clever sailors, bored in the ports, with not enough to do. Traders did better crossing the desert with camels than trusting to the sea. The corsairs, in Tripoli, Tunis, Algiers, did well out of capturing ships and holding crews for ransom, and they did even better when they were paid protection money by the English and the French for leaving their ships alone. Now it is the eighteenth century. But generally there was peace for all this long time, in the empire of the Ottomans.

"It was France that started a terrible part of the story, North Africa divided up by the so-called Christian empires, when Napoleon invaded Egypt. England took Egypt from France, France stole Algeria from its people, and then said it was going to rule over Tunisia, and fought with Spain over Morocco. All of North Africa was taken from the Ottoman empire by the British and the French by the start of the twentieth century, except for Cyrenaica and Tripolitania, which the Ottomans were governing, quite well and quite peacefully, until the British and the French said to the Italians, 'Have Libya; we don't want it'. Why would they? A few old pirate ports, very little land to farm, and a great stretch of desert."

She saw him think for a moment of the great stretch of desert. She didn't interrupt.

"Did you know", he went on, "that in a few years after the first world war, Mussolini's Italians, who said that Libya—they took the name from the Romans—belonged to them, were as cruel in Libya as any colonial power anywhere? Did you know this, Clare?"

"No. I had no idea. On the cruise we were shown some Italian buildings, in Tripoli I think, but no one explained. If there was so little to be made out of Libya, why did the Italians bother with it?"

"Ah. That is not so difficult to tell. A little before the First World War, the Italians wanted to show that they were great, a great power like England and France, with pieces of Africa to prove how great they were. Let us be an empire, they said. We are not long a country, but let us be an empire, an empire again: after all, we are Rome. But the pieces of Africa left when the other empires had taken what would make them money had nothing much that would give a profit to Italy. Eritrea, a desert by the Red Sea, and then more desert, much more, Tripolitania and Cyrenaica, a nowhere place between French Algeria and Tunisia and British Egypt, the nowhere place between Carthage and Alexandria that it had always been."

His history, like hers, was always partly ancient.

"But Italians", he was talking as if he had an attentive audience in a lecture theatre. He did have an attentive audience, of one. "Even poor Italians, didn't want to go to Libya to be farmers of land that grew almost nothing. Would you? Would anyone? It was too hot and dry in Sicily. It was hotter and dryer in Libya. Millions of Italians emigrated in the early twentieth century because Italy was so poor. Only one in every hundred of all those millions came to Libya. And there was fighting from the beginning.

"The Italians told that they were freeing Libyans from the cruel Ottoman Empire. But the Arabs were used to the Ottomans and did not hate them. The Ottomans were Muslims and they had ruled the Arabs for nearly four hundred years, quite mildly, quite carelessly, from Istanbul, a far-away city where few North Africans had ever been. There were taxes. There was no real oppression. When an Italian army came the Arabs fought with the Ottoman soldiers to resist the invaders. As usual, as now in Afghanistan and Iraq, the western invaders didn't bother to find out about the country they decided to conquer. So there was resentment and there was violence, and many people were killed.

"When Mussolini became the dictator of Italy after the First World War, the new Caesar in the new empire, there was a terrible war. The most brave resistance was in Cyrenaica. We had even a hero, Omar al-Mukhtar. He was a Sanusi leader."

"Sanusi?" Clare said.

"They are Sufi Muslims—western people don't know about Sufism which is all the beauty and poetry and art of Islam—pious and originally peaceful. The Wahhabi hate Sufism and destroy the shrines of Sufi masters."

"Like Protestants destroying the shrines of saints."

He didn't hear, or didn't register this.

"Al-Sanusi was a Sufi master, in the nineteenth century, with followers in Cyrenaica, far to the south into the Sahara, and east to the edge of Egypt. Omar al-Mukhtar was a Sanusi, and he fought a guerilla war through the 1920s. His Bedouin from the desert were fighters full of courage. The Italians fought back with every modern weapon of war and murder. They bombed from aeroplanes, like the British in Iraq at the same time. They used poison gas. They put thousands of people in camps with barbed wire, where many of the prisoners died. They executed thousands of fighters and people who were not fighters. In the years of the fighting, a third of the population of Cyrenaica died. Half of the desert Bedouin were killed. The Italians called it Pacification but it was only murder. In the end they caught Omar al-Mukhtar and executed him in front of twenty thousand people."

"What a terrible story, Hakim. And it's so disappointing that the Italians should be so cruel."

"As the British have also been. Not in Libya but in other places, in India, for example. Ayesha has told me."

"I know. I know. I wish—I wish all sorts of things were very different."

"The Italian cruelty was a horrible example to Gaddafi. He executed people not only in front of huge crowds, like the execution of Omar al-Mukhtar, but alive on television, or killed on television I should say. I have seen this."

"How ghastly. Like ISIS."

"The cruel learn from the cruel. And the Italians, some of

the Italians, are proud of this cruelty. A man I know at the Museum went to Tivoli to look at some archaeology that is being done near Hadrian's villa. Afterwards, on his way to Ravenna, he stayed in a little town in the hills called Affile. In this town there was a mausoleum and a monument to General Graziani. He was a very important general in the Second World War. But also he was the commander of the Italian army in Libya in the 1920s and he was responsible for the killing and the concentration camps. He was a war criminal like the important Nazis. The Italians, perhaps some Italians only, treat him as a hero. There were flowers and flags at his monument."

She wanted him to go on, to reach times he knew himself.

"And after the Second World War? What happened to Libya then?"

"Then was the invention of Libya. So late in history, you see. The Italians had lost the war and their empire had died with Mussolini. The winners of the war, America and Britain, knew nothing of Tripolitania or Cyrenaica except the battles of the desert. Burnt-out tanks in the sand they did know. General Rommel who was dead, and many German prisoners. Nothing else. There were ruins, modern ruins. Benghazi was bombed a thousand times in the war. About the people, poor and sick, they did not care. They were kinder to the German soldiers they had captured than they were to the people of Cyrenaica. We were far down their list of matters to be settled. There was India, where millions of people were killed because of the British and the partition. At the same time the French, who liked to think they also had won the war, were murdering Arabs in Algeria. And the British were still dealing with the promises they could not keep, to the Arabs and the Jews, in Palestine, where there were more murders. They argued about us, when they remembered us, until they said 'it is not worth dividing Tripolitania and Cyrenaica between us, and if the United Nations takes charge they will not let us build military bases. We need military bases because we are afraid of Russia so we will make Libya an independent country, and pay it to accept our bases.' So they did, the Americans and the British, without the French. And they chose the old Sanusi imam, head of all the Sanusi, who had once been emir of Cyrenaica, and they said, in 1951, 'You are king of Libya, and here is some money, not much, in return for our bases, to help to make your country.' The people needed everything. Food, schools, doctors, everything."

"And the king—what was he called?—how did he do?"

"King Idris was his name. Kings are not Arab, not Muslim, by tradition. Kings were Jewish once, I suppose: King David and King Solomon. But then kings were modern, European, invented for Arab countries by European empires. King of Egypt, King of Iraq, King of Jordan, King of Saudi Arabia— unhappy results everywhere, except maybe in Jordan—and so King of Libya, unhappiest of all. Idris was a holy man. He was almost like a Sufi master of long ago. He did not want to be a king. He did not believe in Libya as a single country. Everything, everyone was poor, and they quarrelled with each other, the parts of this so-called country. The king could not hold them together. And then suddenly, from, say, 1960, everyone was rich and they quarrelled more."

"But why?"

"Oil."

"Oil again? As in Arabia?"

"Oil again. Huge amounts of money, which should have made everything better, in a poor country, and did make the food, the schools, the doctors, also of course the cars, the refrigerators, soon the televisions, better. But what else does suddenly a great deal of money do? It leads to laziness and corruption and the belief among the powerful that there is no work they need to do and nothing else they cannot do. Poor King Idris. He was holy, as I told you. He was not himself greedy or lazy or corrupt, but it was easy to deceive him. And in the end easy to remove him."

"Like King Henry VI", Clare said.

"Who is he?"

"Sorry. He was an English king, centuries ago. There were civil wars, told"—she was catching Hakim's 'told'—"in Shakespeare. Never mind."

"History doesn't too much change?"

"That's right. What happened to King Idris?"

"He was ill. Because of old Ottoman loyalty he went to Turkey for a better hospital. While he was away a colonel in the army organized a coup. That was the end of King Idris's rule. He was eighty years old. The colonel in the army was Gaddafi. He was twenty-seven years old."

"Goodness! Gaddafi already! When did this happen?"

"1969."

"And Gaddafi was the dictator till just the other day?"

"Until 2011. Eight years ago."

"When you're as old as me, eight years ago is just the other day."

"So you see how short, and how unhappy, is the history of Libya? There was one king, unable to be a good king, for eighteen years, and then there was one dictator, very horrible and mad, for forty-two years. And there has been a civil war, as with your English king of long ago, for eight years now, and it is not likely to end soon. This history is so short that when the revolution happened in 2011, at last to get rid of the dictator, the fighters in Benghazi, where we were proud that the revolution began, carried flags and pictures of King Idris. He was a man of Cyrenaica, and who else could they carry to encourage them? But it was no use. All of it almost no use, except that Gaddafi is dead. Do you remember your Mr Cameron and Mr Sarkozy of France coming to Tripoli because they had saved Benghazi from a massacre? Really they had, and we were grateful. But they came to say welcome to democracy, of which there was no hope. It would be funny if it was not sad. There is not only no democracy in Libya. There is hardly one reliable policeman, one uncorrupt judge."

At last, Clare thought, he has reached the end; he has reached now. But he hadn't.

"And the terrible fighting, which not often reaches the British news, with outsiders joining in as they have for ever, is still happening, and is still between Tripoli, where there tries to be a government, and Benghazi where there is no government but a warlord. Not a real warlord of the old Arab world like Ibn Saud, but a corrupt general with many followers. He is

Khalifa Haftar, who was with Gaddafi from the beginning. He was another rebel officer in 1969. Dangerous boys they were, much younger than I am now. Later Haftar failed to win a stupid war against Chad, across the Sahara, for Gaddafi. So he and Gaddafi quarrelled and Haftar lived in America for twenty years at Langley, Virginia. You know what that means?"

"I don't, I'm afraid."

"It means he was a CIA man, trained to do things for America. What things? We do not know. We do know that he came back to Libya in 2011 to help to destroy Gaddafi. And now he has an army of his own. He calls it the Libyan National Army. Most of its soldiers are from Gaddafi's army. He says it fights IS in Libya, the war on terror again, so he gets weapons and help from America and Britain and France but he gets weapons and help from Salafists also, from Saudi Arabia and the Emirates, and from General Sisi's Egypt. And he gets weapons and help also from Russia. What does he promise all these helpers? No one knows. And he is one dangerous side in a civil war that no one will care to stop with talks or compromise. The other side gets much help from Turkey because Turkey wants its own oil. It is very bad. It is much worse since I left Derna. Who is still alive? I cannot find out. Even Haftar may be dead. There was news in the summer that he had a stroke; perhaps he had died. But it seems he is alive and his army is still fighting to win Tripoli. His bombs fall where they fall, some of them on the camps where the miserable people who are trying to cross the sea to Italy are kept behind barbed wire."

After a long silence, Clare concluded that at last Hakim had reached the end of his story.

"I'm so, so sorry", she said, into the silence as he sat, leaning forward in Simon's chair, looking down at his clasped hands. " I see now", she went on, unsure how she could give him any sense of consolation and support, "that you can't possibly go back until the fighting is over, which surely it will be one day?"

Hakim looked up, his eyes deep with sadness.

"Will it, be over? Will there be peace? No one knows. Perhaps there will be peace when there are two countries after all, Cyrenaica and Tripolitania, as in the ancient times. "

"Which did Gaddafi come from?"

"Ah—that is a good question. The answer is neither. Between Tripolitania and Cyrenaica there is as there has always been a desert space, a long stretch of the coast where the desert comes down to the sea. A nowhere place at the centre of the nowhere place that is Libya. There is a road beside the sea and otherwise nothing. In the middle of this desert coast is a town called Sirte. It was nothing for centuries, a pirate village, a little Ottoman fort, a few Italian officials. But Gaddafi was born a few miles away in the desert, and he made Sirte a modern city, hideous and expensive. His place, his capital, the place that stayed loyal to him longest in 2011, the place where he died such a disgusting death, a propaganda death which should not have happened in that way. Sirte was bombed and nearly all destroyed but now I think is built again. It is where ISIS beheaded the Copts. Oil is nearby."

He stopped, and winced.

"But there is the one real reason to go back."

"What is the one real reason?"

"Ancient times. My stones are the real reason. Who is caring about Cyrene, about the theatres and the temples and the churches? In Tripolitania who is caring about Leptis and Sabratha? Who is there to see if robbers will come and dig for coins and pieces of sculpture, to sell for much money? I have looked at the Internet for sellers of antiquities but where do these objects come from? Of course they do not say the truth. It is not too difficult if there are no guards to lift a whole mosaic floor and carry it away. There are still criminals digging for antiquities in the south of Italy and selling them for many dollars. What hope is there for Cyrene? And who might be checking the columns at Apollonia, where it is simple to cut the marbles at night and take the pieces away in a boat? The cipollino marble is rare to be in such good condition, and the beach is so close."

Clare saw he was on the edge of more tears, so she got to her feet to distract him.

"Now, Hakim. This is all terrible to imagine, I do understand, but these sites have survived for fifteen centuries and

more. They have survived invasions and fighting and archaeologists and robbers. I'm sure they will survive this war.
Almost everything at Cyrene, and even at Apollonia, is too
big and too heavy for anyone to steal, and there's no reason
to think people will damage antiquities just for the sake of
damaging them."

"Palmyra", he said. "The temple destroyed, the beautiful theatre like the theatre in Sabratha, dynamited."

"But that was ISIS, and hasn't it been defeated now?"

"ISIS, no. It is not as visible, as organized, as it was. They
have no territory. But they have not gone, they are everywhere
in the Arab countries, plotting, waiting, killing. When there
was civil war in Libya, ISIS arrived: where were they strong?
In Sirte, because they are heirs of Gaddafi. Where there are
no police who cannot be bribed, where there are no courts
that cannot be bullied, where there is no safety for ordinary
people—and that is almost every Arab country now—the
Salafists will do well."

"So it's good that you're in England, for now, Hakim. At
least—" What she had said struck her at once as glib, not what
he needed since he wasn't concerned about himself. "I'm glad
that you're in England, anyway."

She was still standing, looking at him across the low table
in front of the fire.

" I am sorry Clare", he said, getting up, standing to face her.
"I am very sorry. I have talked too much, for too long. It is late,
and too tiring for you. I must go."

She looked, at last, at her watch. It was not even eleven
o'clock.

"It's not very late. But would you like to stay the night? Your
old room, Matt's room, is just the same."

"No, thank you, Clare. I will go home to my flat. The good
Piccadilly Line. It runs all night on Fridays and I have an early
meeting at the Museum in the morning. I must be ready and
the papers are on my desk in my flat."

She followed him out to the passage that led to the little hall
and the front door of the flat. At the door he turned and said,
"Shall I ask Ayesha to marry me, Clare?"

"Not yet." She answered quickly, without thought. But, on later reflection when he'd gone, sensibly, she decided.

"You will know, she will know, when the time is the right time, if it turns out that this will be good for both of you. It may be. It may not be. It's too early to tell, isn't it?"

He gave her a long look.

"Thank you, for the advice, and for everything."

The hand to the heart and the bent head.

She would have liked him to stay, not just for the night but for much longer. He struck her as more alone than he had seemed all these years, and somehow younger. She knew perfectly well that she was, again, allowing him to fill the empty space in her life that the loss of Matt had left, and perhaps also the different kind of space left by the many boys she had taught over the years, now grown up and gone. She had missed for a long time being able to tell the young things they didn't know and being able to watch them light up in response. Hakim this evening had done the telling and she had listened. The other way round, but just as good. Better, now that she was old.

She watched him down the first flight of stairs and then went to sit at the kitchen table where for a few minutes, as quietly as if there had been anyone in earshot, she cried, for Hakim, for Matt, for the people of Libya, and Syria, and Iraq, and Afghanistan, for the world. Also, she knew, for herself. Loss and growing old: they were the same. And it was beyond her to help Hakim, which she longed to do.

When she had stopped crying she got up, took a tissue from the dresser drawer where she had kept tissues since the children were little, blew her nose hard and pulled herself together. She put the grouse carcasses into a saucepan with cold water and boiled them while she washed up and tidied the kitchen, then turned off the gas under the pan, and sat down again at the table for a moment of quiet, a moment of prayer. She remembered what Hakim had said about Muslims thinking of God, even for a minute or two, five times a day.

She looked round the room, pleased to be in it. She had loved her kitchen at night ever since, thirty years ago, she and

Simon had changed the flat by moving the kitchen into what the converters of the large Victorian house this had once been had intended to be the dining room. In those days, between the wars, there would have been, working in the much smaller kitchen, an invisible cook who would no doubt have slept in the little back bedroom beyond the dining room, which had always been Simon's study. When they first lived in the flat she had cooked in the kitchen and carried everything on trays into the dining room and back to be washed up in the kitchen. Mad, that now seemed. Here in the old dining room, now the kitchen, there was the same table with its William Morris cloth, but room as well for a big, scrubbed pine dresser and an armchair, and two windows instead of the one over the sink in the original kitchen, which was now a useful room with a freezer, washing machine, tumble dryer, ironing board and household odds and ends. The new kitchen—she still thought of it as new—had, like the old one next door, to be at the back of the flat on account of plumbing and building regulations, but at night, with the curtains drawn—more William Morris, but a different pattern and linen instead of cotton—you couldn't see the dreary fire-escaped back of the similar row of tall houses in the parallel street, and the kitchen was cosy and somehow timeless and unplaceable. It could have been anywhere in England in the last hundred and fifty years.

Penny mocked. "Mum, don't you think it's time you did something about this kitchen? Nobody has kitchens like this any more. We could easily help if you think it would be too expensive. We'd love to give you a dishwasher—you really ought to have had one by now, specially at your age. Save you hours. And those curtains are hopelessly old-fashioned, though they don't seem to have faded much, I can't think why." "No thank you, darling. Very kind of you to suggest it, but at my age, as you kindly put it, there's very little washing up. I don't mind doing it and I don't really need to save time. And I'm fond of the kitchen as it is, however bizarre it seems to you, specially the curtains. Your father always liked them." They looked Victorian but of course weren't. They were Sanderson William Morris from the 1960s and she had made them herself.

Sometimes, now that she was, as Penny too often reminded her, pretty old, she would get stuck at the kitchen table in the evening, the *Guardian* crossword finished and the ten o'clock news on Radio 4 over, and almost fall asleep before she summoned up the energy to run a bath and go to bed.

Tonight, however, after all that Hakim had told her, she wasn't sleepy. He had become for her something different from the bright and enterprising boy who had asked for her help and who shared her love, her long love, for what was best and most melancholy in the classical world, the great beauty of what was achieved and acknowledgement of the great cruelty that had made the beauty possible. She had known all along, from his letter, of the death of his father and the almost certain death of his brother. But tonight, perhaps because of the story of Samira and also because of the desperate history of Libya about which she had never bothered to find out, Hakim had become for her a figure of suffering about which she could do nothing, and loneliness about which she could do very little.

Eventually she got to her feet, a little stiffly because she was tired, had a bath and made a hot water bottle. Before she got into bed, she stood, as she did every night, in the window of her bedroom and prayed, for Hakim, for Carrie and Carrie's sister Daisy, so far away on different sides of the world, for David Rose, and then for all her dead.

She couldn't get to sleep. She had drunk too much coffee and there was too much to think about. At one-thirty she got up because she couldn't banish the sadness and anxiety that were more than she could bear, made some camomile tea and found an old copy of P. G. Wodehouse stories about Lord Emsworth which she took back to bed with the tea. After another half an hour, at last she fell asleep.

The next evening, waiting behind two other old women for her turn in the confessional, in the big Carmelite church in Kensington where she regularly came to Mass, she wondered why, exactly, she had decided to make her confession. Was it Catholic, or right, to ask for absolution when what she had to confess was not so much sin as unhappiness? Was either unhappiness itself, or feeling to blame for things she could not have prevented, forgivable, or, perhaps she meant dealable with, by asking for forgiveness?

She smiled to herself as she realized what a tangle she was in after last night. Perhaps what she should be confessing was self-indulgence, allowing herself to give way to the sadness she felt for Hakim, when the sadness was not her own and he had kept it from her for five years, perhaps partly because he didn't want to ask her to share the carrying of it. It would have been like him to think this: kind to her, careful of her, as he had always been. But the sadness, his and now, a bit, hers, wasn't only for the loss of his father, his brother, and Samira. It was also, and more, for the history of his country which wasn't really a country. And the misery Clare had felt in the middle of the night was something separate from Hakim's sadness because it was—what? Regret? Shame? Even guilt? Real unhappiness, anyway, for the part England had played for a hundred years in the story of bad faith, broken promises, greed for power, ignorant interference, that had brought death and destruction to so many in the Middle East and North Africa. And to Afghanistan where Matt had died in a war that shouldn't have happened, and that, years after his death, had left the country more unstable, suffering from more murderous attacks, than it had been when Matt was there.

She, Clare Wilson, sitting on a bench in the church with her hands folded over her bag, as an old man came out of the confessional and shambled away to a pew where, stiffly, he knelt, and the old woman at the top of the queue took his place, wasn't responsible for any of this, wasn't personally answerable to God for the sins, and the folly so lazy as to be sinful, of politicians down the decades. But that England was responsible, and needed truths to be acknowledged and forgiveness to be sought was obvious. Why should she, how could she, take any of it on herself? And wasn't this not so much self-indulgence as self-importance? She almost laughed at herself. But now it was daytime, in which it was always possible to be more sensible, more rational than it was at one o'clock in the morning.

She remembered that confession always turned out to have been good for her, however doubtful the project seemed after she had decided to come—usually she thought, walking the familiar streets to the church, that there really wasn't anything worth confessing to say—so she should stay and take her turn with the other old people who came on a Saturday evening for help and comfort or just because they knew they should. She also remembered that hope is a virtue and therefore despair is a sin. That would have to do.

She looked round the church, lofty, bare, vaguely modern. She wasn't fond of it; she was used to it. Years ago when she was busier and it was possible to park in the small streets round about, she always drove here. Now that she didn't have a car and knew that walking was good for her, she walked. It took her twenty minutes to walk here from her flat, but she liked the walk, a walk she had known almost all her life, and she took a taxi only when it was pouring with rain, and, which wasn't always, she could find one.

Over the years she had seen the shops change in the Gloucester Road and change more in Kensington High Street, but considering how long she had lived in this small part of old, well-off London, the atmosphere had altered remarkably little. Sometimes she walked through smaller streets, where the people living in the houses had, she knew, got richer and richer over the decades. Exotic restaurants came and went, as did shops with one or two smart and obviously very expensive outfits in the window, or two antique chairs, one statue and a piece of velvet artfully arranged. Plainer restaurants, cafés with tables optimistically set on the pavement, and more useful shops often stayed where they had been for a long time. The crocodiles of little children in smart school uniforms on their way to, or back from, Kensington Gardens in the afternoons looked much as they always had, though the teachers shepherding them seemed younger and younger as she herself got older. Battle-axe nannies in navy blue serge, also on their way to the park, pushing high gleaming prams with beautifully dressed babies sitting up in them, had long ago been replaced by pretty young au pair girls, or the occasional, also young, nanny in uniform, pushing ordinary-looking babies in ordinary clothes and ordinary pushchairs, and trying to keep toddlers on terrifying scooters under control.

Kensington.

"Why don't you sell the flat, Mum?" Penny had said, more than once. "It must be worth an absolute fortune by now. You've always loved Yorkshire and I'm sure Michael would let you have a cottage on the estate. You could have a dog and go for lovely walks." It was true that she loved Yorkshire. A couple of times a year she went to stay with Charles and Penny—she was going there for Christmas—and enjoyed being back in the country, but didn't enjoy Penny's idea of people she would like to meet or hadn't seen for years so was bound to want to see again. She couldn't possibly leave the flat now. She was too old and it was too late. Carrie would one day reappear from Nepal; Clare knew she felt happier in her grandmother's flat than in Barnes. She had left the flat to Carrie in her will, and, to make up for it, which it wouldn't, had left to Daisy what there was, quite a bit, of Simon's capital and of what she had inherited from her parents.

Also she depended on seeing David, often, and admitted to herself how sad she would be not to see Hakim, for whom, after last night, she felt more than ever answerable, to God if not to anyone else, though he had said she wasn't responsible for him and she had agreed.

While she had accepted many years ago that we are all pilgrims in a strange land, Kensington was home and that was that.

She didn't know the priest who was hearing confessions that Saturday evening. This was usually the case, and she preferred to make her confession to a stranger: long ago one of the priests in this same church had over several years become a friend who knew everything about her, and Simon, and the ordinary difficulties and sadnesses of their marriage, and letting herself grow used to depending on his knowledge and his sympathy had been a mistake. His illness, in a nursing home outside London where she couldn't visit him, and then his death, became another loss, and one she knew she shouldn't have felt so keenly. Love, she thought, remembering him as she often did, is more a question of being known than of knowing. She hoped, after yesterday evening, that Hakim's life was perhaps a little easier now that he was more properly known by her.

When after twenty minutes the woman in front of her on the bench had had her turn, Clare went into the confessional, asked for the priest's blessing and said it was about three months since she had been to confession. Then she didn't know how to begin.

"I despair sometimes", she had said, to the priest whose voice she had recognized from hearing him say Mass, but whose name she didn't know. "And despair is a sin. In the middle of the night when I can't sleep I can see no hope anywhere."

"Is it for yourself, this despair?"

She thought.

"Not exactly, no. The terrible destruction that the rich world has inflicted on the poor, with the climate changing so quickly and the poisoning of nature—and so little that any of us can do to stop it all. The melting ice and the rising sea."

She was letting the misery of the night run away with her. She stopped, swallowed, sniffed, and went on in a more level voice.

"There's even so little that England can do because we are too unimportant, too small, now, though when we were important it was us who started all the industrial horrors that have done the destroying. And I despair too about England itself. Brexit is a dreadful thing, or anyway it seems to me a dreadful thing, when we belong in Europe, which has done so well since the war to make countries better and more peaceful, and all the young are rightly furious with the old for what they have done, or for what a few lying politicians have persuaded them to do. How can one have any hope, looking at all this?"

The priest said nothing.

"So", she struggled on. "Yes, I suppose the despair is actually for myself, when everything looks dark and I see no light. And it's mixed up with guilt—all of us, if we're lucky and don't have to worry about money, are part of the system of exploitation of the earth and each other that's made all this happen. How much is a comfortable middle-class person like me responsible for people living on the streets? More and more of them there are, one sees them everywhere in London, and more and more of them are dying. And we're responsible too, in the end, for the desperate people crossing Africa and trying to get here. They risk everything to come here, and we don't want them. Everyone just wants to get rid of them." She was almost in tears.

She stopped, sniffed, swallowed, and after a moment went on.

"I'm sorry, Father. What I'm trying to say is that I'm ashamed, that I need, I need because I am to blame, the forgiveness not only of God but of all these suffering people, and of our grandchildren, and their children not yet born who will suffer from the greed and laziness of my generation. And of the young everywhere when we have made such a mess of their world."

Still nothing from the priest.

"I suppose this is sinful really because the scale of the mess the human race has made of the world means that I can't see anywhere, anything, any place or part in it all for God, as if I had lost my faith in him, though I haven't."

"If you had lost your faith in God, you wouldn't be here, would you?" the priest said.

She didn't answer, and waited.

"None of us does enough", at last the priest said. And then, after another silence, "You should thank God for the clarity with which you are able to see all these things. All Christians know about the sinfulness of the world, of what is done against the goodness of God's creation, and against the value of every human being. This of course is the sinfulness of all of us, but not all feel it as you do. That's good, in its way. But you should guard against depression, which is unproductive. And when you find you are experiencing something close to despair, try to remember that to hope is good, and that putting the sinfulness and the harm and the anxiety for the future in the hands of God is the most important thing you can do. Say some simple prayers. That always helps. And do anything you can, subscribing to charities and so forth, that will make a difference to somebody, somewhere, who is having a more difficult time than you are. Keep busy. Remember that time is God's gift to us and we don't have a limitless amount of time. So use it well. And do remember to be grateful as often as you can. Give the glory to God of everything that goes well."

He paused. Was he expecting her to say something?

"One more thing", eventually he said. "Be grateful above all for your faith. You might not have it. You don't deserve to have it. None of us does. It is entirely a matter of grace. Imagine how everything would look to you without it. Now", in a brisker voice, "if you make your act of contrition, I will give you absolution. Your penance is one Our Father and three Hail Marys, for the world as well as for yourself."

What he had said did help, more than she expected. The simple prayers suggestion was a good one. She had a routine of prayers, already simple, that she said every night, standing by the window in her bedroom, between the curtains, closed to keep the light inside the room, and the glass, from which she could see a usually quiet, lamplit London street, and black trees in the gardens belonging to the square, where she used to take Penny and Matt to play when they were little. The priest had told her to be grateful. That wasn't difficult. There was, she knew, plenty in her long life to be grateful for, the company of Simon, who was never dull except when a bit drunk, his amused tolerance of her enthusiasms and her faith, his undifficult death of heart failure that hadn't dulled his mind or his character: he had chosen not to have the big open-heart operation the doctors offered him, because he had seen the devastating effect of open-heart surgery on one of his colleagues, who died anyway, not calmly but frightened and irrational. And then she had for so many years been grateful for David. And was now also for Hakim.

"Give the glory to God of everything that goes well", the priest had said. Augustine, she had thought as she walked home from the church. And she had found, after turning some pages and wishing she had kept her notes instead of chucking them, in her own book, the sentence she dimly remembered.

"Only hold fast to your faithful belief that no good thing can happen to you, to your senses or to your intelligence or to your thought, which does not come from God."

She prayed, as always, for the dead, trying to remember sharply each of those on her list. She made an effort to leave longer spaces between her prayers. Spaces for God perhaps. Compared to the prayer of the many contemplatives she had read about during her life, her own prayers, plural not singular which was already a defeat, were, she knew, childish, pathetic. "God doesn't mind", some priest had said to her years and years ago, "how inadequately you acknowledge his presence as long as you do." This had cheered her always.

Next time, three or four nights later, that she was awake and miserable in the middle of the night, she reached in the dark for the rosary she kept on her bedside table and said the first, the second, some of the third decade until she fell asleep. Was this praying or a way of getting back to sleep? Did it matter which? At least the rhythm of the Hail Marys, which she always said to herself in Latin because, as a convert to the Catholic church at practically the last moment of its Latin centuries, that was how she had learnt the rosary, deflected her anxious mind from half-dreams about floods and lost children and climbing stairs in a building so high she would never find the way out of it.

The rest of the priest's advice she thought about. Charities she subscribed to already, reasonably, she thought, and not excessively which was a temptation in itself: the last thing she wanted was to become short of money and to have to ask Penny and Charles for help.

As for putting it all in the hands of God, wasn't that where everything already was? Perhaps better just to put herself in the hands of God and take not only one day at a time but one half-hour at a time.

"Keep busy." That was the one thing the priest had said that surprised her. No priest had ever said that to her before, in the confessional or anywhere else. He had guessed, no doubt without difficulty, both from her voice and from the fact that practically all ordinary penitents outside the Easter period were old, that she needed reminding there wasn't much of her life left. He was right. She was quite old enough to know that there couldn't be all that many years, even perhaps all that many days and hours left. Not to waste them, that was the thing.

Could she write, during some of those hours when there was nothing particular she had to do? Could she write instead, for example, of listening to Radio 4, which she did too much, more out of laziness than because she was always interested, though often she was? At least, she occasionally thought with some smugness, she had never got addicted, or even accustomed, to watching television. Simon had given up on the television news when the BBC moved the main news in the evening from nine o'clock to ten. "Too late for anyone past a certain age to think straight." Particularly, she didn't say, if they had had by then a certain amount to drink. She had refused Penny's kind offer of a much bigger television: almost nothing nowadays struck her as worth switching on the television for, and she, by herself, never got round to watching any of the old videos and DVDs that she and Simon had acquired in the past, however enjoyable she vaguely remembered they were. It was better to read a book. And, perhaps surprisingly, it was also less lonely.

So she had plenty of time to write. But write what? Her only book was the one she had written on Augustine, nearly thirty years ago. It was only moderately good, she now thought, more or less respectable as an introduction to an inexhaustible subject. She had hoped that sixth-formers or first-year undergraduates interested in the academic gap that persisted between classical and medieval history might read it. But that was before history in schools had become confined almost completely to the Tudors and the Nazis. First-year undergraduates nowadays must be meeting the Greeks and Romans and the Middle Ages more or less for the first time; they couldn't be expected to be even curious about late antiquity. Her book hadn't sold many copies and had been out of print for years.

She blamed the failure of the book entirely on herself—more famous historians had had more success with short books of a similar kind—and not at all on Augustine. She still turned to him when she needed to forget about everything else, not so much because he reinforced her faith, though he did, as because, paragraph by paragraph, he was as interesting as any writer there had ever been. She read him in Latin when she needed to be braced by the effort involved, and always enjoyed finding that her Latin was still more or less there: she could understand him with hardly any dictionary help. But then his Latin was a good deal easier than what she had been brought up to think of as proper Latin.

Cicero. Now that she had stopped ordinary school teaching, she would never have to try to get modern sixteen-year-olds itching to get back to their smartphones to see the point of rhetorical brilliance that had floored opponents in Roman courts two thousand years ago. In her day there were, at least, no smartphones, though Cicero was always a hard sell and probably had been in every schoolroom in Christendom down the centuries. Had all that been worth the effort, her effort? Of course it had. Contact with the intellectual standards of the classical world had to be sustained, even if only for the very few. She remembered with some pride classrooms of such sixteen-year-olds silent with real attention when she read them Plato's account of Socrates's death, or read them back, giving the phrases all the space they needed, the grief and fury of Dido or the story of Orpheus and Eurydice in the *Georgics* when she had taken the class sentence by sentence and word by word through the Latin until they could hear for themselves the beat and the sadness of the lines. Thirty years of teaching. Not a waste of time.

But now, even with all the empty hours of nearly every day, she knew it was too late to write anything remotely scholarly: the very idea of libraries, footnotes, references and copyright permissions made her feel tired and stupid. Might she, if she had made some different choices, have written books that people would even remember, or need to take out of the shelf to consult, after her death? She knew she was clever enough not to be boring, and careful enough to be accurate in detail so as not make a fool of herself. But scholarship had never been her world, though it could have been. It had been Simon's world, yes; it suited him well. And actually she had always been happy to leave it to him, with the exception of her Augustine book, which in any case was only on the outer edge of academic respectability.

But what about now? If she were definitely too old for scholarship, what else might there be? For several days after her confession, she found that she kept returning to the idea of writing something, more as a device for not wasting time than for any more positive reason. She couldn't forget the idea. Or the idea wouldn't forget her.

One sunny day in the middle of September she decided to go for a proper walk. She thought of arranging to meet one of her women friends somewhere for lunch, and then realized that she didn't particularly want to see any of them, didn't want to talk about Brexit or hear about their grandchildren, and that she needed to walk by herself, for the exercise and the fresh air to be helpful for thinking about this writing possibility. She had read somewhere that Wordsworth said he couldn't write poems except by letting the words form as he walked. She smiled to herself remembering this: lots of Wordsworth's poems were very dull. But she had some confidence in walking nevertheless.

She took her walking stick, an elegant black stick with a bone handle set in a chased silver band that she polished from time to time. It had belonged to her father so she was fond of it, and Carrie had said, before she left for Nepal, "You know, Gran, you ought to take a stick when you walk all the way to the park. I know you don't exactly need it, but it's safer, specially because it makes everybody else look out they don't bump into you." Carrie was right, as usually she was, and now, a couple of years after Carrie's speech, she found the stick made walking some distance considerably less tiring. Being old, she knew from observation of her father, and David, and various contemporaries, could be managed well, adequately, or badly. Someone, definitely not Wordsworth, had said that while for most of your life you liked people to think you were younger than you were, there came a point when you liked them to think you were older, and doing remarkably well for your age. She had reached that point, which was fine.

Up Gloucester Road and Palace Gate, across the beginning of Kensington High Street, to the smart corner of Kensington Gardens where in the old days the nannies assembled to set off, three abreast with their prams, along the Flower Walk. She walked up the Broad Walk to the Round Pond and stood for some minutes watching the ducks, being fed by three or four children with bags of bits of bread, and, further away, disdainful swans, too grand to pay any attention to the bits of bread. There were some toy boats close to the edge, with mothers or au pair girls trying to stop them floating out of reach, and a beautiful toy sailing boat in the middle of the water, far out of anyone's reach. Why weren't there many more unrecoverable boats on the water? Did park keepers in waders rescue them in the night? Unanswerable questions. As she watched a scene almost completely unchanged since her own childhood, though the replacements for the great trees that fell in the storm of 1987 had not yet grown to what she would consider their proper height, she remembered her father's story of a party of people on the frozen Round Pond some time in the nineteenth century; every one of them had drowned when the single sheet of ice tipped like a plate and they all slid off it into the freezing water and the ice righted itself. The story was scary indeed, but, she thought, seventy years after hearing it, no doubt no more than an urban myth, not that "urban myth" was an expression of those times, or one that even now she entirely understood.

She walked half way round the Pond and then took a diagonal path across the park towards the north end of the Serpentine. On a weekday morning not in the school holidays there were few people on the less obvious paths, small children and their minders, scooters, tricycles, some dog walkers, and a few old people, like her, walking slowly or sitting on benches in the warm sun. Leaves were not yet falling but their gilding, catching the light on the planes and the limes, was just beginning. London trees she loved. When she reached the statue of Peter Pan, which she remembered thinking, even at seven or eight, hopelessly soppy, like the play, she turned right and followed the Serpentine, glittering and clean-looking with a few solitary rowers in light boats, until she turned right again, to avoid the road across the park and to meet the end of the Flower Walk before the Albert Memorial. More glitter, this time of actual gilding: Albert himself, sitting in his ridiculous yet somehow rather appealing Gothic monstrosity of a monument, had all her life been black until, after a great deal of scaffolding and fuss over several years of restoration, some time ago now, he had emerged gold. Victoria would have been pleased. Clare was fond of the whole thing, the great sculptured groups of the arts and sciences, and of the four continents with their animals, as if Albert had ruled the world. She remembered defending the Memorial when Simon had attacked it as grandiose imperialist tat. Of course Simon was right, in a way, but his refusal to see what was impressive, even moving, in the catching of a confident extravagant moment and in the elaborate workmanship of it all, was unperceptive, and characteristic. Too automatic, too political, Simon was always inclined to be. Another world had created the Memorial, a world well lost, yes, but not without its pathos.

More slowly, because she was tired now, she made her way back to Palace Gate along the Flower Walk, where the Michaelmas daisies, purple, white and pink, and dahlias, some as big as plates, orange, scarlet and yellow against dark leaves, with a background of tidy shrubs, were pretending they weren't in London at all, but in the Victorian herbaceous border of a country house with ten gardeners. Lord Emsworth, in a happy daze of thinking he was at home at Blandings Castle, had got into trouble with a park keeper for picking tulips in the Flower Walk. Wodehouse, so comforting: she had always thought him, after Shakespeare, a long way after admittedly, an important reason for being pleased to be English.

As she walked down the Gloucester Road towards home, looking forward to the particularly good smoked ham and smoked cheese sandwiches she bought for her late lunch in a café she knew well, two phrases the priest had used in the confessional came back to her. Be grateful. That was one. The other was something about the value of every single human being.

When she had let herself into the flat, unwrapped her sandwiches, put them on a plate on the kitchen table, and poured herself some apple juice, she telephoned David. Three rings. Four.

"Hello." His sleepy voice.

"David—I've woken you up. I'm so sorry. What a stupid time to ring. I've been for a long walk and I didn't realize it had got so late. After lunch. Your nap. Which you should have. How silly of me."

"It's quite all right. I really shouldn't have been asleep. I sleep too much in the daytime, and not enough at night. Old age, it's called. But is something the matter, Clare? You don't sound quite yourself. You're not ill, I hope?"

"O no. Absolutely not. I'm fine. Do you mind if I ask you a serious question?"

"Of course not. As serious as you like."

She drank some of her apple juice.

"David. Do you think I'm interesting enough to be the subject of a book?"

A long silence.

Then, "Who is offering to write this book?"

"I am. That's the other half of my question."

Another long silence.

"I think you should explain a little, Clare."

"I'm sorry. Of course. This must sound quite mad. I've been thinking lately that there can't be much time left, much life left, at my age, and what time there is I've been wasting for years. Since Simon died anyway. Days, weeks go by, with no one needing me to do anything in particular—women get so used to it, you know, doing things that other people need, it's the story of our lives—so I do shamefully little. I listen to the radio. Read the newspaper. Go for a walk. Go to Mass perhaps. Ring up a friend to see how her new hip is doing or whether her grandson got into Oxford. Footling. All of it, except going to Mass, I suppose. I want to do some work, and the only kind of work I could do now that I'm too old to teach might be, I thought, to write. Not journalism or reviews. I'm too old, again, certainly too old to start. But perhaps a book? A book basically about me, now, old, in a world that has got itself into such a hideous mess—because, well, because every human life is interesting in its way, don't you think? Even if the person isn't famous or out of the ordinary in any obvious way. But perhaps knows how to write?"

She was over-explaining. Was poor David even listening to all this? If he'd gone back to sleep she wouldn't blame him. She could picture him in the old armchair of all his life, with the raised table like a bridge across it, with books, his newspaper, his glasses, probably a coffee cup on it. She had given him this table last Christmas. It moved easily on casters, over his chair or away from his chair, and meant that he didn't have to have anything heavy on his lap. The telephone was on the other side of his chair, on a small round table with a good lamp for reading.

"David?"

"I'm listening."

"I'm sorry. I'm talking too much. I thought you might have gone back to sleep."

"Not at all. Not at all. Much too interested to go back to sleep."

"So what do you think?"

Another silence.

"Was this your idea or someone else's?"

He doesn't want it to be someone else's: she was half pleased, half remorseful at the slight note of resentment in his question.

"It's my idea. Though a priest told me not to waste time. I didn't think I did waste time until he said it, and then I realized I've been wasting time for years."

"Hardly."

"O yes I have. There's a kind of laziness in just ticking over, don't you think?"

"Possibly. I find these days that ticking over is about as much as I can manage, but then you must remember my considerable seniority. Not to mention my arthritis."

"David! I didn't mean you're lazy—absolutely not. You're not lazy now and you never have been. And somebody looking at me, and how I spend my days, from the outside wouldn't think I'm particularly lazy either. Compared to other old ladies,

I mean. About average for laziness I expect. But 'spend', you see. Spending the days till there aren't any days left—that's what I've suddenly seen, spending as wasting. I could be using rather than wasting the days. But am I capable of writing a book interesting enough for anyone to want to read it? What do you think?"

"I would be interested." Then he laughed. "But if you're going to write it in time for me to read it, you'd better be getting on with it, hadn't you?"

Relief, and, almost, tears,

"O David. Thank you. So you don't think the idea totally idiotic?"

"Certainly not. Foolhardy, perhaps. It will be a great deal of work for sure. But not idiotic. Once you begin, you will soon see whether or not a book is a possible project. If it is, you'll be busy for months, even years." He laughed again. "That'll be excellent, won't it? By the way—"

"What?"

"I hope you'll still have time to come out for lunch occasionally?"

"Of course, of course. I couldn't manage without seeing you. You know that, don't you?"

"Yes, Clare." He cleared his throat. "Now, you should be planning where and how you're going to undertake this great work. So, I shall return to my very long book, about the rise and misdeeds of the East India Company. Excellent, a brand-new book. But it's very heavy, I mean heavy as an object, so it's lucky I've got my table over my knees."

Where had she just heard of the East India Company? Yes. Hakim's Ayesha and Assam. She had seen a review of the book David was reading. How admirably he kept up with what was new.

"Yours, I have no doubt, will be shorter and even better. Do we meet next Friday as usual?"

"Yes, we do. I look forward to it. Thank you, David. And it won't be a great work. But I'll try, and we'll see what happens."

He was right. She needed to decide how and where she was going to write. She walked from room to room in the flat, leaving her sandwiches on their plate in the kitchen, until she made up her mind.

Not Simon's study: too much of Simon still there, with what would have been his amused scorn for this enterprise. Not Matt's room: it was still Matt's room, and Hakim or Carrie might need it at some point. Not Penny's old room, long detached from associations with Penny but full of stuff that had no other home and that Carrie or her sister might one day want. A cot. A sewing machine. Matt's fort with soldiers in khaki mixed up with knights in armour. A rocking horse that had once been the light of Penny's six-year-old life. Her own bedroom? No, because she would need it to be where she escaped from working on the book. Perhaps the sitting room, where there was the old desk with a sloping lid that folded down to make a writing surface, revealing cheerful pigeon-holes and small drawers? She had written her book about Augustine at this desk, with a fountain pen on lined yellow paper, why yellow she couldn't remember. Someone else had typed it out, not entirely accurately and she hadn't checked the typescript carefully enough: mistakes had got through. That was all in the ancient past. Now she had a laptop, which Carrie had helped her to buy, mostly for emails, but she had learnt to type a thousand years ago when she was at Cambridge, so she would write her book on the laptop. And—at last it was obvious and she stopped looking at each room in her flat as if she didn't know all of them intimately—she would write it at the kitchen table, where she felt happiest.

She ate her sandwiches, and they were very good.

That evening after the Archers—he knew she always listened to them—David rang her and said, "Just one thing. Tell the truth. If it seems too simple, or too complicated, never mind. Just try to tell it as it is."

"I will. Thank you again, David."

For a couple of weeks she dithered. The project some of the time looked exciting, an attractive challenge; most of the time it looked evidently impossible, far too difficult for someone of her age who had never even kept a diary.

That wasn't quite true. When she was twelve or thirteen her father had given her for Christmas a leather-bound five-year diary with gilt-edged pages, a lock and a little gold key. It came in a shiny white cardboard box, with Truslove & Hanson in gold writing on the lid. A printer's present. The secrecy, even mystery, implied by the lock had inspired her to resolve on the first of January of whatever year it had been, to write a few lines every evening pinning down the most interesting thing to have occurred, or to have occurred to her, that day. She also resolved not to look back at what she had written until three months had gone by. She was a self-disciplined child and stuck to both resolutions. On the last day of March she read through what she had written so far, three months' worth of half a dozen lines a day crammed into the small space the diary allowed. Her record of things that had happened was boring; her thoughts, as she could see perfectly well, were pretentious and embarrassing. She decided to abandon the project until she, or her life, had become more interesting. She put the diary away somewhere and forgot about it, until now when it had long disappeared and would be useless to her anyway, even if she had gone on for years filling those little spaces.

So how could she begin?

With an event? There were no events in her life. Then there was Penny's telephone call.

Five days after Penny's telephone call, which changed everything, she began to write her story. It seemed obvious to start it with those hours of indecision at the kitchen table when she thought about everything else because she couldn't decide what, if anything, to do about the boy from Libya pleading for help in the petrol station.

At about six, having decided not to ring Hakim, because of Friday prayers and because she didn't want to mix him up with the police or the Home Office, she finally made up her mind to telephone David.

"Are you all right?"

He sounded a little alarmed, unsurprisingly because they had had lunch together and it was unlike her to be ringing him so soon after seeing him.

"I'm so sorry to bother you, after our lovely lunch. I'm fine. But something happened when I got back home."

"You had a fall?"

"No, no, I'm perfectly all right. Really."

David had fallen several times in his house, and now took very great care not to fall again. She had tried to persuade him to wear an alarm button round his neck. He resolutely refused to admit he needed one.

"Penny rang. She was filling up her car on the South Circular when a boy who was cleaning windscreens at the garage gave her a piece of paper. She read it when she got home and it just said 'From Libya Help."

Silence while David took this in.

"What did she do?"

"She didn't do anything. She rang me. She said it was my sort of thing. I think she couldn't quite manage to do absolutely nothing—she does feel some things, you know—but she couldn't possibly get involved herself, because of Charles, or even tell him, come to that. You know what he's like. And Penny's an avoider: if she passed the problem on to me, she could forget about it."

"And what have you done, about this boy?"

"Nothing. I'm far too old and far too much of a coward to try to find him. And of course I don't have a car any more."

"No. And if you did, it would be most unwise to go chasing after a boy who may be in the power of dangerous criminals. Gang masters. Very sinister, one gathers. All the same—"

He stopped. Perhaps to think.

"All the same?" she said.

"This boy may well be in serious danger himself. One reads about asylum seekers, as they're called while no one remembers the meaning of the words, wretched refugees without papers who end up as slaves. Specially if they're very young. And Libya is terrible, even worse for Africans in camps who have struggled across the Sahara than it is for Libyans themselves."

"I know. Penny did say this boy is black."

"That doesn't identify him. He may have crossed the Sahara, from Chad or Niger for instance. Or he may be a Libyan. The Arabs in North Africa have had black slaves since time began. Gaddafi had black mercenaries. If you have mercenaries and don't pay them, they're slaves."

"I knew you would know about where this poor boy might have come from. Not that it makes much difference, probably, by the time he's cleaning windscreens on the South Circular. But do you think there's anything one can do, to help him, I mean, without risking making things worse for him?"

"I doubt it. Anything that gets the police or the Home Office involved would probably do exactly that, make things worse. He might well be sent to one of these dreadful detention centres they have now, a disgrace no one talks about much. It's horrifying that they exist in England. The kind of thing our parents escaped when they got out of Germany. That's why—"

"Exactly. That's why I knew you'd understand."

"I understand. I hate to think of the loneliness and terror of having to live, here, in London, in the way this boy probably has to live. But understanding doesn't get us any further about what to do."

Another silence.

Then he said, "How old does Penny think he is?"

"About sixteen, she thought. But obviously it was difficult to tell. It sounded as if she only saw him for a minute or two."

"Sixteen? He's a child."

"Well, he may be. She said he could be older. Or even younger."

"Clare. We have to find this boy."

"I know. But how? And what could we do, even if we can find him?"

"Have you asked Hakim what he thinks?"

"No. I didn't want to bother him. And I didn't want to risk him getting into trouble himself, specially with the Home Office."

"He's got a perfectly good work visa, hasn't he?"

"Yes, he has. But according to the papers you can't trust the immigration officials nowadays, even to stick to what they're supposed to do. Or rely on decisions made before the referendum. Look at the old Jamaicans who were suddenly told to go home. Just the other day, after fifty, sixty years, when they were asked to come in the first place. Mrs May's hostile environment. I would hate—"

"Clare", he said again. "I know you think a lot of Hakim. I sympathize. I really do. I can see you don't want to put him in harm's way. But do you think Hakim would put his own interests before those of a refugee who may be being treated as a slave by who knows what kind of criminal? From what I've seen of that young man, I'm sure he wouldn't. I think we should at least consult him. After all, he is a Libyan."

"Well, but—"

Trying to stop him was no good now; she could tell from his voice.

"Ask him to meet us, both of us, in the café round the corner from South Ken tube station, at ten tomorrow morning, and we'll tell him about this boy and see what he thinks. He doesn't have to work on Saturdays, does he?"

"There are meetings sometimes, I think. But his weekends are mostly free. So all right. I can certainly ask him. If you really think it's a good idea."

"It's the only idea I've got. And you might try and find out from Penny exactly which garage she's talking about."

David in this mood was not to be argued with. And she was pleased, after her long hours of indecision, to have been presented with a plan.

She rang Penny, on her Barnes number, which Clare had known by heart for twenty years. When the telephone produced only a continuous wail, she remembered they had abandoned their landline because Charles preferred not to be reachable by a number that existed in online directories. "I don't want Penny bullied by constituents wanting to tear a strip off me. Or anti-Brexit journalists. It's not fair on her."

Without much hope of Penny answering, she tried her mobile, having looked up the wholly unmemorable number. The voicemail message. She left a message, asking Penny to ring her when she could. Not important, she said, though it was, because she didn't want to worry Penny, and certainly didn't want to mention the boy or the petrol station for fear of Charles asking questions.

She rang Hakim, who said he had just got home. She apologized for bothering him on a Friday evening—"No, Clare. You know you may call me at any time. I always like to hear you."—and then asked him if he could possibly meet her and David in the morning. Something had happened about which they needed his advice. "I'm so sorry it's such short notice. Of course you may be busy in the morning—a Museum meeting or something?"

"There is no meeting tomorrow. And Ayesha is on duty all weekend at her hospital."

"Could you meet us in the café just round the corner from South Kensington tube station. The dear old Piccadilly Line. Turn right out of the station and it's on the right. Could you get there by ten o'clock?"

"Of course. It will be a pleasure to see you and Dr Rose. I hope I will be able to help you."

His perfect manners sometimes almost made her cry.

She ate some ham and scrambled eggs for supper, drank some apple juice and then some decaff coffee, while she listened to the radio, the angry arguments, almost entirely about Brexit, of the politicians on Any Questions, had a bath and got through her bedtime routine, one statin pill, one tiny aspirin, teeth to be cleaned, moisturizer for her face, too lined for anything to make any difference to it now but it might as well not dry up completely, hand cream. She brushed her hair without looking in the mirror. She felt exhausted by a day in which she had done almost nothing but think.

Before she got into bed she prayed, as usual, between the curtains and the glass of her bedroom window. No one about outside. She heard a street door open. A cat came out and walked across the road to the railings of the square, its tail in the air as if it owned London.

The cat will come back, and be let in, and will probably sleep in a basket in a warm kitchen. Where is Penny's boy from Libya sleeping?

When she left the flat at twenty to ten in the morning to walk to South Kensington underground station, Penny hadn't rung. She wasn't surprised. What with the Tory party conference and the news about an extension to Brexit and possible general election dates changing every day, Penny must have her work cut out keeping Charles calm enough to avoid a heart attack. He was so desperate for Brexit not to be foiled by Remoaners—horrible dismissive word—in the House of Commons that he seemed to care about nothing else that was going on in the whole world. So loyal Penny would be jollying him along: no need for her to worry about a 'not important' telephone call from her mother.

She knew exactly how much time the walk would take her, walking briskly with her stick. She enjoyed it, the exercise, the fresh air, Prince Albert's wide pavements, the weather just after late summer, just before early autumn, the sunshine. Not many people about. The traffic somehow cheerful.

It seemed much longer ago than yesterday that she had walked to lunch with David. Only Penny's telephone call, and hers to David, her fruitless call to Penny, and then her call which did find Hakim, had actually happened since she was last on this same pavement. But the time had been full. How much of life is a mixture of anxiety and memory, the particular combinations of that day, that hour, instantly forgotten. Known to God. The truth of unremembered things.

She reached the café at five to ten. David and Hakim were already sitting at a table on the pavement. David waved. How good, how reliable, both of them were. Hakim got up to greet her with his bow. She gestured to David, with his stick leaning against the arm of his chair, not to try to.

Her capuccino, which both of them knew she liked, was waiting for her.

"Have you—?" she began, to David.

"No. I thought we should let you explain. And you have the first-hand story."

"Something happened to Penny yesterday", she said to Hakim, and told him about the telephone call and the appeal on a piece of paper. "David and I thought you might have some idea about what we could do."

"What exactly did Penny tell you about this boy?"

"About sixteen, she thought he was. Very thin. And black."

"I see."

Hakim drank a mouthful of coffee, thought for a moment.

"He could be from anywhere. There are many black people in Libya, specially from Chad. But for a long time they have found ways of living there, and they know how dangerous it is to try to cross the sea. It is more likely that this boy reached Libya from another country, from south of the Sahara, and hoped to travel to Europe. The camps in Tripoli are so terrible, any danger in a boat he would choose instead of staying in Libya. He would be even more likely to choose a boat and the risks if he has lost his family or left them in his own country, perhaps hundreds of miles behind him. He would be most desperate to cross the sea if he had borrowed or stolen the money at home to pay whoever took him across the desert. Probably he will have promised to send money back, from magical Europe, to his poor family at home. By the time he reached a Libyan camp he will have had no money and no possibility to go back. So he will risk the sea."

"O Hakim, how awful", she said, realizing instantly how weak, how old, and how English she sounded. English and old and weak, a good description of the country now. Unequal to the world we helped to make.

"It is common, this story", Hakim said. "How he may have got to London, who knows? It is very unlikely that he has legal papers. He may not have even a passport. If he is asking for help, he is probably in the power of someone else, who will have taken his passport if he had one."

"But that's really dreadful", Clare said. "So do you think he's likely to be more or less a slave?"

"Almost certainly. At the mosque we have heard of a number of such young men. The mosques here try to help these boys if they do manage to get to London. But it is very difficult to help them, even if families can be found to look after them. If they are caught coming in to the country there are officials and tribunals to face, something called, I believe, the National Referral Mechanism. I have helped a Syrian boy to try to understand the papers he was given. He turned up at the mosque. I haven't seen him again. The system is not fair. There are detention centres to which these people are sent if they are refused permission to be here. Failed, they are called. The detention centres are not as bad as the camps in Libya of course, but they are bad enough. Barbed wire and guards. Often, even if they are very young and have no money at all, the decision is given that they are refused to remain, a negative conclusive grounds decision, it is called, a phrase they do not understand. Naturally, then, while they are kept in a detention camp waiting to be deported, which they are terrified of, they can sometimes escape. They can manage to become lost. And so anyone who gives them a meal or a bed can control them. It is a cruel place, where they find themselves, when they risked their lives to come here."

She was too ashamed, of England, to say anything. So, perhaps was David, who didn't meet her glance.

"Suppose", David said, after a miserable silence, "we were to be able to find this boy, is there anything any of us could do to help him?"

Hakim took another sip from his little cup of espresso coffee and a sip of water from his glass. He looked first at David and then, for longer, at Clare.

Very deliberately, he said, "I think, probably not."

"But surely", Clare said, "one of us could give him somewhere to stay, at least for a short time?"

"The penalty for harbouring an illegal immigrant", Hakim said, "is fourteen years in prison."

Clare felt almost as if someone had slapped her. "But that's outrageous! Even a child? Suppose a boy like this is sleeping on the street with nothing and you pick him up and take him home and give him a bath and a meal and a bed?"

"In the morning, you must report him to the police and they will come and find he has no papers and cannot answer their questions and they will take him away and put him behind barbed wire in a camp. If you keep him for longer, you are a person harbouring an illegal immigrant."

"I never heard anything so dreadful. This is supposed to be

England. I can tell you, Hakim, it never used to be like this. My father, and David's parents came to England from Europe before the Second World War and, as you see, were—"

Were what? She didn't know how to go on. Were perfectly all right? Were welcomed? David's parents weren't exactly welcomed, tolerated and useful as cheap labour, more like. And there was detention at the beginning of the war for David's father. Her own father was a professional already, what Boris Johnson describes as the brightest and best. An alien but not an enemy. So he found work. And, at least before the war, there were no camps, no barbed wire.

Then she remembered what a difficult time the West Indians had in the 1950s, wanted and needed, and at the same time despised for being black, and how some of them, old now and having lived long, useful lives in England, were told only recently that they should 'go home'. That was careless official cruelty. And never mind the Home Office, there had been racism on the streets all her life, racist people frightening and bullying those West Indians after the war, and the Pakistanis later, and all Muslims since the terrorist attacks. And now again the Jews, as a hundred years ago, with the behaviour of Israel an excuse.

David helped her.

"It wasn't altogether easy, as a matter of fact, for refugees then, although my parents and Clare's father were grateful to be allowed to live here when the alternative, at home, in Germany and Czechoslovakia, was so terrifying and became so murderous. But now—"

Hakim leant forward. Clare could see how surprised he was.

"Dr Rose. Do I understand correctly, that your parents were Jewish? And Clare's father too?"

"That's right", David said. "All three of them. If they hadn't come to England, they would almost certainly have been killed, I would almost certainly not have survived childhood, and Clare would never have existed."

Clare met his affectionate look, and smiled.

Hakim looked from one to the other, and back.

"So you are the children of refugees, of people for whom this was a new country, a new language. Was it German, the first language of your parents?"

"It was, yes. My parents were German Jews from Hamburg, where Jews had lived for centuries. Clare's father was a Jew from Prague but his first language also was German."

"So, their language was the language of the enemy, the recent enemy about to become again the enemy?"

"Yes. That's right. They learnt English as quickly as they could."

"That is like Arabic now. Arabic is the language of terrorists. Very fortunately, most English people do not recognize it if they hear it in the street. Or, I suppose, Punjabi. As different as could be, but also the language of terrorists."

So much of Hakim's life in London Clare realized, not for the first time, she knew nothing about.

But he was thinking of her and David.

"Has it been a problem for you, Dr Rose, being a Jew in England? Clare, I suppose you are only half a Jew, is that correct?"

"Yes. My mother was English, extremely English you could say. She was rather like Penny. And my husband was English. So I have always seemed entirely English to most people."

They waited for David to answer Hakim's question.

"No. And yes", he said after a minute or two. "I was a doctor in London all my life, as you know. Perhaps three or four patients in forty years hesitated to trust me. 'I never thought I would have a Jewish doctor. My father would be horrified.' That kind of thing. I imagine they had been brought up to believe that Jewish doctors are charlatans and all Jews are only interested in money. As far as I remember, they acquired the confidence to stay on my list."

He looked at Clare and smiled. Hakim, she thought, will be only puzzled by this.

"But now", David went on, "things are rather different, or they would be if I were younger. I am so old that most of the people I know who are still alive I have known for many many years. But I'm told by the young—"

Who are they? Clare wondered. Or, more likely, who is he? David's life, after all these decades of their friendship, was actually more mysterious to her than Hakim's.

"—that all the old anti-Semitic clichés have reappeared in the last couple of years and are alive and well in this country. The Protocols—you won't have heard of them. A very successful slander invented by the Russians a hundred years ago. Apparently on social media, a closed book to the old, to Clare's and my generation, I'm thankful to say, they tell each other that Jews are plotting to rule the world, that behind the scenes they are running Trump and running Putin, that the money autocrats need everywhere is supplied by Jews, and so on and so on. They say Jews organized 9/11: how or why they don't explain. They even say that the Jews are responsible for flooding Europe with Muslims so that Christian civilization will be destroyed. George Soros, have you heard of him?"

Hakim shook his head.

"Exactly. Most people haven't. But he is supposed to be paying Muslims to come into Europe, paying Central Americans to cross the Mexican border into the US, paying the rescuers of people who should be left to drown in the Mediterranean."

"Who is he?"

"He is a Hungarian Jew who made a great deal of money in the west, and with his money has done a very great deal of good. He was deliberately chosen as a propaganda enemy, a target for accusation and abuse, by the Hungarian Prime Minister who is a right-wing nationalist. The Hungarian Prime Minister, whose name is Victor Urban, has had American fascist help and he is much cleverer than Trump. Not that that would be difficult. He has played on peasant fear of immigrants and ancient Hungarian anti-Semitism to pretend that George Soros is to blame for everything that hasn't gone right in Hungary, and Europe, in the last ten years. Trump loves this scapegoating, one of the oldest populist tricks, and he and his propaganda machine in America, Fox News and all that, have spread this anti-Semitic nonsense across the country while at the same time supporting the extreme settler policy of Netanyahu in Israel, another right-wing nationalist, who permits worse and worse mistreatment of the Palestinians in Gaza and the West Bank."

Hakim, Clare could see, was paying close attention to David. He was good at attention.

"I am not sure that I understand, Dr Rose", he said. "Because you are a Jew, and because your own parents had to escape Germany when the Jews were being murdered, will you not always, even if you live in England, be a citizen of Israel? Is it not said by the Jews that at last in Israel they have a home in the country, or the land, they were forced to leave hundreds and hundreds of years ago? And is not Israel the place where you would like to be when you say that people are more against Jews now, even here in England, than they were when you were young? Why, for example, does what you have told about Mr Soros not make you even more devoted to Israel?"

"O, Hakim. I understand why you ask the question. Indeed I do. It should be a perfectly simple question. But things, you know, are always more complicated than they look, and to the old, who have seen a good deal of history, things are inclined to become more complicated still."

"Please—", Hakim began.

"I'm sorry", David said. "I apologize. I will try to explain. First I will get some more coffee, and perhaps some cake for us all? I am enough of a German to like, occasionally, some cake with my coffee, though I have never lived anywhere except London. I have never, you see, even visited Israel."

Clare put a hand on his arm to stop him. "Don't get up, David. I'll get us all some more coffee. And some cake if it looks eatable."

She left them, to queue briefly at the café counter. She knew David wouldn't start his explanation until she came back, which she did almost at once, with a tray, more coffee for herself and Hakim as well as David, and three plates with slices of cake that were unlikely to be as good as they looked.

"Thank you, Clare", David and Hakim said almost simultaneously.

"When I was your age", David began, "younger than you are, I suppose, I, we, English Jews, whether they were religious or not, and I never was, were tremendously proud of Israel. It seemed to us that by a miracle a place of refuge and independence had been given to the Jews who had managed to survive the Nazis, and that this new country would be a beacon of freedom, democracy, everything good that we were able to imitate from England, France, America, anti-Semitic countries, all of them, by the way, up to Hitler and beyond. It's difficult to imagine now, specially for someone as young as you, that Israel then seemed to us, and to many non-Jews also, a noble enterprise. If you look at the best of what it was trying to do, what, in the beginning, it did, it actually was a noble enterprise. Rather as, once upon a time, and on a much grander scale, America was a noble enterprise. That's if you chose not to be concerned about the people, in both cases, who were swept out of the way for the sake of what was new and to be admired, the shining city on a hill. Those heroic Puritans in America didn't count the Indians as people, just as the settlers in the West Bank don't count the Palestinians as people. No wonder half the settlers are Americans who think they're in the wild west, commissioned by God to push the frontier forward."

He ate a small piece of his cake, drank a mouthful of coffee. Clare and Hakim didn't move.

"Friends of mine went to work on kibbutzim in the holidays from university; some liked the life so much they went back after university for two or three years. One stayed for good."

Clare liked to hear his Hebrew plural, and caught a passing shadow of sadness about the friend who stayed for good.

"When Israel won the 6-day war in 1967, we rejoiced. I think lots of English people who weren't Jews rejoiced with us. It had taken till the 60's for the facts of the holocaust really to be known here. If you had lost everyone, of course you always knew. So to most people the sudden, brilliant victory seemed to be not only a military triumph but also a manifestation of justice, something at last going right for the Jews. I had been too young in the 1940s to understand how terrible the establishment of Israel had been for the Palestinians, and I'm ashamed to say that I didn't realize for far too long, many many years, how wrong it was that Israel insisted on hanging on to the lands conquered in 1967. I also didn't realize for too long how many Palestinians have had to live, into the third generation now, in camps in other countries—camps again. Camps have been the plague of the twentieth century, and now they are the plague of the twenty-first, when the world swore never again."

He broke off another piece of cake, ate it and took another mouthful of coffee.

"If only" he said, "there had been some generosity, some magnanimity - "

"I'm sorry", Hakim interrupted. "This is a word I do not know."

"Yes you do", Clare said. "Latin. Greatness of soul." Damn. The schoolma'am, she thought.

But, without looking at her, Hakim nodded. "Of course", he said. She was careful not even to smile.

"Exactly", David said. "Greatness of soul is what the Jews are supposed to have. They failed then, after the 1967 war, to live up to that greatness. Fifty years ago, they failed. More than fifty years. And they have failed much worse since. The settlers claim to be acting according to the will of God while Israeli soldiers force people out of their homes and off land their families have farmed for centuries. They set fire to their olive trees, an immemorial crime in the Mediterranean as Hakim will know. Sometimes they shoot them, shoot them dead, because they're bored—I have read of such a case, and the soldier who did the shooting was barely punished—this is the use of religion to bully harmless men and women and children, something that Jews suffered at the hands of Christians down the ages."

"But the Palestinians do not stop sending rockets into Israel. Is not that also true?"

David drank the rest of his coffee, put down his cup, put both his hands on the table and smiled at Hakim.

"How long have you been in England, Hakim?" he said.

"Five and a half years", he said.

"Not very long, but long enough to find yourself, an Arab, defending Jews to a Jew who is attacking the way Jews are treating Arabs. Congratulations, Hakim. And some congratulations to England too."

Hakim, perhaps not entirely understanding, shook his head.

"No. I mean it", David said. "You are without bigotry. As am I, I hope. But I have had a lifetime to learn. Now listen. Yes, the Palestinians in Gaza fire rockets into Israel. There is nothing else they can do. But it is very foolish and unnecessary to fire those rockets. Occasionally an Israeli is killed or injured, either by a rocket or because a Palestinian in the street attacks an Israeli with a knife or even a few Israelis die because a Palestinian throws a home-made bomb that doesn't, as is usually the case, do very little harm. Then what happens? There is Israeli retaliation: tanks, aeroplanes, all the equipment of a modern army supplied by America, are sent in to retaliate. Dozens, even hundreds of Palestinians are killed. So—it is foolish and unnecessary to fire the rockets."

More cake. Hakim hadn't touched his cake.

David was still explaining.

"The inequality of resources is so great that the Palestinians should ask for proper negotiations, for a peace to be agreed, having recognized the existence of Israel, which is there, and which is not going anywhere. You see? This would be an appeal to the magnanimity of the Jews which even the present government of Israel would find it difficult, in the eyes of the world, to turn down, President Trump or no President Trump. But will it ever happen? Probably not in my lifetime. Perhaps in yours."

"There is so much hatred", Hakim said.

"I know. I know. It's the same in so many places in the world. The hatred of the generations, sometimes of the centuries. Look at Ireland. Yet sometimes some of the hatred can be dissolved. In good will, which has the power of magic. Ireland again. But then stupid politicians make stupid decisions without thinking of the consequences, and hatred may rise again because it has sunk to the bottom of the bucket but not gone away. Alas."

"I know almost nothing of Ireland", Hakim said.

"Of course. Why should you know about this relic of empire, a small divided country where under a surface which hasn't had time to become strong there is hatred of the old colonial power and a long tradition of the people hating each other?"

Hakim's turn to take a mouthful of coffee.

"This is also a description of Libya." He smiled as he said this, perhaps because he was pleased at having understood everything, or almost everything, that David had said. Clare was proud of both of them, as if she had invented each of them for the other. After all, she thought, in schoolma'am mode, invent means find.

"Is it? Is it really? Ah—the Italians. I'd forgotten about them. But divided?"

"Libya is divided, since the beginning of history. Clare knows. She will tell you about Libya. Also, although Libya is the second largest country in Africa, it is very small in people, I'm sorry, very few in people. Probably as few as in Ireland."

"Surely not? Ireland really is a small country. So, of course, is Israel. Israel is probably a quarter the size of Ireland with twice the population. Vulnerable because it is small, dangerous because it is packed with passionate people. Smallest of all, by far, and most packed with passionate people, is Gaza. The destructive power of hatred has nothing to do with size, and everything to do with history, therefore with decisions made, and foolish, or wicked, policies pursued by people in power."

Silence, between the three of them.

Hakim got his phone out of his pocket and tapped away for only a minute or two.

"The population of Ireland, the whole of Ireland, and the population of Libya are almost exactly the same", he said.

David laughed and said to Clare, "What it is to be young."

Hakim looked a little offended.

"We're not laughing at you", Clare said. "We're impressed. And of course you're not as young as all that, just very much younger than we are."

She finished her coffee. She wanted to bring them back to Penny's boy at the petrol station, but didn't know how to.

Eventually, Hakim said, "So, Dr Rose, with all this hatred in the world, do you think that there is anything that one person, without power, can do? To make the hatred less?"

"My dear boy, there's always very little, I'm afraid, that a powerless person can do. But sometimes there will be the opportunity for some kindness, some good will perhaps, that can make a difference to another person."

Another silence, broken by Clare and Hakim saying at the same moment, "Surely there's something—" and "The boy from Libya—" and breaking off, to smile at each other.

"Yes", David said. "Precisely. One can't do nothing, even if there isn't any obvious way of helping this boy. If he can be found, there may be ways of connecting him with a charity, the Salvation Army for instance, or the Red Cross, or perhaps if he's a Muslim with a mosque, while circumventing the police and the dreaded immigration officials."

"Wouldn't the Salvation Army or the Red Cross have to report him, as Hakim says an ordinary person would have to?"

"I don't know. Probably they would. But if he turns out to be as young as sixteen, or even younger, they might be able to trace a relation or a connection of some kind, someone to look after him, or perhaps find him a foster home for a while. One hears of such things. The wretched boy a couple of years ago, an Iraqi I think he was, who let off a bomb in an underground train, on the District line not far from here, was being fostered by a good English couple who had no idea what he was planning. That shows fostering can sometimes be arranged."

"That boy's father", Hakim said, "was killed by the British in Basra."

"Alas", David said. "How little we know."

Another silence.

"Eat your cake, Hakim", Clare said. "It's actually quite good."

This gave her a minute or two. She knew what David was going to say next.

"I have a car", was what he said. His car was a small old Fiat which he kept on the paved patch in front of the house of someone he knew two streets away from where he lived, someone who didn't own a car, but used his when he didn't need it, which was most days. He drove it rarely but he liked to keep it because his arthritis made the tube and buses difficult.

He had driven Clare to Kew Gardens a few weeks ago, and his driving was cautious but safe.

"Can I borrow your telephone?" he said to Hakim.

When Hakim had shown him how to dial the number, he rang the woman who shared his car. She was in. She didn't need the car.

"I shouldn't be long. An hour or two, I imagine."

He gave the phone back to Hakim

"Thank you. They do have their uses."

"David! You can't go setting off to find this boy! It's too alarming. I haven't heard back from Penny—I had to leave her a message last night, God knows where she is, at the wretched Tory party conference I imagine—so I'm not even sure exactly which garage she was in."

"I'll find it. There can't be many big petrol stations on the South Circular in Barnes. People always get petrol in the nearest place to where they live. I know where Penny lives. QED."

David was excited, as Clare hadn't seen him for years.

"You'll never find him. And even if you do, what happens then?"

"I've no idea. Yahweh Yireh."

"What?"

"Something my mother used to say, because her mother, or probably her great-great-grandmother, long ago in Jewish Hamburg, used to say it. Yahweh Yireh. The Lord will provide."

"David, please! I think it's a mad idea. It could be dangerous. If you manage to find the boy, very unpleasant people may be using him for goodness knows what. There might be drugs, knives, guns, who knows? You really are too old for this."

"I shall go with Dr Rose to find the boy", Hakim said.

"No! Please, Hakim. Not you as well!"

Then she saw that she had almost forgotten the boy. If David were resolved to go, as clearly he was, then much better that Hakim, young and strong and an Arabic speaker which the boy might be, should go with him. She told herself that in broad daylight on a Saturday morning in Barnes no harm was likely to come to them, however sinister the people who might be controlling the boy with the mop turned out to be.

Yet she wanted, desperately, to stop them, to stop them both. Why? She heard Simon's voice from long ago saying that the trouble with women, even clever women like you, is that in the end emotion rules. Well, all right, why not?

It was because of Matt that she didn't want them to go. She had known but never believed that Matt might be killed. When he was, when her beloved Matt was so pointlessly dead, for a while she was more angry than sad, angry with the government which had sent soldiers to Iraq and Afghanistan without any proper idea of why, and angry with herself for letting Matt be a soldier in the first place, though she knew it would have been wrong to try to stop him. She hadn't agreed to those wars, embarked on in her name. She had believed the defence secretary—she couldn't even remember his name—who sent more solders to Afghanistan and said they wouldn't be in danger. She felt like the mothers of soldiers killed in the First World War: no one had explained why they had to go, or what had been achieved by their deaths. Probably the mothers of soldiers in every war since time began had felt the same.

Matt was dead. Simon was dead. Penny was leading a life she found it impossible in all sorts of ways to sympathize with. Carrie was in the Himalayas. Carrie's sister Daisy, whom now she hardly knew, was in Vancouver. She looked across the little café table in the sunshine and saw the two people she felt she had left to love looking at each other as if she weren't there, and about to put themselves in a kind of danger that was difficult to imagine.

Or perhaps not. Perhaps she was letting the memory of Matt leaving the flat for what turned out to be the last time, and her bitter realization ever afterwards that she hadn't taken her farewell to him seriously enough because it hadn't crossed her mind, that day, that she might never see him again, fill her imagination, now, with fear, for David, and even more for Hakim. And yet she knew this was ridiculous. They weren't going thousands of miles away to fight a ruthless enemy in a country of sand and stone and mountains where jeeps full of young soldiers were being blown to pieces by bombs easy to make.

She shook her head vigorously, to dispel all this, which had crowded her with probably needless anxiety in what couldn't have been more than a minute.

"I'm so sorry", she said. "I don't know what came over me. Of course you must go, and see what can be done. It's very good of you, Hakim, to offer to go with David. If you can find this boy, I'm sure you will be a great help."

"Thank you, Clare", David said. He got up stiffly, bracing one knee at a time and gripping hard the plastic arms of his café chair. "I won't keep you a moment, Hakim. I must just—I'll be back in five minutes." He grasped his stick and set off, slowly, in the direction of the Gents.

When he was out of sight, she said, "You will look after him, won't you? He's very brave but he's quite frail, as you can see."

"I will make sure he is not in danger, Clare. But I think it will not be easy to find this boy."

"I'm sure it won't be easy. But if you do find him, you and David are as likely as anyone I can think of to be able to help him."

"We shall try. Dr Rose does know London. I know Libya but that is not so useful." He ate the last bit of his cake. "Dr Rose is a very interesting man. I think he is more of a Jew than he likes English people to see. Would you say?"

She looked at him, at his questioning eyes.

"Yes", she said. "I'm sure you're right. You always notice things, Hakim."

"Maybe as I am more of a Muslim. Some disguise is necessary. And those words in Hebrew, Yahweh Yireh. I have heard them before. They are the name of a place, the place where Abraham was asked to sacrifice his son. The Jews and the Christians say the son was Isaac. Muslims say the son was Ishmael. But the story is the same. So there was God, Allah, Yahweh, wanting Abraham to show that he would sacrifice the person he loved most in the world, his son. Abraham showed that he would do this. And Allah provided. Perhaps Abraham believed that God would provide, a ram for him to sacrifice instead of his boy, because Abraham named the place Yahweh Yireh before he had reached the place of sacrifice."

134

Clare felt dizzy. As she saw David approaching hesitantly from the shadows at the back of the café, she managed to say, "You know so much, Hakim."

"I read", he said.

"Let's go, Hakim", David said as he reached their table. "We'll see what, if anything, we can do. Please don't worry, Clare. This is safe west London on a fine Saturday morning. I'll let you know later how we got on."

She watched them leave the café, Hakim, who hadn't touched her in five years of distant closeness, taking David's arm as they reached the edge of the pavement to cross the road. They disappeared behind the traffic.

She managed, but only just, not to cry, or not to cry noticeably, into the empty coffee cups and the three plates with their cake crumbs. She took a tissue out of the packet in her bag and blew her nose angrily, to stop herself imagining, absurdly she knew perfectly well, that she would never see them, that she would never see Hakim, again. Yahweh yireh. A new prayer. Thy will be done, nearly the same. She crumpled the tissue, put it on her plate and shook her head, to banish what Simon would have regarded as foolish emotion.

She looked at her watch. Nearly quarter to eleven. So much seemed to have happened in less than an hour. Really nothing had happened. Some talk. A new connection between David and Hakim. Was she pleased about this? She was certainly pleased that Hakim had offered to go with David on this errand. Better to leave it at that for the moment, though she was suddenly angry with Penny, as she hadn't been all yesterday afternoon, for throwing at her this plea from a desperate stranger and then vanishing completely.

Where was Penny likely to be?

She had brought the *Guardian* with her in case David and Hakim were late: they had been early. Bless them, she thought, meaning it. She turned a page or two of the paper. The Tory party conference was starting in Manchester tomorrow. Penny and Charles were probably there already. "It's quite fun, the party conference. Loads of wives and girlfriends and a lot of networking. Charles is awfully good at networking, going to the right fringe meetings and all that, and he enjoys meeting masses of people." Penny made it sound like a cross between a football match and the Edinburgh Festival without the concerts. She certainly wouldn't have time to return her mother's not important call. Just as well perhaps.

She read a bit more of the paper. Boris Johnson clearly wanted an election, another election, as soon as possible, presumably because he thought he was likely to win it. If he got a proper majority, he would be able to do more or less anything he liked. The idea of him as Prime Minister for another several years made Clare feel utterly miserable, because he seemed to her, as he had seemed all along, ever since he decided to support Brexit on a toss-up basis, irredeemably lightweight and irresponsible, a clever undergraduate playing with serious questions for laughs and so keen on getting the people in the room to love him that he would say anything they would like to hear. Careless. Not because he dropped things but because he was clearly without care, concern, fellow feeling with anyone about anything. Without good will, as David had called what was, everywhere, so disastrously missing.

She put the paper on the table and looked over to the window, the pavement, the road, the traffic, as if David and Hakim might miraculously reappear.

Ridiculous. Pull yourself together. She looked at her watch again. Five more minutes had gone by. She decided to go home, see if there were any post or a message from Penny, and then, since the sun was shining, find a soothing book that had nothing to do with politics or refugees and sit in the garden of her square for an hour, to kill some time. David wasn't likely to telephone for at least a couple of hours.

Though she had remembered to switch on the answerphone, there was no message from Penny and the post had brought only a glossy account, from the National Trust, of various remarkable places to visit, and her annual membership card.

She sat down at the kitchen table, giving herself ten minutes to think about something completely different before she went out again.

She opened the National Trust report. Beautiful pictures of beaches and islands and cliff-top paths. A Victorian kitchen with shelves of white china and copper pans in some country house. A picture of Housesteads Fort with Hadrian's Wall on the crest of the Northumbrian hills rolling into the distance, where she wanted to go with Hakim and never would.

She decided to remember instead the first time she came across the National Trust, probably nearly sixty years ago. She had a sort of boyfriend in her third term at Cambridge. In those innocent days—it was 1961 but the Sixties hadn't started—it was possible to go out with a boy every now and then for weeks without more than a goodnight kiss, which might, if he was a shy boy, be on the cheek, and perhaps holding hands on a walk in the country. It was a different world: she thought of Carrie and smiled.

Having spent every summer of her life so far on the edge of the North York Moors, she didn't think much of what she had seen, which was very little, of the dull country near Cambridge. But this boy, whose name she couldn't remember though she remembered his nervous friendliness and above all his very unreliable car, took her out for a day in beautiful spring weather, perhaps early May, well before whatever exams each of them was meant to be working for. They drove to a place called Wicken Fen, which she had never heard of, perhaps twenty miles from Cambridge. This was asking quite a lot of his car, which was hot, uncomfortable, rattled, and smelt of petrol.

When they stopped, in a stony space for parking where there was one other car, and he turned off the engine, they got out, into gentle sunshine, gentle fresh air, and silence. At once she stopped feeling sick.

Miles of tall rough reeds, unfamiliar marsh flowers, channels of water, ponds, almost lakes here and there, board paths to walk on, birds she had never seen before flying out of the reeds, more birds swimming on the water, invisible birds calling through the fen, calls she had never heard before, and once, but several times from the same bird, the eerie boom of the bittern. No people. Except for the birds and the faint rustle, all the time, of the reeds, a silence unlike any she had ever come across. A magical silence. She had an idea that "wicken" meant something like "where witches live", but the magic was benign.

In the car park, where the single car was still there when they left, there was a notice board, with pictures of the birds and flowers they might see, an honesty box into which they each put half a crown, and another box with leaflets saying why not join the National Trust, which she had never heard of. She put a leaflet in her bag.

Half way back to Cambridge, the car stalled on a country road and wouldn't start. The young man opened the bonnet, peered unconvincingly into the engine and fiddled with something. With oil all over his hands he shut the bonnet and tried to start the car. It wouldn't start, and the sound it made suggested that it never would. They looked across the flat, unhelpful fields either side of the road. There was one farmhouse, several fields away. When a car came along, the young man stopped it, asked the woman driver if she could call at the next garage and send someone to help. Then, much to his credit, he said, "You're not going to Cambridge, by any chance?" She was, and took Clare back to her college.

She couldn't remember whether or not she ever saw the young man again. But she filled in the form on the National Trust leaflet, sent it with a modest cheque, and had been a member ever since.

She couldn't decide on a book to take to the square, and settled for the latest *New York Review of Books*, which she had subscribed to for years and found properly bracing. She walked down the stairs, quieter than the old lift, crossed the road, unlocked the wrought-iron gate in the railings, locked it behind her, and was pleased to see that no one was sitting on her favourite bench, under a tall tree and at the other end of the garden from the sandpit and swings. She took the *New York Review* out of its cellophane package, got up and threw the cellophane into the empty rubbish bin in its slatted wooden container—the garden was very well looked after—sat down again and tried to concentrate on the first article. It was about politics and refugees.

Where were they now?

She put the paper on the bench beside her.

The garden was nearly empty, towards lunchtime on a Saturday. Many of the, nowadays very rich, people who lived in the square always went away for the weekend. There were two au pair girls at the other end of the garden chatting on a bench while the toddlers they were in charge of played in the sandpit. Beside one of these girls was a pushchair with a baby asleep in it. A third, similar, girl was looking intently at her mobile phone on a nearby bench—impossible to tell whether or not she was in charge of a child. On another bench, half way along the neat path beside the grass, an old man she had often seen in the square, rather scruffy because no doubt he lived alone, was asleep in the sun though the position he was sitting in looked too uncomfortable for sleep.

How admirable of David, never to look scruffy. But he had always lived alone. The old man in the square had probably lost his wife.

On a bench closer to hers a tortoiseshell cat, which she had also seen in the square before, was asleep too, more comfortably than the old man. No cat asleep ever looks uncomfortable.

She found that, sitting under her tree, in the midday quiet of the square and with not much traffic to be heard, she was almost praying. Or perhaps actually praying. Presenting to God what there was in the day of anxiety and sadness. Today there was a lot of both. There was also whatever she hoped, and she had no idea what it could be, that David and Hakim could achieve for the boy who was, at least, alone and trapped in some way she couldn't imagine. Was this prayer? Not really. But she often remembered an old priest saying to her long ago, "Never worry about what's prayer and what isn't. God doesn't."

This happened to her more and more often the older she got. But as her mind became blank, her feelings numb, she found she had lost the fear, almost the panic, of the café table as David and Hakim left. After the last twenty-four hours, not even twenty-four hours, of having no idea what to do since Penny's telephone call, she was relieved that someone else had made a decision, that something she had no part in was happening she wasn't sure where, and that there was now nothing she could do. Perhaps she was just tired. She looked across the grass to the sleeping old man, to the happy cat. Sleep would be good.

She prayed for the old man, for Hakim, for David, for the boy from Libya, that all of them would be safe.

Certainly she was too old to have sensible ideas about a situation in which almost everything was unknown. David was even older. But doctors get used to making decisions that may or may not be right but have to be made. If a doctor's decision is wrong someone may die; if a doctor's decision is right, the patient may still die.

No, she wasn't praying. She was only longing for the safe return to David's house of David and Hakim, whatever they had or hadn't managed to achieve for the boy from Libya.

Later she couldn't remember how long she had spent sitting in the garden of the square not reading the *New York Review*. She couldn't remember deciding to go back to her flat, or whether the sun was still shining, or whether or not she had bothered to have some lunch. Probably she hadn't.

She remembered only waiting for what seemed like many hours, but can't have been as many as two, for the telephone to ring, and, when it did, the disappointment of a recorded message telling her there was a fault on her computer and she needed to—at which she put down the receiver, having been ordered by Carrie not even to allow such messages to get to the end of their first sentence. "They look up your date of birth, you know, so they can aim these scams at old people, Gran. Thousands of pounds you can lose if you don't look out."

Sometime after three o'clock when she had finished the crossword puzzle, almost fallen asleep at the kitchen table, and made herself a second cup of tea, the telephone rang again.

"Hallo."

"Hallo. Clare."

"Hakim. Thank God. Are you all right? Did you find the boy?"

"Clare. I am at the hospital. With Dr Rose. He is not all right. They say he has a severe stroke. I think you should come."

"O no, Hakim. A stroke? I can't bear it. Poor David. Of course I'll come. Which hospital are you in?"

She waited while Hakim asked someone the name of the hospital.

"Chelsea and Westminster Hospital. In the Fulham Road."

"I'll come straight away. I'll be there in a few minutes."

She found a taxi in the Gloucester Road at once.

"You all right, love?" the taxi driver said.

"No. Yes. I'm fine."

She was shaking, shocked but, she realized, not exactly surprised.

In the taxi she did her best to calm down. Deep breaths. Tensing and relaxing. Childbirth exercises. David would smile at that.

The journey took less than ten minutes.

At the main desk she was told that no patient called Dr David Rose was on the computer.

"That means he isn't on a ward. Are you sure you're looking in the right hospital? Has he recently arrived at A and E? In an ambulance?"

"I don't know. I imagine so. Yes. I know this is the right hospital."

"How long ago did he get here?"

"I don't know. Not very long."

"In that case he's probably still in A and E. They'll tell you at the desk there."

She had to go outside and in again at the A and E entrance to the hospital.

At the desk a nurse said, "Yes. Dr Rose has been through the department. He was brought in—" she looked through a pile of forms on the desk, pulled one out and put it on top of the pile—"about an hour ago. Are you a relative?"

"No. A very old friend."

" O. A young man was with him in the ambulance. Mr - " She checked the form. "Husain. He wasn't a relative either. Do you know who the next of kin would be?"

The nurse, with a pen in her hand, waited for her answer. She thought. She knew there was no living relation.

"I'm afraid not. His parents were Jewish refugees, with no family alive after the war. His sister died many years ago and had no children."

"No wife?"

"No wife."

"Well. Not a lot we can do, then. What is your name?"

"My name? Clare Wilson. Mrs Wilson."

The nurse wrote her name down in a space on the form in front of her.

"Would you like to sit down in the waiting area? I'll see if I can get hold of someone to speak to you. " She picked up one of the telephones on the desk.

Clare sat down, among about fifteen others, and tried to work out the implications of what she'd been told. "Through the department"? Shouldn't that mean he had been admitted to a ward? So why wasn't he on the computer at the main desk? "About an hour ago" must mean he was very ill, to have been seen so quickly. She looked along the two rows of the people waiting. Some, as if they had been there for a long time, were apparently almost asleep. Could she ask them if they had seen David go by, on a stretcher, or a trolley, in a wheelchair? She tried to picture his arrival, from the ambulance, with Hakim at his side. No. How would they know? They weren't talking to each other. Only one of them, an old man, was reading, the *Evening Standard*, folded to a sports page. The others, except for a young woman with a sleeping toddler on her lap, who kept looking at the clock over the desk, were staring at nothing.

Ten minutes went by. Two people were called by their names out of the waiting area, by different nurses who appeared from somewhere. Fifteen minutes.

A third nurse appeared, a piece of paper in her hand.

"Clare Wilson?"

Suddenly terrified, she stood up, her knees shaking. She wished she had brought her stick. Walking as steadily as she could, she followed the nurse down a corridor with doors on either side, most of them open, and people hurrying in both directions, into a small room.

"Please wait here. The doctor won't be long."

The nurse shut the door.

Another clock. More minutes. At least this room had a window. The sun still shone on part of a yard at the back of the hospital. A couple of benches. A few dusty shrubs doing their best. No people. Two notices she couldn't read. Probably forbidding smoking. She longed for a cigarette.

She thought she could hear the clock tick as the second hand moved. Perhaps not. The small table in front of her was empty, perhaps waiting for a doctor to put a file, a patient's notes, on it. The doctor's chair had its back to the window. Beside Clare was another empty chair. The doctor would be able to see the faces of the patient and his wife, her husband, the parents of a sick child. They couldn't see the doctor's face so clearly, against the light. The second hand on the clock was moving, silently. So time was going by.

At last, at last, the door opened. A tired middle-aged woman's face, with spectacles, at the door. She looked Indian, or perhaps Pakistani, or perhaps Iranian. Or, come to that, Libyan.

"Mrs Wilson?"

"Yes".

The woman, evidently a doctor, disappeared, opened the door wider, and let Hakim come in to the room ahead of her. He looked drawn, exhausted.

"Hakim—where's David? What's—?"

"Please sit down, Mrs Wilson", the doctor said.

The doctor moved to the other side of the table and sat down, gesturing to Hakim to sit beside Clare in the other chair.

"Mr Husain. Please."

"I'm so sorry, Clare—", Hakim began, not looking at her.

The doctor interrupted him.

"Mrs Wilson, I'm afraid we couldn't save Dr Rose. It's fairly certain that he had a massive haemorrhagic stroke. That means a bleed in the brain. He will have passed away very quickly and he will not have suffered. There will not have been time for him to realize what was happening."

"But—I don't understand. He wasn't ill. This morning, Hakim, in the café, he wasn't ill at all, was he? He was exactly the same as usual. Of course he was old. He was eighty-three.

But he took good care of himself. After all he's—he was—a doctor."

"I'm afraid", the doctor said, "that this kind of stroke cannot be predicted. It can happen at any age, and it can happen to the healthiest people. We have been in touch with Dr Rose's GP practice and it appears that he was taking medication to reduce his blood pressure, but—"

"So are half the old people I know."

"As I say, Mrs Wilson, this kind of stroke cannot be predicted. I am so sorry."

A silence. Hakim sat motionless beside her.

"In Dr Wilson's diary", the doctor said, in a different, more efficient, voice, "he has you written down as his next of kin, or, to be more exact, the person to be contacted in an emergency. You are not related to him?"

"No. I'm a very old friend. That's all. He has no living relations."

"So will you be responsible for the arrangements?"

"The arrangements?"

"The arrangements that are necessary after a death, Mrs Wilson. An undertaker and so forth. His possessions here, in the hospital."

"O, I see. Yes. Of course, if there's no one else. No. There won't be. Yes, of course."

He would have left instructions. He was careful about everything. The instructions would have been written for her. She would thank him.

He was dead. She didn't yet believe he was dead. She had to make herself believe it.

"May I see him?"

"In a little while. If you would like to wait here with Mr Husain. Do you know Mr Husain?"

"O yes."

"That's good. I thought perhaps Mr Husain was with Dr Rose by chance when he collapsed. If, as I say, you would wait here, I will see that someone fetches you when it is possible for you to see Dr Rose. If you would like tea or coffee, there is a machine in the waiting area."

She got up, shook Clare's hand, across the table. Hakim stood, and bowed, without shaking the doctor's hand and without putting his hand on his heart.

With a nod to both of them, the doctor went out of the room, leaving the door ajar.

For a moment she folded her arms on the table and rested her head on her arms. She was trembling but not crying.

She lifted her head and at last looked at Hakim, looked up at him where he was standing by the door.

"I can't bear it, Hakim."

He looked down at her from the sadness of his eyes.

"I know", he said. "I am very very sorry."

She sat upright, opened her bag, took out a tissue and blew her nose firmly, although she wasn't crying.

"What happened?"

"I will tell you everything. May I first fetch you some tea?"

"Yes please." She smiled a little. "The tea will be less unpleasant than the coffee. Perhaps with some sugar, if there is any."

He went out, leaving the door open, and came back only five minutes later, with two cardboard cups of tea.

"With milk", he said, putting one in front of her on the table. "Also with sugar." Her cup had a cardboard stirrer.

He sat down in the doctor's chair, the other side of the table.

"We did not find the boy from Libya", he said.

She had forgotten about the boy from Libya.

"You didn't? Why not?"

It took her a moment to realize how stupid this question was.

"I'm sorry", she said.

Hakim shook his head.

"No", he said. "Please. You should not be sorry."

He drank some tea, and winced because it was hot. No milk in his tea.

"I will tell you everything."

He put both hands, fists clenched, on the table, resolved.

"First we tried to find him, the boy. Dr Rose drove to the petrol station which he said was the nearest to your daughter's house. It was a very big petrol station. Maybe there were twenty petrol pumps, and many cars coming and going. There was no one cleaning the windscreens of the cars that were stopping for fuel. We went together to the paying desk and Dr Rose asked if they had anyone out cleaning windscreens, yesterday or today. The woman at the desk was not helpful. She seemed not to understand Dr Rose's question, and wanted to know why we hadn't filled the car. She said only something like 'We do not have a car wash', and so we looked round more, and when we saw no one else, we went back to Dr Rose's car.

"He drove through the streets until he saw a much smaller petrol station not any more on the main road. It had only two petrol pumps because really it was a mechanic's garage for repairing cars. Dr Rose saw it just by chance, I think. In the yard at the side there were several old cars for sale. A black man was in the workshop, bending over the engine of a car. He was not a boy. He looked older than I am. Dr Rose asked him whether they had a boy helping in the garage, perhaps cleaning windscreens for customers. He shouted for another man, older, white, who came out of a small office. He seemed angry already.

"He said to Dr Rose, 'Is there a problem?' or perhaps, 'You have a problem?' The exact words I do not remember.

"When Dr Rose started his question again, about a boy working there, this man interrupted and said,

'Who's asking?' like a threat.

"Dr Rose started to explain who he was. 'My name is Rose', he said. And then, 'I'm a doctor.' I thought it would be better not to try to explain anything. The man became more angry. He said something like, 'I don't care if you're the Archbishop of Canterbury. I run a garage. I'm not here to answer questions, and I definitely don't need a doctor.'"

"O dear", Clare said. "Poor David."

"No. He was very strong. He was not afraid of this angry man. Afterwards he told that he was sure the man was hiding something, or someone, that he seemed like a man who was guilty. But probably what he wanted to hide was nothing to do with the boy from Libya, more likely stolen cars or changing number plates. That was what Dr Rose thought.

"He didn't give up. He said, 'How many people work for you?' This was a brave question.

"The man was by now really angry. He said, 'How many people work for me is my business, not yours. Clear off, will you, I'm busy.'

"He took a step towards Dr Rose, more threat, and raised a hand. I don't think he would have hit him, but Dr Rose stepped back and stumbled—he had left his stick in the car—and I caught his arm before he fell.

"'Clear off, whoever you are, before I lose my temper, and take the Paki with you. We don't like nancy boys.'"

"O Hakim, that's awful. David will have hated that. And how did—"

"Cruelty will find its target. I've seen it before."

"So you left."

"Yes. We left then, as quickly as we could."

"And was that when you gave up, looking for the boy?"

"No. Dr Rose wanted to find him, more than ever. We drove away and he said to me something like, 'what a world it is out there, one forgets. We have to rescue this boy if we possibly can.' He went a little further, driving through more small streets, looking for petrol stations, and then found the way back to the main road, with lorries and buses, and he turned towards London again. We passed the first petrol station with the woman who didn't understand at the desk, and found another, on the other side, on the left of the road, where we now were. So we drove in. This time there were two young men cleaning windscreens with long, flat mops, so Dr Rose stopped at a pump and put some petrol in his car. 'Ask them,' he said, as he went to pay."

Hakim paused, drank some tea.

"And?" Clare said.

"They were Chinese, Vietnamese, I don't know. They were also very young. I said to one, 'Do you work here every day?' I don't know if he understood. He shook his head. I don't know why but I thought maybe he had been told to say no to every question. He pointed across the petrol pumps to the other boy with a mop, 'He more English,' he said. So when the car he was washing drove away I asked the other one the same question. 'Yes, every day', he said. So I asked him, 'Is there an African boy, a black boy, working here too?' Then—"

He stopped, looking at Clare. She saw tears in his black eyes.

"O Hakim, what? What did he say?"

"'Gone', he said. 'Gone this morning. Police come. Two police and took him in police car. He is gone.'

"I went back to Dr Rose's car. He came from paying. 'I don't like this place', he said. I told him what the Chinese boy had said. He took it badly, like a wound that caused him pain. 'We're too late', he said. 'We might have saved him. We shouldn't have wasted all that time in the café.' He was very sad, and his hands were shaking. I was worried. I tried to say, 'It might not have been the same boy. It might not have been the right petrol station. How can we tell?' But he would not listen. He said, 'I can see what happened. The boy was giving notes to all sorts of people, not just to Clare's daughter. Someone, probably meaning well, told the police. Simple. Now it's too late. He'll be in some detention centre somewhere. He'll be locked up and then he'll be deported, back to whatever country he escaped, where he'll be in disgrace, or back to Libya which would be worse. We have failed him.'"

"Behind us, the next driver was hooting his horn to make us move from beside the petrol pump.

"Dr Rose started the car.

"I said, 'Are you all right to drive?' because I could see he was very upset. He was a little angry with me. 'Of course I can drive. What else is there to do?' he said. Then he said, 'We will send you back. That's what the Prime Minister says. What does he know?'

"He drove back very slowly, very carefully, irritating some of the other drivers on the road, to the house where he keeps his car. He posted the key through the letterbox, and we walked to his house, also very slowly, but now he had his stick. I thought I should stay with him a little, to make sure he was all right, and when we arrived at his house he didn't tell me to go away."

"Thank you, Hakim. You are very good."

"No. Perhaps I could have done more."

He looked down at his hands, unclenched his fists and spread his hands, palms upward, in a forlorn gesture that seemed to mean 'and look what happened.'

"When we got into the house, he told me to sit down in his living room and disappeared for a few minutes, perhaps into the bathroom. He came back. His limp was a little worse I thought, and he sat down very stiffly in what was clearly his usual armchair. He wanted me to think of something we could do to help the Libyan boy. I couldn't.

""We don't know his name, or his age, or where he came from. We don't even know if he was working at the third petrol station. There could have been a different black boy there, or the one who told me he had gone may not have understood my question. I don't think there is anything we can do.' This is more or less what I tried to tell to Dr Rose."

"I'll never forgive Penny", Clare found herself saying. "Why did she have to tell me about that wretched piece of paper? Look what it's done."

"I could not make him calm. He was angry with himself. He said he had failed to answer a chance—he said, 'the only opportunity I have ever been given, and I am too old to be given another'—to do for someone else, someone helpless and alone, what had been done for his family, saving them from death, before he was even born. I think this was what he was telling?"

"That's right, I'm sure it was. That's just how he would have seen it. But it's ridiculous, of course. Nothing was his fault. He did his best. With your help, Hakim. He always did his best."

To stop herself crying, she said, "So then what happened? You talked for a bit, and tried to make him see that he had done all he could to find the boy. And then?"

"After maybe half an hour of talking he was getting very tired. He was telling about other old Jews in London who had come to England as children, and some who had been rescued after the war when the camps were discovered, nearly all of these people dead now, some of them his friends. Why was he still alive? He had not stopped talking when he fell asleep.

I stayed in my chair. I did not want him to wake up and find I had gone. Perhaps he would have been frightened or shocked. I could see he wasn't well.

"He cried out, twice, three times, before he woke. Perhaps he had a bad dream. When he woke, he was surprised to see me there. Then he remembered the day, looking for the boy, not finding the boy.

"He asked me again to do something about the boy. 'You are young. You are clever. You are a refugee yourself. You must know what can be done.'

"I didn't want to say no, again, to say that nothing can be done. So I said I will try. Then—"

"Then?"

Hakim's face crumpled.

"I'm so sorry", he said.

"Tell me, Hakim. Tell me what happened. None of this is your fault. You were kind to him, all day."

Hakim finished his tea and took a deep breath.

"He started to get out of his chair. It was difficult for him. I said, 'Can I do something, get something for you?'

"He lay back in his chair. He asked me to make some coffee in the kitchen. He said, 'You'll find the things' - "

"I went into the kitchen. It was very tidy, very clean."

"Always", Clare said, swallowing tears again.

"I filled the kettle and turned it on. I found coffee."

"I know. In a tin labelled coffee. Typical of him."

"I found a jug to make the coffee in. As the kettle started to boil, to whistle, there was a crash in the sitting room. I did turn off the gas."

He looked down, and up again, meeting her eyes.

"He had fallen, trying to stand up, I think. He had taken hold of the table, a kind of table on wheels to go over his chair, it had been beside his chair when he sat down, and it had rolled away from him so that he fell out of his chair. The table had fallen. There was a heavy book also fallen. I tried to turn him, to put him in the right position—my father taught me—to breathe, for him to breathe, but it was too difficult. I think he had stopped breathing already. I'm so sorry. I would telephone

150

999 to ask for an ambulance, but then I thought, I remembered, that I did not know the name of the street or the number of the house. I had to leave him, to go out of the house, to find these things. I kicked something, a coat, I think, against the door so it would not shut. From outside I telephoned 999 and gave the house number and the street. The ambulance came very very fast. The men came into the house. They did what I should have done, for the breathing. But it was too late. I hoped he did breathe. I don't know. They carried him to the ambulance. I went too. It was only a few minutes to the hospital. They ran with him, doctors, nurses. They were again trying the breathing. It was too late."

Now Hakim was crying.

"There's nothing more you could have done, Hakim. You did everything you could."

"I'm so sorry, Clare." He meant he was sorry to have lost control. But he wasn't sobbing as he sobbed when he told her about Samira. He shook his head and sniffed firmly, then blew his nose. He had a clean white handkerchief. As in Cyrene.

"They asked me about his family. I didn't know anything. I told that I knew his friend. They asked me to phone you and they sent me to wait."

He looked round the little room.

"Not here. Somewhere else in the hospital. I don't know— Then the doctor came to fetch me, when you had come."

He looked at her again.

"I could have done more."

"No, Hakim. You mustn't think that."

His face creased with pain.

"I was a danger to him too. I was a danger to Samira and I was a danger to Dr Rose. I should have said no. You did say no, in the café, and I should also have said no, when he wanted to find the boy. He was too old."

She leant forward, wanting to put her hand on his. She didn't. Years of training in his careful distance.

"We couldn't have stopped him, either of us. He was determined to try. And this stroke—it could have happened at any time. It probably had nothing to do with what happened today."

Something else struck her.

"You know", she said, "he wouldn't have wanted to be alive and incapacitated—I'm sorry—badly damaged from the stroke. Suppose you or the doctors in the hospital had saved his life, just, and he had been perhaps paralysed, unable to move, or unable to speak, or both—You didn't know him well but you could see what he was like, a proud man, a doctor too, used to being alone, to managing his life for himself—his tidy kitchen, how he was never late for anything even though he couldn't walk fast any more. He loved talking—you saw, in the café, how he loved talking—and he was always interested in the world, in politics, in what was happening, however depressing he found it. After he retired, unlike a lot of people, he was more, not less, interested, in the things he cared about. He read more, knew more, than most people much younger than him. He would have hated, really hated, to be alive but not alive. I'm glad, truly, Hakim, that he didn't have to suffer some kind of half life, and didn't even know he was about to die."

"Maybe he did know. I think he did."

"What?"

"I told you. He said it was his last chance, to help, to help someone in danger, as his parents had been helped, and he had missed the chance and there wouldn't be another one. Maybe he was telling only of being old. But maybe he was thinking soon he would die. I don't know."

"I see."

She thought. Hadn't he said to her, about her book, "If you're going to write it in time for me to read it—"?

"Perhaps you're right. Now, we'll never know. But thank God you were with him today. He might have - "

Died all alone, she was going to say, when the door, which had not been closed since the doctor left, opened properly and a nurse came in.

"Mrs Wilson?"

"Yes?"

"You may see Dr Rose now, if you wish."

"Can Mr Husain come too?"

"Of course, if he was also a friend."

"He was."

He didn't look like himself. Pale, tidy, lying under, apparently, a single sheet, with his silver hair neatly combed, he looked not only not like himself but not like a real person. It must have been an hour or two since he died. Was that why?

He's gone, she thought, remembering the nurse when her father died. And he had, altogether gone.

"David", she didn't say. "Where are you?" With God. Of course. At peace. But he had been at peace for years.

After standing quietly for a few minutes, with Hakim beside her, she walked from the foot of the bed, not really a bed, to his head, bent over and with her thumb made the sign of the cross on his cold, dry forehead.

"Goodbye, David", she did say, very softly. "God bless you."

"Amen", Hakim said, pronouncing the word "amin".

She looked up at him and smiled. He smiled back. And as they left the mortuary—a nurse was waiting for them—he put an arm round her shoulders. For this, for so much, she was profoundly grateful.

"Mrs Wilson, just a moment", the nurse said, before directing them towards the nearest way out of the hospital, "I gather you're acting as the next of kin. Have we got that right?"

"I seem to be. Yes."

"It would help us here—the mortuary is very busy, you understand—if you could contact a funeral director's and put arrangements in place as soon as possible. They're all available twenty-four/seven."

It took her a moment to register what this meant: the kind of up-to-the-minute expression David couldn't bear. Picturing his grimace of distaste at the very idea of twenty-four/seven, she understood that death had not taken him from her; she would never forget him.

"Yes, of course", she said. She didn't say, "We'll take him out of your way as soon as possible". Obviously the nurse had to say what she had said.

"Here are his things", she added, giving Clare a full plastic bag. "And here", a large white envelope, "is the medical certificate of death. You'll need it for the funeral director's, and you'll need it to register the death which has to be done within five days. There's a leaflet here too, with the information you'll need."

It wasn't difficult to find an undertaker, even quite late on a Saturday afternoon. A patient, friendly man on the telephone took her through David's details, and hers, asked her for her credit card number, and promised that "we shall begin the necessary arrangements immediately, certainly this evening". So they would collect David's body from the hospital mortuary, not far from their address in the Fulham Road, and then? Put it, no doubt, in the coffin, the simplest and least expensive she had chosen on the telephone, to wait for the funeral to be sorted out. By the time, on Sunday afternoon, that she went to talk to someone in their office, a tactfully soothing room with double glazing dulling the sound of the traffic and potted plants in the window, she had David's instructions to help her.

Hakim had come back to the flat with her from the hospital. He carried the plastic bag, which contained David's clothes and what was in his pockets. He found the key of David's house, put it on the table under the mirror in the hall, and put the bag in the sitting room. Then he left, refusing tea, coffee, supper. "You need to be alone, Clare. I can understand."

That was what he did, understand. Like David.

"Hakim", she said, letting him go. "I'm so grateful to you for all you've done today. Keeping him company—I'm so sorry." She couldn't go on.

"No", he said. "I am happy I was there. I was not there when my father died, far away."

Then he left.

When she had rung the undertaker, and there was nothing else immediate for her to do, she sat down in the kitchen when she had made a mug of tea. She knew that David was dead. She still didn't believe it. She looked at her watch. Quarter past five. Was it only yesterday afternoon that Penny had telephoned? Why, why had Penny told her about that wretched boy? If she hadn't, David would still be alive.

Or perhaps that wasn't fair. Perhaps the stroke had been waiting to happen. Perhaps it would have happened today anyway. Today, or another day. Being angry with Penny was pointless and wouldn't help. But she didn't want to tell Penny that David had died. Not yet. Penny had never understood why she was fond of David, had perhaps even thought that her long attachment to him was disloyal to Simon, which it had never been. Had it? Perhaps it had, a bit.

David's foreignness. That was part of the reason she—she what exactly? Never mind. Simon was so very English. The only thing he had in common with Charles. So was it also that David reminded her of her father? Not really. Her father was always more light-hearted, funnier, less serious about everything, perhaps partly because he had grown up in Prague in the 1920s and '30s—he was born in the First World War but was too young to remember it—when Czechoslovakia was an optimistic and steady place. Before Hitler. Whereas David's whole life, and perhaps now also his death, had been, although lived entirely in England, under the shadow of Nazi terror and Jewish loss.

So she wouldn't tell Penny until things had settled a little and she had got used to the fact of David's death.

Who else was there to tell? She would send a calm email to Carrie, saying that David had died but not telling her the story of the day. She opened her laptop, wrote the email and sent it. God knows what the time is in Nepal. Never mind. You don't have to open emails until you want to.

She took her tea to the sitting room and looked out of the window. The late sunlight from her left was still painting gold the tops of the trees in the square.

She had time to walk up to the six o'clock Mass. That was where she should be. If ever a day needed prayer, connection with God, with all her dead, with the saints who care for us, this was such a day.

She drank the tea, put the mug in the sink, and set off, with her stick.

She even enjoyed the walk, because it was a beautiful evening, because she was used to it, because, somehow, moving one foot in front of the other made it possible to push David's death to the back of her mind, as if it might dissolve, fade into nothingness, and everything might be as if his death, his cold forehead and his combed hair, his absence from his body, had never been.

But when she knelt in the church, much fuller of people, because it was the Saturday vigil Mass that counted for Sunday, than it had been for the weekday Mass yesterday, she was swept at once into sobbing tears, like Hakim's when he told her about his dead love. A man in the same row but across some empty places looked at her with concern. She couldn't quickly disguise her sobs. She left the church and, bent almost double in a dark corner of the porch, leaning over the table with its Catholic Truth Society pamphlets and its pile of diocesan newspapers, did her best to swallow the tears, blow her nose, mop her face. Latecomers to the Mass, which had just begun, brushed past her. One woman, whom she had seen before in the church but didn't know, bent down beside her and said, "Are you all right? Is there anything I can do?"

"No. Thank you", Clare said. "Thank you so much. Someone I know has just died. Today. It's been a shock."

To say these few words she had had to stand up straight, stop sobbing, get her voice more or less under control.

"You poor dear", the woman said, crossing herself. "I know what it's like. Come into Mass when you're ready. It's sure to help."

Touching her arm lightly, the woman left her and disappeared into the church.

The woman's kindness prompted new tears, but gentle tears, and after a few minutes of another couple of tissues, and deep breaths, she returned to the church and knelt through the Gloria and the collect, staying on her knees for the first two readings and the psalm, to hide her face in her hands. When she stood for the gospel reading she was a little shaky still, but calm.

The reading was the story of Dives and Lazarus. She listened, as if she'd never heard the story before, to Jesus describing the careless rich man who pays no attention to the poor man covered with sores, dying at the rich man's gate. There is a great gulf between them in life, and also in death, but in death the rich man has to look not down at the despised poor man but instead, from the depths of where he has been sent to the torments of Hades, upwards to heaven where the poor man is with God. As she sat for the homily at the end of the gospel, Clare looked at those of the congregation that she could see without turning her head. Most of them—not all because it was Saturday and a mixture of people were there for their Sunday Mass obligation—were, like her, elderly, prosperous, English, safe: Dives in his purple and fine linen, and in his complacent failure to see how close by was someone dying, not being fed, not being washed, not being let in.

She thought of the homeless young man wrapped in a dirty duvet asleep with his head on a torn coat who she had just walked past on the corner of Kensington High Street. She thought of Penny's boy from Libya and how David, so definitely not Dives, had been in despair because he and Hakim had failed to find him, to let him in. Perhaps the failure had contributed to whatever caused David's stroke, David's death. She would never know that. No one would. Known to God, like so much we can't be certain of. But of David's goodness, always, she was certain.

"Nay, sure, he's not in hell", she thought. "He's in Arthur's bosom, if ever man went to Arthur's bosom." She smiled to herself, remembering this. Good, deplorable, Falstaff, his death haunting a whole play in which he doesn't even appear. And Mistress Quickly mixing up Arthur with Abraham. Falstaff knows that his ragamuffin soldiers will mostly be killed in the battle ahead, and those who survive "are for the town's end, to beg during life". When she first came across this half-sentence she thought of the first beggars she had ever seen, in London not long after the war, selling matches with notices saying 'EX-SERVICE' round their necks. Now she thought again of the homeless boy on the pavement and the lost boy from Libya.

David didn't share her long, long love of Shakespeare. She was pleased that twice she had managed to widen and improve his idea of Shakespeare. Once, at her kitchen table, she had shown him, on the page, Shakespeare's sympathy for Shylock, Shakespeare's knowledge of what it is to be despised, to be the poor man, however rich, at the rich man's gate. And last summer she had persuaded him to come with her to see Ian McKellen being Lear. She had found the production irritating in various ways though McKellen was terrific; David was bowled over. "I do see", he'd said, "or anyway, I begin to see. How deep he goes."

He seemed to have learnt nothing but science at his London grammar school long ago. "Yes, we did do a Shakespeare play for O level. *As You Like It* it was. I thought it was very silly." She actually smiled now, no longer anywhere close to crying, as she remembered how the topic of grammar schools always got him going: "How would a boy like me, penniless and bright, ever have made it to medical school without the 11 plus?"

She pulled her attention back to where she was, sitting on her church seat listening, but not listening, to the homily. How much one can think, remember, in three or four minutes.

The priest, a different one from yesterday's, was preaching, apparently—she hadn't gathered much—not about Dives and Lazarus, but about something in the first reading that she'd missed. She stopped even trying to listen, and went back to the terrifying, the unbridgeable, gulf between the poor man consoled and the rich man in agony. The story was stark, and yet somehow incontrovertible, as if it embodied an evident truth. It struck her, as it never had before—but this was the day of David's death—how Jewish it was: Jesus's audience of Jews were being told that there was nothing new in what he was saying, that Moses and the prophets hadn't only told—she thought of Hakim who had never sorted out how to use the verb to tell—that the prosperous should pay attention to those who needed help and food and care, but warned them that they must. And, then as now, many of them paid no attention, would not be told, would not even be warned. She picked up the Mass sheet in front of her and read the last sentence in the gospel reading: "If they will not listen either to Moses or to the prophets, they will not be convinced even if someone should rise from the dead."

There, she thought. He was talking about himself. He came, he was sent, for all sorts of reasons, to do all sorts of things, some of them deep in mystery, but it wasn't mysterious or diffi-cult to understand that he came to reinforce God's instruction to the Jews. Love one another. And people, most people, were not convinced, then or ever.

The Mass, after the homily, was straightforward and con-soling. Perhaps, for the moment, she had cried enough, and thought enough. She was glad to be one of forty or fifty people, old, middle-aged, even young because it was the Saturday evening Mass, quietly present at the greatest of the mysteries Christ left, for me, for us, she thought, but also for everyone, for David, a Jew who had died and was with God, like Lazarus in the story.

Ever since she became a Catholic, nearly sixty years ago now, she had liked the randomness of a Catholic congrega-tion, particularly in London. All kinds of people from all over the world, Poles, Irish, Italians, Filipinos, South Americans, Africans, probably some of them understanding as little of the English as, once, most people everywhere understood of the Latin. At the consecration she prayed for the sacrifice to include the offering of David's life. She prayed the Our Father as if it were spoken by David. After all, she thought—had she ever before realized this?—it was a Jewish prayer, also, for the coming of the Messiah: "Thy kingdom come, in earth as it is in heaven". A description of Christ. She prayed the Agnus Dei for the taking away of whatever David's sins had been. And she received holy communion on his behalf because he never could himself receive it. They all shall be one.

Afterwards she walked home in the fading September evening. She knew she had been talking to David too, wherever he was, during the Mass, and she thought that, yes, with the help of God, she would be able to cope, as she had to, with the loneliness of life without him.

Wherever he was. She was grateful again, as she had said to Hakim, that David had not been left alive but damaged by his stroke. An old friend, a woman she had known for many years who was married to a colleague of Simon's and had been widowed a couple of years ago, had had a major stroke like David's last summer. She was paralysed and couldn't speak, but still recognized visitors and smiled. Clare went to see her every few weeks. She never seemed upset by a friend arriving, or a friend leaving, as if she had no sense of past and future but only an appreciation of the moment she was in. "A blessing", the nurses said. But where was she? Where was the person, with a complicated history, as everyone has, and hopes and fears, as everyone has? In the hand of God? And David now, lying in the hospital mortuary before the undertakers took him away, no doubt by some route through the hospital that avoided the groups of waiting patients who might be upset by the sight of a dead body: where was he? Also in the hand of God? What was, really, a person, alive or dead or much diminished by illness or old age? There was something in Augustine that helped answer the question. She must look it up when she got home.

The quickest way to find it was in her own book. There. Almost at the end of the extraordinary eleventh book of the *Confessions*. No one has ever thought more interestingly about time and memory and eternity. "Truly now in the grieving of my days"—yes, now, but not when she wrote the book—"you Lord, my eternal Father, are my consolation. For I have fallen apart in times whose coherence I cannot grasp"—reading this, she thought of the shambles that the world and the country seemed at this moment to be—"and my thoughts, the innermost guts of my soul"—astonishing, Augustine at the top of his form: *intima viscera* were his words for thoughts—"are torn to pieces by upheavals of every kind, until in you I shall flow together, cleansed and melted in the fire of your love. Then I shall stand and be whole in you, in your truth, which gives me form." David, his life completed. The truth of the person God made, in the dead, but also in those who for now, but only for now, are the partly living.

She was very tired and she slept soundly, like the cat and the old man in the square.

The next day, Sunday, after a telephone call early in the morning—"You will go to church?" "I went last night, which counts as Sunday."—Hakim met her at David's house. He had reminded her to bring the key that he'd taken from David's pocket.

The streets were sunny again, and very quiet: most people in South Kensington were no doubt still in bed or drinking their coffee over the Sunday papers.

Hakim was sitting on the steps, waiting for her. He stood to greet her.

"I have seen the man who lives below Dr Rose", he said. "He left the house and came back five minutes later with newspapers. He looked at me as if I should not be here. It will be better if you would explain."

"Of course. I don't know him but I have met him once or twice with David."

She rang the bell of the basement flat and when David's tenant appeared at the door, a middle-aged man in an old jersey who probably looked quite different on weekdays in a suit, she said, "I'm so sorry. You won't remember me. I'm an old friend of Dr Rose. I'm afraid I have to tell you that he died yesterday, quite suddenly."

"O—that is a shock." The tenant put a fist up to his mouth and bit the side of a finger. "I'm really sorry to hear that. Was he—how did he—how did it happen?"

"He had just come back from being out, not far away, and he collapsed here, at home. Luckily he wasn't alone."

The tenant looked at Hakim, who was standing on the pavement, waiting.

She saw deductions, false deductions, being made, but it wasn't the moment to object.

"The ambulance took him to the hospital in the Fulham Road, very quickly. But they couldn't save him."

"Was it a heart attack?"

"Apparently it was a massive stroke."

"I see. He hasn't been looking well recently, but I assumed it was heart trouble. He was—of a certain age."

"Yes indeed. He was eighty-three."

"Quite. A good age, I suppose, people would say."

He looked for a moment awkward, almost sheepish.

"Well, thank you for letting me know. I imagine—"

"Yes?"

"I imagine there'll be a funeral?"

"Yes of course. I'll let you know", she said, though she thought he had been about to say something else. Probably something like, "I imagine it's too early to know what will happen to my tenancy?" This was, after all, where he lived. So she added, "I'll let you know anything he may have arranged in case he died, about the house, your flat, and so on. He was a very careful man."

"I know. Whatever—whatever happens, I shall miss him."

"So shall I."

"Thank you, Mrs—?"

"Wilson. My name's Clare Wilson. I live quite nearby and I was for many years Dr Rose's patient."

"I see. My name is Parker, by the way, Philip Parker. Well, you'll be in touch, won't you?" He was retreating, closing his front door.

"Of course. Goodbye for now."

She returned, up the steps from the basement, to Hakim where he was waiting on the pavement.

"He thinks I am the Pakistani boyfriend, so the man in the garage thought."

"Never mind him. It doesn't matter what he thinks. Actually he seems quite a nice man. Now. Come on, Hakim. We must see what we can find."

It wasn't easy, going into David's house without David opening the door and holding it for her to walk through, as he had done dozens, probably hundreds, of times in the years since he retired. It was even less easy to see, lying on its side by his chair with two of its casters in the air, the table she had given him so that he could read without a heavy book on his lap. And there was the heavy book he had been reading, until yesterday morning, face down on the carpet, splashed open, a few of its pages bent. The first thing she did was pick it up, smooth its pages, close it, and put it on the table which Hakim had righted.

Hakim went towards the kitchen.

"Shall I make coffee, as Dr Rose asked me?"

"Why not? I think he would like us to have coffee."

She waited, her hand on the back of David's chair, until Hakim, after the whistle of the kettle—David had never got an electric kettle—and a bit of opening and shutting cupboards looking for things, came in with David's old cafetière, very like her own, and two small cups and saucers on a tray.

"Well found", she said. "Not just a jug. Thank you."

With a cup and saucer in her hand, she looked round David's sitting room, tidy as it always was. Where was he likely to keep important papers?

His desk was under the window, facing the little garden which, she knew, for years the tenant in the basement, Mr Parker as she now knew him to be, had looked after. This wasn't David's old desk from the consulting room downstairs, with an in-tray and an out-tray and lots of drawers and plenty of space for folders of notes and in the end the big computer he had had to get, much though he disliked it, not long before he retired. This desk was just a table, with an old, fringed, plush tablecloth, dark red, that looked as though it had been in an overfurnished flat in turn-of-the-century Hamburg. Probably it had. Probably his mother brought it to London just before the war. She had never noticed this tablecloth before. There wasn't much on the desk: an old blotter with leather corners; a laptop, not new, but adequate for emails and looking things up on Wikipedia. A basic printer was on a small chest of drawers at the end of the desk: she and David had arrived at about the same degree of accommodation to technology. On the floor by the desk was a pile of half a dozen issues of the *BMJ*, on top of them one *New York Review of Books*, hers: she always passed them on to David. He understood the science essays that she had to skip. On the blotter was a diary, open at the week gone by, today, Sunday, the last day of the week. Yesterday had a pencilled entry. "Meet C and Hakim S Ken café 10." Today was empty. The entry on Friday said, "Lunch Clare. V & A. 1.30." The day before yesterday. The world before Penny's telephone call.

She looked round the room again. No filing cabinet any-where. No box files in the bookshelves. Ah—she lifted the front of the plush tablecloth: there were two drawers side by side beneath the table top. She opened the one on the right. A box of paper for the printer, nearly full, some postcards, not written on, from museums—they reminded her of a couple of the exhibitions they had been to together—and from Edinburgh, where David had been a medical student in the 1950s and still had one or two friends he had visited until quite recently. Envelopes of different sizes, some of the larger ones used but carefully opened to be usable again. Pencils, a rubber, a pencil sharpener, an old wooden ruler, felt-tip pens, red, black, blue. Two books of stamps, one first class, one second. Nothing important.

The two drawers looked the same. Each had a brass handle in the middle with, above it, a keyhole. The drawer on the left was locked.

"Hakim. This could be where he keeps, where he kept, papers and things. But I can't open it."

Hakim rattled the drawer.

"No. This is a strong lock. Definitely locked. We could break the drawer from underneath."

"I would hate to do that."

They stood side by side, looking at the desk with the plush cloth folded back.

"His key", Hakim said. "Maybe he kept it in his pocket-book—what is it in English?—with his money and his cards?"

"His wallet. Of course. It was in the bag with his clothes. I brought his things here, except for the clothes." Oxfam, she had thought, when she could face it. She had put the other things the hospital had produced in a much smaller bag, and brought it in her basket. "I haven't looked at his wallet."

It felt wrong, even now, going through his wallet. Two twenty-pound notes and one ten-pound note. A bank credit card and a debit card. His driving licence, with a photograph that made him look too old. A medical identity card with a younger photograph and reference numbers. An Oyster card and a Waitrose loyalty card. That seemed to be all. She shook the wallet. Nothing fell out. What else was in the bag? No telephone. She smiled: he had a mobile phone, not a smartphone, but, like her, he hated it ringing and usually left it at home. A clean handkerchief. An unopened packet of tissues. His reading spectacles in a black case. A cheque book in another, soft, black case. She had a cheque book herself, in her bag, but she knew that no one under 60 used cheques any more. A small diary with almost nothing written in it, but the first page filled in with useful telephone numbers, his doctor, dentist, plumber, electrician, solicitor—that number might be useful—a local minicab firm, the AA, his car registration number, passport number: all the mechanics of a regular, orderly life. At the bottom of the page was a section headed In Case of Emergency, with her name, address and telephone number. There were spaces for two names; he had put in only hers. For a moment, she was pleased there wasn't a second name. She shook her head to banish the unworthy thought.

"It's no good", she said to Hakim, who was watching her go through the bag. "These must have been all the things there were in his pockets."

"May I please look at the wallet?"

She gave it to him. Under the place for credit cards there was a concealed section she hadn't noticed. It was behind the slots for cards, most of them empty, and had a slim leather fastener. Hakim opened it, felt inside, and carefully took out a very old photograph. And then a key. He gave her the photograph without looking at it, held up the key and tried it in the lock of the drawer, which opened easily. The photograph, black and white and folded in half so long ago that there was a worn strip across the middle, was a wedding photograph, taken in a studio, of a young man in a wide-lapelled 1930s suit, who looked very like David when she had known him first, and his pretty, smiling bride in the fairly hideous fashion of the time but with a bunch of flowers in her hands and more flowers in an urn on a pedestal beside her. David's parents. In faded ink on the back was the date. 12 March 1933: Hitler was already in power in Germany but a Jewish wedding was still allowed.

She showed the picture to Hakim.

"David's parents."

He looked at it with his usual attention.

"Long ago", he said.

"So long ago. Another world. The Jews in Hamburg were reasonably happy and allowed to live in peace before the Nazis.

David told me there had been Jews in Hamburg for four hundred years, more Jews than in any other German city. David's grandfather fought for Germany in the First World War. Hitler decided to kill them all."

"But Dr Rose's parents came to England."

"That's right."

He gave her back the photograph. She put it on the table by his chair, gently.

"Look, the drawer is open."

"O, well done, Hakim, for thinking of his wallet."

She opened the drawer to its full extent. There were two small loose-leaf files containing bank statements, and, neatly stacked and labelled, seven or eight large buff envelopes. Tax. Pensions. Insurance. Medical. Family. Money. Legal. It was typical of David that none of these envelopes was sealed: documents, letters, forms might be added, or subtracted if they weren't any longer needed, without upsetting the tidiness of his simple system.

"This is correct, this is what you need?" Hakim said.

"Yes, exactly as I hoped."

Hakim took his coffee to the other side of the room and sat on the little sofa where she always sat to talk to David. He got up, picked up from David's lap table the heavy book that had fallen, took it to the sofa, sat down and opened the book.

Watching this, she thought, not for the first time, that in a long life she had never met anyone as tactful as Hakim.

Back to David's drawer.

Again it felt wrong to open any of the envelopes. Again she knew she had to.

She opened the envelope labelled Family. His parents' German marriage certificate: Bernhard Rosenberg, doctor of medicine—this was before the Nuremberg Laws—married to Rebekka Katz. His own birth certificate, registration district Marylebone, David Rosenberg, 14 June 1936. They must have changed the family surname later, perhaps when war broke out. His medical qualifications. The death certificates of both his parents, and of his sister, this, issued in Marylebone again, was dated more than twenty years ago when she was not even sixty. She looked at it more carefully. "Ursula Rose. Born Hamburg, Germany, 1934. Occupation: Nurse. Retired." "Cause of death: carcinoma of uterus". She folded the single sheet of paper, all that was left of a childless life, and put it back in the envelope. "She wasn't easy, my sister. But she was an excellent nurse, like my mother. Unlike my mother, she didn't laugh much." A smaller white envelope contained a few photographs: black and white school photographs from the 1940s. Ursula, with pigtails, at about twelve; David, cheeky, but also looking as he looked all his life, at nine or ten. She put these back, with a few others, for later.

She looked at the labels on more of the envelopes. Tax, Pensions, Insurance, Money: she put these in a pile on the table. There were no doubt things in them that would have to be dealt with—she remembered vaguely a list of things she had had to do when her father died—but she would need a lawyer's advice about them. Medical she opened. Almost nothing inside. A local GP surgery's list of prescriptions: blood pressure pills and statins; nothing else. Three opticians' reports, and prescriptions for spectacles, from the last eight years. A booklet from the Chelsea and Westminster hospital about cataract surgery, which, she had forgotten but now remembered, David had had several years ago. She looked out over the garden, the papers in her hand. He was well, for his age. In spite of his arthritis, there were no painkillers or sleeping tablets on the list. But he had always said, "the fewer pills the better". And now he was dead. She shook her head, to make herself get on with what needed to be done.

Legal. Here was the tenancy agreement for the basement flat. She had never before seen a lease, if that was what it was, but it looked like standard legal language, making almost incomprehensible what was probably quite straightforward. The tenant was Philip Parker. The date was 2007. David had retired at seventy, in 2006, and at once turned his surgery into a flat, so Mr Parker was almost certainly his first tenant. Good. They must have got on well. She looked at the agreement again. Something about six months' notice on either side. Did that mean that whoever bought the house—presumably it would be sold—would have to allow Mr Parker to stay for six months? She had no idea. Again, she would need advice from a lawyer.

Ah, a slim buff envelope, also not sealed, with *The Last Will and Testament* printed on it in legal Gothic script, and "of Dr David Rose" and his address filled in on dotted lines. Again she hesitated. Had she read something somewhere about wills having to be opened in the presence—of whom? The family? A lawyer? Most likely she'd read this in a novel. And there was no family. So she opened the envelope. A single sheet of paper, as simple as could be, headed, in Gothic writing again, *This is the last Will and Testament*; the spaces below the heading, after *of me*, for name, address and date, were filled in in David's handwriting, and were followed by the names of two executors, the first Clare Wilson, with her address, the second a lawyer, with his firm's address in Kensington High Street.

She looked at the garden again. Had she agreed to be David's executor? Probably. Years ago. She dimly remembered. The date of the will was 8 September 2009. Almost exactly ten years ago. After Simon's death. Two years after Matt's death. Just before she went on the North African cruise.

And the substance of the will? Two sentences. The first leaving the house to "my friend Clare Wilson, on condition that my tenant, Philip Parker, if he is still living in my basement flat, may continue his tenancy as long as he wishes", and the second leaving "all my other possessions and any money remaining in securities or bank accounts to my friend, Clare Wilson, who will therefore be able to pay my funeral expenses and any debts I may leave".

There. It couldn't have been less complicated, and as she turned over the will, blank on the other side, and folded it to return it to its envelope, she realized that the sheet of paper and the envelope were a kind of kit, no doubt bought from somewhere like W. H. Smith. So like David. Why waste money on exceeding what was necessary?

The witnesses to the will were a woman whose address was the house next door, and Mrs Mary Hunt, with a Battersea address. Clare remembered Mrs Hunt, David's Cockney charlady, long dead, who used to clean the house and iron his shirts once a week. For solidarity she had gone with David to Mrs Hunt's funeral, in a grim crematorium somewhere in south London, with five other people there.

She was distracting herself from the extraordinary news the will had just given her. It couldn't be right that David should leave her the house. These little streets south of Walton Street used to be quite modest, the small houses, brick and stucco with narrow gardens behind them, were lived in, when she first knew David and her children were babies, by all sorts of people, working-class couples who had seen the war through in bombed London, artists, journalists, photographers, owners of little galleries, editors of ephemeral magazines, people who didn't mind how small the houses were, and didn't have cooks or proper nannies. David, she knew, when, in the early 'sixties, he had set up his practice and put his brass plate on the door with an arrow pointing down to the basement, had bought the house for fifteen thousand pounds. It was now worth probably a million.

Penny, she thought at once, would want her to leave the flat and move into David's house. "So convenient, Mum, don't you see? Nearer the tube, nearer Harrods and Peter Jones, nearer everything. And so much more suitable than the flat." So much smaller, is what she would mean. And Penny and Charles would love, now that the children had gone, to swap their house in Barnes, bigger than they needed and itself worth a fortune, for the flat, so much easier to get to the House of Commons from, as well as closer to Harrods and Peter Jones.

How had she and Simon managed to produce Penny? This was a familiar question. It was twenty-five years of the Tory party, and her passion for horses, and the limitations, to put it kindly, of Charles that had turned Penny into a Sloane Ranger, not that anyone used the expression any more.

"And think", Penny would go on to say, "of how easy to manage David's little house would be."

Well, for Penny, or for David, or for anyone, she wasn't going to leave the flat. And she couldn't sell David's house, even when everything to do with his will and his money had been sorted out, and she remembered the time probate had taken when her father died, because Mr Parker must stay in his flat in the basement.

"Is it all right?" Hakim said, from the sofa, "What you have found?"

"Yes, it's all right. It's fine. As I expected, he had thought of everything. Though I had hoped—"

She was about to put back the tenancy agreement and the will in the big envelope labelled Legal when she saw that there was an ordinary white envelope still there. She took it out. It was sealed and addressed to her. Clare Wilson, in the event of my death.

She winced. A new reminder that David was actually dead.

In the envelope was a postcard. A painting by Claude of Aeneas at Delos, very classical, very peaceful. She and David had stood together in front of this painting two or three times in the National Gallery. She remembered saying, "Virgil is much sadder than this, you know." "I don't, but I'll take your word for it. What a beautiful painting, anyway."

She turned the card over.

"My funeral", it said. "Talk to the rabbi at the synagogue in Rutland Gardens."

That was all.

"Well!" she said.

"It is still all right?" Hakim said.

"Quite all right. Better than all right. This card says I should talk to the rabbi, the rabbi in a synagogue not far from here, about his funeral. You see what that means?"

"It means the rabbi knows him, knows Dr Rose? So he was after all more of a Jew than you thought? So that is good?"

"Of course it is. It may explain—"

What was she trying to say?

"Explain?" Hakim said.

"It may explain, a bit, why he didn't seem lonely, although he was alone, didn't see many people, couldn't walk very far."

"Like you."

"Me?"

"You are alone. But you are not lonely because you are a real Christian. You are saying that perhaps Dr Rose was a real Jew?

And that is good?"

"Yes, Hakim, that is good."

That afternoon she went to talk to the professionally helpful man in the funeral directors' office in the Fulham Road.
He not only knew about the synagogue in Rutland Gardens
but actually knew the rabbi. "We have dealt with a number
of Jewish funerals. There should be no difficulty at all. It is
usually possible for them to take place much sooner than if a
church service needs to be booked. Perhaps, as the next of kin
responsible for Dr Rose's funeral, you would be good enough
to speak to the rabbi yourself tomorrow, and also to go to the
registrar to obtain the death certificate so that we can proceed
with the arrangements?"

"Of course, yes. Thank you. There seems to be quite a lot
to do."

"I'm afraid that's always the case, particularly with a sudden
death. May I ask you one further question?"

"Please do."

"No doubt Dr Rose intended his funeral expenses to be
covered from the resources of his estate. It normally takes
a certain amount of time, weeks, sometimes even months,
for the legal formalities to be cleared such that moneys may
be liberated from the estate of the deceased. May I ask you
whether you are in a financial position yourself to cover the
funeral expenses until such time as it will be possible for you
to be reimbursed from Dr Rose's estate?"

"What?"

This man wasn't even a lawyer.

"O, I see", she said. "Yes. I can pay the bill."

She wished David could have heard this exchange. Perhaps
he had, she thought. Was the thought absurd? Childish?
Probably. Never mind.

"Thank you, Mrs Wilson. So we'll await instructions as to
the funeral once you have spoken to the rabbi."

Next morning she went to the register office in Chelsea Town
Hall as early as they could give her an appointment, and then,

armed with several copies, which the hospital instructions said she would need, of David's death certificate, she went to see the rabbi.

The best single thing about David's death was the discovery that the rabbi at the synagogue knew him quite well, had talked to him several times, and was expecting to organize his funeral.

"He asked me last year whether I would accompany such a bad Jew to his grave."

She wasn't sure what to make of this, but then saw that the rabbi was smiling.

"My impression, Mrs Wilson, was not that Dr Rose was a bad Jew. Certainly not. My impression was that here we had a good man, who now that he was old wished he had paid more attention to God over the years, but a bad Jew, no. In any case who are we to judge what can be known only to God?"

She smiled. "Well, yes", she said. "Of course that's true."

To her surprise, it turned out that there would be no service in the synagogue but only a short service at the Jewish cemetery in North London. The rabbi would say the prayers.

"But who will come?"

"Faithful members of our congregation will come, to accompany"—that word again—"a Jew with no family, and to join in the saying of Kaddish."

She was for a moment acutely sad that her father had been cremated, as he had wanted, and that she had scattered his ashes, also as he had wanted, on a wintry Yorkshire moor. She wished he had ever been connected to a Jewish community.

"Is it—would it be all right for me to come? I'm not Jewish." She couldn't embark on an explanation about her father.

"Indeed you must come, Mrs Wilson. You were Dr Rose's friend, and the loving prayers of family and friends carry the dead to God. We shall welcome you. I shall speak to the funeral directors. It should be possible for the ceremony to take place tomorrow. At Golders Green, you understand. I will let you know the time."

"So soon?"

"It is the Jewish custom not to delay a funeral."

"Isn't Golders Green a crematorium?"

"Indeed it is. I'm afraid an actual burial in London is rare and difficult nowadays, and Reform Judaism has no objection to cremation though extreme Orthodox Jews do not allow it."

"I see." The same old story. Disagreements, no doubt bitter, within the faith. Jews, Christians, Muslims, all supposed to be peaceful, all disagreeing, quarrelling with each other, sometimes, at least Christians and Muslims, murdering each other.

"But the ashes will be scattered in the Jewish cemetery", the rabbi added.

When the rabbi had telephoned her to say that the funeral would be at three on the next day and that he had spoken to the undertaker, she walked to David's house and posted a note through Mr Parker's door. She was so tired when she had done this that she found a taxi to take her home.

She took less time than she expected to get to Golders Green on the tube, the District Line to Charing Cross and then the confusing Northern Line, which she managed to get right, so for half an hour she sat on a bench in the garden outside the crematorium, watching two other funerals come and go, and feeling calm among the silent dead.

She found the funeral in the carefully non-Christian, non-anything chapel, with about a dozen men from the rabbi's congregation present, and no Mr Parker, nearly as soulless as her father's in Mortlake had been.

David seemed far away. But at the end, after the coffin had disappeared, they recited Kaddish. They gave her a leaflet with the Aramaic text—Aramaic, the language Jesus spoke—and a translation, and she saw that the prayer was a great hymn of praise to God with nothing of sadness or mourning in it. And that seemed entirely right.

She got home just before six o'clock after a crowded rush-hour journey back. She was given a seat on each train. People, mostly youngsters, boys and girls, black, brown and white, are kind to old ladies on the tube, kinder than middle-aged men in suits who almost never offer you their seat. She didn't read the *Evening Standard* which she had picked up at Golders Green tube station: the front page was about the Tory party conference and some cloud hanging over Boris Johnson. The party conference. Of course. Penny and Charles were presumably still there. But she was thinking about David.

Did he know how important he was to her, specially since Simon died? Perhaps he did. Perhaps he didn't. She had thought for a long time that he would rather not know. But there was the will. David didn't have any relations, and apparently didn't have any close friends either: the men who had come to the funeral and carried the coffin didn't seem to know him well, though it was hard to tell. Two or three of them were quite young and read their Kaddish pamphlets as carefully as she did. The rabbi must have let them know?

The funeral director had wanted her to put an expensive death notice in the *Times* or the *Telegraph*, but she had said no. She didn't think David would want to appear in either paper, and no one read death notices in the *Guardian*. She would have told David's friends in Edinburgh if she had known their names. Perhaps they would have seen a death notice, but they might read only the *Scotsman*. One way or another it was no doubt her fault that so few people were at the funeral. This she knew David would forgive her.

That she should be going to own his house, the house that she'd known since Penny was born, and had been fond of for so many years, seemed quite extraordinary. She wasn't yet used to the idea. She would be rich if she sold it. But she wouldn't sell it. She didn't want to be rich. In any case, there was Mr Parker. And, she had already thought, there was Carrie, who wouldn't be in Nepal for ever. What a thing it would be, to be able to let Carrie live in David's house one day. Meanwhile there was Hakim. Perhaps—but she felt she shouldn't even think about Hakim in David's house. He must be allowed to lead his own life.

When she got home she made a mug of tea and sat, with relief, at the kitchen table. She had put the *Evening Standard*, still unread, in the recycling box and taken the *Guardian* out of her shopping basket where it had been under some leeks, some butter and half a dozen eggs since the morning.

The cloud at the party conference turned out to be about Boris Johnson groping some woman's knee years ago at a dinner. So unsurprising as not to be remotely interesting. And then there was his affair with an American go-getter. Ditto. Penny thought Boris Johnson wonderful.

She really should tell Penny about David, even if she had to leave her a message.

But Penny answered at once, against the noise of a room full of people.

"Hello, Mum" she said, before Clare had said anything: she knew that Penny's telephone flashed up the number of the person ringing. "Are you OK?"

"I'm all right, yes, but I'm afraid—"

"O good. We're having a terrific time at the conference. I always forget what fun it is. Charles made a brilliant speech at a fringe meeting last night and important people keep telling him it's time he had a job. His new thing's the northern power house. Perhaps Boris will—"

"Just listen a minute, Penny. David died on Saturday."

"What? David Rose? He died? I'm so sorry, Mum. How sad for you. But he was quite old, I suppose, wasn't he?"

"He was eighty-three. He spent his last morning looking for your boy."

"What boy?"

"The boy from Libya."

"From where? I'm sorry, Mum. I can't hear you properly. There's a hell of a racket in here."

"O never mind. You'd better get back to Charles's networking, or whatever you're meant to be doing."

"I've lost him, actually. There are so many people in here. Hang on a minute."

A silence, full of noise.

"O there he is. Miles away. He wants me to come over. I'd better fight my way through the mob. Sorry, Mum. Anyway, you're all right?"

"O yes, I'm all right. We'll talk when you get back to London. 'Bye, darling."

""Bye, Mum. Lots of love."

Part 2

28 February – 4 March 2020

She hadn't realized that she was afraid it would happen again, the telephone ringing inside her flat while she searched in her bag for her key, until it did. Almost exactly five months later, and also on a Friday afternoon, though not, alas, when she'd had lunch with David, she had been to Mass and then walked home through the wet streets because there were no empty taxis in Kensington on account of the rain. Her umbrella kept her more or less dry but she got very cold in the sharp wind. Perhaps her umbrella would be blown inside out: as a child she'd been told by her old nanny that the wind could do this. There was a picture in a children's book, she couldn't remember which, of an inside-out umbrella with the little girl holding it lifted into the air. She had never seen an umbrella do this, and, sure enough, hers survived the walk the right way up.

As quickly as she could she opened the door, propped her dripping umbrella against it when she'd shut it, and got to the kitchen to answer the telephone. If it were Penny she would think she had run into some kind of spooky kink in time.

It was Hakim.

"Clare, how are you?"

Polite as always, but his voice didn't sound quite right.

"Hakim. How nice to hear you. I'm fine. Rather wet. I've just come in."

"I'm sorry. May I see you? On Sunday, after you have come back from the church? Will this be difficult for you?" There was definitely some strain in his voice.

"Difficult? No, not at all."

She thought. Penny and Charles sometimes asked her to Sunday lunch in Barnes but she knew they were going to Yorkshire for the weekend. Flying, for heavens' sake, because the trains were all over the place. So much for Charles's "O, we're all very green nowadays."

"Come to lunch, Hakim. It will be good to see you."

"Thank you, Clare. I have a problem. You will help me, I know."

"I'll do what I can, of course. Come at about one o'clock on Sunday. I look forward to it."

"Thank you. I will be there. It will not be easy, Clare. The thing I have to tell."

As soon as he had rung off, she wished she had arranged to see him sooner. But since he had chosen Sunday, she saw it was best to leave the plan as it was. The last thing she wanted was to become part of the problem by sounding over-anxious. It was unlike him, to say on the telephone, but without explaining, that he was in some kind of trouble: always so thoughtful, he would ordinarily have spared her worry by saying nothing until they met.

So, two days of not knowing. Patience, patience I need. That was King Lear. Let's not exaggerate: she heard David's voice, as she often did.

Since David's death, she hadn't had anyone to talk to about the horrors of politics, of Brexit, of the arrogant dangerousness of the government, of her feeling that the whole country was becoming more and more unpleasant, less and less governed. The poorest people were still suffering dreadfully from austerity, local government having no money, the horrors of universal credit which had actually driven a number of victims of illness and bad luck to suicide. In the election in December hundreds of thousands of people who had never before voted Tory had given the dreadful, irresponsible, deeply careless, if one can be deeply careless, Boris Johnson a big, solid parliamentary majority, good for five years because they had been deliberately tricked, again. "Get Brexit done." A hollow recommendation, or promise, or lie.

The result of the election had made her, if anything, more miserable than the referendum result itself. The election, again, like the referendum, was unnecessary. If the Labour party had had a sensible, pro-European leader, one of Mrs May's soft Brexit deals would have got through the House of Commons, where a majority of MPs had always been in favour of staying in the EU, and there wouldn't have had to be an election. Now there wasn't a single Tory MP allowed not to be a Brexiteer, Charles and Penny were crowing, and there would be a year of squabbling and confusion probably ending with no deal at all and many many people broke and broken. Looking back over the last six months, she found it hard to understand exactly how the country had been allowed to arrive at the worst possible outcome.

And Boris Johnson clearly cared as little about climate change and the fate of the planet as he cared about anything else. No one was bothering much about the crucial international meeting in Glasgow in the autumn and no one strong enough had been put in charge of it.

She was sitting at the kitchen table looking at the telephone and worrying about Hakim. She shook her head, got up, gathered together the small brown loaf she had started yesterday from the bread bin and, from the fridge, half a Camembert, some lettuce and a tomato, which would taste of nothing because it was February, and sat down to eat some lunch. The first Friday in Lent. A frugal lunch, but her usual kind of lunch.

She was no longer hungry enough to eat anything, so she made a cup of tea.

What could be the matter with him?

She had seen him not long ago. How long exactly? Nearly three weeks, it must have been. They had had lunch in the Museum because she was there taking school groups on Greek and Roman tours on a Monday afternoon. He was cheerful, full of news about work he was doing on finds at the Yorkshire Roman town on the A1, and he mentioned Ayesha here and there in a relaxed way that indicated all was well between them. "Ayesha says I think too much in the past. The Greeks and the Romans are too long ago to help with the terrible things now in the world. It is not quite true."

He had never again mentioned the question of marrying her. Perhaps the pair of them had talked about the possibility and agreed to shelve it, to wait until they had a clearer idea of where their lives might take them in the next year or two. Whether or not the idea of marriage had ever reached the surface between them, Hakim seemed happy with their relationship, however it was, as it was. For several reasons this part of Hakim's life was to Clare almost impenetrable. She wouldn't have dreamt of asking him a direct question about it.

"How is the mysterious Mr Parker?" Hakim had said over their Museum café table and their only fairly good Museum salads.

Clare smiled, as she often did at his now almost comically idiomatic English.

"The mysterious Mr Parker, as far as I know, is perfectly all right", she said.

In the months since David's death, she had had to talk to Philip Parker several times. She wasn't at all sure that she liked him, but David's solicitor who had helped her through the formalities which have to be coped with after any death—probate still wasn't granted, not that, even after dealing with her father's death, she entirely understood what this meant—had recommended her to agree when Philip Parker had asked if a friend of his could be her tenant in David's part of the house until she needed it for a member of her family. The solicitor said the lease could be drawn up so that, with six months' notice, she could ask the tenant to leave. He also confirmed what Clare already thought, that Mr Parker was, after nearly thirteen years as David's tenant, certainly to be trusted. He had always paid the rent, looked after the garden and made only reasonable requests for repairs and maintenance.

Clare's plan, which had occurred to her as soon as she read David's will, and at their first meeting put to the lawyer as what she would like best, was to let Carrie live in the house when she came back from Nepal, perhaps eventually with Daisy when she in turn came back from Vancouver, if the two of them were getting on well enough and both wanted to be in London. Or perhaps Carrie with the American boyfriend, or another boyfriend if the American had vanished from the scene: like David, she found the word 'partner' hard even to think, let alone utter out loud. She hadn't said anything about this plan to Penny because she knew Penny and Charles would disapprove of any arrangement that would make less than the maximum amount of money out of the extraordinary piece of luck that was David's bequest.

She hadn't said anything about the house to Carrie either. When David died she had emailed Carrie with the news, without explaining the circumstances. Carrie's email in return had cheered her so much that she kept it on her laptop and had often opened it in the months since.

Hi Gran—I'm so so sorry that David's died. And so suddenly too. What a beastly shock for you. You've had too many people dying, poor Gran. Of course I remember Matt and Grandpa, but I was only ten and twelve when they died, and David I knew properly as a grown-up, or nearly a grown-up. So I'll miss him as well. He was a lovely man and you'll be lonely without him I know. I'm planning to come back next summer, probably for good, so I look forward to seeing you then. Nepal is still brilliant and the people are lovely. V. much love as ever, Carrie.

Dear Carrie. She looked forward to seeing her again. She was an understander, and there weren't many in her life now that David had gone.

She had hoped briefly that Mr Parker might become a new friend, but she was quickly certain that he wouldn't. He was an accountant in a city firm, so there was absolutely nothing for them to talk about. In any case, either too shy or too constricted in some other way even to meet her eye when they had to meet, he was beyond her speculation as a character, though he had clearly been fond, or at least respectful, of David. Gay no doubt, and perhaps unable to cope with women of whatever age or kind, he had politely and formally, with a letter to the solicitor, asked about the tenancy in David's house for a friend. Well, why not? Much better than the house being empty. It still had most of David's things in it, though she had taken the linen home and sorted his clothes, neat and clean as they of course were, for Oxfam. As long as she could get the house back for Carrie.

When she met the friend, her prospective tenant, she liked him better than she expected, and better than the lawyer did. Also a great deal better than David, she knew, would have liked him.

"An acquired taste, I would say, Mrs Wilson", the lawyer had said. "But he's a rich man and I'm sure he'll pay the rent. I don't think he's intending actually to live in Dr Rose's house himself."

She was puzzled by this until all became clear.

S. H. Steinberg—"Please, Mrs Wilson, call me Sol. They all do."—was a large sixty-five-year-old New York Jew, with a thatch of wavy white hair, a very pale green tweed suit and a red bow tie with white spots. He had a formidable hand-shake. He ran a small, expensive art gallery in Walton Street, ten minutes' walk away, and was effusively enthusiastic about David's house. "It's the most darling house I could ever have imagined. I cannot believe, ma'am, that you're able to resist living here yourself. And look at all these books, and these wonderful prints, so English, so in period." On David's sitting room walls was a good set of early nineteenth-century prints, of Edinburgh. "Are you really leaving all this here for your tenant? What awesome self-denial! What do you think, Miles dear? Could you have believed that such a dream of a little house could have come our way?"

Miles was perhaps twenty-five, a tall, blond English public school boy who didn't do effusion.

"It's very nice, yes", he said.

"I have to let the house furnished at the moment", Clare said to Mr Steinberg. "I hope you'll be able to look after it, the house and the things too."

"Sure, ma'am, sure", he leant forward earnestly. "Beautiful objects are our life! Isn't that so, Miles? No way will we allow any harm to come to a single thing you leave here. Will we, Miles?"

"No. Definitely not", Miles said, without looking up from the book he had opened on David's desk.

"Do you think all this is reliable enough?", Clare asked the lawyer later. "Mr Steinberg is perhaps—well, perhaps a bit over the top?"

"More than a bit, yes indeed. But I asked him for a couple of references. He gave me them, from most reputable people I must say. I followed them up, and I'm certain he can be trusted."

There had been no problems since Miles moved in, and, without saying so, Clare was relying on Mr Parker to let her know if he thought any harm was coming to the house.

At Christmas in Yorkshire, where Clare had gone to stay for a few days with Penny and Charles as she had every year since Simon's death, she said almost nothing about David's house. "O, I've let it, just for the moment, while the lawyer's sorting things out. We haven't even got probate yet."

"And won't for months, I don't suppose. The bureaucracy in this country is getting worse and worse. Slow. Inefficient. Expensive. Another thing we should be able to get a better grip on once we've left the wretched EU."

This was Charles—as if the EU had anything to do with English probate rules which were probably invented by Henry II—and this was the theme-tune of the holiday. Charles was cockahoop because of the thumping election success of Boris Johnson and the Tories less than a fortnight before Christmas. Clare had voted Liberal Democrat, though she knew the party leader had, maddeningly, thrown away any prospect of making an impact on the Brexit nightmare. The Liberal Democrats did well in Kensington, increasing their vote and coming a respectable third. But this was useless of course. The wretched system was as usual to blame: either/or, like the referendum itself. And Charles had put up his majority, or Boris Johnson and Get Brexit Done had put it up for him, as the Machiavellian party propaganda outfit had achieved for practically all Tories in country constituencies, as long as they had undertaken to be in favour of Brexit for ever and ever, amen. As Charles had been ever since the word was invented, though that was only a very few years ago. Not to mention the old Labour constituencies where people trying to survive had been bamboozled into thinking Brexit was going to solve all their problems and therefore voted Tory for the first time ever.

Now there was nothing left to hinder or temper Brexit. And nothing to hinder or temper Charles's complacency. Always pleased with himself, after the election he seemed to think he was only one step away from the cabinet. Johnson's reshuffle of the cabinet had come in the middle of February, ten days ago. The new cabinet was unimpressive, to put it kindly, but Clare was thankful that it wasn't unimpressive enough for Charles to have been given even a junior job in the government.

Meanwhile he was convinced that everyone in the constituency was delighted, delighted with Boris Johnson and delighted with Brexit, for which indeed a majority of his constituents had voted in the referendum, and therefore delighted with him. As with most things in Charles's life, the truth was more complicated than he was capable of imagining.

For example there was a sad conversation Clare had had on Christmas Eve; she didn't attempt to describe it to Charles.

She had borrowed Penny's old Land Rover, mostly used for towing the horsebox, and gone, alone, to the remote top of a dale for a walk, a favourite place since her childhood. It was a damp grey day and the lines of the flat-topped limestone hills, one behind the other, faded into the distance like lines of grey watercolour paint on soft paper. She walked among the scratchy black and brown clumps of dead heather and the dank dead bracken, rusty orange, putting up the occasional grouse, and smelt the moor on the wind, a smell like nothing and nowhere else. Driving back down the dale she stopped when a farmer who was standing in the drizzle talking to an old gamekeeper she had known for years opened a gate for her. She got out to greet the keeper.

"Hallo, Geoff."

"Afternoon", he said. "O, it's you, missis. Long time no see. We was wondering. Nobody comes up here in this weather. You here for Christmas? Staying with that son-in-law of yours?"

"That's right", she said, putting a hand on the damp head of the farmer's friendly sheepdog, which was looking up at her and thumping its tail.

"This lady's daughter's married to our MP, the marvellous Mr Roberts", the keeper said.

"O aye", the farmer said. "Is she now? Well, nobody's to blame for who other people marry." He looked at Clare, amused rather than hostile. "You'll be from London then?"

"Well, yes. But I've been up here for holidays all my life."

"She's part of the Harrison family", the keeper explained.

"O aye."

"This is Frank Teasdale", the keeper said. "That's his farm." He pointed down the track that led from the road. A small stone farmhouse with a red pantiled roof like the others scattered in the dale. A barn. One or two outbuildings. An old Land Rover like Penny's. A quad bike. A trailer.

"How do you do?" said Clare.

A nod from the farmer.

"Will he be planning to get us out of this mess, then?" he said. "Your son-in-law. Eh? All we've got up here's sheep. All we've ever had. Look there." He waved an arm towards the steep hillside. Grey grass with here and there stone outcrops, bracken, water running down in little becks, sharp reeds by the water, black heather above where the moor began, sheep in the drizzle. "Nowt else will do any good. Less favoured area they call us. Not bloody favoured at all's more like it."

She had thought of these moorland farmers and their sheep often as she sat in her comfortable kitchen in Kensington, listening to the news, or to Farming Today with her first cup of tea if she couldn't sleep beyond five-thirty in the morning which was more and more the case. She knew no other kind of farming was possible up here, or in the sweeping fells of the Dales, with their stone walls and stone barns, on the far side of the A1 after you climbed beyond cattle and horses and Wensleydale cheese.

"There's to be tariffs on lamb, apparently", the farmer went on. "Forty per cent I've heard. Market'll pack up. Nobody thought of that did they? We weren't told the half of it." This was a speech, she could tell, he had made before. He looked at her again, now fiercely. "What does your Mr Roberts have to say about tariffs then? Come to that, what does he know about farming? What does a city man know about sheep? About weather? Just look at it, the wet. It's never stopped since

October." He remembered who he was talking to. "Nothing personal, mind."

"No, of course not", she said.

After a brief, awkward silence, the keeper said, "To tell the truth, looking back we weren't told 'owt. Empty promises on that bus. All that money for the health. Have our cake and eat it. A lot of rubbish."

"That's a fact." The farmer couldn't stay quiet for long. "Were we told hill farmers'd be hung out to dry? No we weren't. The subsidy'll stop and then what? Farmers won't be able to cope. There've been suicides. Two from round here. There'll be more."

"Farmers should have thought harder before they voted for Brexit", the keeper said. "Too late now."

A gloomy silence. Then the farmer said, "Nature they want. Nature they'll get. We'll be the last up here, you mark my words."

The last, the last. The last whale, the last polar bear, the last lapwing, the last skylark. Now the last Yorkshire sheep farmers. And this, the fate of the farmers, nothing to do with global warming or the destruction of the planet, only to do with Tory politics and totally unnecessary.

"I'm so sorry", Clare said, feebly, she knew. "I wish none of it was happening, I really do. I wish the wretched referendum had never been invented." She took her hand from the sheepdog's reassuring head and looked at her watch. "I must go. It's getting dark and I'm supposed to be decorating the tree. It was nice to see you both. I hope you have a good Christmas. As good a Christmas as possible. Goodbye, Mr Teasdale. Goodbye, Geoff." She shook their hands. "I'm sorry", she said again.

On the way back to Penny's house and the Christmas tree, she thought all over again how thoughtless, careless and dangerous it had been to risk a referendum that could be manipulated, as it had been, by people interested only in how much power they could get out of it for themselves. Surely it was obvious, to anyone with basic common sense and any idea of English history, that it was always better to let members of parliament sort out problems for the rest of the population? Not that the EU had been much of a problem for most people until Nigel Farage had persuaded them that it was responsible for all their difficulties. The Brexiteers in the House of Commons, not yet so called when they were bullying John Major and then wretched Mr Cameron, had been outnumbered for forty years. Until now.

After tea she and Daisy decorated the Christmas tree, lights, tested and working, first, then baubles, mostly chosen by her years ago for the tree in Barnes when Carrie and Daisy were little, then tinsel.

Daisy was back for Christmas from Vancouver, looking healthy and sporty—she seemed to have spent most of the last few weeks skiing—and American, though Clare knew that Canada, where she had never been, was different from America. It was good to see her: Christmas, without any actual children except for the younger cousins in the big house, was made more cheerful by her presence. But she wasn't Carrie.

"What do you think about Brexit?" Clare asked her, as they disentangled lines of tinsel from each other and from a nest of the wire loops that attached baubles to the tree "We really must get some new tinsel next year."

"Actually Gran, this tinsel's horrible. Let's chuck it and skip the tinsel. Mum won't notice."

"What a good idea. Wrap it up and put it in the bin. It's so ancient it even smells rusty."

Daisy stuffed it into the waste paper basket.

"Well, where are you on Brexit?" Clare said.

"Brexit's the most boring thing I ever knew. Dad never stops banging on about it, though I notice it's stopped being topic A for most people over here. About time."

Daisy was choosing silver and gold balls and stars out of a heap on the floor and fixing wire hangers to them as they talked.

"Sorry, Gran. I know you're interested in it. I suppose I should mind about it but really I just don't know enough, I'm afraid. I thought it was quite boring before I went to UDC. That was nearly a year and a half ago. Now it's actually happening, even though they keep putting it off, you'd think at least Dad would shut up about it. What's happened to the big star that goes on top?"

She searched the heap.

"Here it is. Good. I'll fix it with a light underneath it."

She stood on a chair to reach the top of the tree.

"In Canada Brexit doesn't come up much, you can imagine. You certainly don't get people having rows about it like here. Anyway it's really just about over now isn't it?"

"I'm afraid it isn't. There are a whole lot of very complicated issues that've got to be negotiated and Britain and the EU are miles apart on a lot of them. Boris Johnson swears it can all be done by the end of next year, but they're not going to be even talking till March, and no one else thinks it's possible to get it done, or decently done, so quickly. And if it isn't done—"

Daisy, like half the country, Clare thought, didn't wait to hear what would happen if it weren't done by the end of the year.

"Really?" Daisy interrupted. "Then why does Dad keep saying things like 'We did it, didn't we? They all tried to stop us but we did it.' He makes it sound like some kind of rugby match. His side won, the other side lost, and that's that. End of story."

"Your father's not always very realistic. And you're quite right. About the rugby match. Brexit became something very un-English, an all-or-nothing issue, my side totally right, your side totally wrong, whichever side you were on."

"A zero-sum game", Daisy said, taking two silver balls off the Christmas tree, putting them in different places and standing back to assess the effect. "That's better."

"I've never understood what that means, a zero-sum game."

"Game theory, Gran. You know. Basic maths. All gain for one side equals all loss for the other. Nothing left over." She moved a gold bauble shaped like a torpedo.

"Well, there you are. Not basic maths in my day. And perfectly idiotic if you apply it to politics."

"Is it? Dad thinks Brexit all gain. You think it's all loss. Zero sum. Seems to me to make sense."

Clare, surrounded by cardboard boxes and bits of tissue paper, was kneeling on the floor beginning to tidy up.

She sat back on her heels.

"Except that politics isn't a game. It's about people's actual lives, so the consequences of decisions are mixed and complicated and can't always be made to turn out as you want them to. If the referendum had gone the other way, nothing much would have changed and everyone except the ghastly European Research Group would have more or less forgotten about it by now. Even your father, I dare say. Students would have gone on going backwards and forwards between European universities and ours, strawberry pickers from Lithuania and plumbers from Poland and care workers from Portugal would have gone on doing stuff no one in England can be bothered to do, and Muslims who live here for reasons that never had anything to do with the EU one way or the other wouldn't be nearly as hassled and bullied and scared as they are now. And the farmers up in the moors would have gone on looking after their sheep with a European subsidy to keep them afloat. Perhaps there wouldn't have been obvious gains, but there wouldn't have been obvious losses either. Now there will be."

"Exactly. All loss, you think. All gain, Dad thinks. Zero sum." She wasn't really listening, or she didn't care, or both. "Anyway, what's the European Research Group?"

"O Daisy, what it is to have been abroad all this time. They're the Tory MPs who think the only thing in the world that matters is leaving the EU. Nothing to do with research. It was a little group of plotters, disloyal to the main Tory party for years. All for Brexit and the harder the better. Now for all I know it's half the Tory MPs. Your father didn't used to be one of them, though by now he may well be."

"So it's just in Parliament? Just MPs?"

"I think so, yes."

"Such a shambles Parliament seems to be. I suppose that's why Carrie didn't want to work for an MP", Daisy said. "I thought it might be quite fun, watching them quarrelling away. Carrie always just wants everyone to agree to save the world.

I'm going to switch the lights back on, to see what it looks like now."

She switched the tree lights on by the socket in the wall. The simplest cheering effect.

"There, look. I think that'll do, don't you?"

"It looks lovely." But Clare was nearly in tears. She looked round her at the debris on the carpet, cardboard boxes, tissue paper, a couple of baubles with their tops broken.

"O dear", she said.

"Leave it, Gran. I'll do it."

"All right. Thank you, Daisy. Give me a hand to help me up, could you? I'm getting too old for the floor."

Daisy pulled her upright and she sat in a comfortable chair. "That's better."

Daisy swept together the odds and ends from the tree decorations, threw the broken baubles into the waste paper basket on top of the tinsel and piled the rest into a supermarket plastic bag.

"There. I'll put that in the cupboard under the stairs till we take the tree to bits."

"Sit down a minute, Daisy."

Daisy looked startled, like a child realizing a ticking off was imminent and not being sure what it was for. She put the plastic bag down and sat beside it on the carpet, cross-legged, with her athletic back straight, looking up at her grandmother.

"It really matters about Brexit, you know. People of your generation will have to—"

Looking relieved that the ticking off was only going to be about Brexit, Daisy interrupted.

"O, I know we're all supposed to be terrific remainers. Carrie went on and on about it after the referendum but she hadn't said much about Brexit before it happened. And she didn't even bother to vote. Nor did plenty of other people her age. I was too young, thank goodness, so you can't blame me one way or the other."

"I wouldn't dream of blaming you, darling. Or Carrie. Or anyone young. It's all the fault of the politicians who didn't explain properly what was at stake, and didn't give your contemporaries, or anyone, actually, a sense of the good and brave achievement the EU has actually been after hundreds of years of war in Europe, and specially after the two worst wars in the whole of history. Perhaps you had to be old, like me, to remember all that, but one of the things that was so disappointing was that lots of old people voted for Brexit because somehow Boris Johnson and co gave them the idea that because we won the war we should never have got mixed up with all these unreliable foreigners who'd either been the enemy or had feebly given in."

"Dad thinks that, more or less, doesn't he?"

"He does, and he isn't even old."

"But how I see it, being young, I mean, and being at uni in Canada, is that all that history's part of what makes it difficult to mind about Brexit like you do. Europe's such a mess, isn't it? Always has been, everybody fighting each other and hating each other and burning each other at the stake. Not to mention imperialism, stealing from people, their land and whatever, and despising them, all over the world. All of that was the Europeans, including the British of course. I think Europe's done. It's quite rich, or lots of its countries are quite rich. But except for Germany it's been pretty useless at looking after all these poor Syrians and people trying to get into Europe. Including the UK. Canada's been much better. To tell you the truth, Gran, it's been quite nice to be on a different continent and as far away as the Pacific."

Clare didn't know where to start.

"I do see—I realize, of course I do, how bad we've been, how bad most of the EU countries have been about the Syrians, and all the wretched people, from Africa and Afghanistan and Iran and Iraq, from Libya where—anyway, people from all these places where there are wars, who've been trying to come to Europe to be safe." She stopped. She wanted to pull the discussion back to the positive. She tried.

"But in spite of all that, Daisy, there is, there has been, so much that's good, interesting, in the EU countries, with deep roots in history. You mustn't forget you're English yourself, and European as well. Both are lucky things to be, even nowadays, and with the luck comes—"

"Sometimes I wish I wasn't. English, I mean. And I don't feel at all European."

"Your great-grandfather was a Czech Jew."

Daisy looked blank. "What? How do you mean?"

"My father was a Czech Jew, who escaped Hitler, I'm not sure how, and came to England just before the war. He married my mother who grew up here, exactly here, well, not in this house, in Michael's house. Michael's grandfather was her brother. Didn't your mother tell you anything ever about my father, her grandfather? She loved him when she was little. He was brilliant with children."

"No. Yes, she might have done. I'm afraid I can't remember. I'm sorry."

"No, Daisy. Not your fault. There's no reason why you should remember such ancient history."

Daisy thought, and then said, "So I'm an eighth Jewish. Is that right?"

"That's right. A dash of Jewish in the genes is always meant to be good, for brains, for music, for jokes, so I hope you're pleased."

"I suppose. There are quite a lot of Jewish students at UBC. Some of them are very brainy, science, maths, IT, all that. Rather like the Chinese students, But they're more fun than the Chinese, like you say. They're awfully touchy, though."

"How d'you mean, touchy?"

"A few of them are from Israel and lots of other students are always campaigning for the Palestinians and asking for boycotts and things against Israel and then everyone else starts talking about anti-Semitism and it gets quite nasty."

"O dear. That's happened here too. With the Labour party for one thing. But it's so much more complicated than people realize, and so terribly sad."

"Is it? I suppose it is. I'm afraid I don't know much about it. Israel and the Palestinians, I mean. It seems like another mess from the past no one can do much about, and it's too far away for students in Vancouver to make much difference anyway."

"But they're right to care, you know."

Daisy shrugged. "It's more a bit of a fuss to show how cool they are, don't you think? It's woke to be pro-Palestinian and anti-Israeli."

Clare had only a vague idea of what "woke" meant, but let it go. She leant forward in her chair.

"Daisy, what are you going to do when you've got your degree? What exactly are you studying?"

"O, this and that. Some computer science, some Asian Studies. A programme on the environment. My main thing next year's going to be Gender, Race, Sexuality and Social Justice."

"Goodness. What a lot. So what might all that equip you to do when you've finished university?"

"I've no idea yet. Stay in Canada if I can, at least for a few years. If I do reasonably well I might be able to stay at UBC and do a master's. Dad would be impressed. And I know I won't want to leave when it comes to the point. It's a really brilliant country, Gran. Wild and beautiful and pretty much empty, but with good cities. Vancouver's a great city. Toronto's meant to be good too. And the people are lovely. Quite like Americans, I suppose, endlessly friendly and jolly, but much more sensible."

"More sensible?"

"Well, look at Justin Trudeau. He's a good egg—even you would think so, Gran. The Canadians would never have elected Trump. But the Brits practically have: look at Boris. And, while we're on Europe, there are worse people than Boris in other European countries. There's a clever girl in my dorm—it means student house, not dormitory like in an English boarding school—who's doing politics at UCB, and she says Europe's basically had it. Her grandparents were all from Ukraine. I don't understand the issues. I suppose I don't know enough history. But this girl thinks we—I mean Canadians—should forget about Europe and concentrate on China because the future is China. I chose the Asian Studies programme more or less by accident but it's jolly interesting."

"O Daisy, China. It sounds so sinister in so many ways."

"Well, exactly. It probably is, as sinister as anything. So we need to know about it, don't we? Not about Europe."

"But don't you think we can only cope properly with the future if we don't forget about the past?"

"I expect you're right, Gran. But nobody can learn about everything, can they?"

"Well, perhaps there are some priorities, like—" She got no further. The door, pushed by Penny's foot, opened, and she came in with a tray with a few glasses on it and a cereal bowl with peanuts. She put the tray on the piano.

"O, well done. The tree looks lovely. Did you decide against tinsel?"

"Too old. Tatty", Daisy said. "We chucked it."

"Probably quite right. I've been cooking for hours. Would you like some sherry, Mum? I'm going to have a g. and t. Daisy?"

"I'll get a coke."

That evening, after dinner, Clare, by herself and borrowing the Land Rover again, went to what should have been Midnight Mass in the dull little Catholic church where all those years ago she had got married. The Mass was at nine, no doubt because most of the congregation were old and didn't want to be out too late. There was the familiar crib that was brought out every Christmas, and candles and holly, and the church, with new electric heaters bright red and high on the walls, was much warmer than it used to be. But she was too sad for Christmas.

Sometimes, specially sometimes at Mass, she felt stricken, all over again, by the loss of David, as if it had not happened until now, or as if she had entirely forgotten and suddenly remembered it. Three months had gone by since that weekend, and she had written about it as accurately as she could in what might or might not be going to be her book, but she hadn't got used to David being gone, being nowhere, being not any longer in the world. As she had never got used to the loss of Matt. That, obviously, was because Matt was too young to die, and because losing a child is always against the proper order of things. But David had been old, and less well than she had noticed, and there was nothing against nature about his death. So why did she miss him quite so much when she had got accustomed to the absence of Simon, even after nearly forty-five years of marriage, more easily and with fewer moments of black grief? Was it because Simon's death hadn't been a shock—indeed, because of his illness, had been in its way a relief? Partly, no doubt. But it was also because David had been company, for years and years but particularly since Simon's death, in a way no one else, in her now long life, had ever been.

She remembered, as she sat in the little Catholic church on Christmas Eve, hearing a homily about babies and new life that she wasn't listening to, a visit with David a year ago, more likely two years ago, to the National Gallery. "Do you mind if we start with the Pieros?" she had said. "I haven't seen them for ages." He hadn't even answered, and they had walked through nearly empty galleries—it was a Tuesday morning in winter—not stopping for any of the wonders on the way, until they came to the spot where, from some distance, they could see Piero della Francesca's Baptism of Christ. Side by side they walked very slowly towards it.

For a long time—how long? Perhaps ten minutes that seemed much longer—they stood in front of the painting and said nothing. No one else was there.

When a man by himself came close, they turned, together, to look at Piero's Nativity on the wall to one side of the Baptism.

Was it because it was Christmas Eve that she was now remembering so vividly this strange Nativity? Mary, kneeling, quiet, with praying hands. The child naked and defenceless, lying on some dark stuff, holding up his arms to his mother. Angels playing lutes, gentle music. But on the roof of the stable a raucous crow, a portent, an omen.

They walked slowly back through gallery after gallery and down the stairs to the café, side by side, saying nothing. Over coffee, and David's cake, he said, "It's the discordant note that does it, isn't it?"

"The crow. Of course."

"And in the Baptism not exactly a note but something else, movement, against the miraculous stillness of Christ and the dove and the watchers and the Baptist balanced on one foot— the movement of the man taking off his shirt."

"All of us, perhaps, stripping off our sins, to receive grace."

"The painting does it without those words."

She felt a very slight rebuke.

"Without any words", he added. "And just for that one moment, the held moment. The watchers are angels. They will vanish."

That's what angels do. She remembered what Hakim had said about the boy, or the boys, in *Waiting for Godot*. Now she remembered, too, the boy on the beach who told Augustine that trying to understand God was like trying to pour the sea into a small hole in the sand. Then he vanished.

Looking at paintings with David. Never again. She had followed the Mass, joined the rest of the people in the church in the words of the Creed, the Sanctus, without noticing. She knelt for the eucharistic prayer and pulled her attention back to where she was and why. Christ coming into the world.

Christmas Day came and went like so many other Christmas Days. Charles and Penny went to church in the village. They all had lunch in the big house, where Michael and Sarah, his wife, were hospitable and kind and three of their four children were young enough to be over-excited and noisy. The oldest, a girl of about fourteen, was sulky and silent. "Is Flora OK?" Clare said to Sarah before lunch. "O, she's fine. In a mood, you know. Girls of fourteen. I got her the wrong thing for Christmas. Fatal."

Clare was sitting next to Michael and while everyone was finishing huge plates of turkey, stuffing, roast potatoes etc. etc, said, with enough noise at the table for no one else to hear, "Is poor Flora a bit low? She's not eating much."

"O, Flora. She's inclined to be in despair about something. These days I think it's the environment. All through the summer holidays she was counting, birds in the garden, birds on the farm, bees, butterflies, bumble bees, even wasps: not enough of any of them, according to her, and all our fault. For having a Range Rover and oil-fired heating. She'll get over it."

"The world may not", Clare said, but Michael didn't notice. He was getting to his feet, saying "I'd better have another go at the turkey for the starving hordes. Billy!" A shout down the table to his youngest, aged six. "Don't feed Bear at lunch, OK? You know it's bad for him." Bear was an ageing golden retriever of great gentleness, called Teddy by the toddler Flora when he was a puppy, hence Bear as more dignified.

Michael, her cousin's son, was a nice straightforward fellow, Clare had always thought. Penny, a bit older, had liked him since they were children, and he had been pleased when Charles became the local MP. Michael wasn't interested in politics, was in favour of Brexit in a mild sort of way, and had always been a Tory because he would have found it inconceivable to be anything else. He ran the small estate he had inherited, was a race-starter at the two reasonably nearby racecourses, and nowadays was also a JP. He was good with dogs, horses, tenants and, to be fair, elderly widows who arrived for Christmas.

Eventually Sarah brought in the Christmas pudding, the blue flames of lit warmed brandy dying down too quickly for the children—"It's gone out, Mum"—and the grown ups ate some of it while the children were allowed ice cream instead. Sarah went out to the kitchen and reappeared with half a Stilton. Michael fetched a decanter of port from the sideboard. Once a glass of port was in his hand, Charles got to his feet.

"A toast", he said, loudly enough for even the children to shut up and look at him. Clare looked down at her lap, wishing she were somewhere else.

"To 2020, the year of Brexit at last!"

Daisy said, "Dad, for goodness' sake", and more quietly, "I hope 2020'll be a bit more exciting than that", and simultaneously Flora scraped back her chair, left the dining room and shut the door behind her with a bang.

"O dear", Charles said. "I've upset the radicals, and Carrie isn't even here. I'm so sorry, Sarah."

"It's quite all right, Charles", Sarah said. "Politics is inclined to send her off the deep end I'm afraid. Take no notice." But Sarah picked up a pile of dirty plates and followed Flora.

"To 2020 anyway", Charles tried to rescue his toast. "And may we all have a good and prosperous year."

Well, which? Clare thought.

Michael stood up to help. He gestured with his glass towards Charles at the other end of the table

"To 2020! Thank you, Charles."

Clare and Penny and Daisy raised their glasses and muttered an echo.

"Dad, can we get down?" Billy said.

"Yes, of course you can. Vanish. Go and play with some of those fantastic presents. Try not to break them, or anything else."

The children clattered out of the room.

Boxing Day was grey, chilly, blustery. Penny, dressed to the nines in gleaming hunting clothes, shortly to be covered in mud, took her horse, the horsebox and the Land Rover to the meet in the town seven miles away. Michael, even smarter in his scarlet coat because he had been MFH, would be there too, on his big, shiny chestnut horse which Clare had been to greet in the stable after lunch on Christmas Day. Charles drove in his car to appear at the meet, look enthusiastic about hunting—he had no idea how to ride a horse—remember the right people's names and stand in the market place with a glass in his hand looking as important as he could when huntsmen, twenty or thirty horses and riders, some of them children on ponies, and a pack of not very disciplined hounds, moved off towards the soggy edge of a wood somewhere. Clare wasn't there but could easily picture a scene familiar from all her life.

She went, instead, for a demanding walk, out of the village and up through the dripping wood to the top of the long hill from which she could see the moors to the north, and if she turned right round, the line of the Howardian Hills to the south. In each direction she could also see a couple of small villages on the flat fields below, hedges, old trees here and there, some of them dark with ivy, and a few farms. It wasn't a spectacular landscape but she had known it always and knew where its secrets were: the old, low bridges across the becks, and the hidden railway, where when she was a child a steam engine two or three times a day pulled a couple of carriages and a guard's van full of stuff between the market towns and as far as York and Scarborough. Over the sixty years since the trains had stopped and the track was taken up, the railway had become a wide green path with oaks and sycamores and crabapple trees beside it, for undisturbed birds, wild flowers in the spring, and for walking, far from roads and cars.

There were village churches, mostly out of sight among cottages and trees, though she could see the top of one modest square tower. She knew these churches. Two of them had Saxon stones as well as Norman and later walls and windows, and so were a thousand years old. And she could in her imagination or memory (one of Augustine's topics, this elision) travel with exactness the lanes that let to a third, her favourite, which was invisible below the wooded sides of a narrow dale, and was more than a mile from any village. Over the low, wide door, like an old door into a house or a small barn, was a Saxon sundial, sheltered now in a rough porch, announcing in still clear letters that the church was rebuilt before the Normans came, so most likely it had been built originally in the seventh century, before the Vikings came, the raiders from the sea who no doubt pulled it down. This little church hid in its small, quiet valley, with its quiet graves stretching away, old leaning tombstones near the church, the inscriptions on some now indecipherable, and further from the church newer, more upright stones, only a few of them unpleasant polished granite, with legible inscriptions, and, to Clare, many familiar names. Her mother, her grandparents of whom she had only faint memories, Michael's father who was her first cousin, other people she remembered or remembered the names of. Standing a little below the top of her hill to avoid the worst of the blowing rain, she pictured the graveyard—she had been there at least once each summer for eleven years—with sheep among the stones cropping the grass, and a few bright or fading flowers on the freshest graves.

Matt was there. When she thought of the church and its peaceful graves, she always did this, let her imagination wander down the paths, along the rows of stones, until she reached Matt's stone, quite far from her mother's and her grandparents'. The army had brought him back from Afghanistan and the colonel of his regiment and four other soldiers, one a bugler to play the Last Post, had come to his funeral. Simon was there, of course, holding her elbow to steady her as they followed the coffin through the graveyard. Afterwards he seemed grateful for the ceremony and the sense of occasion. But when he was dying he was definite that he wanted to be cremated, that he didn't want his ashes scattered, that he didn't want any kind of service or memorial. "I've written all this down. You know I have. Don't let anyone persuade you to organize anything. I definitely don't want one of those concerts where people have obviously struggled to find poems to read between the music. I want a clean finish, and I don't really belong anywhere, do I? Never have." She had wanted to say, "a stranger on the earth, like all of us", but she knew Simon would think this an attempt to turn his realism into something Christian, and said nothing.

So Matt was buried near at least some of his relations, unlike—and she often thought of him when she thought of Matt—the last soldier in the family, before Matt, to be killed: her mother's brother, Michael's grandfather. He was buried in a cemetery in Normandy, his grave one among hundreds with their white stones, not far from where his tank had been blown up like Matt's, a week or two after D-Day.

Below the graveyard was a beck that as a child she had regarded as magical. If it had rained on the moors, the water flowed strong and clear, speeding over stones, a proper river. If the weather had been dry for a while, the water disappeared completely, the stones were dry, flat, almost regular slabs, as if someone had laid them and, but for birds, sheep and a very occasional car on the lane beyond the graveyard, the silence was absolute. She knew now that the river hadn't dried up but had disappeared underground, to reappear downstream where once it had even powered a corn mill: limestone watercourses, she had read somewhere, quite often behaved in this mysterious way.

She thought, for an impractical moment, that she might walk to the church and the graveyard. She realized at once that she was too old, the day was too wet, and because, as usual, she had no mobile phone to ask someone to fetch her, she would have to walk all the way back. There most likely wouldn't be a signal in that narrow dale in any case.

So, after a few more minutes, looking at each thing she could see from her hilltop, to remember it as if—it occurred to her: why?—she might never see it again, she made her way back through the steep wood, carefully. You know you're old, she thought, when it's more difficult going down than going up, hills, stairs, everything. There wasn't much of a path, her knees were a bit shaky, Penny's wellington boots were too big for her, and if she fell and broke her leg or even sprained her ankle she would be—no mobile phone: what would Penny say?—a real nuisance for several hours until someone came to look for her.

When she got back to the house, cold and very wet, she was pleased that no one was there. Charles was probably following the hunt half-heartedly in a warm car, stopping on some verge to exchange chat and a drink with others who had lost track of horses and hounds. Daisy, she remembered, was being picked up in the middle of the morning and taken to some distant pub for lunch by a local boy she had sounded delighted to hear on the telephone.

She had a bath, put on dry clothes, and sat at her dressing table with her laptop to write about her walk. It was as if she had been to the church in the narrow dale and the graveyard, though she hadn't, and she thought about it more: what was it that made it such a very special place? Matt, yes. All the graves, yes. The strange river. But most of all, it was the long, long centuries during which the church, or at least a church, had been there.

When missionaries, who were also monks—the church, though always very small, was called Minster—had arrived in the seventh century, probably from Lindisfarne or somewhere else in Northumbria, this must have been a frightening pagan wilderness. After four hundred years of more or less orderly life, even here in the distant north of their empire, the Romans had left. Two centuries later when the monks made the clearing by the limestone beck, the Romans' farms, their comfortable houses, must have almost completely disappeared. In that wide landscape she had been able to see, or nearly see, from her hilltop, the places only a few miles apart where three Roman villas had been discovered at different times. It was both poignant and somehow almost comic to remember that each of these farmhouses, nearly two thousand years ago, had mosaic floors and bathrooms and piped hot water—unheard of again until well into the nineteenth century. Just the other day, Hakim would smile at her for saying. Under the fields and woods there might well be the foundations, the floors, of more villas. This was gentle farming country for the families and the retainers of Roman officers in York, perhaps sometimes senior figures who had come south from the fiercer hills of Hadrian's Wall.

The Romans went. The Anglo Saxons came, worshipping trees, thunder, the sun. Gradually the sun and thunder and trees returned to the natural world, kind or unkind but not divine. The monks had brought Christ into the forests and hills. Also the monks had brought back Rome, with their Latin bibles and prayers, and the Latin Rule by which as time went by they lived their lives. St Gregory, the patron of this little church at the back of beyond, was a grand Roman official in the tradition of Cicero before he was the bishop of Rome: in his life responsibility for the city shaded without a definite boundary between the earthly city and the city of God into responsibility for the souls of the citizens of both.

When she was a classics teacher, in another world it now seemed, so depleted had English education become, she used to read, in spare classes after exams were over, some chapters of Bede's History, or St Benedict's Rule, or even Augustine, with bright sixth-formers who found the Latin wonderfully easy. That Bede's monastery, across the Tyne from Hadrian's Wall and so even further towards the edge of the world than St Gregory's Minster, was Roman, as were Bede's mind and Bede's writing, were among the reasons for remembering with warmth and admiration him and his account of the coming of Christians to these dales. Not long ago Hakim had told her of new discoveries at Tintagel in Cornwall, amphorae from Cyprus and Asia Minor that had held olive oil and wine, glass and pottery from Spain, North African coins, all from later than when the Romans were supposed to have disappeared from eastern England. Civilized life at the court of King Arthur?

More likely just civilized life beyond the reach of Angles and Saxons.

She stopped writing and looked out of her bedroom window at Penny's grey wintry garden, at some cottage roofs beyond the trees, and the low grey clouds. What she wanted was to bring Hakim up here, to take him to the church in the narrow dale, to show him that there were other ways of connecting with Virgil's Rome, humbler than the fallen cities by the blue Mediterranean but no less moving and in their way longer lasting.

She smiled as she realized that she had never even thought of David as someone to show this landscape to, these beloved places of her whole life. David was urban, a Londoner from first to last. She couldn't imagine him in country clothes, plodding up a steep, muddy path in wellington boots. She couldn't imagine him at a bonfire or a picnic. He was a man of café tables and quiet galleries at carefully chosen times of day. And although his affection for her had led him through her book on Augustine with a certain amount of understanding and sympathy, he would have thought all she had seen and remembered and imagined, looking from a rainswept hill at an apparently dull expanse of winter countryside, fanciful, romantic, much too English for him.

But Hakim, in most ways a great deal more foreign than David, was used to reading landscape, used to remembering the Romans or the Greeks however much their time in a place was overlaid by the sediment of history. He would have understood.

Sitting at her dressing table, alone in the house, she missed Hakim acutely.

That evening, after Penny, sopping and tired, had had a long bath and a rest, and Charles and Daisy had reappeared after tea from their separate days out, they had an easy supper. Clare had laid the table, got out of its layers of wrapping the smoked salmon she had brought from London and arranged it on a plate with quarters of lemon. When Penny appeared—"O brilliant, Mum. You are a star"—Clare made toast and scrambled some eggs and Charles shouted upstairs for Daisy who came into the kitchen still talking on her telephone.

"You know, Charles", Clare said as they ate, "Some of the locals I've been talking to are really worried about Brexit."

She was leaving the next morning: Penny was taking her to York for a train and the others were staying over the New Year. She couldn't any longer resist a modest attempt to get Charles to think a little harder about what he, as a Tory member of parliament if not part of the government, was actually doing to the people who had elected him.

"Farmers, I suppose."

"Farmers, yes, and an old keeper I've known since he was a boy opening gates for the hunt."

"They'll complain about anything, you realize, or maybe you don't. They always complain. Farmers have been feather-bedded in this country ever since the war, and all they do is grumble and say it's impossible for them to make a decent living however hard they work. Perfect nonsense. Have you noticed the cars their wives drive nowadays? There were several at the meet this morning. As far as I can see, they're doing very nicely thank you. Not worth being a dairy farmer they say. Not worth being a pig farmer. The prices aren't right and the bureaucracy stifles everything. That's why they voted for Brexit. And now they're complaining because Brexit is actually happening. They'll all be better off in the end, you'll see."

"Charles. If Boris Johnson and co are so stubborn that there's no deal by the end of the year, there'll be a forty per cent tariff on lamb going into Europe and no sheep farmer here will survive. It's no good just telling them to keep the moors beautiful for tourists. They do that anyway. But telling a farmer not to produce anything—it goes against the whole of history, don't you see?"

"Produce is the point, Clare. I know economics isn't your thing, in spite of being married to an economist all those years, but this one isn't hard to grasp. Do you know what proportion of British GDP's in agriculture?"

She didn't. .

"Well, do you? No. Of course you don't. Point nought six five per cent. Practically negligible in statistical terms."

"The price of everything and the value of nothing", Clare said.

"What?"

"Never mind. The point is that these are people, not numbers. They voted for Brexit because no one explained to them what it would mean, and because they were promised that everything would get better not worse, and they voted for you because you're their Tory MP and that's how they always vote. But they're frightened now, even despairing. There have been suicides. They think if there's no deal—"

"Don't exaggerate, Clare. There's no need for the farmers or anyone else to get their knickers in a twist about no deal. Boris'll get a deal for sure. We've got a date, the end of next year. He won't extend, and once the blasted Europeans have got that, they'll have to play ball. What people like you, Clare, have never understood is that they need us a lot more than we need them. Boris has said all along—"

"Why anyone should believe anything Boris Johnson says I have no idea."

"Mum!"

Clare had been aware of Penny getting increasingly annoyed with her during this argument with Charles. Never mind. Now she sounded affronted. Like Mrs Tabitha Twitchit in Beatrix Potter.

"You can't say that! Look how brilliantly he's done, specially in the election. The biggest Tory majority since Mrs Thatcher—that's not nothing, you know."

"Of course it's not nothing. But is it something good? Much more doubtful. I'd have thought you'd have been more sympathetic to the farmers, Penny."

"A proper Tory majority means the stupid hunting laws can be chucked. About time."

This was too much for Daisy.

"Honestly, Mum, with the world going to hell in a handcart, you really can't go on fussing about the hunting laws. Were they ever anything to do with Europe? They don't seem to have made any difference anyway."

"Ridiculous, the whole hunting business. It was all a fudge in the first place", said Charles. "Tony Blair pleasing one lot of people by abolishing hunting and the other lot of people by not abolishing hunting. Quite clever, really."

"Yes", said Clare. "What a pity you didn't follow his example and vote for Mrs May's deal, pleasing one lot of people by doing Brexit and the other lot of people by not doing Brexit. It's called compromise and managing it used to be thought of as an essential political skill."

"Well done, Gran", said Daisy.

This didn't help. Charles looked actually angry.

"I give up, Penny", he said, as if talking to the Speaker. "Perhaps your mother will see the point of Brexit in a few years, when everything in the country is going better than it has for half a century."

Clare laughed.

"I doubt if I'll live that long, Charles", she said. "Which is probably just as well."

"Don't say that, Gran", said Daisy. "We all want you to live as long as possible, don't we, Mum."

"Yes, of course we do. Now, who'd like a mince pie?"

"Any brandy butter left?"

"Lots."

That night, just before getting into her warm bed—she had switched on the electric blanket after supper—she turned out the lights in her pretty room in Penny's house and stood, as always, between the curtains and the window to pray. She opened the window. The dark became a little lighter as her eyes got used to it. "The dark is light enough." Who said that? Or was it the title of a book? She couldn't remember, but she liked it.

One of the things she always enjoyed when she stayed in Penny's house was the difference between the night she could watch and hear in the country and the familiar London night. Beyond the silent trees of the square, the occasional passing car, and rare footsteps on the pavement, there was, in London, always the hum of traffic from the Gloucester Road and the

Cromwell Road, the roar of the odd motorbike or revved-up fast car, and the sirens now and then of a police car or an ambulance. There was always also the orange haze of street-lights, so no star was ever visible. Here there was real darkness and a deeper silence.

Once, perhaps last Christmas or in the summer, she had seen from this window on a moonlit night a barn owl glide across the garden, pale like a ghost and so utterly noiseless that its passage only intensified the silence. Not tonight. No moon. She wouldn't see an owl if there were one, though she could just see the trees against the still cloudy sky.

But here, always, there were also more sounds than in her London square. She listened. A faint rustle. And another. Then, perhaps answering each other, the wavering faint hoots of two tawny owls in the woods above the village, one nearer, one further, with pauses as, maybe, they also listened. Nearer, the harsh double squawk of a woken pheasant. What was prowling in the dark? A fox? A silent fox with its mouth full of fur—she had seen two rabbits in Penny's garden—or feathers? Audible only with the window open, the church clock in the village struck eleven. She counted, and then listened to the living silence resettle when the last chime had died.

She smiled as she remembered the hopeless conversation over the smoked salmon and scrambled eggs. There was no point in even trying to shake Charles's sense of deserved vic-tory. Penny didn't do either doubt or complexity and never had. And Daisy, muddled and patchily informed, was quite understandably all for youth and the future and sorting out the climate, and leaving behind, to the old and sad, Europe, the Middle East, the past, the unresolved consequences of the sins of history. There was no longer David to talk to. At least, she thought again, there was Hakim, who was young but also carried in him, in his mind and his soul, so much of it all.

She prayed for Hakim, ruefully for Charles, Penny and Daisy, for Carrie so far away—she had managed to telephone yesterday to say Happy Christmas to her parents and had sent her love to Clare—and for David and all her dead.

Christmas seemed long ago now, and Yorkshire far away. She had several times since those few rainy days wondered why she had had such a strong foreboding: she might, she would, never see those places again. Was it only the sadness that almost never left her now—sadness about the world, about Brexit, about David? Perhaps, because she wasn't sad about the approach, inevitable of course though as far as she could tell not imminent, of her own death. How entirely lacking in logic, not to be sad about dying, leaving everything but in some unfathomable way finding in eternity those who had died, but to be sad about never again seeing those fields and hedges, farms and trees, with the churches and streams hidden and the line of the moors in the distance.

Sitting at her kitchen table, displacing anxiety about Hakim with what she remembered of the last couple of months, she was struck all over again by the most dispiriting memory of all, the lonely night here in her flat, the night, which she had tried and failed to forget, of the thirty-first of January, the third time within a year when the politicians had promised that Brexit would take place: March, October, January. Third time lucky, Charles and his friends would think.

She was in bed by half past ten, with a mug of camomile tea and a whole Lord Emsworth novel that she hoped would soothe her, as Whiffle on *The Care of the Pig* soothed Lord Emsworth, so that she could fall asleep and forget all about it. She didn't have to pretend to be tired: since David's death she had found the days more tiring than she used to, though this may have been an illusion caused by sadness. Or just a reality caused by old age.

Before she was properly asleep the fireworks began, and went on, near and far, from what seemed like all over London, for at least an hour, making it impossible not to be not only wide awake but furious and miserable, furious because the people celebrating had been led to believe that something glorious was taking place, miserable because what was taking place was absolute loss.

Most depressing was the fact that while what had happened that night was indeed the end of belonging to the EU, it was by no means the end of arguments, negotiations, deals, concessions and so-called victories which would go on for months, quite possibly, whatever Boris Johnson unreliably promised, for years, and could not deliver a result for the country which was better than staying in the EU would have been. It was as simple, and as unnecessary, and as destructive, as that. And the people letting off fireworks and singing "Rule Britannia" in pubs had been sold a delusion to put in power people who didn't deserve to be trusted with anything.

Eventually she went back to bed with a new hot water bottle, and sometime after two in the morning went to sleep.

She woke confused, perhaps from an actual nightmare, perhaps just from fireworks and despair, and couldn't think of anyone to ring up who might cheer her, at least a little, by feeling as she did. Her women friends weren't interested in politics or had been in favour of Brexit—one was half in love with Boris Johnson whom she'd never met—and the one who, like her, had minded bitterly about the referendum result was now too ill to think about anything except the next round of chemotherapy. And David was dead. As for Hakim, although there was so much they shared, the pain of Brexit meant little to him. Britain, France, Italy, then Germany when it was Rommel's soldiers marching across the desert, were to him the colonial powers who had brutally and lazily parcelled up North Africa between them for their own profit and glory, or used it as an imperial battlefield, and he couldn't see that European unity since the end of the Second World War had done anything good for the lands and the people he knew best.

Hakim: what could have gone wrong? She knew from his voice on the telephone that there was serious trouble of some kind in his life, but she had no idea what it could be. She must wait until Sunday to find out. But she was pleased that, whatever it was, he thought she might be able to help. And perhaps trying to help him would make something real for her to do in Lent.

It was already two days after Ash Wednesday, and she had so far failed to make any serious connection with Lent.

On Ash Wednesday itself, when it hadn't rained, or hadn't rained much, she had gone to the early Mass at 8 in the morning, pleased to walk there and back in chilly sunshine, and queued with quite a number of others to receive the cross of ashes on her forehead. As the congregation left the church, dissolving into mere people one by one scattering into the streets of Kensington, into buses, taxis, no doubt also into underground trains to get to work, she felt them, with the ashy marks on their faces to be visible carriers—of what? Of a reminder of the mortality that most people would always prefer to forget? So carriers of the truth of death, the universal plague, a bit like medieval lepers with their bells, except that death itself isn't nowadays usually catching. Also carriers of their identity like carriers of the yellow star in Nazi Germany. Not that a Catholic identity would be recognized by most people now, still less hated, though it remained suspect to a few. Some of the congregation would no doubt wash off the sooty mark before they appeared in an office or a classroom or behind the counter of a shop or a desk in a hospital, so as to look like anyone else, like themselves on any other day. She wouldn't wash away her ashes until she had a bath before going to bed. She had never, on Ash Wednesdays in the past, washed off her ashes till the end of the day, to Simon's irritation. "It's barbaric, that black cross on your forehead. Gives me the creeps." "Remembering death. Not creepy, just realistic, don't you think?"

Ash Wednesday was easy. Catholics had to eat no meat and not much of anything else. As she rarely ate meat and rarely ate a lot, one of the great merits of widowhood being that you didn't have to think about food, it wasn't difficult to have a cup of tea rather than coffee when she got home, and a boiled egg and one piece of toast for an early lunch. After lunch she decided to walk up to the park to see, although it was another cold day, whether there were any signs of spring in Kensington Gardens, crocuses, perhaps even daffodils.

On the way she met people coming out of St Stephen's church in Gloucester Road, black crosses like hers on their foreheads. Anglo-Catholics. Of course they would do ashes on Ash Wednesday, as they did so much else that was Catholic while letting themselves off the obligations that came with loyalty to the church that was united only because it was under the ultimate authority of the pope. A loyalty that was still, among both liberals, who regarded Catholics as brainwashed bigots, and patriots who regarded them as potential traitors, unpopular in England, at least among people of a certain age. The young mostly knew little and cared less about Christianity itself, never mind sectarian differences. When, long ages ago, actually nearly sixty years, she had been dithering about whether to ask for instruction from the Catholic church, she had gone a couple of times to an Anglo-Catholic church in Cambridge. Little St Mary's: could it have been called that? She had taken against the atmosphere, heavy with incense and lace and gilding, though she wasn't sure why. Once, also years ago now, she had looked inside St Stephen's in Gloucester Road, not when a service was going on, and had recognized the atmosphere at once. After she and Simon had left Cambridge, when she knew more about the history of the church, and particularly when she had read a biography of Newman, she understood that Catholics in England, accustomed to dull, even ugly, churches, bad music and worse statues and paintings, would always find Anglo-Catholic aesthetics irritating. "Well", some Catholic she'd met, she couldn't remember where, had once said to her, "having their cake and eating it: the perfect definition of Anglo-Catholics".

Like Boris Johnson on Brexit.

Now and then, walking past St Stephen's, she remembered that it was T. S. Eliot's parish church when he lived, in a mansion flat less nice than her own because built later and not as part of a proper house, in a street on one of her routes to Kensington High Street. Miserable man: for all the never-to-be-forgotten lines, there was something deeply negative about him, even about the kind of Christian he made such a performance of becoming. More Anglo than Catholic, in any case. Would he have been a Brexiteer? Probably. She couldn't remember him saying anything anywhere about actual Catholics, though probably he thought, as most snooty WASPS thought, that Catholics were really Italian, Polish, Irish, to posh America inconsiderable, foreign, and poor, like Jews when they first crossed the Atlantic in steerage. And about Jews he was terrible, two or three times, but two or three times is enough.

Anglo-Catholics still didn't like "Romans". When she was on the committee that looked after the garden in her square—she had resigned when she reached seventy-five—she had met two of the St Stephen's Anglo-Catholics, neighbours in the square, a retired soldier and an obviously prosperous businessman, also retired. She knew their wives by sight. The soldier's wife had a black labrador and was always dressed as if she were setting off to watch a shoot. The businessman's, clearly second, wife was probably twenty years younger than him, and too smartly dressed ever to sit on a bench in the garden, let alone risk her shoes on the grass.

Chatting over coffee after a meeting, she had discovered that both soldier and businessman were sidesmen at St Stephen's and were passionately anti-European as well as anti-Catholic. "Shouldn't have joined the wretched Common Market in the first place. Not a British thing to do, asking for favours from the Frogs and the Krauts. At least we avoided the Euro." This was the businessman. The soldier chimed in. "The whole thing was invented after the war by a bunch of Catholics from the battlegrounds between France and Germany, the Rhineland, Belgium, Alsace, Luxembourg. Neither one thing nor the other themselves, not really French, not really German, wanting to bring back the Holy Roman Empire. Most un-British thing you could imagine. Good Queen Bess got us shot of all that." "Quite right. High time we got back to standing on our own feet. What we always did best." It seemed so long ago, though it was only shortly before the referendum, when she had listened to this conversation and one or two others like it. For the sake of a quiet life she hadn't objected, and had thought that at least most people with these ideas would soon be dead. It was odd, and very depressing, to remember now that in those days, four years ago or so, younger people, even mindless Conservatives like Charles and Penny, never talked about Europe. Beyond the nostalgia of old fogeys like the members of the garden committee, Europe wasn't an issue until the referendum made it the only issue. She stopped at the top of Victoria Road and almost groaned aloud.

She worried about all this much more at two or three in the morning when she couldn't sleep than in the daylight when she could more or less forget about it, or, at least, sit at the kitchen table and write another paragraph or two of her book.

She had written, more easily than she had expected, several thousand words. She had begun her story with Penny's telephone call on the Friday before David's death, because this was David's book. If he hadn't died, she might never have collected the courage to begin anywhere. As it was, the empty space his loss had left in her days—much more painful than she would have imagined when he was alive—had been at least partly filled by writing. The book, if it ever became an actual book, was for him, though he had gone, and for him because he had believed she could do it. She had often remembered, with pain, that he had said something like "You'd better get on with it if I'm going to read it". A premonition? Or light encouragement? Perhaps both.

No one else had any idea she was trying to write a book, or would be interested if she told them. She found that she enjoyed writing, and enjoyed even more going over what she had written the day before, taking a few words out, adding a few words, changing the order of paragraphs, listening, over and over, as she had always told her pupils to do, to what she had written. She was enchanted by the ease with which all this could be done on a computer, almost laughing, alone in her kitchen, when she remembered writing her book about Augustine with a pen, with crossings-out and additions, some in tiny writing crammed sideways into margins. And then trying to type it herself and failing, because she made too many mistakes and couldn't bear the misery of starting all over again with a page and its two carbons, so she had got it typed, not well enough, by someone else. So long ago. Now there was no excuse for failing to produce a piece of writing that was not only correct in every possible way but as good as she could make it, sentence by sentence after revisions she couldn't count and of which there was no record. Wonderful. And so quiet. Best of all, she loved the quiet.

The book she was writing for David was a companion, a friend, occupying at least some of the space, the emptiness, he had left in her life.

She had been to Mass today, as she often did on Fridays, but with perhaps more resolution than usual because it was now Lent. There had been a long reading from Isaiah about how much more pleasing it is to God to be doing some actual good rather than going about looking penitent because of it being the official time to fast. Sitting in the church listening to this, she had decided to think of something useful to someone else to do during Lent. She was old, yes, but not ill, not incapable; wasn't her orderly, quiet, undemanding life actually only selfish?

Then there was a very short gospel reading, John the Baptist's obviously penitent, obviously fasting followers asking Jesus why his followers looked cheerful and weren't fasting. Jesus's answer struck her as if she'd never heard it before: "they're not fasting because I'm with them; when I'm taken away from them, they'll fast."

On the walk home she had puzzled over this. Wasn't he always with us? Or hadn't we, this side of the grave, and perhaps beyond—she had always found the idea of Purgatory not terrifying but consoling—always lost him, always had him yet to find? Were both his presence and his absence true at the same time? That this was a proper theological question she couldn't answer, and that it had something to do with time and eternity and that therefore Augustine would help, was as far as she had got when she reached the door of the flat and heard the telephone ringing.

After sitting at the kitchen table for half an hour—she looked at the big clock on the wall and then at her watch; they agreed—she decided she should eat some lunch. So she made a little good vinaigrette, sliced the tomato into a few lettuce leaves and mixed up a small salad which she ate with a piece of toast and some cheese.

With a bit of food eaten and a cup of strong coffee in front of her—the last she would allow herself in the day because of sleeping at night—she realized she was almost pleased that Hakim needed her help or advice or whatever Sunday would reveal.

She was lonely, she knew. Penny didn't need her. When Penny remembered, which, to do her justice was perhaps twice a week, and quite enough, she rang to see if she was all right. As she always was. And, as Penny's life at this time of year was all-consuming, Monday to Thursday in Barnes with Tory party networking, fundraising and heaven knows what else, mainly, probably, gossip, and the weekend in Yorkshire with hunting on Saturdays, there wasn't much to talk about.

"Have you heard from the children?"

"Nothing from Carrie, needless to say. No news is good news. Daisy's fine. I'm all for Vancouver. Safe as houses." A pause. Then, "All right, Mum? We'll chat again soon. Lots of love."

Women's lives, or the lives of women of her generation: they were always being talked about, but no amount of talk could change the basics. It was all supposed to be different now, though, she suspected, it wasn't, for almost everyone, as different as all that. Whether or not you have some kind of career, unless you are one of the very few with an all-consuming ambition that shuts out everything else, you are needed for decades, by husbands, children, grandchildren, old parents who decline and die, friends if you're lucky, and then, perhaps quite suddenly, you're not needed at all. Your parents are dead. Your husband is dead. Your grandchildren are grown up and, in her case, at the ends of the earth. She wished, as often she wished, that Matt had married and had children before he died. His family would have needed her, his children would have needed their own grandmother even if their widowed mother had married someone else and had more children. But this, like so much that came in and out of her head to be dismissed at once as pointless wishful thinking, and sentimental too, was indulging a sadness that wasn't attached to anything that had happened, that was therefore no more than indulgence. Really.

To be ashamed of. She thought of that morning's gospel again. Don't think of mourning while I am with you.

Hakim needed her, and that was good.

Later she tried and failed to remember what happened during the rest of that Friday and all of Saturday. So, presumably, nothing much did happen. Probably it rained. It seemed to have rained almost every day that winter, and sometimes with winds that even in London were quite alarming. Yes, now she remembered that on the Saturday it was too wet and blowy for her to stay out longer than it took her to collect some milk and some kippers, a treat, from Waitrose. Her *Guardian* was still delivered to the door of the block, where Mr Clements, the grumpy part-time caretaker, who cleaned the stairs, sometimes, and changed bulbs on landings, distributed papers and post to the pigeon-holes in the hall.

On the Sunday, with Hakim coming to lunch, she went to the eight-thirty Mass. There was still a gale blowing but she walked, rather unsteadily and depending on her stick to keep going, up to the church and, after mostly praying that she would be able to help Hakim, down again. On the way back she bought the wherewithal to make a straightforward Sunday lunch of the kind Hakim liked best, a small shoulder of lamb, some potatoes to roast, and some leeks. She wouldn't attempt anything Levantine which she would get slightly wrong, but Hakim was keen on ordinary English cooking, especially roast potatoes. On Saturday evening she had got out of her little freezer some blackcurrant purée she had made in the summer, so she also bought some cream to make it into a fool, a kind of pudding unknown to Hakim until she had given it to him once before.

He arrived punctually: she had never known him to be late for anything. He was looking older and thinner. Before he said anything he greeted her with his usual hand to the heart and slight bow. She had never got used to this and the gesture always moved her.

"Clare. Thank you", he said. "I am glad, so glad to see you."

She almost said, "Poor Hakim. Tell me all about it", but realized in time that it would sound like a mother sympathizing with a child in trouble at school. So instead she said, "Come in, Hakim. Do take your coat off—it's very wet. I'll hang it in the cloakroom."

"I'm sorry to be wet. Only from the tube station to here—it is five minutes, but the rain is bad."

"Wretched weather. It never stops raining. People in the north have had terrible floods."

She took his coat. When she came back to the kitchen he was standing with his eyes closed and his head bent as if he were praying, or perhaps deciding how to tell her whatever he had to ask her about.

"Sit down", she said. She had laid the table properly, and put in the middle of it, in a glass vase, a few daffodils, nearly out, from the supermarket.

At last, when he had eaten a few mouthfuls, he said, "This is very good, Clare. Thank you."

He put down his knife and fork, drank some water, and began.

"It is Ayesha. She has almost completed her examinations; in two weeks will be her last examination so she is working very hard. She has almost completed all of her training. She should wait to hear that she has become a qualified doctor, which she would be told in some more weeks. But she will not wait. She says she must go to Assam, to her home, as soon as possible—she told me this on Friday—because the government of India is killing her people. She says she will go after her last examination. They will tell her from London to India that she is now a doctor."

"What? How can the government be killing her people? I thought India—"

She wished again that she knew about India.

"I do remember something in the news", she said feebly, "a couple of months ago, something about Muslims and a new law? Is that it?"

"Yes. That is it. That was it, I should say, at the beginning. It is so far away, I know, but for Ayesha it is close, it is her family, specially her father. I will tell you."

217

She watched him eat some more, while he decided how best to explain.

"In December—this is what you heard in the news—there was a new law in India. This new law pretended to make the treatment of refugees kinder. People coming into India for asylum from Pakistan, from Bangladesh, from Afghanistan, would be allowed to stay if they belonged to any religion except Islam. Muslims, this law pretends, cannot be persecuted in Muslim countries. This is obvious, the government said. But it is not true. Different kinds of Muslim are persecuted in Muslim countries. The Rohingya, the most persecuted and the most harmless of people, have taken refuge from the cruel Burmese in Bangladesh. But already Bangladesh is a poor country and tries to chase the Rohingya into India. So the new law is to stop them coming. But the riots in Assam in December were not mainly about these desperate refugees, though there are too many and poor people always resent refugees, as we know here even in England, but because Muslims who have lived for generations in that part of India, next to Bangladesh, are told they must prove their citizenship or they will be deported. And first they will be put into camps—more camps, more barbed wire and sick children dying, like the ones the Rohingya are trying to escape, but these camps are for people who have been Indian for all their lives."

"I don't understand. Why is this happening so suddenly? I wish I knew more about India."

"I knew nothing about India until Ayesha told many things to me. I will try—"

He ate some more. So did Clare. When he had finished his plateful, he drank a little more water.

"The answer to the question is one man, Narendra Modi."

"He is the Prime Minister?"

"He is the Prime Minister. He was democratically, that is correctly, re-elected last year. Millions and millions of Hindus in India think he is a great leader. He is not a dictator. But, Ayesha is afraid, even if he is not yet a dictator, that he is nearly becoming one. He is strong, and cruel, and popular with a big majority of the people, and that is how dictators begin. It is how Mussolini and Hitler began, though Ayesha does not know these histories. It is even how Gaddafi began.

'What is terrible is that Mr Modi does not—as things in his life of the past have shown—actually think that Muslims are human beings. Twenty years ago he was in charge of a part of India where thousands of Muslims were killed by Hindus and he did nothing to stop the killing. Possibly even he encouraged it. Now he has produced this new law, a Hindu nationalist law, which is a disguised, though it is a badly disguised, attempt to make India a Hindu state where Muslims become bullied second-class people, and many of them are told that they are not even citizens. The home minister, who here would be the Home Secretary, has called Muslims termites, crawling ants, destroyers. This is language of fascism. Mr Modi's government has even tried to make schools teach a history of India that pretends the Mughal empire never did exist. This also is fascist and very shocking. The Mughal empire existed for two hundred years and was a civilized and tolerant Muslim empire. It was like the Ottoman empire. And now Muslims are beaten and raped on the streets and police do nothing."

"But Hakim—surely that can't be possible in India? Isn't there a constitution, a model secular constitution we're all supposed to admire, for all the people, for so many different religions and languages, designed to be equal, to be fair?" She remembered David, who always knew much more history than she did, talking about Nehru and the foundation of India after the British left. But she couldn't remember exactly what he'd said. Something about religion putting India in danger, when Nehru had thought religion would fade away. Is this persecution what he meant, although he had died before the new law Hakim was talking about?

"You are quite right. This wicked treatment of Muslims should not be possible in India. In spite of Partition and all the horrible things that happened then, there are more Muslims in India than in the whole of Pakistan where almost everyone is Muslim, and from the beginning there was supposed to be no political distinction, no political discrimination, in India between one person and another. There is a supreme court which is supposed to guard the constitution but it seems to be powerless, or afraid. I don't know which. Ayesha doesn't know, I should say. She has told me all of these things.

"And now, in just a few years because of Mr Modi and his Hindu party, persecution is not only possible, it seems to be almost what the government wants. There have been mobs beating and killing Muslims, even in universities."

"This is terrible, I do see. I haven't been paying enough attention to the news. I do concentrate when I hear anything about Libya."

Hakim laughed, with some bitterness. "There is almost never news here about Libya. The war in Syria, indeed. The war in Yemen also. The killing in Afghanistan. The war in Libya almost never. Perhaps it is not as bad as Syria, as bad as Yemen, as bad as Afghanistan. It is bad enough. I will tell you what I—But first India and Ayesha."

"Yes. I'm so sorry. I've distracted you. You were saying that Ayesha feels—" Damn. That sounded so English.

Hakim stood up.

"May I eat some more, Clare, please? Your food is so good."

"Of course, Hakim, of course. Help yourself."

He was good at carving.

"And for you?"

"No, thank you. Well, perhaps some leeks." To keep him company while he ate.

He took her plate, returned it with a spoonful of her chopped up, buttery leeks, and sat down to his own plate, almost full, and with the last three roast potatoes. At least he wasn't too upset to eat. Youth.

He ate while he thought for a few minutes.

"In December when the cruel law was passed and the violence began, Ayesha wanted to go home, to help her father who was looking after people in their city in Assam, some of them wounded but many more terrified and confused. Thousands of poor people, she told me, do not have the right papers, or any papers. Perhaps they do not read. Perhaps they never knew that they should apply for papers, though they might have lived in the same street since 1971 when their grandparents or great-grandparents were refugees from the war that separated Bangladesh from Pakistan. Those refugees, nearly fifty years ago, were welcomed by India. Now, suddenly, they are told that they are not Indian unless they have papers. It is a terrible thing, and Ayesha, almost a doctor now, wants to help her father to help these people. In December her father was arrested."

"Arrested? Why?"

"Because he was out on the streets with people who were trying to escape the Hindus. Because the police were arresting anyone they could. They accused him of inciting violence. They let him go after a few days and they did not torture him, but in those few days Ayesha didn't know where he was or if he was alive because all the telephones and the Internet were closed down."

"But she didn't go home in December?"

"She had to finish the last part of her course. Now she has almost finished."

"I see." She looked at Hakim's tired face, the grief in his black eyes something she had seen only once before.

"So now it's possible for her to go home. Is it also possible for her to stay here? For her career, I mean?"

"Yes it is possible. If everything in India had been normal, she would stayed for another six months, maybe another year, for what is called an F1 job. I don't know exactly what that means, a first hospital job as a doctor, I think. Her father always wanted her to do this. There is a hospital, another London hospital, where she has been hoping to work next. But she says she must go to India."

"Aren't things quieter now, a little better in Assam?"

"The streets are quieter in Assam because the Muslims are afraid to move, afraid to speak, afraid to be noticed, while the government builds detention camps for those who will be told they are not citizens. Who will be forced into these camps? Who will escape? They live in fear so they are quiet.

"But in Delhi they are not quiet. In the last few days there have been riots, terrible attacks on Muslims in Delhi. Fifty people have been killed, some of them police because in Delhi police are at least trying to save some Muslims. And faithful Hindus and Sikhs are saving Muslims also. These people have lived side by side in the same streets for all their lives. Many many poor people have watched their houses set on fire, altogether destroyed. If they maybe had papers for their citizenship, the papers have been burnt. Ashes cannot prove who they are. It is for this, for these people and how much they suffer, that Ayesha says she must go home. I understand."

He stopped because it was difficult to go on. He went on.

"But I am too sad, to lose her. She maybe will never come back to England. It is as it was for Samira. I should say it is as it was for me when it was Samira. We say goodbye. We say see you again very soon. She goes. She will be killed, as Samira was killed, only for trying to help—I bring this bad luck, this bad fate. Also there was Dr Rose. He also was trying to help."

"No, Hakim. No." Clare got up, took his plate and hers and put them on the draining board. Then, still standing, facing him, with both hands flat on the table, she said, "Listen to me, Hakim. You mustn't think like this. You bring what is good to people, not what is bad. You brought into Samira's life the sunlight and love that she brought into yours. You know you did. And her death was an accident of war, not in any possible way your fault. Dr Rose was ill when we didn't know he was ill. Yes, he was trying to help by looking for the boy from Libya. He would have gone alone to find him, but it was so much better that you were with him, and your kindness meant that he didn't die alone. You were there in his house and in the hospital, and you did everything you could. Again, you were good, not bad, for my old friend."

She was talking herself into tears. So she stopped, sat down opposite Hakim across the kitchen table, and took a couple of deep breaths.

Hakim put both hands over his face and shook his head.

"No, Hakim. This is all true. I promise you."

He shook his head again, but did take his hands from his face, and looked at her.

"They died", he said. "And I couldn't help them."

"Yes. But it's true of all of us, of every single human being, that people we are close to die and, almost always, we can't help, we can't prevent their death. For Samira and for Dr Rose in different ways you did all you could, and now all we can do is to remember both of them in God. But Ayesha—"

His face crumpled again.

"Ayesha is alive", he said. "She is young, and good, as Samira was. She is a doctor like Dr Rose. Almost a doctor, she would say. She wants to help people in trouble. I understand that she does. If she thinks that the best way she can help people in trouble is by going home to India and working with her father, then that is what she must do."

He stopped and looked straight at Clare.

"I must let her go."

Clare took another deep breath.

"Perhaps you should go with her."

She didn't want Hakim to suspect what even this suggestion was costing her.

But he did.

"Clare. You are generous, a most generous lady. Five years ago you have saved my life. And now you suggest that I should with Ayesha leave England, when I know—"

She was grateful to him for not finishing the sentence.

"Yes", he went on. "I decided to go with her. After she told me she would go home, after I called you on Friday—I was hoping to come to lunch with you today to tell you that I would go to India with her. I have done much research. It is not possible."

"Not possible? Why?"

She hoped the question disguised her relief. It had. She was sure it had because he answered immediately.

"Because I cannot be given a visa. A Libyan can apply only in Tripoli, only himself in front of the official. In person the website says. I had to look up 'in person'. How can I go to Tripoli? If I go to Tripoli, the Indian embassy might refuse the visa—no country wants Libyans, now or ever—and then how am I sure that I am able to come back to England? The Home Office—"

"O the Home Office. To be avoided at all costs." She ran through what he had just told her.

"I see", she said. "How very difficult the world is. I'm so sorry."

"Then I think I must go, go there after all, to Libya."

"What? But you've just said that if you go to Libya to get a visa you might not be able to come back, if the Indians won't give you a visa. Isn't that what you said?"

Perhaps she hadn't understood him, for once.

He shook his head, in confusion rather than denial.

"No. Yes. I am sorry, Clare. I have thought too much. I have not talked to Ayesha since she was telling me she must go to Assam, and by myself I have thought too much. Excuse me."

He got up and quickly left the kitchen, for the bathroom. He flushed the toilet, ran the tap in the basin for a few moments, and came back, obviously having rinsed his face as well as his hands.

"I am sorry, Clare. I will try to explain better."

"It's all right, Hakim. There's plenty of time."

She remembered her blackcurrant fool.

"I've made something I know you like."

She fetched pudding bowls out of the cupboard and the fool, looking dark purple and very good in a glass bowl, out of the fridge, and put them on the table.

"There."

Then, seeing him swallow tears again, she wished she hadn't remembered the wretched fool.

"Never mind. Perhaps later."

"Later, yes. But thank you again, Clare."

For a few moments he sat still, looking down at the table-cloth, before clasping his hands together on the table and beginning again, in a firmer voice.

"When I found I must go to Tripoli to ask for a visa for India, at first I said no to myself, no, no, Tripoli I hate, and, as I told just now, if I had gone out of England and then I tried to come back I might be stopped at the airport by the Home Office and not permitted to return. Then I thought, if I stay and if Ayesha goes to India, for years maybe, I will be too sad in London, too alone as I was before—before I found her."

He drank some water.

"I will never want to go to Tripoli, even if in the war there is now in Libya the government that tries to govern in Tripoli is less lawless and wicked than in Benghazi is the army of Haftar who calls himself Field Marshal. This army does not even try to call itself a government. But Tripoli, Tripolitania, is not my country. You know this, Clare. Benghazi, or not Benghazi itself but the Greek and Roman places of Cyrenaica is where I must go. I must do what I can while the ruins are in danger. Many of them are in danger in the other countries where there is war, but it is Cyrenaica I know, and so it is Cyrenaica where I can be maybe useful. I have almost counted the tesserae in the mosaics of Cyrene."

Clare, in turn, poured herself some water and drank a little, for calm.

"I know, Hakim, I know. I do understand. But why now? The war is no better, is it? I know the papers here, and the news, tell us very little about Libya, but when other countries try to arrange negotiations, they always fail, and there are UN resolutions and agreements to stop delivering drones and bombs and guns to Libya and they go on being delivered. Turkey, Russia, the Emirates—I don't know who else, but they all send arms, they all interfere and make things worse. Isn't that how it is?"

"It is. All this I know also."

"Of course you do. So I wonder why you want to go back now, when the war shows no sign of ending. And when you have been here so long, and—fairly happily, I hope?"

She was determined not to talk, at all, about herself, and determined not to cry.

"I have been happy, yes", he said. "And more happy since I have Ayesha, since I have met Ayesha. But without her I shall never be happy in London. She will go to Assam—she will not go for some weeks, until she receives the results of her last examinations—and I shall go to Libya, to look at my stones, to be sure they are not damaged and to see whether any carving or mosaic has been stolen. I cannot leave them any more. I have been too comfortable in London, for too many years."

She didn't move or speak, but perhaps he caught an inner flinch.

"Clare", he said. "You saved my life when you made it that I was able to come to England. I thank you always. But now I think, is my life, the one life of Hakim Husain, so important? I think maybe while I have this life, while I can choose, I must use my life, spend it for something that is good, and not save it. There is such fear and suffering, and it becomes worse not better, everywhere in the places I know. In Syria, for example, America has betrayed the Kurds, again. They always betray the Kurds. In Iraq, another place where they betrayed the Kurds, because of America there is no government that is honest and fair and people die, and in Iraq America kills Qasssem Suleimani, so more people will die. But it is not Americans who will die. When was it right for a country to order to be killed a foreign general, even if he is a bad man, by assassination, while the country who gives the order is entirely safe?"

"Hakim, I don't understand about Suleimani. I hadn't even heard of him when suddenly he was killed."

"Suleimani was a very brilliant soldier, a most powerful fighter for the ayatollahs in Iran. He was no doubt a bad man, but a clever man. He, much more than the Americans or any other people, defeated the Taliban in Afghanistan, all those years ago when they were defeated. After 9/11 if the Americans had not been so ignorant and stupid they could have made an ally of Iran. But no. President Bush said Iran was part of the axis of evil. And they were enemies again.

"And in the last few years it was Suleimani again, much more than the Americans, who defeated ISIS in Iraq and Syria. Do you remember what I have told about Sunni and Shia? Saudi Arabia and Iran? Well then. Sunni ISIS defeated by Shia Suleimani. And now the Americans lie about why they killed him. One American mercenary is killed. He is killed by Iraqi militia, so America kills twenty-five of the militia soldiers. There are demonstrations at the American embassy. Benghazi, America thinks, where the American ambassador was killed, not by Iranians but by Islamists. So they kill Suleimani with their drone, because they can. I read on the Internet that he was on his way to Riyadh where he was going to talk to the Saudis about calming hostility between Saudi Arabia and Iran.

Imagine if he had succeeded, only a little. It is like Musa Sadr again, but this time it is not Colonel Gaddafi but President Trump who does the murder. And this is another humiliating death of a famous Muslim. There have been too many of these deaths: Saddam Hussein, Osama bin Laden, Gaddafi himself, al Baghdadi, Morsi, all bad men, except Morsi, but these humiliating deaths and boasting about them in America—in the case of President Trump, lying about them—bring only new supporters for these bad men. And now a general is assassinated by a cowardly drone, and more lies are told about why."

"I didn't know all this", Clare said. "Somehow things always turn out to be worse when you know more about them."

He wasn't listening. She could see that now he couldn't stop.

"And Afghanistan is most terrible of all, with more and more deaths, this year, last year, every year. There is a peace agreement yesterday—did you know this, Clare?"

"Yesterday? No. I can't have been listening properly to the news."

"A so-called peace agreement between America and the Taliban. America makes concessions. The Taliban make no concessions. The government in Kabul is ignored, left out of the agreement. This is all for President Trump to say, 'I have ended America's longest war. I am a wonderful president. Elect me again.' But the agreement is not real. There will not be peace. There will be a worse civil war. More people will be killed. There will be more refugees."

"But Hakim, what good can one person do? If you go back to Libya, and I can see why you think you should, there'll be nothing you can do, even there, let alone in other countries, to stop these wars. Will there?"

"All these people are my brothers, my family, Kurds, Syrians, Iraqis, Afghans, Yemenis, dying in more refugee camps. They are Muslims, all of them. Why should I be safe in London while they die? Can you remember what Dr Rose said before we went to find that boy?"

She had pulled herself together and banished her own feelings, for the moment.

"I do remember."

I will never forget, she didn't say. Instead she said, "Perhaps the answer to your question, the question why you should be safe in London, is that you should stay safe here for Ayesha when she is able to come back? Then she will find you, perhaps for a future that you might be able to share?"

Was this going too far?

No. Apparently not, because after a moment or two he said in a calmer voice, "Maybe also I shall go to the Indian embassy in Tripoli if I can get to Tripoli, if the embassy is there, if it is open—who knows?—and see if they would give me a visa."

There. His primary reason. She considered for a moment before she ventured to say, "Hakim, I think you're in a bit of a muddle." Sometimes it was useful that she was so much older than him.

He looked at her, puzzled.

"A muddle?" he said. "How, a muddle?"

"I'm sorry", she said. "What I mean is that you've been thinking about a number of different reasons for going to Libya, for leaving England, and possibly you've added these reasons together to make an argument that isn't as strong as you think."

"I don't understand."

"Of course you don't. That's my fault. I'll try to explain."

More water. She sat up straight on her chair, and clasped her hands on the table, as Hakim might.

"You are very sad and angry about what's happening to so many innocent, harmless people in countries you know well, and specially in Libya. You are quite right to be sad and angry. But because you are sad and angry, and there is so little you can do, here, to help these people, and because you are yourself a Muslim and a refugee, it seems to you unfair that you are working safely in London. You are not in danger, not being bombed, not trying to persuade any officials to let you stay. This makes you think you have a duty to go back home, to share in the suffering."

He nodded. So far so good.

"At the same time Ayesha, who has made you happier in London than you have been since you came to England, says she must go back to India to support her father and her people.

You don't want to be in London without her, but also if she has decided to put her people and their troubles first, you are thinking you should do the same. But you know, don't you, that if you were back in Libya you might be able to do something for your stones, the ruins that you love, but you could do very little for the people. You might be killed yourself. Would that do any good? Really? Would it do any good to the stones, or the people? And—most importantly—wouldn't your death be a terrible loss for Ayesha?"

He nodded again, miserably.

Should she try to make it even clearer?

"Isn't there really only one reason to go to Libya?" she said. "What you most want is to be with Ayesha wherever she is, and going to Libya to get a visa for India in your Libyan passport is the only way to join her. Do you think that's right?"

"Yes. No."

She saw that he was trying to decide whether or not she was right, and whether or not he should allow what she had said to shake what he had thought was his decision.

"You have told three reasons for me to go to Libya, three reasons I have thought or, or I have felt, because of Ayesha's choice to go to India. But you think they are too different, and none of them is a good reason?"

"No, Hakim. Each of them is a good reason, as far as it goes. But you have arrived at each of them from where you are now, here, in London, horrified at what is happening in the world, and very unhappy that Ayesha is going home. What you haven't done perhaps—I'm only suggesting that you think again about all this—is imagine what is likely to be the result of the decision. If you can get back to Libya—and, by the way, how easy is that? Won't you have to fly to Tripoli, where you don't want to go, and find yourself unable to reach Cyrenaica because of the war?"

"I have found that it is still possible to fly from Cairo to Benghazi. At least it is possible sometimes. According to the conditions of the war. But usually it is possible, because Egypt is on the side of Haftar."

"I see. I understand." She was determined not to look or

sound as if his decision affected her. He might go. It was possible for him to go. She might have to cope with it. But it was still worth trying, for his own sake, to get him to sort his head out.

"What does Ayesha think?" she said. She saw him relax a little, and realized that she should have asked him this sooner.

"Ayesha wants me to stay in London in case one time, one day, if her father is OK and life for the poor people of Assam is not so bad after all, she will be able to come back. Then, maybe—"

"Then maybe you might get married?" She was instantly annoyed with herself. Jumping the gun: Michael's expression.

But Hakim smiled, almost for the first time since he had come in, wet, from the streets.

"Maybe. We have talked about being married. Yes. Of course. We talked even about being married quickly, now, in London, maybe to make a visa more possible. But Ayesha is too careful, after only one year and a half in England, she is too English. 'One thing at a time', she says. This is most English. And it is against all Indian, all Muslim, custom not to have a wedding that is an important celebration. For her father and her family she must one day have a celebration wedding, even if I would be alone there, with no family."

He stopped, imagining, she could see, such a wedding. "So in case she comes back, she wants me to be here in London. But she understands, like you, Clare, that I must go home to Libya for a while because I—because—I am not sure how to say in English—"

Now Clare was able to smile.

"Hakim. You always know how to say things in English."

"Not today", he said. "Not now. What I am for my stones is what Ayesha is for the poor Muslims in Assam—there is a word. "

"Responsible. You feel responsible for the stones of Cyrenaica. Ayesha feels responsible for the people suffering in Assam."

"Is this the right word? Responsible means I will answer, I should answer. Is that correct? I should answer the need of my stones?"

"Almost, but there's more in the word. A responsible person is a person who can be trusted. To be responsible is to take on yourself what is asked of you, accepting that you will have to answer for how you do, how you carry out—O, English is a difficult language—what you have been asked to do."

He looked at her, puzzled again.

"I'm sorry. That's not very clear", she said. Where were her old classroom skills?

"Yes", he said. "I think I understand. But who must we answer? Who asks how we have done, have carried out, what we must do?"

Now she had to think. There was no avoiding the answer.

"God", she said.

He looked at her for a long minute across the kitchen table.

"Exactly", at last he said. "That is why we must go, Ayesha to Assam, I to Libya. This is the one reason that is good, that is strong, even stronger than the visa."

He smiled again, and said, with finality, "I know this." And, after a minute or two, he said, "Maybe now we have some of the delicious—"

He gestured, his open hand palm upward, over the glass bowl. She saw he couldn't remember the idiotic name of her pudding.

She gave them both some fool.

Before he ate any he said, "May I ask you something else, Clare?"

"Of course. Anything."

"I would like, I would much like, you to meet Ayesha before—before we have to go."

She had thought he would never ask.

"I would love to meet her, Hakim. Bring her—what would you like to bring her to? You know I almost never do anything. Most days are quite empty. What would suit you, and her of course?"

Shut up, she told herself. She was gushing. She didn't want to turn, after all these years, into an old woman who gushed.

"Soon I will bring her. She is working still in the hospital for, I think, one more week. She has on Wednesday the afternoon free. May I bring her on Wednesday? I will ask Mr Roberts at the Museum if I may be allowed to leave early."

"Wednesday is perfect. Come to tea. At about four o'clock?"

"At four o'clock. Ayesha will be so happy. I have explained you to her of course. Also she likes tea."

"Hakim. Have some coffee. I'm so sorry. I should have made coffee before."

"No. This fruit and cream is so good. Yes, I would like coffee. Stay, Clare, in your chair. I will make coffee."

He put some water in the kettle and switched it on, prepared the cafetière with the right amount of coffee, collected their bowls, glasses and napkins, put the bowls and glasses in the sink, the napkins in the bin and the fool back in the fridge. When the kettle boiled, he waited the statutory fifteen seconds, laid down for her decades ago by David, for the water to stop boiling, and then made the coffee. He looked on the top shelf of the cupboard where there were sometimes chocolates and took down a box of After Eights Clare had been given for Christmas by one of Michael's children.

He knew how the kitchen worked.

"I'm sorry, Hakim, I must—", she said, leaving the kitchen because now, after all, she was crying.

She had so much enjoyed having him about the place when he had lived in the flat for those months after he first arrived. And now—

In her bedroom with the door shut she blew her nose, mopped her face, looked in the mirror without conviction— she hardly ever looked in the mirror these days, except very briefly to comb her hair—sniffed hard, and did comb her hair. She thought she looked a hundred years old, though she knew this was partly the way the afternoon light fell on her face, and she told herself that she refused, refused absolutely, to put any pressure on him to stay. He was young. His life was his own. She had no responsibility for him, even to God, except that she would pray for him every day until she died. He certainly had no responsibility for her. And what he must do of course he must do.

She went back to the kitchen.

"Your coffee", Hakim said. He had made good, strong coffee, and poured some into two small cups. "And I found these chocolates."

"Quite right. I'd forgotten all about them. One of the children in Yorkshire gave them to me for Christmas. Have one. Have two or three. They're very thin."

He took two.

"I wish I could see your home, your mother's home you told me, in Yorkshire. Now I will not see it. But I have been, I have told you, to York three times."

"I remember."

She had wanted to go with him each time, but saw that she couldn't. He was there for the Museum, looking at finds on building sites, checking, advising. Her presence would have been an embarrassment to both of them.

"York was the most Roman city I have seen in England. London was a greater Roman city, I know, but London is always layers and layers of more recent building, and York still has the Roman street lines, the actual stones of the headquarters building where Constantine was announced to be emperor, under the great church which is so beautiful, and there is Roman building stone still possible to see in the city walls of later times and the embankments of the river. And they find new inscriptions, gravestones, shop signs, all sorts of Roman things, every year more. You know, I told you, Clare, they are planning to dig a large important site the other side of the river from the great church where the Roman bridge was, in the centre, the heart of the Roman city. I have done some work already for them on how in the first century the Romans would have—"

He was talking, she saw him realize, to cover the shock he had given her. So he stopped.

"Clare, I am sorry. I am so sorry. I will come on Wednesday with Ayesha, and you will maybe understand—"

"I do understand, Hakim. I really do. And—you mustn't worry about me. I am old and I am entirely used to being alone. I shall be OK."

He looked at his watch, partly, she realized, to deal with the silence.

"I should go back to my flat now. I have to write a report for the meeting on Tuesday, and I must deliver it tomorrow so that the committee will have time to read it. If they do read it."

"Meetings. One of the things about being old that I enjoy most is remembering that I don't have to go to any meetings, don't have to read—or, much worse, write—any minutes, and don't have to sit there seeing half the other people either talking too much or going to sleep."

He laughed.

"Are all meetings like this?"

"All. Most meetings are twice as long as they need to be. And there are far too many of them. An old headmaster of a school I worked in years and years ago said to me once that if everyone knew that only ten per cent of meetings were going to take place, the running of the school as well as the meetings would be much more efficient."

He took this in.

"Shall I tell them this in the Museum?"

"Certainly not—meetings are the breath of life to lots of people who work in large institutions. You would be very unpopular."

Then she remembered he was leaving, the Museum, the country, her.

He got up. He always noticed.

"I am sorry, Clare. I should go. I will find my coat." He looked out of the kitchen window, at the yard and the visible bit of sky. "It has stopped raining I think."

By Wednesday she had more or less accustomed herself to the loss of Hakim. On Monday and Tuesday she had walked up to the midday Mass, to use as much of the day as possible. On Wednesday she went to the early morning Mass instead; all she had managed as a resolution for Lent was that she would try to go to Mass every day. She went to the early Mass so that she could get ready for Hakim and Ayesha coming to tea. This was ridiculous, she recognized, as it would take her twenty minutes at most to tidy the kitchen and the sitting room, both always tidy anyway, and put on a couple of plates the little

French éclairs and macaroons she had bought, after Mass, at the best pâtisssserie in Kensington High Street. Simon would have laughed at her.

"You always think food will make the whole difference. Most of the time nobody notices what they're eating, specially if it's a tricky occasion. You have to be on holiday to appreciate food."

Wrong, she had thought then, and still thought now.

Would it be a tricky occasion? Probably not for them, though Hakim would want her to like Ayesha, even if—She tried not to pursue the thought.

At Mass on those three days she had tried to put into practice something an old priest in a church in Hampstead had recommended when her father was dying. "When you come into the church and cross yourself with the holy water, think of the moment as washing away all your anxieties, worries, fears. You are coming to meet Christ in the Mass. That's all, for the next half an hour. Follow him through the readings, whatever they are; follow him through the streets of Jerusalem and at the Last Supper and up to the cross and into the morning of the Resurrection. When you leave the church you will find what is difficult in your life seems a little more manageable."

On Monday and Tuesday in the middle of the day she had, indeed, walked back home feeling less weighed down, calmer and more hopeful, and after lunch had put in a couple of hours at the kitchen table, writing. Making her mug of decaff tea and sitting down on her usual kitchen chair she remembered, as often, a favourite instruction or reminder of her father's, a single word, *Sitzfleisch*, which means all of: sit on your bottom and get on with it. It always works. He was right.

On Wednesday it was more difficult. She cried at Mass: among the dozen scattered people there, no one seemed to notice so it didn't matter. When she got home with her white cardboard box tied with red paper ribbon from the pâtisserie and some early, too early, yellow tulips she had bought in the Gloucester Road, she hoovered and polished and thoroughly cleaned the whole flat as if it were going to be photographed for *House and Garden*, and managed to laugh at herself for this when all that was happening was that two young people, one of whom she'd known for years, were coming to tea. She put the tulips in an old Italian pottery jug on the bookcase in the sitting room.

They arrived, punctually of course, and Hakim, as if coming home and so without his usual greeting, introduced Ayesha before they had taken their coats off. "Here is Ayesha. Ayesha, this is my friend, Mrs Wilson."

Ayesha put her hands together as if in prayer and bowed her head slightly, a gesture as foreign and nearly as moving as Hakim's, but then shook hands with Clare and said, in an unusually gentle voice, "Mrs Wilson, it is so kind of you to invite me."

"Not at all. It's lovely to meet you, Ayesha." Clare smiled at her, and then at Hakim, who looked less tired, less thin, and a good deal younger than he had looked on Sunday. "Take your coats off, both of you. Leave them here."

"Go into the sitting room, Hakim, with Ayesha, and I'll bring the tea in a minute."

But Hakim, having shown Ayesha the square from the sitting room window—"It is beautiful when the spring flowers are coming"—left her there and came into the kitchen.

Clare smiled again, and nodded her approval.

"Perhaps you could take this tray. I'll bring the teapot."

Hakim took the tray, with cups and saucers, teaspoons, plates, milk, sugar, napkins and the little cakes on a plate. Clare followed him.

"What kind of tea do you like, Ayesha? I have several—"

"Thank you, Mrs Wilson. I like builder's tea best."

"Really? I thought perhaps—"

"Hakim likes very weak tea and always wishes it is mint tea. In India we have strong Indian tea with milk and sugar. We make it in a different way but builder's—which most of us have all day in the hospital—is close."

"Good. Builder's it is. I'll make Hakim some peppermint."

She took one cup and saucer, and when the kettle boiled made Hakim's peppermint and in the teapot strong Assam— she had bought a packet of Assam teabags specially—for

Ayesha and her. She waited a minute or two and took Hakim's, minus teabag, and the teapot into the sitting room, shutting the door with her foot.

"There."

She gave Hakim his cup—"Thank you, Clare"—and put the teapot on the tray.

How to help things along?

"Hakim told me on Sunday, Ayesha, that you're going back to India?"

"That's right." She looked across the tray on the low table to Hakim. "I am sorry to go but I must go. There are bad things happening and I should be with my father if I can help him."

"That's very good of you."

She poured Ayesha's tea.

"Is that strong enough? Help yourself to milk and sugar."

"That is perfect. Thank you."

"Do try these. They're quite good."

Ayesha took an éclair and a macaroon and put them on a plate. Hakim shook his head.

"How soon will you be going, do you think?"

"I must do my last exam, in ten days from now." She smiled at Clare. "I should be working now, at my terrible notes, not eating such a good tea."

She ate an éclair, took a napkin, wiped cream from her mouth and fingers.

"So good. And I must find a ticket for a flight. This should not be too difficult. I have saved some money and my father has sent some to me as well."

Clare looked at Hakim, but he was used to this idea and his half-smile of pride in Ayesha didn't fade. She took a macaroon and ate it, to keep Ayesha company.

After a minute or two, having munched her macaroon, Ayesha said, "Mmmm. These are good too. Real almonds. Not like hospital biscuits. Try, Hakim."

He shook his head, but sipped his peppermint tea.

"And when do you think you will be going, Hakim?" Clare thought her voice sounded fairly normal.

He put down his cup and saucer.

"Soon. I have told the Museum. My boss is very helpful, more than I hoped. He has asked me to prepare an official report on the current state of the antiquities of Libya in this time of war. This will be good work for some weeks, probably two or three months, for which the Museum will pay me, while I—"

He looked at Ayesha.

She smiled at him, and said, "While you try to get a visa for India."

"Yes. If I can travel to Tripoli."

Ayesha winced.

"If you can—", she said.

"I will", he said. "I will travel to Tripoli, to the embassy."

"Only if it is safe, please, Hakim."

"If it is safe or if it is not safe, I will travel to Tripoli."

Ayesha looked at Clare with an appeal in her eyes. "He must be careful", she said. "That is the most important."

Clare smiled.

"Of course he must be careful", she said. "He knows that, don't you, Hakim?"

He stood up, perhaps a little irritated, a man being fussed over by women. Suddenly she wished Penny were more like Ayesha. Penny never fussed because Penny never noticed.

"Clare", Hakim said, "May I leave you a few minutes with Ayesha? I want to say goodbye to the garden."

"Yes, the dear old square, of course. The daffodils are just coming out. We'll be fine, won't we, Ayesha?" Don't gush, she said to herself. To Hakim she said, "You know where the key is."

She heard him take the key from its hook in the kitchen, open and close the door of the flat. He probably ran down the stairs, though she couldn't hear that and there was the red carpet on the stairs. When she heard the front door open she went to the window.

"Look, Ayesha, there he goes."

Ayesha came to stand beside her. They watched him unlock the gate, shut it behind him, pause, looking to right and left, and then set off to walk on the path between the lawns, not cut yet, with drifts of daffodils nearly fully out. He disappeared behind a bed of bushy shrubs.

Ayesha turned towards Clare.

"I am so sorry he must go to Libya. You will be sad, Mrs Wilson. And it is my fault."

"My dear girl, it's absolutely not in any way your fault."

Clare left the window.

"Come and sit down. He'll be a few minutes saying goodbye to the garden."

Clare sat in her usual chair, Ayesha on the sofa. They left empty Simon's chair, where Hakim always sat.

"I'll miss him, yes. But that's life when you're old. And he must do what's right for him—I'm quite sure that to follow you to India is what he most wants. And what he most needs. You are more important than anyone in his life. "

Ayesha put her head in her hands.

"Of course you are."

After a moment she looked up, and smiled at Clare through tears.

"Also", Clare went on, "he needs to see what's happening to his beloved stones. He's been worrying more and more about his Roman sites, I know he has, through these years of war. It must be difficult for you to understand—"

"No. It is not difficult. These ruins were his whole life in Libya, and Syria, and Lebanon, where he studied, all these countries where things have been so hard for the people for many many years. He has told me very much that I did not know. I think the story of the suffering of people in these places, most of all in Libya which is his home, is all joined in his mind with the ruins being neglected when he is trained to care for them. He must do what he is trained to do. Like a doctor must."

Hakim had found a girl who deserved him.

"I see" Clare said, "That you do understand. That is so good to know."

"Thank you, Mrs Wilson."

"Would you like some more tea, Ayesha? Another little cake?"

"Yes, please. This is such a lovely tea. So English."

"Well, the cakes are really French."

Clare poured them both another cup of now sinister-looking tea. Ayesha put in milk and sugar and took another éclair.

"Can I ask you something, Ayesha?"

"Yes, please do."

"How old are you?"

Ayesha laughed.

"That is an easy question. I am twenty-six, nine years younger than Hakim, which my father thinks is a good difference."

"So you've told your father about Hakim?"

"Of course. I know my father will like him. He is so pleased that, in London, I find a Muslim who is an educated person, a professional man, and who is even not a doctor or a lawyer."

Clare laughed. So Jewish, this sounded.

"Well, I'm glad to hear that. And what about Libya being his country, and that he has no family? Isn't this a problem for your father?"

"My father knows nothing, knew nothing, I should say, of Libya. Now he knows a little of the sad history, and that Hakim's father, who was another doctor, and his brother have been killed. He understands such troubles. India has had them also."

Clare sipped her much too strong tea.

"May I ask you something else, Ayesha?"

The girl looked up at her from her teacup, clearly hearing something different in her voice.

"Does your father want you to come home?"

This was more difficult for her, Clare could see.

Ayesha put her cup and saucer back on the tray, wiped her mouth with her napkin, folded it and put it on her plate.

"Mrs Wilson, I have not said this to Hakim, but my father wants me to stay here. He says he would like me to be far away from the hatreds in Assam, and he has always wanted me to be first an English doctor and then come back later to India when I shall be able to get a senior job. I don't know whether what he says is what he really means or what he feels he should say. It is so difficult—"

She looked unhappy, and her eyes pleaded for help from Clare.

"I was sure it was right to go home. I told Hakim I had decided. Now because I am going home he is going to Libya which is so dangerous, and I think perhaps my decision was the wrong decision."

"But it's not too late, is it? You could stay after all, and if you did stay, he would stay too?"

Calm, Clare told herself, keep entirely calm, for her sake, poor girl.

"It is too late. I have seen him change because he wants to go, he so much wants to go to where there is war and danger and work for him to do, because he thinks London is too safe and too easy. It is too late, now that he has decided. I have seen the decision make him happy. So I shall go to India—and when I arrive my father will be happy of course—and Hakim will go to Libya and when it is possible he will come to India also and then—"

"And then perhaps you will get married?"

The smile returned.

"We shall get married, and the wedding will be at home. Hakim is worried because he has not much money, but this does not worry my father."

Clare was for a moment beside Hakim as he walked through the daffodils in the square.

"He will miss London", Ayesha said, as if Clare had spoken. "England has been kind to him. Also England has been kind to me, with some exceptions."

"Hakim told me. I'm sorry, so sorry, that you've run into the prejudices of stupid people. Old people like me are ashamed that the behaviour of such people has recently got worse when there were many years of it getting better."

"They think all Muslims are terrorists. That is really stupid, isn't it?"

"Of course it is. And I believe it's encouraged by a lot of wicked nonsense on the Internet. Social media: I'm glad to be too old to know what that even means."

"I don't like it, so I leave it alone. More people should. But I was surprised, in London where there are so many Indian and Pakistani people of so many different kinds, and some are

MPs and even cabinet ministers and the mayor of London, to find in the streets sometimes people shouting at me and calling horrible names, telling me to go back home. English people drink too much."

"Yes. That's often part of the problem. I'm sure there are many ways in which you'll be pleased, yourself, to be back home."

"It will be complicated. I don't know. I have—"

Ayesha was talking when Clare heard the door of the flat open—Hakim must have left it on the latch—and he appeared, smiling at both of them.

"Here I am", he said. "You have had a good talk?"

He meant us to make friends.

"We have", Clare said. "How was the square?"

"The square was very nice. No people, or maybe two old people and two mothers with children. It was very peaceful and very green. I shall remember how green it is today, and gold, with the daffodils."

"Do sit down, Hakim."

"No, Clare. We should go now. We have many things we have to do."

Ayesha stood up.

"Hakim is right, Mrs Wilson. I have too much revision I should do and I must be back in the hospital tomorrow and I have also weekend shifts."

Were they leaving, so soon?

"Will I see you again, Hakim?"

He looked at the floor before he looked at her. So unlike him, to be awkward.

"I don't know. I am sorry, Clare. I must go soon to Libya if it is possible."

"Yes, you must. I understand. The sooner you can get to your stones, the sooner you can get the work done and get your visa for India."

"Thank you, Clare."

He held out his hand to Ayesha, palm upwards, not for her to take it, and she didn't take it but went to stand beside him.

"Thank you", he said again to Clare, as if she had given him Ayesha.

They went into the hall, took their coats and put them on, then turned to say goodbye.

Clare managed to say, "It was so good to meet you, Ayesha".

"Thank you, Mrs Wilson."

"Tell Hakim to give you my telephone number if he leaves England before you do, just in case."

"I will. Goodbye, and thank you for the tea."

Hakim followed her on to the landing and looked back for a moment as Clare stood in the doorway, his eyes deep.

"I am sorry", he said softly, and, in his ordinary voice, to Ayesha, "The stairs are better."

She waited until she heard the front door open and shut. Then she closed the door of the flat, went into the sitting room, and watched them walk towards the Gloucester Road, side by side, not holding hands, until they were out of sight.

Good children.

She sat down in her chair, with the tray of tea still on the table, and cried.

Part 3

17–19 April 2020

It was still early, about eight-thirty in the morning, when she came in from doing the shopping and collecting the paper. The supermarket was reserving the hour between eight and nine for the old, carefully spaced along the aisles and in the check-out queues, to do their shopping before everyone else was allowed in.

Her walk to the shop through the bright early sunshine had done a good deal to banish the grief and fear of the evening before, Ayesha's terror that something bad had happened to Hakim, and her increasing unhappiness that she couldn't do more for her patients. A new day might bring news from Hakim, and that would make the misery of the Covid ward easier to bear.

Ayesha had left for the hospital before Clare had seen her. She had put a note on the kitchen table.

Dear Mrs Wilson,—Clare hadn't yet persuaded her to call her Clare—*I shall be later tonight. The shift does not end until eight o'clock and then there is a short meeting for the FI doctors. Please do not wait for me to eat supper. I shall find a sandwich in the canteen. I am sorry about last night. Ayesha.*

The last thing she should be was sorry. She was being so brave that it was probably good for her occasionally to burst into tears, to let Clare see what she was coping with.

And actually she would be hungry when she came in. Clare was going to make spinach soup and she knew that if she offered Ayesha a Welsh rarebit as well, she would certainly eat it. Luckily, like Hakim, she enjoyed English cooking.

Clare washed her hands thoroughly under the hot tap, as recommended. While she put the shopping away she thanked God, as she did several times a day, that in this time of pestilence, when the old were supposed to be locked in isolation, she had Ayesha to look after. It should, of course, have been the other way round. Ayesha, at twenty-six, should have been looking after Clare, old and therefore vulnerable to a disease that was more dangerous the more ancient you were, even if you had nothing else the matter with you. Because she had smoked for decades she imagined her lungs to be in poorish order, though she hadn't coughed since she gave up, and she was obeying all the instructions for keeping safe. Except that she had Ayesha, who was part of what the radio kept calling "frontline NHS staff", living in her flat, and she couldn't have been more pleased, to have her company most evenings, and to be taking care of her, for herself and her patients and also for Hakim, wherever he was, and for Ayesha's father in India who was probably dealing with Covid 19 patients of his own.

Clare remembered that at the beginning of Lent she was feeling more or less useless: she had no idea what she could do to prepare for Easter except decide to go to Mass every day. Forty days, Lent lasted. It was now five days after Easter, a week after Good Friday, yet the beginning of Lent seemed months and months ago. Years ago.

At the beginning of Lent everything was still quite ordinary. It was easy to go to Mass every day. She had walked back from Mass on Ash Wednesday thinking that the black mark on her forehead was not only a *memento mori*, a reminder of death, as it was meant to be, but also something that would identify a Catholic as the Star of David had identified Jews in Nazi Germany. Figures of suspicion. That had been then. Now anyone at all might be suspected of carrying coronavirus, and everyone must stay two metres away from anyone else.

Then it was possible, as it always had been, to walk up to the Park for no particular reason and wander about among the spring flowers and the children on scooters and in pushchairs for as long as one liked. It was possible to sit on a pavement terrace outside a café on the way home and spend half an hour over a capuccino watching the world go by. It was natural to greet people in the street or in the square's garden without thinking of the distance there had to be between one person and another. Hakim was still living in Wood Green, still working every day at the Museum. A whole week of Lent had already gone by before Hakim and Ayesha had come to tea and Clare from the sitting room window had watched them walking away, so very much together.

And then Hakim had gone, and, for a week or so after that, each day felt emptier, though she hadn't seen him or spoken to him again until the day he left. Looking back now, only a few weeks later, it was difficult to get straight the order in which things had happened, so quickly had the virus changed the way she, along with everyone else, was living, and the way she was thinking too, because there was so much anxiety everywhere, and so little other news. It was certainly not much more than another week after Hakim left England that the churches were shut and her life became emptier still.

A couple of days after the first Sunday without Mass, parliament closed early for Easter because of the virus, and wasn't going to sit again for at least a month. Penny telephoned from Yorkshire.

"Mum. Are you OK?"

"I'm perfectly fine, thank you, darling."

"O, good. Well, we thought it might be nice for you to come to us for the lockdown. Charles is coming up tomorrow so he can be in the constituency—not that he's meant to be meeting people exactly, but finger on the pulse, you know—so we'll be here for the duration." Naturally, Clare thought. Nicer in Leckenby with the horses than in Barnes. "He'll be working from home as they say."

"I can imagine."

"Mum! MPs always have tons of work, you know, and with the office closed in London—I'm sure there'll be all sorts of emails and things. There's supposed to be going to be virtual meetings—you know, tiny pictures on your screen with people taking it in turns to talk one after the other—it's really funny,

247

a little yellow frame pops up round the picture of the person talking. Not a hope, I imagine, with the broadband, or lack of broadband, in the village. But Mum, the point is, Charles could drive you up tomorrow, and then you'd be here. We could look after you and you wouldn't be lonely."

Clare thought, but only for a few seconds.

"That's very kind of you, darling, and very kind of Charles. But I think honestly I'd rather stay here. I'm entirely used to being on my own, after all, and I've got stuff to do which will keep me going."

"Really? What sort of stuff?"

"O, sewing for instance. I bought some canvas and wool ages ago to redo the seats of those two old chairs in the sitting room. Now I thought I'd actually do the embroidery. And I'm always quite happy in the flat, messing about and listening to the radio."

She wasn't going to tell Penny about her book, probably ever.

"Well Mum, it's up to you of course. If you're sure you'd rather stay—Charles says it's only going to be three or four weeks anyway. But do look after yourself, won't you?"

"Yes I will. I always do, you know."

"I know you do. You're amazing. Michael and Sarah send their love by the way. We'll keep in touch. Lots of love for now."

Twice a week, as always, Penny telephoned, usually after tea. Clare hadn't told her that Ayesha was living in the flat. She could imagine only too easily what Penny, and Charles, would say. "A doctor, mum, at the moment? In and out of the germs every day? You must be quite mad." "I wish your mother had a bit of common sense."

She had heard nothing from Ayesha since the pair of them had come to tea at the beginning of March, and imagined she was at home in India, hoping that Hakim would be able to get his visa in Tripoli.

Three days after Penny's invitation, with another long Mass-less day ahead, Clare was sitting at her laptop in the kitchen taking herself, sentence by sentence, through the Christmas holiday in the rain in Yorkshire, when the telephone rang.

"Mrs Wilson?"

The voice was familiar but she didn't immediately know whose it was.

"Yes?"

"Mrs Wilson. Hello. This is Ayesha speaking."

"Goodness, Ayesha, what a surprise. How nice to hear you. Where are you?"

"I am in London, in Islington where I have been living. But the landlady of my house does not want me to stay."

"What? But aren't you about to go to India? I thought you had probably gone by now."

"No. I am staying, to help with Covid 19. But my landlady does not want in her house someone who is working with coronavirus patients. She says it will be dangerous for her."

"Is she old? Or perhaps not very well?"

"She is not old, no. Perhaps she is fifty, and I think she is quite well."

"But Ayesha, that's awful."

"She wants me to leave at once. Even today, though I have not yet seen a Covid patient. Could I please stay with you, Mrs Wilson, for a few days, while I find somewhere else that is not afraid of a medical lodger? Would this be possible? You would perhaps be afraid?"

"Of course you can stay here, Ayesha. You can stay as long as you like. I will be very happy to have you. Matt's—that is, the room where Hakim stayed when he first came to England, will be comfortable for you I hope."

"But when I am working with Covid patients, I may catch the virus, and then—"

"Then I might catch it from you and I am old? Yes of course, you're quite right. But there's a risk of catching it anyway, isn't there? And really, Ayesha, you mustn't worry about me. If I catch it, I catch it, and it will be good, something I'd be nothing but pleased about, if I'm able to help with the effort everyone's making to deal with the virus. There's very little I can do, but I can give you a nice room for as long as you need it."

"That is most kind of you, Mrs Wilson. Hakim has always said how kind you are. Will you decide what rent you would like me to pay you?"

"There's no question of rent, Ayesha. Absolutely no question. It'll be nothing but a pleasure for me to have you in the flat."

Another few days later Ayesha, who had been able to give her address as Clare's flat, was assigned to the Chelsea and Westminster Hospital, where David had died. This was presumably because whoever was arranging these things wanted to make these very junior doctors' journeys to and from work as short as possible. Twenty-five minutes' walk or fifteen minutes if Ayesha took the bus. "It's very good not to be afraid of coming home", she said.

Clare washed her hands again, made some coffee and sat down at the kitchen table with the paper. She already knew the worst of the news from listening to the Today programme before she went out. The numbers of people dying in the whole country were every day a kind of shock, though in the last few days they hadn't much changed, seven or eight hundred people a day. Seven or eight hundred people, each of them alone in hospital, separated from their families through their last hours, no doubt a few without families at all, the nurses doing what they could to be with them as they approached death, or as death approached them.

This seemed a terrifying number of deaths, but apparently wasn't as many as had been feared, which meant that the doctors and scientists and politicians she heard every day at teatime were becoming cautiously hopeful that what they kept calling "the peak" might even have been reached or would be reached very soon. It also meant that one way or another, including keeping practically everyone inside their houses except for an hour a day, they had managed to prevent the hospitals from being what they called "overwhelmed". The pictures of what had happened to the hospitals in Italy, and what was still happening in New York, lorries full of coffins on the streets of Manhattan and huge pits being dug to bury them, like plague pits during the Black Death, had shown everyone what could happen if the ordinary systems for dealing with illness and death broke down.

Meanwhile it was obvious that there were many more deaths than the official total because deaths in homes for the old and in hospices, where by definition people were bound to be particularly likely to die, weren't being counted in with hospital deaths. It was also obvious, though the government didn't admit it, that either there weren't the resources to test people dying in care homes or hospices, or, come to that, in their own homes, or someone had decided that as they would probably have died soon anyway it was pointless to waste a test on them.

She put down the paper. Her coffee was very good.

She got up, took her coffee and sat down at the other end of the kitchen table where her laptop, plugged into a row of sockets on the floor, the spaghetti of leads organized years ago by Carrie, was waiting for her to start work on her book. She opened it. One email, from Carrie. She hadn't heard from her for weeks, the weeks in which everything had changed.

Hi gran,
Mum says you're doing the lockdown in London.

Carrie always wrote emails as if she had been talking to you that morning.

Quite right. Staying with the parents for weeks on end would definitely have driven you nuts. Though I suppose even Dad has had to shut up about Brexit now. About time. What do you think will happen about Brexit? After all that fuss the Tories are going to look pretty silly if they can't do it after all. But how brilliant that would be! I might even come back to hopeless old England if it's still in the EU. Just joking—of course I'll come back anyway, probably at the end of the summer. The wretched virus should be over by then.

I'm fine here. We're getting on really well with the village. They're using the school we built already. The children are too sweet for words. I'm teaching them some English. You'd love it here—the spring flowers in the mountains are amazing.

There's hardly any virus in Nepal, certainly none up here, and I don't think anyone's died of it. It sounds really scary in London so you must be careful, Gran. I wish I was there to do your shopping and make sure you stick to the rules—though I know you will anyway and knowing you I expect you're managing fine.

Let me know you're OK.

    Love you—Carrie

Darling Carrie,

How lovely to hear from you. You are lucky to be in your beautiful mountains, with such good work to do, and far away from the horrible virus. I can imagine you teaching the Nepali children in their new school. Lucky them.

I'm quite OK, as you would expect: I'm happy by myself by now, or in any case used to being almost entirely by myself. I do miss chatting to David, though if he were still alive it would have to be only on the telephone at the moment. Your mother keeps in touch and is delighted to be in Yorkshire, horses and sunshine (there's a bit of a heatwave, at least for April) just up her street.

London is very strange, quiet, cautious, everyone being careful to have two yards' distance between them and the next person. I get to Waitrose every morning at 8. They have a special hour for the old to do their shopping, which is very civilized, and I get the Guardian (mostly for the puzzle—you remember how I enjoy it) as well as a few supplies. I walk round the square's garden for an hour in the afternoon which is allowed, even recommended, to stop us all seizing up completely. I must say people are being remarkably sensible and obedient, so far anyway. They may get less obedient as time goes by and they get more fed up. I feel very sorry for mothers cooped up in small flats with children off school and tetchy husbands trying to work from home.

Brexit. I've no idea what will happen now. I don't suppose anyone has. Everyone in government and in Brussels too has got quite enough on their plate dealing with the virus to fuss about Brexit. It seems years and years ago that we were all so worked up about it. I expect you know that Boris Johnson nearly died of the virus last week. I suppose it's possible that the experience of being so ill will sober him up, even make him a more sensible politician. Do leopards change their spots? Not often, alas. And ghastly Gove, the cleverest politician to be so wrong that I can remember in a long life, will go on saying Brexit can be done by the end of the year, which quite obviously now it can't.

I'm so glad you might be back after the summer. I do miss you, darling, but you know that.

Much love,
Gran

She said nothing to Carrie about Hakim or Ayesha. "Almost entirely by myself" was truthful as far as it went. She didn't want Carrie telling Penny that Ayesha, of whom, of course, neither Carrie nor Penny had ever heard, was living in the flat.

Yesterday evening, Thursday evening, had been the third time when even a good many of the sedate and inhibited inhabitants of the square had opened their windows or gone down to the pavement to clap and cheer for the doctors and nurses of the NHS at eight o'clock. Clare got up from the kitchen table where she and Ayesha were having supper. She had failed to register this demonstration last week or the week before but this time had left the sitting room window open so that she could hear it if it happened again.

"Come and listen", she said, taking Ayesha to the window. Ragged clapping and cheering, and one person banging something, perhaps a saucepan with a spoon.

"This is for you, Ayesha, to thank you, you and all your colleagues, for the wonderful work you're doing."

Ayesha, beside her at the window, had cried a little. "We are only doing what we are trained to do, you know. Like any job."

"Not like any job."

After supper, when Ayesha, sitting in a corner of the sofa, was holding in both hands her cup of strong, sweet, milky Assam tea, and Clare in her armchair was doing the same with her camomile, Ayesha had said, "Mrs Wilson, may I say something to you, about what I have learnt in the hospital?"

"Yes, Ayesha, of course you may."

"If by bad luck you catch Covid 19, which I pray you will not, I would like to ask you please to allow me to look after you here in your flat. The ventilator is a very cruel thing, almost like a torture thing, and I would not wish you to suffer it. Also, after the ventilator, they say it is not easy to become truly well again."

Clare looked across the low table. She met Ayesha's concerned look, and smiled.

"That's a very kind thought, Ayesha. But it's all right. I've decided about it already. If I get it, I'll definitely stay here. The GPs are very nice." They were. They were not David but they were good girls. "I can talk to them on the telephone. If I get better, that'll be fine. If I don't get better I won't agree to go to hospital. I'd rather die in my own bed. The hospitals need all the beds there are for people who may get better, and I have some money saved so I could get an expensive nurse to come to help me until I die. Oxygen and morphine and so forth. From what I gather, it would only take a few days. You couldn't look after me because of your work in the hospital, though it's good to know you will still be living here."

After a moment, Ayesha said, "You are very brave".

"Not brave at all. Not nearly as brave as you're being, volunteering to look after people with this very frightening illness that's so easy to catch. That was properly brave of you, Ayesha, very much braver than an old person like me being realistic about death."

"I don't think it is very brave. It is what I have been taught by my father and all the doctors I have worked for in India and here. A doctor must always try to take care of whoever needs her most. I thought the women at home in the villages needed me most. But now this has happened in London, where the NHS has been so good to me, and the women in the villages will still be there when Covid 19 is over. You know, many more people are dying with the virus in London than in all of India."

After another moment, she said, "What does being realistic mean, if it is about death?"

"Ah", Clare said. What did it mean? Ayesha was surrounded every day by the possibility of death, if her patients were moved into intensive care. Most of them were old, or not well before they caught the virus, or both. But some were young, as young as her.

"I suppose", Clare said, "it just means being prepared to die, acknowledging that we all have to die and that when you're old your death can't be too far away, even if you don't know when or how it will happen. It should be easier for the old even if, usually anyway, they are nearer to death than the young are."

The readiness is all, she thought. Hamlet. And he was young.

"The patients in the hospital in India were not so afraid. There is more death in India. It is a familiar thing. I think here it is more difficult, not to be afraid. In the hospital I see old people who are more afraid, not less, because they know that death is already near to them."

"It's often difficult, I do know, of course."

Clare looked carefully at Ayesha, who was leaning forward with her mug in her hands. She looked interested, not, at least for the moment, upset. Perhaps it was helpful for her to talk about this.

Better to stick to herself, perhaps, Clare thought.

"How afraid you are may depend a bit on what you've seen of death." Ayesha had no doubt seen many more deaths than she had, but of strangers.

"When you're as old as I am", she went on, "and when you've known well several people who've died, and who themselves haven't been afraid, it helps—well, it helps to take the fear out of the prospect of dying." David, she thought. And her father.

"The death I was closest to was my father's. My mother had died several years earlier, and I wasn't there when she died. When my father was dying, the GP said the hospital wouldn't be able to make him better and I could look after him in his flat, which my father very much wanted, but I didn't know how to look after someone as ill as he was by then, so the doctor found me a nurse to help. It only took two weeks. A few hours before my father died, the nurse said, 'He's ready to go.' And I'm sure he was."

It was almost twenty-five years since those weeks and days, and she remembered them almost hour by hour, shopping in unfamiliar Hampstead shops, collecting his paper from the newsagents where the kind Pakistani lady asked her every day, "How is your father today, Mrs Wilson?", cooking in his little kitchen to make sure the nurse had decent meals, dealing with the washing, of which there was a great deal, dozing in the chair beside her father's bed in his nearly dark room while the nurse had a night's sleep, sleeping herself in the daytime on the sofa in the sitting room so that the nurse could have the second bedroom. She remembered the sense of peace, of relief, when he died, when she was sitting beside his body, almost like the sense of peace when your baby has been successfully delivered—or, more exactly, when you have been successfully delivered of a baby. Birth and death, not so different, for women. Helping a person into the world. Helping a person out of the world. Both with a good deal of pain, which is then over.

"Hakim told me you are a good Christian", Ayesha said. "Do you think you can be brave about dying because you are a good Christian? I think a good Muslim would be brave in the same way."

"O, I don't know. I expect it helps, to believe in God. Though I'm sure plenty of people who don't—but how does one know what's going on in someone else's soul? My father didn't believe in God, or thought he didn't, but he was as brave as could be about his own death."

She remembered her conversation about death with Matt, and hoped that perhaps it had helped him with the deaths, very few as far as she knew, of soldiers he had known. Of his own death he had known nothing, but he may have feared it. Now, in this same room, here was Ayesha, even younger than Matt had been then, and surrounded by more deaths than any very junior doctor could have expected to cope with.

"I think", Clare said after a minute or two, "it does help to believe there's a real connection between the living and the dead, a connection which can only be real if God is real. If you do believe that God is real, death becomes less of a final, frightening thing."

"In the hospital the chaplains are very good", Ayesha said, "and which religion they belong to—there are imams and

Catholic priests and Protestants and rabbis—doesn't seem to make any difference to how they talk to the patients. The chaplains have to wear all the PPE for Covid—masks and gowns and gloves, you know—as we do, so I think some of the patients don't know they are chaplains when they talk to them. That may be good if the patient is afraid of religion as well as afraid of death. I have seen this in my other hospital here."

"O dear", Clare said. "That I can easily imagine." She thought but didn't say that the chaplains looking indistinguishable from doctors wouldn't help a frightened old Catholic on a Covid ward, thinking that death was imminent and looking and hoping for a clerical collar.

Ayesha didn't notice that she had said anything. Clare was pleased that she was talking and talking.

"Most of the patients I see on my ward are old. I understand that it is reasonable for them to be afraid. They see that other patients leave the ward for ICU and they know they may have to be taken to ICU themselves if their breathing becomes too difficult. Mostly they don't know what ICU means but they hear it talked about. They know it is not good. Also when we help them on the ward with oxygen, some of them are frightened. It is difficult not to be frightened when it is nearly impossible to breathe and you have a mask over your face. Some of them are getting better, more able to breathe, on the ward. But some get more sick very quickly. I don't see them after they have left the ward unless they come back to us, which some do, though there are different wards. The ones who come back will recover and they will be discharged. But half the patients who are taken to ICU will die. If a patient is alert enough to notice what is happening on the ward, to count for example, he will be frightened. It is hard for all the patients that the family is not allowed on the ward, even a patient's wife. And those who understand that they might die, also know that they are not allowed to say goodbye."

"That's very hard", Clare said, "One of the cruellest things about this awful disease, though I suppose it must be necessary. It must be very hard for the families too, for old couples who may have been married for decades, for people's children." And very hard also for the doctors and nurses, she didn't say.

In the silence between them she thought, prayer. How weak it often seemed.

She was missing Mass since all the churches had been closed. Why? She found it hard to know exactly why. It wasn't that one couldn't pray outside a church: she knew that one could. She did, after all. Perhaps it was a question of presence. Just that. Being present, where Christ is present. Very Catholic. All those years ago when she became a Catholic she had found the presence of the Blessed Sacrament in Catholic churches, close to the light which never went out, always friendly, always comforting, even when nothing else was happening, no one else was there, and when, in front of the statue of Mary holding the infant Jesus, she had to light the only candle herself. The single story, from the Annunciation to Easter, told in a single building, however otherwise undistinguished. And being present at the Mass, where Christ came, and spoke, in the words of the gospel, the words of the priest, and was on the altar as he had been at the table of the Last Supper, had simply after so long become necessary to her. And it had been more acutely necessary precisely when it became suddenly impossible, because for those three weeks, half of Lent, she had stuck to her resolution and gone to Mass every day, and had been pleased to find that quickly it had become a habit about which she didn't have to think or choose. And it had helped her to cope with Hakim's going away.

Whenever she paused, as now, to have a cup of coffee and think, every word of her last contact with him came back to her.

One morning, only a few days, eight days, after he and Ayesha had come to tea, he had rung her in the middle of the morning. She had been back from Mass an hour or so, and was at the kitchen table working on her book.

"Hakim, where are you?"

"I am in the airport, Clare. I am telephoning to say goodbye. My flight will be called soon."

She said, as soon as she could, "Are you in Heathrow?"

"Yes. Exactly where I arrived, such a long time ago."

She saw him walking in his suit, with his case, among the holiday arrivals from Egypt, recognizing her and greeting her with his bow and his hand to the heart.

She couldn't speak.

"I shall come back, Clare", he said. "With Ayesha, when we are married. I shall come back. The Museum will want me to do my job again when I have written a very good report for them. Ayesha's father will want her to be a doctor in London, at least for some years. We shall see you then."

"I hope so, Hakim. I do hope so."

She thought, wildly, they could live in David's house.

"I must go now. The notice of my flight has changed to Boarding. Goodbye, Clare, and thank you, for my life."

She just managed to say, "Goodbye, Hakim. Take care of yourself. Take care."

Going to Mass every day, the walk there and back as well as the demanding Lent readings and the rhythm of the same thing at the same time every morning, had helped.

Then, suddenly, because of the virus, Mass had stopped, stopped dead as it were, killed by the necessity to reduce infection as much as possible, in the middle of Lent. The priest at the Mass on that Friday—it must have been four weeks ago from today but how much longer ago it seemed—had said, "Today, I'm afraid, is the last day when we shall be able to celebrate Mass with a congregation in the church, while the government thinks it necessary to order that there must be no gatherings of people. Mass will continue to be celebrated, of course, and I hope you will find it comforting to be with the community in spirit at the altar while physically you must stay at home and look after yourselves."

She had tried. She knew there was something called live-streaming of Mass from various churches, but she couldn't make her laptop provide her with anything that she could hear or see properly and she had soon given up trying. At teatime every day she read the readings she would have heard at Mass, and imagined what she might have said about them if she had been a priest having to deliver some kind of homily that day. She enjoyed this exercise: it made her think like the teacher she had always been, and it was good for her because it made her look seriously at the readings and at the connections between them that someone somewhere, when they were chosen, had thought helpful and interesting. It also made her sympathize more than she had ever bothered to before with priests wondering what to say, day after day, year after year, to fewer and fewer, older and older people. How often did those who heard them say thank you, or well done? How often did she? Not often enough. Hardly ever. A lonely task, she thought, alone as she was with her weekday missal.

"Ayesha", she had said last night, over their cups of tea. "Do you miss the mosque being open for prayers?"

"I do. I would more miss the mosque being open if I had known a mosque near here. But the mosques had already closed when I came to stay with you, Mrs Wilson, so I don't know where one is. On my ward, even though I am so junior, not a proper doctor yet as they remind us every day, there is too much to do to think of prayer very often, though I see bad things happening to patients and I often pray for a moment for them, more than five times a day I think. You know—"

"That Muslims are supposed to pray five times a day—yes I do, Hakim told me. How good, I thought when he told me. If everyone belonging to any religion would only remember God five times a day, how much better the world would be."

Then she couldn't resist saying, "I don't suppose you know, Ayesha, what the word 'religion' actually means?"

"No. I don't think so. What does it mean?"

"It means 'reconnection'. So you see, reconnecting ourselves to God is right at the heart of it, of all the religions, certainly of yours and mine."

Ayesha smiled. "Really? I am glad to know that", she said, reminding Clare slightly of her own children long ago, or of Carrie and Daisy. If Ayesha were laughing at her a little, that was good.

Then Ayesha yawned, politely into her hand, and said, "I am afraid I should go to bed, Mrs Wilson. I am quite tired and I must get up early."

"Of course you must go to bed, and get some proper sleep.

You're working so very hard. You've had a bath, haven't you? So you can go straight to bed. No. I'll do that—just leave it."

But Ayesha had put the mugs on the tray with the teapot, milk and sugar, and was carrying it back to the kitchen.

As she washed the mugs, nearly as at home in the kitchen now as Hakim had been, she said, "It is so sad that there are people in England who hate Muslims. One of the boys at the hospital, one of the very junior doctors who are not quite doctors, like me—I suppose they are the same age as I am but they seem younger—told me today that on social media there are people saying that Muslims have only pretended to close the mosques and that crowds of Muslims are secretly gathering at mosques to spread the virus deliberately. It is not true, but lots of people believe it. There are even photographs of crowds of Muslims being beaten by police. These photographs are from India—where things have been very bad, you know—but people pretend they are in London."

"Really? That's shocking." Clare had seen something about this in the *Guardian*, but not taken enough notice. She had also heard on the radio that because the two senior doctors advising the government in Paris about the virus were Jewish, French social media were saying that Covid 19 was a Jewish conspiracy. Would nothing ever dissolve these stupid hatreds, even in countries that are supposed to be educated, liberal, tolerant?

"Have you seen this yourself?" she said.

"No. I am afraid of social media. It has horrible messages. We have had two patients who were crying when they arrived on the wards from the ambulance, an old lady on Wednesday who I was told about, and today a man not so old on our ward. They were crying in fear, because social media has told them that we are killing Muslim patients in hospital."

"What?"

"Yes. 'Don't let your parents go to hospital', these messages say. 'You will never see them again. The doctors will murder them.'"

"I never heard anything so awful, so destructive. Surely these messages should be taken off the Internet or wherever they are?"

"I don't know how it works, how things can be taken off, deleted. I don't know why some people want to tell these lies. But if people are afraid, it is easy to make them more afraid, and there must be bad people who enjoy doing that. Does it make them feel powerful? Like President Trump, who enjoys making people feel afraid. I don't know. Of course I have a smartphone like everyone, but I never go to the social media parts. I don't want to read these wicked messages. Also I don't want people to know who I am or where I am. It scares me."

"Quite right. Stay away from it all. Real people are enough, don't you think?"

Ayesha gasped and bent her head into both hands and the tea towel she was holding.

"O, Ayesha, I'm so sorry. What an idiotic thing to say. Have you heard from him today?"

She swallowed a sob, raised her head from the tea towel, and looked at Clare in desolation. "Not today. Not yesterday. Not for four days. I don't know—"

With difficulty, she stopped herself crying. And all the evening she had been calm, in control.

Since Ayesha had arrived to stay in the flat, ten days ago, Clare had been careful not to ask her about Hakim. There had been one day, five days ago, when Ayesha had come back from the hospital looking different from usual, lit up, half excited, half nervous. Her normal expression was composed, thoughtful, often sad, breaking sometimes into her hesitant smile. But that evening she came in almost laughing and also almost crying. It was Holy Saturday. The day before, Clare hadn't been able to find on her computer a Good Friday liturgy that she could hear properly, and she was relieved that Holy Saturday was the one day of the year when there was no Mass, until the Vigil Mass which she wouldn't even try to find now that Ayesha was back for supper.

"Something has happened? Something good?"

"He has sent me an email. The first since I came here, Mrs Wilson. He must have found wifi somewhere. I have tried to call him, but I think there is no signal wherever he is."

Clare, in as ordinary a voice as she could manage, had said, "How is he?"

"He is well. He is very busy. He says it is very good and very bad to be back in his country. He has been in Derna, the city of his home, and has found some people he knows. They are sad and worried because there is no peace, and there is no real government. There is a so-called government in a place called Tobruk but Hakim says the only power is fighters. So there is often robbery and there have been many bombs. He says there is much work to do for his report because there is no one taking care of the ancient ruins now. There are no tourists since the revolution so there is no money to pay the people who should be looking after the stones. He says he is leaving today for other sites that he knows."

She stopped.

"I can imagine" Clare said, pointlessly she knew, "how difficult it is for him to check the stones, to find out if there's been stealing, for instance." She had often in the last weeks imagined him on his hands and knees studying the edges of a piece of mosaic pavement, in Cyrene perhaps. "It may help, in a way, that there aren't any tourists. Neglect took care of the Greek and Roman sites for hundreds of years."

Ayesha wasn't listening.

"It is good to know that he is well and safe", she said.

It was good but it wasn't enough, Clare saw. Or something else was wrong. When they were having supper a little later, she said, "Ayesha, was there something in Hakim's email that upset you? Or worried you, perhaps? Did you think it sounded as if he is in danger?"

"No. Not definitely. But—"

"But?"

"It is difficult to describe." Her eyes were anxious, almost pleading, as she looked at Clare across the table. Clare said nothing.

"I think he was not alone when he wrote the email."

A chill came over Clare.

"Not alone? How do you mean? What made you think that?"

"It is not how he has emailed me before. On the first day he was in Libya, and then ten days later, he sent me emails which were like him talking to me. Those were the two emails I received before I came to stay with you. They were—" She hesitated. "They were in the same voice as his talking voice. Do you understand what I mean? It is not easy to explain."

"I understand. Yes, I do understand."

"Also, some of what the email is telling me today he has already told me. Why would he tell me again? Also—"

Clare could see how hard it was for her to go on. She waited a minute or two and then said, very gently, "Also?"

"There was nothing in this email just for me. Nothing— nothing private."

"I understand, Ayesha. So you think perhaps he was a captive of some kind? Or perhaps under some pressure we can only guess at?"

Ayesha, now almost in tears, took a tissue from her pocket and blew her nose.

"I don't know. How can I know? Would he have been allowed to send an email at all, to keep his phone even, if he had been captured? And who would want to capture him? For what? A ransom? He has no money for a ransom."

She had clearly been imagining frightening possibilities since she read the email. Clare waited another minute and then said, "Do you think perhaps he's lost his phone, and he wrote this message on a phone he borrowed so he had to keep what he was saying as public and ordinary as possible?"

Ayesha brightened a little.

"Do you think that is what has happened, Mrs Wilson? That would be so much better."

"I've no idea, of course. It's impossible to know what's happened. But it does seem at least something that could have happened."

Ayesha's face was hopeful, questioning.

"Could it?" she said. "Maybe it could."

"Have you tried to ring him", Clare said, "tried an ordinary telephone call, to speak to him?"

"I have tried many times. Before he left he told me to email because it was better. But I have tried to call him, just to hear his voice, you know, but he does not answer. It is always only the message telling me that I should leave my message. Nothing else. And when I looked on the Internet to see if I could discover anything to help me speak to him, I found a place where it says that mobile phones in Libya do not work well. In most places they do not work at all. Do not take your mobile phone to Libya, it says. Although—" Ayesha managed a smile. "Although it also says do not go to Libya for any reason whatever."

"Does it? Well, I suppose it's bound to." Clare thought on. "You know", she said after a minute or two, "if mobile reception in Libya's as patchy as that, there may be even another possible explanation of your email. If he's in a place with no signal, he might have borrowed a phone belonging to someone else who was going to a different place where mobiles work, and he might have left your email for this other person to send. Perhaps he thought that any way of getting a message to you that he's all right was worth trying, even if he had to make the message rather plain, rather public. Is there—" Clare didn't know anything about smartphones. "Is there a way of telling, when you read an email on your phone, whether it came from one particular phone or a different one?"

"I don't think there is. Excuse me, Mrs Wilson."

Ayesha got up from the table, went to her room and a couple of minutes later, clearly having mopped her tearful face and rearranged her hijab, came back with her phone.

"Look. Here is the email of today."

Clare took the phone, put on her reading glasses but even with them could hardly see the text and certainly couldn't read it. She could see that at the top it said From Hakim Husain, but there was no email address.

She gave the phone back.

"I'm afraid there is nothing I can do", Ayesha said, "to discover whether he has used his own phone or another."

Clare suddenly saw more implications of this failure to communicate properly with Hakim.

"Ayesha", she said, in what she realized was a rather sharper voice than she intended. "Does Hakim know you're still in London?"

Ayesha spread her hands wide over the kitchen table in a gesture of hopelessness.

"I don't know", she said. "That is the terrible thing. I don't know if he knows or not. I have told him, in emails and in messages on the phone, but I have no way to be sure that he knows. In the email that came today he says nothing about me or about anything I have told him. As I said to you, I have tried to speak to him but it is never possible. I sent him an email message on the day when the exams were cancelled. That was soon after he left and I didn't know where he was, but it was after his second email. I don't know if he got the message."

"And after that?

"Then too many things were happening too quickly because of the virus getting worse so fast. I was trying to find for myself a flight to India that was not too expensive, but the information was changing all the time until it became almost impossible to fly. I still was looking for a flight when Mr Modi announced the lockdown in India, and on the very next day all of us, all of the final-year medical students whose exams had been cancelled, were asked whether we would volunteer as F1 doctors to help with Covid 19. We will not be F1 doctors until the summer, but the hospitals need us now so they are counting us as doctors. It is good experience, well, it is experience, some of it very bad, but it is also an honour for us, you see. I telephoned my father and he said, you must not try to come to India now, it is not the time to come and if you are being asked to help with the epidemic then that is what you must do. So I said yes, I would volunteer."

Clare, who had heard most of this already, understood that Ayesha was going through the account she had not been able to give to Hakim.

"And Hakim?"

"I emailed him again, to say that I was staying in London to help with Covid 19 and my father was happy for me to stay and I hoped he would be happy too because now he could come back to London when he has done his report. But now—"

Perhaps Ayesha also was looking properly, for the first time as Clare was, at the implications of Hakim not knowing she was still in London.

"Now?"

Ayesha picked up her glass, swallowed a mouthful of water, and took a couple of deep breaths before going on, "And now, you see, he doesn't need to go to Tripoli, so that he can go to the Indian embassy to see if they will give him a visa. He doesn't have to cross Libya from one side to the other of the civil war which does not stop. But how do I know he isn't trying to do this dangerous journey today, tomorrow, the next day, because he didn't get my emails? How do I know he isn't travelling to check his ruins on roads where there are soldiers and fighting? There are not many roads in Libya, he has told me. There is one big road along the coast, and that is where nearly all the ruins are. I don't know if he is driving along this road. I look at the map online. Most of Libya is in the power of this terrible man Haftar, and then there is a line where the fighting must be. And on the other side of the line there is the government in Tripoli but the fighters for the government are all sorts of militias, not like a real army. And where is Hakim? I don't know anything."

"Well, you do know that when he emailed you earlier today he was all right. Wherever he was, or wherever the email was sent from, he was all right when he wrote it. That's a lot to know."

"But where is he? How can I find out? I ask myself the question all the time."

She took another tissue from her pocket, blew her nose, got up and put both tissues in the bin, and sat down again, a little calmer.

"My email also told him that I had come to stay with you, Mrs Wilson. He would have been so pleased with this news that I know that if he received my email he would have said something about this, about me being here in your flat. How kind of you, how safe I shall be, something like that. But he has said nothing. So he can't know."

There was no arguing with this.

Clare thought, again, not for long.

"Look, Ayesha. Send him a much shorter email, just saying you're in London, staying with me and helping with the virus patients in the nearby hospital—he knows the hospital—and asking him to answer. Nothing else."

She looked at Clare with surprise and fresh hope in her eyes.

"Do you think that will work?"

"I've no idea. I'm afraid it may not. But it's the only thing I can think of. Make it plain, simple, so as not to complicate anything for him, wherever he is."

"I'll do it now, before I go to bed."

Tomorrow is Easter Day, Clare thought when Ayesha had gone to her room, and she had finished tidying the kitchen. She looked at the clock. It was long before the complicated blessing and lighting of the Paschal candle, the spreading of the new fire, and the midnight singing of the *Exsultet*, with, this year, no ordinary people to watch, to hear, to be there. Perhaps tomorrow, on the most marvellous day of the year, something will reconnect Hakim and Ayesha, there will be some new light, some hope for them as there was, and is, hope for the world. She prayed, easily, before she got into bed.

That was six days ago. There had been no sign that Ayesha had heard from him since, and the last thing Clare wanted to do was to upset her by asking.

She also hadn't told Ayesha that on Monday night, two nights after that conversation in the kitchen, she had been unable to sleep and at five in the morning, by then Tuesday morning, she had got up, as she often did, gone to the kitchen in her dressing gown, and switched on the World Service while she boiled the kettle to make camomile tea and fill a new hot water bottle. The combination, with an undemanding book, usually sent her back to sleep for an hour or so. Matt's room, Ayesha's room, was at the other end of the flat. She wouldn't be woken by the radio.

On the world news, as the kettle came to the boil, she heard "In Libya—", switched off the kettle at the wall to stop it making a noise and stood stock-still to listen carefully. "—the fighting of the last few days in the west of the country has intensified. There are reports today that the forces of the UN-backed government in Tripoli have regained control of some coastal towns west of the capital from the so-called National Liberation Army commanded by General Haftar. These towns include Surman and Sabratha."

The news moved on to something else. She made her mug of tea and sat down at the table.

She had already deduced from what Ayesha had told her of Hakim's email on Saturday that he must have been in the part of the country more or less under the control of the government or he wouldn't have risked what he said about Haftar. So he might already be west of Tripoli.

Sabratha. She remembered it so clearly that she felt she could have walked along the straight paved road from the museum towards the sea, through its ruined streets, across the forum, into the remains of temples, baths and markets, and then back a little way into the wonderful theatre where she could turn to look up at its towering, arched façade, at the dazzling blue of the sea behind the three tiers of sunlit arches, and then down to the curved stone base of the stage, with scene after scene carved in relief, of harvest, countrymen, corn and grapes, gods and heroes, including Paris deciding between the three goddesses, and no warfare. She had read in the guide book that it was the most beautiful theatre left in the whole of the empire, so she had found her way there while everyone else on the cruise was listening to one guide or another, one young man or another, telling them about the town.

She was for a few minutes alone in the theatre, hearing the ghostly voices of actors of two thousand years ago, playing the lines of Terence, perhaps, Terence the African, the Berber slave, born not far away, whose plays, with the plays of Plautus, were at the very beginning of Latin copying Greek and becoming a civilized language. Then the groups of cruise passengers began to wander into the theatre, looking and pointing at the carvings and the arches, and the actors' voices faded into an English murmur of appreciation.

There were churches in Sabratha too, mosaic floors and fallen columns; one church, very large, was built in the second half of the fourth century, when Augustine was growing up. Perhaps when he was a bishop he came here. Perhaps he preached in this church.

Sabratha, a city and a port for a thousand years, Carthaginian, then Greek, then Roman, and, after the Arabs came, a book of ruins under the encroaching sand for another thousand years, to be read only recently when archaeologists rescued it from the sand, not many decades ago. They were Italian archaeologists, reclaiming another Roman city for Mussolini. Never mind. They reclaimed it for everyone. And now—

She had loved Sabratha. Even though it was in Tripolitania, Hakim loved Sabratha. They had talked about it more than once. He worried about it, not only because of the civil war but also because of the sea, changing its currents, coming and going, crumbling the buildings near the shore. He thought Sabratha more beautiful, more fragile, and more interesting than Leptis Magna, perhaps because many of its buildings are older than Septimius Severus's great demonstration of imperial power.

Septimius Severus, the emperor with the unforgettable African face. And the appalling sons. At Sabratha Clare had seen on the wall of some once-impressive building an inscribed tablet with one name chiselled out of the stone, leaving a rough empty patch: the name had been Geta, Severus's son, who was supposed to rule the empire with his brother Caracalla after their father's death. Caracalla ordered the murder of Geta and then took his name out of every inscription in the empire. On the unsuccessful holiday in Northumberland with Simon and Penny and Matt she had seen the same chiselled gap in an inscribed Roman stone reused in the Saxon crypt of Hexham Abbey. She had never forgotten that scar in the stone: such was the emperor's reach, from the Sahara to Hadrian's Wall, probably two thousand five hundred miles. And obedient legionaries everywhere in between chiselled out the name of Geta. Rome at its most pitiless.

Hakim of course knew about Caracalla and Geta and the inscriptions. She remembered telling him when he was going to visit York for the first time that three emperors had stayed in the city, Hadrian, Septimius Severus, who died in York, and the young Constantine, and he was so delighted by this news that he set off as if he were the fourth. But even then he had said, "Yes, Septimius Severus and his arch, to be admired, naturally. Leptis Magna is a remarkable city but Sabratha is a place of many times, not only one emperor's work. The first theatre at Sabratha was built soon after the defeat of Carthage—there are ancient stones in the foundations—and the great basilica was rebuilt under Justinian, centuries and centuries later. The mosaics are very fine."

Clare had seen the huge mosaic pavement of Justinian's church.

She shook her head, alone at the kitchen table at ten past five in the morning of Easter Monday, not that it would be a holiday this year for anyone, to pull herself back to the almost unfaceable present. She could not imagine that Sabratha was not on Hakim's list of places to report on. "Fighting has intensified", the BBC had just said. But to imagine Hakim caught in this fighting, she knew, was to give way to irrational terrors: he might be anywhere, might at this moment—she looked at the kitchen clock—be waking up to a sparkling Mediterranean morning in someone's house near the sea at Apollonia, the fighting hundreds of miles away. But he had said in that peculiar email that he was leaving—leaving Cyrenaica?—for other sites, and he had also, because if she and Ayesha had guessed rightly, the email was being read by someone in or near Tripoli, criticized the Haftar non-government in Tobruk. Perhaps he was walking, waiting for the sunrise, among the stones of Sabratha.

What could she do? Nothing, except worry more, pray more for his safety, above all say nothing to Ayesha.

Since she had heard fighting in Sabratha mentioned, only once on the world service, three more days had gone by. There had been no news of Libya in the *Guardian*, but there was at the moment hardly any news from anywhere, the virus taking all the space there was. She wasn't good at the Internet, but she'd tried her best to discover more information about the war in Libya, and had failed to find anything more recent. She hadn't told Ayesha what she'd heard, and in any case the names of Roman towns in Libya meant nothing to her until she looked them up on an Internet map: Clare didn't want her to see how far away Sabratha was from Derna.

But Ayesha had had no message from Hakim, and last night, only last night, here she had been in the kitchen, after she should have gone to bed, unable to stop talking about him.

Clutching the tea towel under her chin with both hands, she had said, "I still don't know, you see, whether he received my emails. He has said nothing, about the cancelled exams, or about the virus, or about the work in the hospital, or about me staying with you, Mrs Wilson. He would have said something, if he had read my emails. Wouldn't he?"

She was about to start crying again.

"Sit down a minute, Ayesha. Give me that tea towel."

Ayesha looked with surprise at the crumpled tea towel in her hands.

"I'm sorry", she said. She carefully dried the two mugs on the draining board and put them on their hooks on the dresser. Clare watched her, her own eyes stinging with tears. Then Ayesha shook the tea towel, hung it over its rail on the cooker and sat down at the table. She clasped her hands in front of her on the table, as Hakim often did.

In a steadier voice, and looking down at her hands, she said, "The most important thing of all is that I don't know whether he knows that he must not go to Tripoli, because now there is no need for him to ask for a visa. You see, Mrs Wilson—"

She raised her eyes to Clare's. Clare waited.

"It was because going to Tripoli was the only way to get that visa that he first thought of going back to Libya. It was all my fault. I decided to go to India. And it was a silly decision. My father didn't want me to come home even before Covid 19 became so serious. He always wanted me to be an English doctor for two or three years, and then to go back home. If I hadn't made that bad, bad decision because I saw the pictures of the horrible things happening to Muslims at home, Hakim would have stayed in London. I know he would. And we would have been happy, as we were happy before—before everything became so difficult. It was my fault that he decided to leave. And now—"

"No, Ayesha. You mustn't think it was your fault. Really, you mustn't. As soon as he thought of going back to Libya—and yes, perhaps it was the visa that was the beginning of the idea—he understood how much he had been missing his stones, his sites, all that he had worked on and learnt about since he was a schoolboy. Those places are who he is, Ayesha, as you know because you said so that day when he brought you to meet me, and he had to go back to be there, to check on them, to discover whether there had been damage and looting, once he had seen that it was possible. And the Museum giving him the report to do, and making him feel safe about coming back to his job was what made it certain that he'd go. None of this was your fault. Nothing would have stopped him going, once he'd made up his mind that he had to go." She hoped more than ever that the Museum had been right about his job and his being able to get past the awful-sounding Border Force when he came back to England: she wouldn't put anything past the Home Office.

"Maybe", Ayesha said, one of Hakim's favourite words. "Maybe you are right. I think that I don't know anything any more, and too many of my patients are dying. When the oxygen reading is going down and down and there's nothing we can do—Then they have to go to ICU and quite often they die very quickly."

"Ayesha—"

But she wasn't going to listen.

"Early this morning before I went to the hospital I tried again to telephone him. Now the message says, 'This mailbox is full' and then the telephone only makes a long sound like a whine. The mailbox is full of my messages, that's why it's full, asking him—but if he had heard them he would have emptied the mailbox. Then I emailed him once more. I said, Please tell me you have my messages. Nothing. And the ward was worse, more sad, today. There is so little we can do."

She's too young, Clare thought, too young and too far from home, to be coping with the nightmare of the Covid ward and the disappearance of Hakim all at the same time.

Clare got up and held a hand out to Ayesha.

Ayesha took her hand and stood up herself, then fell into Clare's arms and sobbed against her shoulder.

When the sobbing had become convulsive sniffs, as with a small child, Clare took Ayesha by the shoulders, stood her up straight, got her a tissue from the box in the drawer, and said, "You must go to bed and have as much peaceful sleep as you can manage. I'll make you a hot water bottle. It always helps."

She took her hot water bottle from Clare, hugged it to her and said, "I am so sorry, Mrs Wilson."

"No, Ayesha. What you are dealing with would be too much for almost anyone. Now go to bed. I'm sure you're tired enough to go to sleep straight away."

She wanted to go with her to her room and tuck her up as if she had been six years old but of course couldn't.

When she was on her way to bed herself she stood, in her dressing gown as every evening, between the curtains and the glass of her bedroom window to pray, for Penny, for Carrie and Daisy, because she always did, and then with a new weight of care for Hakim—where was he? How was he? How would they ever find out if there were nothing but silence from him?— and for Ayesha and her patients. She opened the window and looked out over the pavements and the dark square, London much quieter than it used to be, no one about. *Fidelium animae per misericordiam Dei requiescant in pace.* May the souls of the faithful through the mercy of God rest in peace. It was the prayer for the dead, and, as on every night, she remembered her way through her list of the dead, many more names to recall than the names of the living she prayed for. She tried to give each of them a moment of attention, of deliberate memory, so that none of them was just a name. David's was the last name on the list because he had died most recently, and as well as praying for him, she found, as often, that she was asking for his help, looking across a café table at his face, amused, intelligent, sympathetic, realistic. Realistic, that word she'd used to Ayesha about death.

She listened for David, talking in her head.

"You have to have faith, Clare. You're good at faith. That boy is a survivor. Look at what he's been through already. He's much too sensible to let the random fighting of a sporadic civil war get near him. And after all he's in his own country." She heard David as if they were in the café in the V and A and he was about to complain about the coffee. But then she thought, the slings and arrows of outrageous fortune. What if the car or the truck or whatever Hakim was travelling in were blown up by some homemade bomb as Matt's jeep had been? "Don't imagine, Clare. Such a waste of fear to imagine. And the Taliban were out to get British soldiers in jeeps. No one's out to get Hakim." David. May he rest in peace.

"And all who died today", her list always ended. Today there were Ayesha's patients who, after the doctors and nurses on Ayesha's ward had done their very best, had got worse and had to go into ICU and, after more doctors and nurses had done their very best, had died. She didn't know how many had died today, in Ayesha's hospital, in all the hospitals and care homes and in people's own houses. Several hundred, for sure. She didn't know their names. It didn't matter. She often remembered, from when she first read the book many many years ago, Father Zossima in *The Brothers Karamazov* talking about those who died today. It is good, he said, more or less, to the novice Alyosha in the monastery, that a soul standing before God today should know that somewhere someone is praying for him, even from the other end of the earth.

So for everyone everywhere who died of the virus today, worn out by the effort to breathe, *fidelium animae per misericordiam Dei requiescant in pace.*

And then be quiet, she told herself. She had read somewhere of some old priest, a real one not a character in a novel, who had said something like, if you keep talking how can you listen to God? So a moment of silence, of only listening. Nothing, but the presence of God which never leaves us.

As she shut the window, closed the curtains and turned back to cross the room towards her bed, her anxiety for Hakim rose up at her like darkness itself. She reached her bed, switched on her bedside light, and as she climbed into the warm comfort of her bed, she managed to think, with gratitude, that Hakim and Ayesha were also faithful souls who needed the mercy of God to sleep in peace. She gave them into the care of God, switched off the light and turned over, too tired to worry herself awake.

And now it was the morning and Ayesha had already gone to the hospital, after, Clare hoped, a peaceful night and a decent amount of sleep.

What she needed herself was to walk up to the midday Mass in Kensington Church Street, to leave behind as she crossed herself with the holy water by the door all the sadness and fear that was weighing on her, and to concentrate her attention on the readings and the coming of Christ to the altar. *Benedictus qui venit.* But the church was shut.

So she brought her daily missal from the sitting room to the kitchen, made another cup of coffee and found the right day. Friday in the Octave of Easter. Suddenly and unexpectedly, as if he'd just come into the kitchen, as if he were standing behind her chair looking at the open book in front of her, she heard Simon's lightly mocking voice: "They're bonkers, these Catholics. Why stick to an old Latin word for the week after Easter when most people think an octave's eight notes on the piano, if they happen to know anything about music which most people don't. Octave of Easter, I ask you." Simon's voice saying this, which maybe it had at some point in the long past, was neither spooky nor irritating, but somehow reassuring. He hadn't left her, either. He had always been at bottom on her side, however ridiculous he thought the most important thing in her life. Ridiculous mostly, not wicked. It would have been harder not to mind if he had thought the Church wicked but luckily he reckoned its wickedness was in the past. If he had lived to see so much disgrace and hypocrisy revealed all over the Church in the last few years, the cruel exploitation of frightened children, the cynical neglect and concealment of appalling behaviour, it might have been different. But he had died before all this had come out of the shadows to stain the Church, as greed and corruption and cruelty had stained it in the past. People, as David used to say, can make a mess of anything.

She read the gospel for the day, the story of Jesus on the shore of the sea of Tiberias, the miraculous draught of fishes, and then Jesus, many days after the Resurrection, cooking breakfast on a fire by the lake and giving Peter and the disciples bread and fish to eat. Somehow it had always been the cooking that made, in this scene, the extraordinary reality of Jesus's resurrection more real, the smoke from the fire, the sizzle of the fish, the smell of them grilling. And John, the author of the gospel that tells this story, was there.

Because of the Raphael cartoon in the Victoria and Albert, she could see the first part of this story, the fishing itself, happening as if it were a memory of a scene she too had witnessed: Jesus is sitting calmly at one end of a little boat, Peter is on his knees in the boat, pleading, perhaps for understanding—he isn't yet sure who this is—and another disciple is on his feet making the boat, already full of fish, rock in the water. Two others are pulling fish into a second boat and a third fisherman, with a long pole and a worried expression, is trying to steady it. And, between all of them and the person looking at the picture, are three dark birds, vigilant cranes, standing and watching from the rocks. In the sky over the lake four other birds, black, more sinister, ravens perhaps, are flying towards the fishing boats, coming closer, threatening. This is also the scene in which Jesus tells Peter that one day he is going to be taken prisoner and killed.

She remembered the calm of Jesus and the confusion of the disciples who don't recognize him, the blessing of the present moment, all the fish they have suddenly caught, and the shadow over the future. Jesus will disappear and Peter will die a martyr's death in Rome.

Why did people who saw Jesus after the Resurrection fail to recognize him? There had already been Mary Magdalene in the garden and the two on the road to Emmaus. Now here were Peter and the others at the lake. Jesus must have been changed, yet also himself. None of the gospel writers attempts to explain.

She loved this picture. Life suddenly goes well. The empty nets are full of fish. She thought of a good hour, writing her book, the enterprise going for a paragraph or two unexpectedly well, something to be thankful for. And there is foreboding also, the ravens in the sky. Do we fail to give the glory to God? It was her second-favourite of the cartoons. The one she liked best was the painting of Jesus commissioning Peter to feed his sheep, part of the same story, the next thing that happened after the breakfast by the lake. Perhaps this would be tomorrow's gospel reading? She turned a few pages in the missal. No. Just a few bare sentences from Mark's account of the appearances after the Resurrection.

She carefully remembered the other Raphael, again as if this too were a scene she had witnessed. *Christ's Charge to Peter*, it was called. Charge. A strange word. The world is charged with the grandeur of God. Peter is charged with responsibility, a charge like electricity, a current from Jesus to Peter, his answerability for what will be the Church. Authority. She thought of Simon again, and his mocking contempt for all the terrible popes. "What a crew—honestly, darling, how can you take such an institution seriously?" People can make a mess of anything.

Never mind. There in the painting is Jesus, still calm, but standing, poised as if about to leave, to go back to God, telling Peter, kneeling once more, now on the stony path by the lake, to look after his sheep, for ever. There are peaceful sheep grazing behind Jesus, and behind Peter are ten anxious disciples, huddled like more sheep, who seem to be begging Jesus to stay. He won't stay. He will go. Peter will die, will be crucified upside down in Rome, so far away from this quiet lake. The last disciple, dressed in red, has his face hidden. Perhaps he is John, who lived to be old, and wrote all this down.

Clare had once, after lunch in the V and A café, taken a reluctant David—"Really not my cup of tea, Clare"—to the cartoon gallery, the Raphael Court. "I know they're too Christian for you but there are plenty of Christian pictures you like, and he's so good at putting you absolutely in the place where the story's happening."

It was not a success. "It's no good. I can't warm to them. Such a polished achievement of realism, that's the problem.

Doesn't it make you long for the cool geometry of Piero, or the messiness of Titian? These make one almost sympathize with the pre-Raphaelites, at least in theory, much as I deeply dislike their paintings. Raphael's too late, that's the problem."

"How do you mean late? Didn't Raphael—" she went up to look at a label on one of the paintings. "I thought so", she said. "Raphael died half a century before Titian did. I didn't realize he died so young." She looked at the label again. "Thirty-seven when he died. Goodness. So how could he be late?"

"I mean late in the sense of a skill over-developed in one particular way. Titian became messier and more and more wonderful when he was old, because he was old instead of late. Quite different. Michelangelo the same."

David made one think. "That's very complicated", she said. "I suppose I see what you mean."

But after they'd walked about, separately, a bit more in the huge empty space that was the cartoon gallery with, that early weekday afternoon, no other visitors in it, he had been surprised into something like admiration by another of the paintings, lateness or no lateness.

"Now that's more like it", he said, stepping back to see it properly. She left the *Charge to Peter* to join him. "Look", he said. "No mysterious Jesus. A brave, impressive Jew giving the philosophers what for."

This was the painting of St Paul preaching in Athens, a tall, commanding figure, standing on a marble pavement at the top of three steps, his arms raised with a mixture of conviction and demonstration, as if he were saying "There you are, you see", or "QED". A small crowd is listening. There are three old men at the front of the crowd, interested, dubious, grave, a middle-aged man, nearest the person looking, is kneeling on the steps, his hands raised in a gesture echoing Paul's. The columns of Raphael's imagined Areopagus are green, the colour uniting Paul's green tunic under his red toga, the green tunic of one of the philosophers, and the sleeves of the man kneeling on the steps. Perhaps, Clare hadn't said to David, Raphael's green columns were cipollino marble from Euboea which he could have seen in Rome, the marble of the columns of the ruined churches in Apollonia, where Hakim—

"What's he saying to them?" David in the V and A that afternoon had asked her, as, side by side, they looked at St Paul in Athens.

To her shame, she couldn't remember exactly what Paul had said. "Something about the unknown God, I think."

"That sounds promising. Next time you come to tea, bring your New Testament and we'll see what he said. Quite a challenge for the old boy, Athens."

So she took her pocket New Jerusalem Bible to David's house, and he got her to sit at his desk and read to him, with the window on the garden behind her, the eighteen verses of *Acts* which tell the story. Before she began, he said, "Hold on a minute, Clare. *Acts of the Apostles*. What do we know about this book? Do people think it's moderately accurate history?"

"Luke wrote the book. He also wrote one of the four gospels. St Luke the evangelist. He was a doctor - which is quite a recommendation don't you think?—and he travelled quite a lot with Paul, so people have always thought him a pretty reliable source."

"Really? So he's a better source on Paul than on Jesus? He wasn't one of the twelve apostles, was he?"

"No, he wasn't. Matthew was, John was. But Luke wasn't, and nor was Mark, though his gospel is always said to be the earliest." Hakim had told her that St Mark was born in Cyrene. She didn't say this. "But Luke is supposed to have been one of the two on the road to Emmaus who found Jesus had been walking with them though they didn't recognize him."

"Do I know that story? O yes, *The Waste Land*. Who is the third who always walks beside you? Mysterious Jesus again."

"That's right. Jesus after the Resurrection, like in those two Raphael pictures by the lake."

"Good. At least I remembered that. So come on, Clare, read me what Paul said in Athens."

It took her a couple of minutes.

She shut her Bible and looked across to David sitting in his usual armchair facing the window.

"Well", he said after a silence. "There's a lot going on there, isn't there? "

She said nothing, seeing he was thinking.

"The collision of two worlds, you could say. Practically the clash of civilizations—what an appalling phrase that was, by the way, doing untold harm by confusing politics with religion."

She wasn't sure she understood this, but couldn't interrupt him.

"But wasn't it clever of him, Paul I mean, a Jew from nowhere as far as the Athenians were concerned, to start from the unknown God? He must have understood that the philosophers in Athens were much too intelligent to think that the idols, the gold and silver and stone, were actual gods capable of paying any attention to human beings. You can't imagine Plato or Aristotle having any truck with idols. Think of Plato's cave. So he establishes some kind of unity there." The green paint, she thought. "Where he goes wrong of course, Paul, not Plato, is where he swerves from the one unknowable God, the creator of everything who can't be confined by anything human, representation, definition, words, let alone statues and pictures—all very Jewish this, by the way—into Jesus rising from the dead. The mysterious Jesus reappears. God as judge of us all is one thing; Jesus, a Jew crucified by the Romans and coming back from the grave to be that judge is something else. No wonder they laughed in Athens, or most of them did."

"Alas", Clare said, thinking of Simon.

"Well, yes and no. They did have a point, the philosophers. They thought the idea of someone who was dead being alive again was simply preposterous, and you can't say that was an unreasonable view."

"No. I suppose you can't."

"I wouldn't laugh, Clare", David said, "if I were the philosophers now, because for you what Paul's saying to them is what you believe is true, what in a particular way you even know is true. I realize that. But if he'd made that speech a bit differently, he could have held on to the Athenians' attention a little longer. Perhaps if he'd actually read some of Plato and not just heard about what his wool-gathering followers had written centuries later, it might have helped. It's a fascinating moment, whichever way you look at it."

He smiled at her.

"Did he win the argument? Yes and no, again. He did win it in a way because it didn't end. Even the Enlightenment didn't bring it to an end. It's gone on ever since Paul made his speech in Athens, or really ever since Aristotle profoundly disagreed with Plato, and no doubt it'll go on till the end of time when we'll all find out who was right."

Remembering this, she felt, as she so often did, the absence and the presence of David at the same time. She did miss him. How English he was, as well as how Jewish, which Hakim after a couple of conversations had seen. RIP, she thought, as she did every night.

And now—what could she do? She couldn't find Hakim. Ayesha couldn't find Hakim. A simple, insoluble, problem. One young man in a country where nothing was safe, nothing was steady or reliable, where he had grown up, yes, but where he hadn't been for more than five years, years, in Libya, of violence and confusion.

She shut the missal and moved again to the other end of the table and her laptop, with a hope that she knew to be wholly irrational that he might have sent her an email. Nothing. Of course.

What else could she do? Since she was being irrational she might as well try his mobile as well: nothing to lose, after all. She did. A long, continuous whine told her that the mobile had run out of power or was for one incomprehensible reason or another no longer reachable. Perhaps he had had a different number, which perhaps he had given only to Ayesha, for when he was abroad. Or perhaps that was a hopelessly out-of-date idea. Useless speculation.

She sat at the kitchen table with the long empty day ahead, feeling half irritated at being so out-of-date, so left behind by the world, and half pleased, amused even, to find herself left behind in the land of the old where David had for so long been her left-behind companion. At least it was possible for the old, or anyway for those whose memories were reasonably sound, to remember all sorts of things now being quickly forgotten.

She thought how wrong the children were—Carrie, Daisy, Hakim, Ayesha—to think that in the new super-connected world no one could lose touch with anyone else, could be beyond communication wherever they were on the planet. But wasn't the smartphone actually the one too-vulnerable basket into which the young put all their eggs? If they lost it or even couldn't find somewhere to charge it, they were totally sunk. No address book, no diary—Clare had had a small address book and a small diary in her bag since time immemorial and still had—so without the phone they had no idea of everyone else's forgettable mobile numbers, or anyone else's equally forgettable email address. They couldn't read a map unless it were a tiny section on a tiny screen, and in any case without a mobile they didn't know where they were or where they were going. Mostly they didn't even have a watch. She remembered asking Carrie if she'd like a really nice watch for her twenty-first birthday. "You mean a wristwatch, Gran? That's really kind, but no one does watches any more." However, setting off for Nepal a year or two later, she had said, "Gran, you know that watch you once offered to give me? I thought perhaps in the Himalayas it might be more reliable than a phone."

Hakim had a watch, but he was a bit older. Did Ayesha? She smiled at herself again, imagining nurses of the past in starched caps with watches pinned to the bosom of their uniforms. Anyway, Ayesha was a doctor, not a nurse. She always seemed to know what the time was but Clare didn't think she had a wristwatch.

And in what everyone nowadays called this interconnected world it turned out to be as possible as it had ever been for someone to disappear completely, as Hakim had disappeared.

There had been a time, not long ago it seemed to her, ancient history to the young, when if you had any idea where someone was you could telephone from your landline to another, in those days just called telephones, and leave a message with an actual person, on the reception desk of a hotel for example, asking your friend, your husband, your child, to call you back.

But of course this only worked if they were the kind of person who stayed in hotels. That kind of person was already old or middle-aged when her children were growing up. Students didn't stay in hotels. If you didn't know where they were, you just had to consign them to the care of God and wait patiently for them to get in touch, usually if they'd run out of money. Matt, thirty years ago, before he joined the army, had gone to India and then to Tibet, travelling on unpredictable trains and buses, on hired bikes, on foot, first with a school friend and then, when the other boy had had enough, by himself. She and Simon had had, for months on end, no idea where he was or whether he was all right, or even whether he was still alive, though they vaguely assumed that if a person with a British passport got into some kind of trouble his parents would eventually be told.

Remembering this, she thought that Ayesha wouldn't have been so desperate about Hakim if it weren't for the mobile phone she had thought an infinitely dependable way of staying in touch with him. Matt, after six months in India and Tibet all those years ago, had reappeared with some hair-raising stories—he had been bitten by a rabid monkey at the Taj Mahal and thereafter had to travel with injections that needed to be kept in fridges until he had, as instructed by a doctor, used them up—but all right. So Hakim, much older than Matt had then been, and in his own country, would probably also be all right.

Wouldn't he? But there was a war in Libya. If Hakim had been killed, or wounded, in some muddle obscured by the fog of war—as Ayesha clearly couldn't help imagining—how would they ever know? He had a Libyan passport. There would be no reassuring British consul, however harassed, in Tripoli to make contact with Ayesha or with her. Would he anyway have put Ayesha or her in his passport or any other document as someone to be informed "in case of accident"? Who else was there in Hakim's life?

The Museum. Of course.

Feeling at once more hopeful, she got up from the table, put on the kettle, went to the bathroom, combed her hair which, in lockdown, it was easy to forget to do, made a face at herself in the mirror because her hair, with no hairdressers open to cut it, was too long, would soon be witchlike, and came back to the kitchen to make more coffee.

Why hadn't she thought of the Museum sooner? Hakim was careful, as David had been careful. She could see now the orderly folders in David's locked drawer. Hakim would have left some instructions, surely, with his notes for his report, so that if he were injured or killed someone, anyone who found them and had some sense of responsibility for the stones of Libya, or just for honouring a basic human connection, would send his notes back to the Museum, or perhaps try to get in touch with someone there. Was this expecting too much of a random militia fighter in a lawless country in the middle of a civil war? Probably. But someone finding Hakim's work might think his notes worth some money to an institution that sounded as solid and rich as the British Museum. An ordinary landline call? An email to some standard Museum email address that must exist?

She reached for her bag, found in her address book a short list of telephone numbers under BM, mostly extension numbers or mobile numbers for people she knew there. They were presumably, with the Museum shut for the last four weeks, working from home or furloughed in this new world of the pandemic, and so should be findable. The one most likely to have heard something from or about Hakim was the head of his department, who had given him his job in the first place and been pleased to have him on the staff. He had an ordinary London landline number. She fetched the telephone, and sat for a moment looking at it resting quietly in her hand. Was she being absurd? Interfering? Over-protective, when Hakim was a grown-up doing a serious and properly authorized job for the Museum? Just old and foolish? I am a very foolish, fond, old man. Lear. Fourscore and upward. So even older than her. Then she thought of Ayesha sobbing last night, and tapped in the number.

His wife or daughter or partner—how could one guess, nowadays?—answered.

"I'm afraid he's out. Walking the dog, which is allowed, you know."

"O, I'm sure it is. I'm so sorry to bother you."

"I can get him to call you when he comes back if you like."

"Thank you so much. It is—it is to do with work."

"It always is. Who shall I say?"

"This is Clare Wilson. A colleague at the Museum. Thank you so much."

"Colleague" was stretching it a bit, but whoever was guarding him wasn't at all friendly.

She tried to concentrate on the crossword puzzle, waiting for him to ring back.

Half an hour later, the telephone rang, which startled her because she was expecting it.

Penny.

"Hello, Mum. Are you all right?"

"I'm fine, thank you, darling. Absolutely fine. I'm actually waiting for—"

"I thought I'd ring you in the morning for a change. To make sure you're in, and keeping safe and all that. The Aga's on the blink which is maddening and I'm waiting for the chap who's meant to be coming to fix it. That's why I'm in. Of course I'll have to talk to him from the doorstep and then leave him in the kitchen to get on with it by himself. Masks and gloves. Everyone looks like a surgeon nowadays, even the chap mending the Aga. It all seems a bit ridiculous in the middle of the country, but Charles says we've got to do exactly what the rules say because MPs, you know—they can't be saying one thing and doing another."

"No, of course they can't." In case someone finds out, she thought. "Look, darling, could I ring you back a bit later? I'm—I'm just in the middle of something."

"O, sorry. I thought you might be getting quite bored by now. Might be glad of a chat. But if you're busy, never mind. I'll ring you after tea. Maybe tomorrow."

"Thank you darling. Bye for now."

"Bye, Mum."

If Penny had said "What? What are you in the middle of?"

she had no idea what she could have said.

Five minutes later the telephone rang again.

"O, hello. How good of you to ring back. I'm so sorry to ring you at home."

"That's all right, everything's at home now, isn't it? What can I do for you, Mrs Wilson?"

"Well, it's probably silly of me, but I'm worried about Hakim."

"Hakim?"

"Hakim Husain, the Libyan who works in your department on inscriptions and so forth."

"O Husain, yes of course. But he's gone, you know. He insisted on going, to Libya, to see what's happening to the antiquities. I thought he was quite mad—Libya's a shambles, has been for years, and the Foreign Office says no one should go there—but since it's his own country and he cares so much we let him go, gave him some money and a report to write, and promised to hold his job for him. He went just before the lockdown I think. The flights were still working, anyway. Now heaven knows when he'll be able to get back. We've got various people stuck in the wrong countries at the moment. But as practically all the staff are furloughed it doesn't make much odds. I've no idea how he's getting on. Has he been in touch with you?"

"No, he hasn't. That's why I'm worried. He—" She realized just in time that the story of Ayesha, the emails and the mobile phone would bore, even irritate, this man she scarcely knew, so she said only, "A few days ago he sent an odd email which didn't appear to be from him or from his phone. Then silence. So I wondered whether you'd heard anything from him?"

"I don't think so, no. I'm getting my own emails of course but emails to the office have been a bit all over the place as things are at present. I'll ask my secretary. She's more on top of what's coming in than I am. If there's anything from Husain I'll let you know. I wouldn't worry too much if I were you. He's probably right as rain. He's quite a survivor, isn't he? In fact I look forward to hearing about what he's been up to out there when he gets back."

"Yes, I'm sure. I expect—"

"OK, Mrs Wilson? We'll be in touch in due course."

"Thank you so much. I do apologize for bothering you."

"Not at all. Goodbye now."

He must have been years younger than her. Why did he strike her as old-fashioned, someone at whose way of carrying on Carrie would have cringed? "Out there": that was it. He'd sounded like someone talking about the Raj.

Damn, she said to herself, shaking her head, annoyed, with him, with herself, and because she should have asked him whether Hakim would have had with him details of how to get in touch with the Museum. She couldn't possibly ring him back, and then she saw that she was not only fussing, which one should try not to do, but becoming almost hysterical. After all, hadn't he said, like David, "He's quite a survivor"? Had David said that, or had she only imagined him saying it?

She must get out of the flat, go outside, walk round the square's garden for a bit, even sit on a bench with the *Guardian* if there were few people about. An hour's exercise a day was not only allowed but encouraged, and sitting at the kitchen table allowing herself to spiral downwards into imagining things that were very unlikely to have happened was useless to her, to Ayesha, and to Hakim himself wherever he was.

When Ayesha came in that evening, it was nearly nine o'clock. She appeared in the kitchen looking worn out, with her eyes dulled and sunk into her head, and dark rings beneath them. Clare knew she had to leave again at seven fifteen in the morning. It was too much.

"Ayesha—are you all right?"

"O, Mrs Wilson, it is good to be back. I am very tired. It has been so long, the day."

"Do sit down. Perhaps you'd like some tea before you have something to eat?"

"No. I'm so sorry. No thank you. I must put all these clothes, and the gowns I have here"—she held up a carrier bag—"in the washing machine now, so that I can dry them for the morning. If that is all right?"

"Of course it's all right. It's always all right. You know that.

And do have a bath or at least a shower. It will make you feel a bit better I'm sure."

"I will. Thank you. I won't be very long."

Clare heard the bath running.

Surely an actual doctor, however junior, shouldn't have to wash at home the protective work clothes she'd had to wear in the hospital? But for several days Ayesha had come back to the flat with a bag of washing, and Clare, after sending her to bed, had stayed up long enough to put on the tumble dryer. She had heard on the radio stories of there being hold-ups in the supply of gowns, masks, gloves, all the things that made a chaplain indistinguishable from a doctor or a nurse, all the things that must be making it so difficult to give the dying the smile, the touch, the warmth of another human being at their side, on their side, when their wife, husband, son, daughter couldn't be with them. She knew Ayesha was finding the sadness of this the most difficult thing of all to cope with.

Clare heard her switch on the washing machine next door. She came back into the kitchen, looking a little better, in her dressing gown, an old, warm, candlewick dressing gown Clare had lent her for breakfast and supper times, when she didn't have to be properly dressed and could even leave her hijab in her room. "At home, with only another woman to see me, I do not have to cover my hair, you know."

"What would you like to have? There's some spinach soup, or I could make you scrambled eggs?"

"Thank you but I am not hungry. Could I have a cup of tea please, with lots of sugar? I can make the tea."

"Certainly not. Sit down, Ayesha. I'll make the tea."

She sat at the table. Clare put the kettle on.

"At the meeting they told us we have new shifts next week. From Tuesday I shall be on the night shift. I like night shifts because there is a little more time. And on Monday I have the whole day off, and Tuesday until the night shift starts. So maybe I shall have some extra sleep. It is so—it is so quiet, here in the square."

Her voice wasn't the same as usual. it sounded constricted, perhaps just with exhaustion. When the kettle had boiled,

Clare said, "Was it a very difficult day?"

"It was very long. And also I—"

Clare turned towards her. She was clearly on the edge of tears.

"Here." She gave her a tissue out of the dresser drawer. "There's no need to tell me. But it might help a little if you can—"

Ayesha blew her nose, mopped her eyes, took the tissue to the bin and took a clean tissue out of the box in the drawer. Then she sat down again. Clare had made a mug of Assam tea, and a mug of camomile for herself. She waited three or four minutes and then took out the teabags and put a little jug of milk and the sugar bowl beside Ayesha's tea, so that she had to add the milk and spoon in the sugar herself. She did, stirred her tea and at last said, "Thank you." After a pause she said, "You see, there was this boy today."

"A boy? I thought your ward was a men's ward?"

"Yes. It is the same ward. He came into the hospital yesterday. The nurse at the desk said that when the ambulance brought him to A and E he told them he was nineteen. He told his name"—she had caught this "told" from Hakim—"but no address. He is not English and he had no papers, no passport, no phone, nothing. They had picked him up in the street where he had collapsed. Someone had telephoned 999 for an ambulance but they had not given their name and this person had gone when the ambulance found him. They put him on our ward because he said he is nineteen. He is coughing very badly and he has very high fever. I think he is only fifteen or sixteen."

For a moment Clare put her head in her hands. Then she looked up. Ayesha was sipping her tea. She made a face because the tea was still very hot but she was looking a little better than when she came in.

"O dear. You think he's only a child?" Clare said. "I wonder where he's been living. And why no one's looking after him."

"I couldn't find out anything about him until just before the meeting tonight, when I—"

She stopped, and then said, "I'm sorry, Mrs Wilson. I should not be telling you about this boy. We are always told not to talk about our patients outside the hospital. There is patient confidentiality."

"I understand that, Ayesha. But this boy sounds as if he doesn't have anyone to take care of him and it's only good that you're concerned about him. Telling me about him can't possibly do him any harm, can it? And perhaps it might make your job which is so difficult at the moment a little easier, if you can talk about what's happened in your day."

"Do you think—do you think the consultants wouldn't be shocked if they knew I had told you about this boy?"

"I'm quite sure they wouldn't. For one thing, they're far too busy themselves, and for another thing, from what I know of doctors, they would be pleased you have someone to talk to."

"Maybe you are right. And my father would agree, I think. He has said he is very happy that I am staying with you. So—"

Clare saw her collecting what she was going to say.

'It's all right, Ayesha. You don't have to hurry. Try a little more tea. It'll be cooler now."

She did. Her face brightened a little. "Thank you." She looked down at the table, and then across to Clare.

"He is black, but he has very little English so he is not a London boy. I checked him this morning. He is very thin and when I put the stethoscope on his chest he jumped as if I had hurt him. His lungs are not good. I asked him where he was born, but he only shook his head. He may not have understood. He is very frightened because of the breathing, and I think because of other things as well."

"Do you know his name?"

"Ahmed is his name. I don't remember his other name. It was written down at the desk but I saw it only for a moment. An African name."

"Will he get better, do you think?"

Her lip trembled again.

"I don't think so. I hope but I don't think—this evening he is worse, his cough is worse, his oxygen is still falling. For a few minutes I could sit with him. I held his hand, my hand in its horrible glove of course, but he calmed down a little. He opened his eyes once, when he was not coughing. He saw me,

I think he saw me through the visor of the mask, and he said, 'Help me please'. I can't help him. We can't help him, except with more oxygen, and it isn't working. It was difficult to let his hand go. He was holding my hand too tightly."

Now she was crying. But she sniffed, shook her head, blew her nose, and went on.

"When we were coming off shift", she said, "I asked one of the nurses if she had found out anything about him. I asked her because I saw her washing him earlier in the afternoon. I'm glad I did because she had really talked to him. Excuse me, Mrs Wilson—"

She used the crumpled tissue in her hand to blow her nose again, and dry her eyes.

"This nurse is lovely, she is so kind to the patients even when there is so little time. She is old enough to be my mother, even almost my grandmother. She is from Africa, from Nigeria, but she has been in London many years. She told me that she asked the boy where his parents are. He said Niger—I think she said Niger. I had not heard of the country. It is not the same as Nigeria, but the nurse told me it is the next country to the north, a desert country. In that part of Africa there is a language, Hausa, which many people speak. She asked him a question in Hausa, which was her language when she was a child, and he knew the language. He told her that he left Niger to be rich in Europe. His parents saved up the money. He crossed the desert in a lorry. He crossed the sea in a boat from—" More tears.

"I can guess, Ayesha. From Libya. Is that what he said?"

She nodded miserably, swallowed her tears.

"Then I had to go to the F1 doctors' meeting. I could not be late. So that is all I know."

"Too much, I can see. This poor boy, alone—"

"Imagine how much loneliness, how much danger in his life, Mrs Wilson, and if I am correct about his age he should be still in school."

She drank a little more tea, to help her to go on.

"Hakim told me about these people in the middle of Africa, in countries where there is no work, no proper government, and there is not even oil. The people are so poor that they will risk their children's lives in journeys like this boy's journey, for the chance of them sending money home from Europe one day. Many of these boys die in the desert, some of them die in the camps in Libya, if they are ill, if they are bombed. Hakim says the government in Tripoli is paid by the European countries to keep the Africans in the camps to stop them coming across the sea. European countries do not want them. European countries do not care if they die. If they find a boat to take them they often die anyway, because the boat turns over in the sea. And now this boy who has managed all that, who has stayed alive, who has got to England, is—"

She had done so well, to keep talking, even to mention Hakim without cracking again. She couldn't go on.

She folded her arms on the kitchen table and laid her head down on her arms. She wasn't even crying. Clare reached across and moved her mug, still half full, further away from her arms. After a minute or two she saw that Ayesha was asleep.

She sat quietly, watching the sleeping girl, for half an hour. At ten o'clock she boiled the kettle again, filled a hot water bottle and put it in Ayesha's bed, and then woke her as gently as she could, though she was so fast asleep that Clare had to shake her shoulder until she was startled awake. If Clare had been a man, she thought, if she had been Hakim, she would have picked her up and carried her to her bed without waking her. She led her, dazed with sleep, along the passage to her room and this time did tuck her into bed like a child.

She stayed in the kitchen until she heard the washing machine spin Ayesha's clothes and then stop. She looked up Niger on the Internet. Ayesha had been right. A huge empty country, almost all of it desert, out of all the countries in the world the very poorest, with a terrible French colonial history through the twentieth century. No wonder its wretched people, the few who could scrape together the necessary money to pay the traffickers—a horrible word for a horrible thing—who had trucks to cross the Sahara, wanted something different, something better for their children. Something, alas, more French, though the French, if the children got that far, would put them in camps and promise the British, who didn't want them either, not to let them cross the Channel. And for them Libya had been nothing but another hostile place, another filthy, hot, competitive place of detention and hunger, to be escaped from by any means possible, however dangerous.

Where was Hakim?

She moved Ayesha's things to the dryer, had a quick bath, and set her own alarm for six forty-five so that she could wake Ayesha in time for her to have some breakfast and get to the hospital for the eight o'clock shift.

Looking out at the square after eleven o'clock, she prayed for the boy, for Ahmed, whoever he was, whichever boy he was. She heard David's voice: Don't let's exaggerate.

He was young. Perhaps he would after all recover. Dear God, look after him.

In the morning, Sunday morning, it was difficult to wake Ayesha. She looked as if she had hardly moved all night, though she must have, because she had dropped the hot water bottle on the floor and thrown back the duvet as if she had been at some moment too hot.

Clare had brought her clean clothes and her hospital protective kit. She put them on the armchair and the dress-ing-table chair in her room. When she was sure Ayesha was awake enough to get dressed, she left her, saying, "Breakfast in the kitchen. You should eat something before you go to the hospital."

She heard her have a shower in the bathroom, and then she took a few minutes to get dressed. When she came into the kitchen she looked drawn, her eyes glittering. Clare could see that now she wasn't just tired, as she had been in the evening, but properly ill. When she sat down and shook her head at the idea of eating anything, Clare got up, stood behind her and put her hand on her forehead. It was dry, burning hot.

"Ayesha, you can't go to the hospital. You have a fever. Let me take your temperature."

There was an old thermometer in the tissue drawer. It had been there since Penny and Matt were little.

Obediently Ayesha accepted the thermometer Clare put in her mouth. Clare found her glasses and took the thermometer to the window to read it.

"Just over 103", she said. "I thought so. That's—" She remembered no one did Fahrenheit any more. "That's"—she looked at the thermometer again—"39.5".

"O", Ayesha put a hand to her mouth. "I'm so sorry", she said. Then she hurried to the cloakroom by the front door. Clare could hear her retching.

She came out shivering.

"Go back to bed", Clare said. "Get undressed, get into bed, and in a few minutes I'll bring you a hot water bottle and a jug of water with some ice. And you must tell me who I should ring at the hospital to say that you can't come to work."

"I must—I will telephone the ward myself. I will tell them, and I must find out—"

About the boy.

Clare gave her ten minutes and then knocked and went into her room with the hot water bottle and the iced water. She was sitting up in bed, her phone on the bedside table, and she was crying.

"O, Ayesha. I'm so sorry."

"They moved him to ICU last night. He died early this morning. I'm sure he was ill before he caught Covid. He was too thin."

"I'm so very sorry. It's the saddest thing, I do understand how miserable it is for you, after all he'd been through, poor boy. Poor Ahmed. I'm sure everyone in the hospital did their very best for him."

A great deal better, Clare thought, than almost everyone he'd met on his way from Niger to London, especially, no doubt, police and officials everywhere.

"Thank you", Ayesha said, "for remembering his name."

"And what about you? What did the hospital say?"

"The ward sister told me to stay in bed. She said I should take paracetamol for the fever. I am young and strong she said. I should get better. I said maybe it is not the virus, just the flu. Maybe if I sleep a lot I shall be better for the night shift on

Tuesday. She said don't come in till you are better. She also—"

She hesitated. Clare waited.

"She asked me if there was anyone at home to look after me." She raised her eyes, appealing, more than ever the eyes of a child.

"What did you tell her?"

"I said yes. But now I think I was wrong. I should have said no. You must not come near me. You could catch the virus and—"

"Now listen to me, Ayesha." Clare sat down on the end of the bed. "You are not to worry about me. Not for a moment. Yes, I'm old, of course, and I'm quite likely to catch the virus anyway—just by picking up a jar of coffee in the shop which someone with the virus picked up and put down again before me. If I do catch it, I might die—and at my age, as we agreed the other night, that's not a terrible thing. But I might very easily get better. Anyway, it may not be the virus that you've got. I'm not going to worry about it, and nor must you. I shall take sensible precautions and do a lot of washing my hands, and I have some good sanitizer in the kitchen. So you were right to say yes, you have someone to look after you, and I'm very pleased you're here, and not where you were living before with your frightened landlady. Imagine—"

Ayesha smiled, almost laughed, for the first time in what seemed to Clare like days.

"You are very very good. Hakim—"

She stopped, and managed to go on.

"Hakim would be happy to know that if I am ill, I am here in your house."

She shivered.

"I am hot and cold together. It is the fever. One more thing, Mrs Wilson, may I ask you?"

"Anything."

"I wonder if you would be able to telephone my father, to tell him that I am not well? If you speak to him first he will know that he can talk to the person who is taking care of me. Then he will not be too worried, I hope."

"He knows you're here, doesn't he?"

"Yes. He knows you have also looked after Hakim when he first came to England."

"Of course I'll talk to him. What time is it in India?"

"Four and a half hours ahead of London. I don't know why the half an hour. So—" She looked at her alarm clock but couldn't do the sum.

"A few minutes past twelve", Clare said.

"He is always at home for lunch. Maybe in twenty minutes? I will give you the landline number. Then he will know it is not a patient calling him."

"That's fine. I'll come back when I've talked to him. Here are some paracetamol. Take a couple. Drink lots of water and have a little sleep."

Ayesha's father answered the telephone himself, far away in Assam, his voice as clear, though with a little delay on the line, as if he had been the other side of the Park.

"Hello. Dr Gupta. I am Clare Wilson, in London. Ayesha is staying with me."

"Ah, yes, Mrs Wilson. Ayesha has told me of your great kindness. Is everything all right?"

"I'm afraid Ayesha isn't well. She is extremely tired and is finding the work with coronavirus patients very demanding, so I think it's possible that exhaustion has made her ill. She has a fever and has vomited. She is asleep now and has no work in any case until Tuesday evening."

A long silence.

"Are you there, Dr Gupta?"

"I am here. Does Ayesha have a cough?"

"No, she doesn't. I haven't heard her cough at all."

More silence.

"Not yet, perhaps."

"I am so sorry. She is young and strong. Even if it is the virus, she's very likely to get better, isn't she?"

"She has been very much exposed."

"She has been so brave and good."

"She is a good girl and I always thought, from when she was a small child, that one day she would become a good doctor."

Clare waited.

"Has she had any news of young Mr Husain?"

"I'm afraid not. I'm sure he will be in touch soon. He is in his own country and he is a survivor. But—his being out of contact has added to the stress for Ayesha."

"So it is not possible for you to let him know that Ayesha is ill?"

"I'm afraid it isn't. Communications in Libya, like everything else, are very difficult."

More silence.

"Mrs Wilson, am I correct to think that you are not young yourself?"

"Yes, Dr Gupta, you are correct. I am seventy-seven."

"Are you quite well, in general? Excuse me, please, for asking you this."

"Yes, I'm well. I'm very lucky and have nothing wrong with me beyond a little rheumatism."

"That is good. I have not seen any cases of Covid 19 virus here. We have been most fortunate. There have been very few cases in the whole of Assam. I thank God for this because already in parts of India Muslims are blamed for the virus. We have enough trouble here without this."

He paused. She waited for him to go on.

"But Mrs Wilson, I have read enough about this virus to know that you should not be taking care of Ayesha. I am very grateful that she is in your house, but will you please be extremely careful, with towels and taps and glasses and plates and the handles of doors and toilets, everything she touches? Will you wear a scarf over your nose and mouth when you are in Ayesha's room? If she does not have Covid 19, there is no harm in precautions that turn out to be unnecessary. We would not wish you to become ill also."

"I will be very careful. I do understand how easily the virus spreads."

"And may I ask you to telephone me again to let me know how Ayesha is progressing?"

"Of course, Dr Gupta. I will telephone in a day or two anyway. Is this time of day good?"

"It is perfect. Thank you very much, Mrs Wilson, for what you are doing for my daughter."

"She will telephone very soon. She wanted me to talk to you first."

"Of course. Thank you, Mrs Wilson."

In her bedroom she chose a fine cotton scarf to cover her nose and mouth, and tied it at the back of her neck. In the kitchen she took out of the drawer a new box of tissues, unopened, and a new packet of paracetamol for Ayesha's bedside table, and went to tell her, waking her again from a deep sleep, that she could now ring her father, and that he had been calm and sensible when he heard that she was ill.

At nine o'clock she went into Ayesha's room again and found her asleep once more. She went back to the kitchen, wrote a note saying she would be out of the flat for a few minutes, and put it beside her phone and her glass of water.

Then she went downstairs to where the grumpy caretaker would be sorting the post by the pigeonholes, and, two yards away from him, asked him if he could, for what she thought was a generous bribe, do a little shopping and get her newspaper every day while she was looking after someone who might have the virus.

"Yes, Mrs Wilson. I dare say I can manage that." The bribe was obviously big enough. "I'm doing the shopping for Commander Morris and Mr and Mrs Blake already. One more lot won't make much odds. What's your paper?"

"My paper? O, the *Guardian*."

"Well, it would be, wouldn't it?"

He had been an ardent Brexiteer and was the only person she had ever come across who read the *Daily Express*. On hot days she had seen him asleep in a deckchair in the yard behind the house, the *Daily Express* spread over his face. Four years ago, before the referendum, they had had one or two quite fierce arguments. No one would ever be able to change his mind.

"If you leave me a list here"—he pointed to an empty pigeonhole at the end of a row—"before four in the afternoon I'll do your shopping next morning. I'll leave it at your door and ring your bell to tell you it's there. I'll keep a proper account and you can write me a cheque at the end of each week. I know the likes of you still favour cheques."

"That's very good of you, Mr Clements."

"Well, we've all got to muck in a bit at a time like this, haven't we?"

"Thank you so much." She turned towards the lift and he called after her, "Mrs Wilson, you won't have got your Sunday paper, will you? Not if you're stuck in your flat. I can get you one when I go for my dinner if you like. There's no Sunday *Guardian* is there?"

"I usually get the *Observer*. That would be lovely. How very kind of you to think of it. Thank you again."

Astonished by Mr Clements's conversion to the human race, she decided to go back to the flat up the stairs, for exercise.

Ayesha was still asleep, so Clare took her note to the kitchen and threw it away, and then found in her Sunday missal the Mass for the second Sunday of Easter and sat by the open window in the sitting room, resolved to pray her way through all of it.

The readings were positive, joyful, of course because it was still only just after Easter: the joy of faith in what we believe although we have not seen. Reading on, into the eucharistic prayer, she almost fell asleep herself.

There was something peaceful and calming about knowing she was responsible for this sick girl from so far away, lying asleep in Matt's room. She couldn't go out now, because of the isolation rules. So she would write a bit more of her book, or rewrite some of what she had already written, a process which seemed to be one of almost infinite possibility, and she would look after Ayesha.

She would keep her safe, for her father and for Hakim, and do her best to make sure that, even if she had caught the virus, Ayesha would get better.

Part 4

22–30 May 2020

Clare was sitting at her kitchen table, her laptop in front of her and a mug of coffee beside her. She was looking at a passage on her screen, in a large font so that she could read it easily, recording one of those late evening conversations she had had with Hakim, listening to him talk while she learnt so much from him. It was too long, though she had already shortened it, and she knew there were important bits of what he had told—told, tell, his favourite word—that she had forgotten.

She saved the few small changes she had made, shut her laptop and looked across at the clock. Nearly ten. She resisted the temptation to turn on the wireless and hear more news of the virus, now receding, at least in London, as the figures of deaths across the country had come down to between four and five hundred every day. The government, nevertheless, seemed to be increasingly all over the place, increasingly inconsistent and liable to change its mind, and nowhere near where it had promised it would be with testing and tracing people's contacts. Also, obviously much too late in the course of the pandemic, it was saying it was planning to quarantine everyone arriving in the country.

Would Hakim be able to fly back to England? If he could find a flight, afford a ticket, perhaps he could be isolated for a fortnight here in the flat? This was probably much too much to hope for.

What did she have left but hope, unanchored in any evidence? She wasn't even sure which country he was in.

Was he alive?

She didn't need the ten o'clock summary of the news she'd heard too much of already. She opened her laptop again and immediately shut it.

Was there any point in her trying to improve what there was of her book, any point in trying to plan a way of finishing it? Every morning she made a new effort, and every morning she felt her confidence in the enterprise leak away a little more. She was too sad to work, and yet she had almost nothing else to do, though after the fourteen days of isolation compulsory from the day Ayesha had been taken into hospital she had gone back to doing a little shopping and fetching her *Guardian* every morning at half past eight. She had stopped waking up, not only in the mornings but several times during each night, wondering whether, or when, she was going to run a temperature, start coughing, lose her sense of taste. Why she hadn't caught the virus she had no idea, but she hadn't. She had stopped expecting to die without being able to go, once more, to Mass, without, probably, a last Confession. And now she was allowed to walk up to the Park in the afternoons as long as she was careful to avoid getting near anyone else. There was still no Mass to go to. July, they had said, for churches to be allowed congregations.

After a few blank minutes she reopened the laptop and tried, as she tried every morning, to pull her concentration back to what was in front of her. If all this had ever been worth the attempt, and David himself, after all, had in the first place encouraged her to make the effort, then it should be worth trying to improve it now.

Had she remembered accurately what Hakim had said on that evening that now seemed many years ago though it was only a few months? Had she checked the facts thoroughly enough to be sure she hadn't reported him as saying something actually untrue? Would anyone be interested in these conversations now or ever again, when 2020 was going to be remembered always for the pandemic and nothing else? Except perhaps, with everything in the unsafe hands of Boris Johnson and an inept, inexperienced set of ministers, that it might be remembered even more for the worst possible kind of a crash-out Brexit at the end of the year. She tried, like, she suspected, practically everyone in the country, to push Brexit to the back of her mind as if it were a nightmare from which she had woken up. But it wasn't. And whenever Boris Johnson or Michael Gove said anything about it, the line was as unbending, as populist and stupid, as ever. No, we won't ask for an extension at the end of June. The Europeans are to blame. If there is a disastrous crash-out, the virus will be to blame.

And where was Hakim?

In the last month, since Ayesha became ill, she had tried as hard as she could, with nothing but the *Guardian*, the BBC and the Internet—which after all did amount to quite a lot of sources of information—to find out what was happening in Libya. There had been bits and pieces of news, none good. It seemed that the forces of General Haftar had recently been pushed back a certain distance from the suburbs of Tripoli. The Tripoli government, with help from Turkish planes, shells, mortars and drones, had recaptured not only Sabratha but more towns along the coast towards Tunis. Was this a good thing? Impossible to tell. Haftar's planes and drones and shells and mortars, apparently supplied by the UAE, Egypt and Russia, had retaliated with strikes against Tripoli, seventeen attacks on hospitals and health centres since the start of the year, according to a UN report she had come across on the internet. It was said that Syrians, from fighting on both sides in their own civil war, had come to Libya to fight on each side in this civil war, paid as mercenaries. Who was paying them? Russia, the UAE, the Saudis, plenty of money there, for Haftar; for Turkey and the Tripoli government there was plenty more money from Qatar. Perhaps these Syrians, with no doubt nothing left to lose, were fighting harder for Tripoli than for Haftar because Tripoli was more Islamist? Remembering all Hakim had explained to her about Libya, was there any prospect of things improving if either side in the civil war actually won it?

In the last few weeks, since Hakim had sent Ayesha that sinister email, there had been a number of deaths, and many more casualties, on both sides, as well as deaths and casualties among people on neither side. She couldn't forget discovering a few days ago that a five-year-old Bangladeshi boy had been killed in a Haftar attack on one of the camps in which the Tripoli government held migrants desperate to cross the Mediterranean. What was a Bangladeshi child doing in Libya? Presumably his parents had travelled all the way from the other side of India to escape poverty. To work in the Gulf perhaps? But in Libya? The people in those camps were the victims of so much. And even the few who made it all the way to England—

She felt tears rising again. Would there be a day before too long which she would get through without crying? For Ayesha, for the boy, for each boy. Perhaps if Hakim turned out to be still alive?

At least Penny wouldn't ring today because yesterday, after tea, she had.

Penny and Charles had been in Yorkshire since the lockdown began towards the end of March. MPs had been told to work from home for the time being, and when fifty of them came back to the House of Commons after Easter, Charles wasn't important enough to be one of them. The broadband in Leckenby certainly wasn't up to connecting him by Zoom, which Clare had read about—seeing a number of people at the same time on your computer screen struck her as a very unpleasant thought—to Prime Minister's questions, or, as far as Clare could tell, to anything else. So, presumably, deprived by the lockdown rules of any opportunity for the networking Penny always said he was so good at, he had done practically nothing for months—"he says the office is really busy answering emails"—while Penny rode every day, dead-headed the daffodils and learnt how to make bread, a new skill she was very proud of.

She telephoned a couple of times a week to make sure Clare was OK, and Clare had managed to conceal from her everything that had happened in the last month.

"Are you sure you're all right, Mum? You don't sound brilliant."

"I'm fine. The whole thing does rather get one down, you know, specially in London. You do hear an awful lot of ambulances, and they seem very loud when there's practically no other traffic."

"Yes, I suppose that must be a bit grim. There doesn't seem to be much of it round here, though I gather a few people have died in York and Scarborough. Mostly old people with five other things the matter with them. Lucky you're so fit for your age."

"Yes, well, fingers crossed."

Just lately this kind of conversation had changed a little.

"Charles says we must go back to London for Parliament starting up again after the half-term break. Rees-Mogg is ordering them all to reappear on the second of June. Though I don't see how they can have everyone back in the House because of social distancing so I suppose we'll have to sit in Barnes waiting for the call for Charles to say something on Zoom. Quite boring. Though if they start changing the rules a bit we might actually be able to see you again one of these days, have you to Sunday lunch like old times."

"That would be lovely, darling."

She wouldn't have been able to pull the wool over Carrie's eyes if Carrie had been in London, but she was still in Nepal and, when last heard of, had said only that she would be back perhaps in August, *when there are bound to be flights. Poor old England. I do feel a bit bad about being away so long while you're all having such a beastly time. Well, not Mum and Dad, obviously.*

She got up from the kitchen table, feeling, for no specific reason, old and stiff as she tended to every morning, getting out of bed after a patchy and unhappy night with not enough sleep, too many bad dreams and too many bad memories. It was after ten and she'd been out and come back, so she shouldn't be still stiff, specially as she had walked up the stairs instead of taking the lift. This was tiring so it must be good for her.

She did some tidying in the sitting room, which was tidy already. She picked up and put down again her sewing, the large square of canvas which was supposed to become the seat of one of the two eighteenth-century chairs with ancient worn tapestry, that her mother had inherited and that she, in turn, had taken from his flat when her father died. She had managed about twenty square inches of a moderately nice and suitably sober Bargello pattern—primary-school embroidery—which she would have to expand considerably before Penny came to the flat. "You must have had loads of time, Mum. I thought you'd have finished redoing those chairs by now."

She walked slowly through the flat, going into each room, except Simon's study, as she did every day, seeing that the kitchen, the laundry room, the cloakroom by the front door, the bathroom were clean and tidy. Her bedroom was as she had left it before she went out shopping, her bed made and her clothes put away or dumped in the washing basket. Penny's room was the same as usual, cluttered but reasonably clean. At the closed door of Matt's room she hesitated. It would probably make her cry, again.

She had thoroughly cleaned and tidied it on the afternoon of the day the ambulance had taken Ayesha to the hospital. She had washed everything washable, sprayed sanitizer over all the surfaces, remade the bed, and had the room ready for Ayesha to come back to when she was better. In a small zipped bag that used to be Simon's one-night bag for lecturing outside London, she had put Ayesha's alarm clock, smartphone and the charger she found plugged in by the bedside light, some night clothes, a cashmere cardigan of her own—remembering that there are few things more dispiriting in hospital than being cold—a couple of hijab scarves, a new sponge bag Daisy had given her for Christmas with Ayesha's toothbrush, toothpaste, comb, hairbrush and tissues inside. She added, from the table by the window, a small book in Arabic and English, called Salat, which was obviously a prayer book.

She had had to pack this bag very quickly.

The ambulance had arrived a quarter of an hour after she had rung 999. Two paramedics, a man and a woman dressed as for space in protective suits, helmets, masks, gloves, had come into this room, taken Ayesha's temperature, not with a thermometer but with some modern device Clare hadn't even seen, and heard the cough which she had had for two days and which had got worse all night, as she struggled more and more painfully to breathe.

When the woman had, with her gloved hand, gently wiped the hair off Ayesha's forehead, she said, "But don't we know you? Aren't you Dr Gupta?"

Ayesha had nodded, and said, finding with difficulty enough breath to say anything, "I'm sorry."

"Have you been looking after her, Mrs—?" This was the man. Clare couldn't see his face properly, particularly as he had ordinary glasses under the visor he was wearing.

"Wilson. My name's Clare Wilson. Yes, I have. She's been ill for six days, but in the last twenty-four hours her breathing has got—well, you see what it's like."

"I'm afraid we'll be taking her to the hospital. Would you put a few things together for her? I'm sorry but you can't come with her. At the moment it's—"

"Not allowed. Of course. I understand."

She found the bag and packed it, showing Ayesha each thing as she put it in. Ayesha nodded, and smiled when she showed her the cardigan and then the prayer book. Then she stood watching while the woman paramedic helped Ayesha out of bed and into Clare's old candlewick dressing gown, her pretty Indian slippers, and the hijab she hadn't worn for days. Her cough made it difficult for her to stand upright.

The man had watched Clare pack the bag. "A small towel, if you've got one?"

"Of course."

She found a small towel and a face cloth in the airing cupboard, and put them in the bag.

"One more thing might be helpful", Clare said, leaving Ayesha's room for the kitchen and hoping she could find—yes, in the dresser drawer, were still three or four brightly-coloured old-fashioned luggage labels with string knotted through a reinforced hole. She pulled one out, wrote on it Dr Ayesha Gupta and the address of the flat, and tied it to the handle of the bag.

As they left, with Ayesha between the paramedics, and the man carrying the bag in his other hand, he said carefully but firmly, "You're a vulnerable person, Mrs Wilson, if you don't mind me saying, and you've been exposed to a possible Covid patient. I see you've got your face covered, which is good, but I have to tell you that you need to isolate strictly for fourteen days from now. Don't leave your flat for any reason. And you should be extra careful with hygiene, in Dr Gupta's room and elsewhere in your flat, in the bathroom for example. "

"Yes. I'll do my best."

She stood in her doorway and watched them into the lift. Before they reached it, Ayesha turned her head, and whispered, "Thank you." The man pulled the old gate shut with its metallic clang, and the lift creaked downwards.

She hadn't been able to give her even an encouraging touch, let alone a hug.

After lunch that day, when she guessed that Ayesha's father would be at home after his day's work in Assam, she telephoned him. He answered immediately, as if he had been expecting her to ring. Two days before she had told him that Ayesha was now coughing and still had a high fever.

"Yes, Mrs Wilson, Ayesha is worse?"

"Dr Gupta. I'm so sorry but I'm afraid she is. Her breathing was getting more and more difficult and this morning I had to call the ambulance. They have taken her to the hospital where she has been working. "

"I understand."

She waited.

"This is the Chelsea and Westminster Hospital?"

"That's right, yes. It's a very good hospital."

"Naturally. I have found on the internet that the National Health Service in UK is doing a most excellent job with the Covid patients, although it is not good that there are so many."

Another pause.

"I am so sorry, Dr Gupta."

"Mrs Wilson, you have been exceptionally kind to my daughter. You must not think that you are in any way to blame. Ayesha chose to work with the Covid patients. She knew that it was dangerous to do so but as a doctor she was correct to make that choice, and it is most unfortunate that she has contracted the virus, which it is likely that she has. But she is young and strong. I shall speak to someone at the hospital tomorrow to find out how the disease is progressing. I am sure that they will not hesitate to inform me how she is because I am also a doctor as well as her father."

"I wish I could visit her."

"I also wish that you could. But naturally you may not. I am sorry for that. But it is important that you take care of yourself, Mrs Wilson."

"I'll do my best", she said, as she had to the ambulance man. "Thank you Dr Gupta. I shall pray for Ayesha. Goodbye. We'll be in touch."

So it was her father who, a week after this telephone call, rang to tell her that Ayesha had died.

Clare had rung the hospital the day after the ambulance took her away, but once she had got through to the right ward, she was asked whether she was a relative—"Only a friend but Dr Gupta has been—" Then she was cut short with the information that Ayesha was being given the best care.

Three days after this, Dr Gupta had telephoned from Assam to tell her than Ayesha had been moved to ICU. She knew, because Ayesha had told her, that half the people who went from the wards to ICU died. She prayed and prayed because there was nothing else she could do, that Ayesha would be one of the half—half, after all, was a lot—of the patients in ICU who recovered. But she had known, known by some instinct without actually knowing, even though she had hoped throughout that it would not be so, that Ayesha was going to die, at least since the long night before she sent for the ambulance, and perhaps even before that, when they had talked about death, though she had tried to confine that conversation to the subject of the old and death, really the subject of herself and death.

She remembered Hakim saying, when he first told her about Ayesha, that he couldn't ask her to marry him because he brought death to everyone he loved. Of course he didn't. Of course he hadn't. In fact, if Ayesha had gone to India, as she had decided to do before Hakim left England, so that he could join her there, so that they could get married there, she would still be alive. But Clare knew that if, when, he came back, to the telephone, to the email, back to life, back even to London, and she had to tell him that Ayesha had died, he would think, say, "There, you see, I told you", or perhaps—she heard his voice—"There, you see, I told it to you, about Samira and Dr Rose, and now it is Ayesha. It is what I feared exactly."

She wished, it seemed to her all the time without stopping, that she had died instead of Ayesha. She couldn't have died instead of Matt. There would have been no reason for her to wish to die instead of her father, Simon, David, all older than her, all, variously ill and all not afraid of dying. She was still alive partly to remember them. But instead of Ayesha? She was so much more likely than Ayesha to die of the virus if she caught it, and she'd been so likely to catch it because of looking after her. For the first days she had been as careful as she could manage, had worn the scarf over her nose and mouth, and gloves which she kept washing. But that last night she had abandoned scarf and gloves to cool Ayesha's burning forehead and hands with a flannel wrung in cold water, and to be able to smile at her properly when she opened her eyes to apologize. So why was she still alive?

Which brought her to God.

She knew perfectly well, from the dozens of homilies she must have heard in nearly sixty years on the subject of why bad things happen to good people, that God, in whom are both justice and mercy, doesn't inflict injustice on those who die of a disease or are drowned in a flood or killed in a car crash when those who love them think they deserved to live for many more years. Or on those who grieve for them. Accidents, natural disasters—wrong to call them "acts of God"—and illnesses are just that, accidents, natural disasters and illnesses. War, which had killed Matt, is war, for which human beings are always to blame. But the "special providence in the fall of a sparrow" is God's love and care for every single one of the victims of all of these, victims who, as victims, whatever complexity and sinfulness their lives might have held, are as innocent as the five-year-old in Libya two weeks ago.

Ayesha was twenty-six and had spent seven years of hard work becoming a kind, skilled, thoughtful doctor. Hakim loved her, and would have become the father of her children. Why was she dead while Clare, nearly seventy-eight with her life over and no one needing her any more, was alive? It didn't make sense in any ordinary human terms but as some old rabbi, according to David, had written, "Who said it had to make sense?"

With gratitude for their presence on the earth, their presence in our lives, we have to return them to God who made them, to God who allowed from the beginning the world to be dangerous, imperfect, transient, bound by time and accident, while the souls of his children live with him in eternity.

Either, she thought, all this is true, or nothing is. She had held this dizzying alternative, this choice—but was it a choice? Wasn't even the perception of it a gift from God?—somewhere in her mind, her soul, for many years, perhaps ever since she had read somewhere that either everything means something or nothing means anything. She was sure that this was so, had been sure for most of her life that it was, but she didn't often have to remember it to keep herself steady, to keep herself going, just about, through the next hour, the next day.

At least she knew, because Dr Gupta in Assam had told her, that before Ayesha died an imam, a chaplain in the hospital, had said the prayers for the dying beside her and that he was sure she had recognized that he was there. And an ICU nurse would have been with her too. It was the imam who had telephoned Dr Gupta to tell him that his daughter had died, and to reassure him that she would be buried, very soon in accordance with Muslim custom, in the huge Muslim cemetery in south London called Eternal Gardens.

"I would like to bury her here at home beside her mother", Dr Gupta had said to Clare, "but it is not practical because of the virus. Most fortunately the imam is there to undertake the formalities required. I shall send the money for the funeral as he has instructed me."

"I am so sorry, Dr Gupta. This is extra hard for you at such a sad time."

She waited. She was now used to these pauses when she was talking to Ayesha's father.

"One more kindness I would ask of you, Mrs Wilson."

"Anything."

"The hospital has requested that someone should remove Ayesha's things. I understand there is a small bag. Would you be able to arrange for this bag to be collected? I know that you yourself cannot leave your isolation."

"Don't worry, Dr Gupta. That shouldn't be a problem at all."

"Thank you once more, Mrs Wilson. You will dispose of Ayesha's things as you think right, I know."

She had rung the local minicab firm she had used in the past to take her to King's Cross. "We can do that for you, Mrs Wilson. We have the PPE. We'll ring your bell downstairs and leave the bag at the door of your flat. Will you be paying by card over the phone?"

"Yes of course."

"We're sorry for your loss." This clearly wasn't the first time they'd collected the possessions of someone who'd died in the hospital.

She had made a small package, in a jiffy bag, of Ayesha's slippers, her smartphone, well wrapped, a beautiful silver necklace she had left in a drawer, and her prayer book, and Mr Clements had posted it to Dr Gupta. Ayesha's clothes she put away in a cupboard in Penny's room, to take to a charity shop later.

In the afternoon she walked up to the Park. There were more people about, though they were still carefully keeping the statutory two yards away from each other. There would probably be even more over the weekend and on Monday. Though the schools were still shut, half term was beginning, Monday was a bank holiday, and the poor parents struggling to keep their children doing school work at home could stop for a few days and take them outside to play. The government had so badly muddled the lockdown message in the last couple of weeks that the atmosphere, even in Kensington Gardens, not exactly a place of dissidence or unrest, was already different, as if people were observing the social distancing rules less because they were doing as they were told, more because they were still nervous of each other, partly perhaps on account of the shadowy possibility of "symptomless carriers", an unpleasant phrase apparently used all over horrible social media for scapegoating immigrants, Muslims, even people working in hospitals, some of whom had been actually attacked.

No longer "Stay At Home" but "Stay Alert": the government's latest maxim, no doubt from the same source of magical mantras as the empty promises "Take Back Control" and "Get Brexit Done", was just an empty slogan, since one of the few qualities of the virus that was certain was its invisibility. She watched the widely separated people walking down the Broad Walk towards her. She was supposed to be "alert", to what exactly? She had heard this morning on the Today programme that Dominic Cummings, the author of all these magical mantras, had travelled with his family two hundred and fifty miles from London to Durham, knowing he had the virus, in the worst patch of the epidemic when "Stay At Home" was meant to be mandatory for everyone, specially if they were ill. So much for trustworthiness. Penny had announced on the telephone. "Charles says MPs can't be saying one thing and doing another." Well, for once, good for Charles.

It was another sunny day. All through May, since Ayesha's death on the first day of the month, the sun had shone, it hadn't rained, and London was getting to be dry and dusty with the melancholy that overtakes anywhere accustomed to rain when no rain comes. The grass in the Park was turning yellow, as if it were late August in a dry summer. Clare had wished several times in the last two weeks since she had been able to come outside, and wished again today, for green country and the sound of water. She thought of her piece of Yorkshire, at its most beautiful at this moment in the year, with new leaves on the oaks and beeches and birches, and the brilliant green of new grass, and new green mixed with hawthorn blossom on the hedges, and bluebells and starry white wild garlic going over in the woods, and the running becks under the trees, and, somehow most evocative of all, the creamy lace of cow parsley high on every verge. If she could only replace Penny and Charles, when they came back to Barnes and stay alone in their house in Leckenby for a week or two—but she saw she couldn't possibly. Old people were still not supposed to travel anywhere because of the virus, and Penny would, reasonably, be offended if her mother only wanted to be in Yorkshire if Penny and Charles weren't there.

She had, after all, been more or less contented alone in her flat since Simon died, and since Hakim had come, and gone to Wood Green. Even after David's death had brought a different quality to her aloneness, she had been, as she always said to Penny, "fine". How long ago that seemed.

She sat on a bench in the Flower Walk, knowing no one would attempt to share the bench because of social distancing, and watched the people going by, not many people, long gaps between them, mostly the au pair girls or nannies with children in pushchairs or on scooters that had replaced the nannies of the past with their huge, shiny black prams. Since she was a child herself, brought here in the late 1940s by the old nanny who had looked after her mother as a child in Yorkshire and then looked after her in London, the Park, she thought as she often did, had changed little and the people had changed a great deal. Even in Kensington Gardens, and certainly a bit further west or north, along Kensington High Street or in Hammersmith or Shepherd's Bush, the mixture of faces, languages, kinds of people would have astonished anyone accustomed to come here seventy, fifty, even thirty years ago. This was good, very good, and the virus, for all its devastation, had reminded people, at least in London, how much they depended on the mixture of people who kept the hospitals and the care homes going. Even this dreadful government had had to change its mind, in less than a day, when it had ruled that while the families of immigrant doctors and nurses who died of the virus could stay in Britain the families of immigrant hospital porters and cleaners and care assistants who died of the virus couldn't. Soon they would have to change their dire decision that after Brexit no one could come to work in Britain who would earn less than twenty-five thousand pounds. Who would staff the hospitals and care homes then?

Not that you saw these indispensable people in the Flower Walk. The au pair girls and nannies might be English or eastern European or Filipino, the children they were looking after might be English or Indian or Russian or Arab, but neither the girls nor their charges were likely to be black. Clare thought of the black single mothers trying to home-school three or four children in flats in tower blocks in north Hammersmith or Paddington, and, worse, coping at the same time with an irritable, perhaps violent, cooped-up man, and with deaths from the virus in their parents' or grandparents' generation, among uncles and aunts and friends. She prayed for them and their children. She knew that, as with her nightly prayer for all who died today, it didn't matter that she didn't know their names. She thought of the Nigerian nurse who had talked to the dying boy from Libya in Ayesha's ward, and the imam who had prayed with Ayesha, and the nurse who, she was sure, had held her hand as she died.

She was hot and tired when she had walked home so instead of going at once up to the flat, she found in her bag her key to the square's garden, sat down there on another empty bench, her stick beside her, and stayed for half an hour doing nothing at all, not even thinking, not even praying. Perhaps it was a blessing brought by beginning to get really old that it was possible sometimes to do nothing without going to sleep and without worrying about things one should be doing.

She went up in the lift, for once, and heard from outside her door that agitating sound of the telephone ringing. This was, in all these months since September, only the third time this had happened. She fumbled for her key, found it, opened the door, and reached the kitchen as the telephone stopped. She dialled 1471. "The caller did not leave a number."

Damn. Damn. Damn. Why had she spent that empty, pointless half hour sitting in the square? Why hadn't she, for once, left the answering machine on?

She was certain, though she had no reason to be, that Hakim had tried to call her and failed.

If he had managed to telephone once, presumably he would be able to try again, wherever he was. All she had to do was to wait.

This convinced her for perhaps twenty minutes. Then her confidence left her. Probably the caller who didn't leave a number was one of the scam organizations she had learnt she should fear, though there had been many fewer such calls than usual during the pandemic.

She had given up hope and switched on the PM programme, in the middle of the regular, dispiriting Downing Street coronavirus briefing that began every day at five o'clock—hundreds of people were still dying every day and different ministers, told what to say, or what not to say, were each afternoon put in front of the press to say almost nothing—when the telephone rang again. Penny? It was her time of day for ringing, but she had rung yesterday. She turned off the wireless with one hand and picked up the telephone with the other.

"Hello."

A short silence.

"Hello Clare."

"Hakim—I don't believe it. How wonderful. Where are you?"

She sat down, her heart thudding, though she was not even surprised.

Another silence. A delay on the line.

"I am in Benghazi."

He knows. In his voice she could hear that he knew about Ayesha. She realized she wouldn't have to tell him, and was at once ashamed of the thought.

"Are you all right, Hakim?"

"No, Clare. I have talked to Ayesha's father."

"O, Hakim, I am so so sorry."

"Why did she stay in London when she said she would go to India? Why did she put herself in such danger? Clare, do you know why? I thought all through the weeks there have been that she was in Assam."

"It was too difficult to fly to India because of the virus. And then doctors just qualified like her were asked to help in the hospitals, so she did, of course she did. You know she would have. It was very brave and good of her."

"And it was very foolish. She did not ask me—"

"How could she, Hakim? She tried and tried. She sent you messages. I know because she was living here in the flat from the beginning of April."

"Stop, stop. I am sorry, Clare. She was in your flat? Why?"

"Because her landlady was afraid of the virus. She asked Ayesha to leave her room so Ayesha came here. I was so pleased to have her. She sent you emails, a lot of emails, and you didn't answer so she thought you were dead, kidnapped—that something terrible had happened to you."

A long silence.

"Hakim, are you still there?"

She heard him breathe in. He's crying.

"Yes. They took my phone. I begged them to let me send her a message. I did. It had to look like my first message. It had to say Haftar was bad. Then they took the phone away. Also they took my iPad. I had no way to email, to phone."

"We knew you were in trouble. Ayesha guessed there was something not right about that message. She was desperately worried."

Another long silence.

"I should never have let her—have let myself—I told you, Clare. I told you I am—"

"Hakim, you must not think that. She died because she was a good doctor who wanted to help. It was not in any possible way your fault."

He said nothing.

"Have you been in Benghazi all this time?"

"In Benghazi? No. Not until today, where I can buy a new phone."

"Where have you been?"

"Everywhere. I have done very much work in too little time. Until they captured me. I will tell you."

"Are you coming back? To London?"

"Now. Yes. I was going to try to reach Assam if Ayesha was there, although I would have to wait somewhere until there are flights to India. Even I have a visa for India. Now I discover that if I can find a way to get to Cairo, there is a flight to Frankfurt on Wednesday. Frankfurt is close to London. But a ticket is very expensive."

"How expensive?"

"One thousand dollars."

"Have you got any money?"

"No. They took my money, my American Express, everything. I still have my passport, which is a miracle—it is good luck that a Libyan passport is worth nothing—and I have my USB notes and photos, all the work I have done, which did not interest the fighters. My old professor in Benghazi has helped me since this morning. He has found me clothes and given me money for this phone. I can borrow the dollars from him for the air ticket, and for getting from here to Cairo, which is not simple. But I need to know that I am able to pay him the money before too long. Otherwise I should not take it. There is no university money in Benghazi to help me."

"Hakim. Listen. I will talk to the Museum. They may be willing to pay for the plane ticket. They're sure to want you back safe and sound. If they won't pay, I will. Don't worry. I can, quite easily."

She thought. Be practical. Sensible.

She said, " Can you send an email from that telephone?"

"Yes. Of course."

"Ask your professor exactly how he would like the money to be paid from London—bank details or whatever is necessary, and send the information to me in an email. Can you do that?"

"Yes. But Clare—"

She waited.

"I do not wish you—", he said.

"I know you don't. But it's not the time to fuss about money. I have some, which is lucky. So does the Museum. That's all. How much will the journey to Cairo cost?"

"Excuse me, Clare."

Voices, confused, for a minute or two.

"Clare. The professor says I will have to find a driver to take me to the frontier, and then an Egyptian driver to take me to Cairo. And some bribes at the frontier. The professor thinks five hundred dollars. It is a lot of money. I am sorry."

"Don't worry about it. Tell the professor that I'll make sure he gets the money on Monday."

She had no idea how this kind of thing was done, international money transfers, banking on line, but knew that it happened. She would have to appeal to the Museum to get the money quickly to the professor in Benghazi, and promise to pay them back if necessary. At least they had known her for years.

"Hakim. How will you travel from Frankfurt to London?"

"The trains are going from Frankfurt to Brussels and the Eurostar to London also."

"You must be able to pay for the trains as well. Ask the professor to give you an extra two hundred dollars. In fact, tell the professor I will make sure that he gets two thousand dollars on Monday, so that you will have enough to get back here for sure, with some dollars to spare in case anything goes wrong. "

"Clare I am not pleased for you to—"

She knew what he was trying to say: his English had slipped a bit in what had been nearly three hard months in Libya. She felt like saying, "Hakim, shut up and do as you're told", as if to a small child, but didn't.

"I said, don't worry about the money. Only worry about getting yourself to London." Then she added, "Are you all right yourself? You're not ill or anything?"

"I am not ill. I was injured. I was in a hospital in Tripoli, which was not good. I am not ill. I have lost Ayesha. I must work. It is all I have. So I must go back to London. Also I must leave Benghazi tomorrow. I must not put into danger the professor and his family."

"Certainly you mustn't. Injured? How?"

"You will see. I will tell you all the story."

"All right, Hakim. I hope to see you very soon. Take care."

Would she? See him very soon? It seemed difficult to believe. That there was a flight to Frankfurt from Cairo when she thought there were no flights from anywhere to anywhere was unlikely enough. But that he could somehow be driven all the way from Benghazi to Cairo, seven hundred and fifty desert miles, through lawless Libya to police-state Egypt, governed by an authoritarian general liable to chuck people into prison for no reason, with frontier guards demanding dollars between the two, and heaven knows how many roadblocks manned by twitchy teenagers with machine-guns—it seemed hardly possible and very frightening.

Neither of them had said anything about how the virus might affect the journey. Probably he had no idea of how strange London had become, and no doubt Frankfurt and Brussels too. But he was starting in his own country, his own part of the world, his own language, so he was likely to be able to manage, if anyone could, the road to Cairo, with dollars to help, and no doubt he would be put right about masks and distancing and all the virus precautions in Germany and Belgium and nearly empty European trains. So she should hope he would make it.

She could. She did. He was alive.

After she had made a cup of tea, she opened her laptop and Hakim's email with the name of the professor and the instructions for sending money to a bank account belonging to the university in Benghazi had already arrived. Modern communications could work at this extraordinary speed. Or not. Ayesha cut off from Hakim, and never again hearing his voice, never again reading an email that was properly from him to her, because they, whoever they were, wherever they were, had taken his telephone and his iPad, which, Ayesha had told her, he had bought specially to make the notes for his report on the stones.

Clare looked up exchange rates on the Internet to see what two thousand dollars was in pounds. What was the time? Quarter to six, the kitchen clock said. Could she ring the only moderately friendly head of Hakim's department at the Museum? She would, anyway.

This time he answered the telephone himself.

"This is Clare Wilson. I'm so sorry to bother you again."

"That's all right, Mrs Wilson. I'm in the garden. Hold on a minute. I can hear better in the house."

Noises for a brief moment.

"Mrs Wilson? Good. What can I do for you? I'm afraid we haven't heard a peep from Husain."

He had remembered. That was something.

"He's just rung me, from Benghazi."

"Has he stayed in Cyrenaica all this time? I gather the World Heritage people are more concerned about Sabratha."

"He's certainly been further west, and he says he's done lots of work but he's had a very difficult time. He was captured, I don't know by who, and he's been in hospital in Tripoli with some injury. He's desperate to get back to London, and he's found a flight, from Cairo, but—"

"He's got no money. Is that it? "

"Well, yes. I'm afraid so."

"We've got no money either. I don't know whether you've noticed—there's been a bit in the papers about it—the Museum's being rottenly treated by the government. We're called an arms-length institution, as you probably know, and because of that we seem to have fallen into some sort of bureaucratic swamp between the DCMS and the Treasury, and we've got the unions on our backs as well. So the whole furlough thing is going to cost us an arm and a leg. I simply daren't commit a bean to anything extra at the moment. The finance people would have me for breakfast."

"I didn't expect there'd be any spare money. I'm happy to pay for the plane ticket and the rest of his travel to get him back."

"Are you sure, Mrs Wilson? How much money are we talking about?"

"Two thousand dollars. About sixteen hundred pounds."

"Good heavens. That seems a bit steep. We'd like to have Husain back, of course. He's a useful chap and a proper workaholic. But wouldn't it be more sensible for him to stay where he is for the time being—he's in his own country after all—until all this Covid stuff settles down and there are normal flights?"

"From what he said, I think he's in considerable danger. He's also just out of hospital and I don't know how bad his injuries are. If he stays in Benghazi he'll definitely make things dangerous for his old professor who's helping him at the moment. He needs to get out of the city as soon as possible. The professor will give him enough money to get him to England, but he needs to be paid back as quickly as can be managed. Libya isn't at all easy for anyone at the moment, you know."

"I do know that, and I understand what you're saying but I really don't see how I can help."

"I was hoping you might just allow your office to help. I can produce the money, but I'm too old to be any good at the Internet, so I was hoping you'd be kind enough to ask your secretary to deal with getting the money to Benghazi. I can pay the Museum back immediately."

A pause. Please God, Clare said without speaking.

"It's very generous of you, I must say, but I suppose you know what you can afford."

"I do, yes." This sounded sharper than she meant it to. Damn.

Another pause.

"Mrs Wilson. Are you absolutely positive it was Husain on the telephone?"

"What do you mean? Of course I am."

"There are all sorts of dodgy people about, you know. Plenty of crooks cashing in on the virus. Pretending to be stranded in some impossible country and asking for money is an old trick."

"No. I mean, you're quite right to ask me. But no. I'm sure it was him. I do know him pretty well."

"Well, the risk is yours. And you seem to feel some sort of responsibility for young Husain, though I've no idea why you should."

She couldn't answer this, so she waited.

"All right. Have you got the bank details and so on?"

"Yes, I have. From the professor himself."

Another pause.

"OK then, I don't see why not. Here's my secretary's email." He rattled it off, and Clare, ready with a pencil, wrote it down. "She's at home of course like everyone else, but she is working, dealing with emails and so on. Husain's not the only one stuck in the wrong country. She'll certainly know what to do."

"I'm most grateful. Thank you so much. I'll put a cheque in the first class post tomorrow morning."

"That sounds very old-world, but I suppose the Museum can still cope with cheques, though the whole place is bolted and barred at the moment except for the security people. You'd better have my secretary's snail mail address as well. I expect she knows what to do with a cheque. Hold on while I find it." Three or four minutes went by before he reappeared. "Sorry, can't find anything in this house. Here it is." He rattled off an address in Fulham.

"Thank you again."

"Not at all. I think you're quite mad but if that's what you want to do, it's no skin off my nose. Goodbye now."

Thinking that both his wife and his secretary had a good deal to put up with, she wrote a calm, orderly and grateful email to the secretary, and received a friendly, obliging reply a quarter of an hour later. "Yes, we can do that. And we'll expect your cheque asap—the post is a bit peculiar at the moment. I'm glad to hear Hakim's OK. All the best, Holly."

Good Holly.

What in that conversation had reminded her of David? Certainly not the man himself. Ah, yes. DCMS. The Department of Digital, Culture, Media and Sport, the government masters of the Museum, the British Library, the National Gallery, the Royal Opera House, the National Theatre among much too much else. "For heaven's sake", she could hear David saying. "So much for civilization. Leave out the first comma and you have a description of most of what's in the heads of practically everyone these days. They change the minister every five minutes, choose people who've never read a book, and whoever they choose will spend most of their time thinking about football and Rupert Murdoch and how to do in the BBC."

Saturday, Sunday, Monday, Tuesday somehow went by, very slowly. She went out each morning early, as usual, for a short a time as possible, leaving the wretched answering machine on, checking it at once when she got back. Nothing. Silence. A call from Penny after tea on Sunday, saying her soda bread was even better than her ordinary bread. "And the first roses are nearly out." Never mind the roses. If she'd been in Yorkshire herself, Hakim would never have found her.

He was dead, after all. The car he was in had been hit by a Turkish shell from a drone fired at Haftar's militia. He'd been kidnapped for a huge ransom on the desert road to Egypt. He had gangrene and was dying of sepsis. His dollars had all been stolen at the border.

He rang in the middle of Wednesday morning.

"Hakim. I'm so glad to hear you. Where are you?"

"I am in the airport at Cairo."

He sounded very tired.

"Thank goodness. Was the journey very difficult?"

"It was—complicated. I will tell you. But I am here. I will be able to be on the plane for Frankfurt, which is flying quite soon. I am not permitted to leave the airport in Frankfurt, so the trains are not possible, but there are two or three flights every day from Frankfurt to London. I will call you again to tell when I am able to arrive."

"Any time will be very good. Take care."

Where would he sleep if he couldn't get on a flight tonight? In the airport? People do.

He must have, slept in the airport, because there was more silence for another day and a half, until he telephoned at five-thirty on Thursday. Not Penny but Hakim.

"Clare. I am at Heathrow."

"Thank God."

He sounded brighter, less exhausted.

"I shall be at your flat in an hour or so."

"Are you getting a taxi?"

"I will go to my friend the Piccadilly Line. I hope I will—if there are no problems with the immigration officers."

"O, Hakim. Have you got anything to show them from the Museum?"

"I have a photograph on my phone of the money transfer from the Museum to the university in Benghazi. I had left Benghazi when the money came but the professor sent me the photograph."

Good Holly. And resourceful professor.

"Let's hope that's enough."

"They can look up my permission to stay, permission to work, all these permissions, on the Home Office computer. The Museum money and the permissions should be enough."

Please God, again Clare didn't say.

"Also I had enough dollars to buy a Covid 19 test in Frankfurt airport. It was very expensive but it was negative, so I have the test result to show also. Clare, I should tell you that I am looking terrible. I look like a Barbary pirate."

"I don't care how you look. At least you are in England."

"I will be outside the flat very soon."

She went back to Matt's room, as she had done over and over again since Friday, to make sure there was no trace of Ayesha to be seen or detected. She opened the window wide. Early summer in the square. She thought of Hakim at the beginning of March, going alone across the road with her key to say goodbye to the square. She and Ayesha had watched him. That was before anyone in England was saying anything about the virus, though it was now clear that they should have been. If the country had been locked down ten days earlier than it was, some of the scientists were now saying, half the people who had died would still be alive. Hakim would never have left London, and perhaps Ayesha— it was no good, she knew, imagining what grand historians nowadays called counterfactuals. What had happened had happened.

She looked to her right, seeing again Hakim and Ayesha walking side by side along the pavement, out of her life, she had thought, at least for a while.

It was after half-past seven when the intercom bell rang from the street door of the building. She had done her best to assume for those two hours that no news was good news.

"Hakim. You've arrived."

She pushed the button to open the street door and went out of the flat to wait by the lift.

He came out of the lift, carrying a plastic bag from Frankfurt airport. He had a black patch over one eye, a white mask over his nose and mouth, and his left arm in a sling. He bowed. No hand to the heart because of the airport bag.

"Clare. I am so happy to see you."

"Come in, Hakim, I can't tell you—"

She couldn't go on, and didn't have to say anything for a few minutes as he left his bag in the hall, said, "Excuse me, Clare", and disappeared into the cloakroom.

He emerged eventually and said, "It is difficult to wash one hand properly. Would you want me to wear this mask?"

"No, Hakim. Take it off. You've tested negative for the virus, and I'm not going to get it now—I may even have had it without any symptoms. There was no problem with the immigration people?"

"Not really. A small delay. But because I was with arrivals from Frankfurt and I had been tested for coronavirus, they didn't seem to worry about Libya. They looked me up on their computer and all was OK."

"Thank God."

She smiled at him, then pulled herself together.

"What would you like? There's tarragon chicken for supper, but would you like apple juice or mint tea or coffee first?"

Not knowing when he would arrive or what he would feel like, she had cut up the chicken and left it, in its sauce, with cream and mushrooms, in a warm oven.

"I would like coffee please, Clare."

"Sit down in the sitting room. You must be exhausted. I'll bring some coffee, and you can start to tell me—"

She made some strong coffee for Hakim and some camomile tea for her, and took them into the sitting room where Hakim was standing with his back to the door looking out of the window.

He turned as she came in.

"Please. Tell me about Ayesha."

Now he did sit down, in his old chair, Simon's chair, and with his right hand picked up the coffee cup from its saucer. He listened, his head down, the cup in his hand, his coffee untasted, the eye Clare could see shut, as motionless as if he had been a carved stone figure.

"I see", at last he said, without looking up. "If I had been still in London, I could not have stopped her working for the coronavirus patients, could I?"

"No. I don't think you could."

"Where is she buried?"

"I know the name of the cemetery. It's somewhere on the edge of London. We'll be able to find out exactly—"

For three or four long minutes he said nothing. Then, still without looking up, he said, "I loved her, Clare. I loved her also. I thought after Samira died that I could not. But I did."

"I know."

"I should not have left her for my stones. She would not have been so sad, so afraid, when it seemed I was lost and it seemed I might be dead—I could have been dead—and if she had been more calm maybe she would not have caught the coronavirus."

"Hakim, you mustn't blame yourself. Really, you mustn't. Many doctors and nurses have died of the virus, though of course many more haven't. It was only bad luck that she caught it and became so very ill. Even her father thought it was only bad luck."

"I should have been in London."

At last he looked up, his one visible eye full of misery.

Clare, sitting opposite him in her usual chair, with her back to the window, raised a hand in a hopeless gesture, and let her hand fall.

"Your eye, Hakim", after a while she said, "What's happened to your eye?"

"My eye is gone."

"What?" For a moment she thought she might be sick. She put her hand to her mouth, swallowed. "O no, Hakim—how dreadful."

"It is gone. A very good doctor tried to save it but it is gone. There was debris, shrapnel, after the truck I was in was shelled. It was shelled from a Turkish aeroplane, on the road to Tripoli from the south, from the desert, where I was taken after the battle in Sabratha. Something hit my eye, with much pain, very much pain."

"How horrible. I can't imagine—and how terrifying."

"I don't remember, except for pain, what happened until I woke up in the hospital. There were cloths—what are they called in English?—the cloths for dead bodies in ancient Egypt—?"

"Bandages?"

"Bandages, yes. There were bandages round my head, round my eyes. I could see only darkness. I was afraid, of course. I could hear people near me, groaning, one man shouting. I was trying to take the bandages off. My hand, one hand, was covered in bandages too. I knew nothing, where I had woken up, what had happened to me. Nothing."

"Where was the hospital?"

"The hospital was in Tripoli. Once it was a special hospital for eyes, with very good doctors, but now most of the patients have all sorts of different wounds from the fighting. The professor for eyes was still in the hospital. He tried to save my eye but it was impossible."

"Your glasses? How can you see?"

"My glasses I lost. I must get a contact lens for my eye, the doctor said. That will be now in London."

"Was the hospital terrible?"

"Not terrible, but too many patients. The doctors were doing the best they could. Most of the wounded people were much more ill than I was. There has been so much fighting, in Tripoli, near Tripoli, along the roads, at the airport, hospitals bombed and the camps for the people trying to cross the sea to Europe bombed also. Most of the bombing and killing is done by Haftar from Cyrenaica, with planes and tanks and armoured cars from Russia and Egypt, paid for by the oil emirs in the Gulf who think there are Islamists in Tripoli. There are, Islamists in Tripoli, but they are not the important fighters. The important fighters are Syrians, Syrians from their civil war fight on both sides in Libya, for money, and the planes and other machines of the war, that fight against Haftar, planes, drones and more tanks, are Turkish. This is new. Turkey's help to the government in Tripoli is now defeating Haftar and his Russians. One whole year there has been fighting in Tripoli, near Tripoli. Now Haftar has almost lost. That is how I got back to Benghazi, with Russian fighters who are giving up the fighting in Tripoli. I was three weeks in the hospital. I had no money so why they could look after me I don't know. I think the Russians had money to pay. Two of them were in the hospital also, one with both legs broken. The other one, who could walk, came to find me and told me we have to leave Tripoli as soon as possible when a truck was going. He would come to tell me. He did. We left the man with broken legs. What will happen to him I fear. The truck was going to Tobruk. They took me to Benghazi which is on the road."

"Goodness, Hakim, what a story. How lucky you were to be rescued and looked after in the hospital. I can hardly believe it. But I don't understand who captured you in the first place and took your telephone and your money. That wasn't Russians?"

"That was Syrian militia fighters. I was in Leptis, but only for two days. I wanted to get to the other side of Tripoli, to Sabratha because I was told in Leptis—there are in Leptis some people still taking some care of the stones, official people, paid by the government in Tripoli—that Sabratha had had much fighting and the site is damaged. So I got a lift with some GNA fighters—that is fighters for the government in Tripoli—who were in a convoy going to Sabratha. On the way Syrians fighting for Haftar ambushed the truck I was in, the last truck in the line, and killed the fighters. I was a prisoner because I was not a fighter and they were surprised to find me. Maybe they thought someone would pay a ransom for me. Then in the battle in Sabratha I escaped—that was easy because there was only chaos, not in the stones but in the town, and I hid in the stones with some families, women, children, old people who had been too afraid to stay in the town. They had even a little food.

"When there was no more noise in the town they went back. They hoped that their homes were not bombed. I don't know. I stayed in Sabratha two more days, looking, looking so carefully and trying to remember what I saw. Then I went to the road, the empty road, hoping I don't know what, for help, any help, also for food—and Russians came, escaping south into the desert because they had lost Sabratha. They picked me up. I was afraid of them. The GNA soldiers had told me the Russians had nerve gas. They had gassed and shot GNA fighters. But they also were surprised to find me, and they were good to me. One even spoke a little English, better English than Arabic. He had fought everywhere, this Russian, in Crimea, in Ukraine, in Syria of course. The Russians had fought IS in Syria and cleared them out of Palmyra. That was good. In Libya fighting for Haftar has been not so good. But he told me the Russians think Haftar is finished, has lost too much. President Putin will support Saif al-Islam instead."

Hakim raised his hand, palm upwards, in what would have been his old gesture of rueful despair if his other hand hadn't been bandaged and in a sling.

"Saif al-Islam?" Clare said.

Hakim leant forward. "Saif al-Islam Gaddafi. The Great Leader's son. The only one alive."

"Heavens above—", Clare said, "Gaddafi still?"

"Still."

"Is he as bad as his father?"

Hakim's hand, turned over, outstretched, see-sawing.

"He is more complicated. He is less mad. Everyone in all of Libya knows him, and he is younger of course than Haftar. For Putin who wants power in Libya he might do well. But he might be very bad for Libya. He is not to be trusted, not at all. He is a friend of important people in Europe and America but he is not honest. He has a doctorate from the LSE—is that what it is called?"

"Yes, my husband was—"

Hakim could not even pause.

"But the doctorate was not real. Other people wrote his thesis. And, much worse than a dishonest doctorate, he has ordered torture in Libya, as his father did. In the past, but a torturer is a torturer."

Suddenly he stopped talking, as if all his energy had been used up. His head dropped.

"Hakim. You're so tired. Come and have something to eat. And then you must go to bed and have a long, peaceful sleep."

He raised his head and looked at her as if he wasn't sure where he was. Then understanding returned as he registered what she had just said.

"Yes. Thank you, Clare. It was cold, sleeping on a chair in the airport. But nobody told me to go away."

He wasn't too tired to be hungry. He ate like a child who is so pleased with his favourite food that he can think only about one thing at a time, which is that he is enjoying it. She asked him no questions.

After supper he said, "That was very good. Thank you, Clare."

"Now go to bed, Hakim. It doesn't matter when you wake up."

By the end of the following day Hakim's life, and therefore Clare's life, were for the time being settled.

In the morning—he hadn't appeared until after eleven, when he came into the kitchen, apologetic and polite as ever—he had spoken to his boss on the telephone about fetching his work laptop, his briefcase, and the clothes he had left in his suitcase in the Museum. "All I possess is in that case. I took it from Wood Green to store it in the coat cupboard of the department until I came back to London with Ayesha." Clare had said it might be difficult to get into the Museum to fetch his stuff on account of lockdown, though some rules had been relaxed in the last week.

"He seemed surprised to hear me. 'So it was you', he said. I didn't understand. But then he seemed a little pleased that I am back, and when I told him I have my USB sticks and I need my work laptop he said he would ask security to let me into the building by the nearest door to the department, so that I can collect my things."

While he was out, with his mask for the Piccadilly Line, she got Simon's study ready for him to use as an office while everyone was working from home. She hadn't felt so positive, so cheerful, so pleased to have something constructive to do since she had got Matt's room ready for Ayesha nearly two months ago. Ayesha—She shook her head, and went to fetch a dustpan and brush and a duster.

She had asked a colleague of Simon's, all those years ago when he died, to go through the books, files of notes, papers on his desk, in case anything might be useful to anyone at the LSE. The colleague had taken a couple of boxes away and Clare had chucked the rest of the papers and files, incomprehensible to her or to Penny as they were and would remain. Most of Simon's books were still on the shelves but his big kneehole desk, with lots of drawers and a filing cabinet built into it, a present from his parents when she and Simon had moved into the flat more than fifty years ago, was cleared and empty. Hakim hadn't needed a desk when he first lived in the flat and was always working in the Museum. Now he did, and here one was. The room wasn't all that neglected-looking. She had hoovered and dusted it from time to time all these years, so that it didn't disappear under Miss Havisham cobwebs, and the old Persian rug on the floor was the same as ever.

She looked round the small room as if she'd never seen it properly before. It was an indoor sort of room. The window, like the kitchen window, looked across the yard to the back of the next tall, uninteresting row of large nineteenth-century houses similar to this one. In the past, no doubt, this had been where the cook, probably an overworked "cook-general", had slept, in the days when no one would have lived in this kind of flat without at least one servant. Whoever they were, between the wars, say, would have probably had a daily charwoman as well, and, if they had children, a nanny, sleeping alongside the youngest child in Penny's room, the night nursery, with Matt's room the day nursery. Before the first war the whole house—the terraces that formed the square were built in the 1870s, in high Victorian prosperity—would have had a single family and lots of servants living in it. *Upstairs Downstairs*. A world well lost.

Simon had always liked to have his desk sideways on to the window, so that he wasn't directly looking into bright sunshine—the back of the building faced south—and so that if he raised his head from his work he could look across the desk to a wall with two bookcases to the ceiling and between them a large framed map of Yorkshire in the sixteenth century, a present from Clare's mother long, long ago, which he liked in spite of not much liking Yorkshire itself, and, on a lower bookshelf across the middle of the wall photographs of Matt in military uniform and Penny as a pretty VI Form schoolgirl which he'd had in his room at the LSE. Clare had taken these off the bookshelf and put them away in a drawer in her bedroom. There was a reasonably comfortable small armchair beside a standard lamp, a solid Windsor chair at the desk, an old Anglepoise on it, and ancient red and gold linen William Morris curtains, which she had washed the day before yesterday in the hope that Hakim really would manage the journey. It was a room that was at its best at night with the curtains drawn, in the silence of the back of the building.

Would Hakim be still here in the autumn? In the winter? There was no telling. Neither he nor Clare had needed to say anything about him staying, now, in the flat. Here he was, and he had for the time being nowhere else to go. Over the coffee and toast and marmalade—"I had forgotten marmalade, how good it is"—he had told her that several bones in his hand as well as two fingers had been broken in the shelling of the truck, he had no idea how. Because they were trying to save his eye, no one in the hospital had done anything about his hand for several days. It was now set and in plaster but because of the delay it wasn't going to look right, though they had told him in Tripoli that he should be able to use it for most things. Clare had made him a clean sling.

That afternoon over cups of tea, mint and camomile, she asked him about his stones.

He had come back with his suitcase, into which he had managed to stuff his briefcase, with his laptop inside that. He was delighted with Simon's study and the empty desk. He hadn't seen the room before, though he had lived in the flat for months.

"It is wonderful, Clare. The desk—it is not sad for you if I use the desk?"

"No. Not at all. My husband would have been very pleased for you to use it."

Suddenly he looked stricken.

"I wish—"

He didn't finish the sentence.

"Of course you do", Clare said. "Peace be upon her, Hakim. All we can do is pray and remember."

"Yes", he said. "I know."

He bent his head.

After a minute she said, "Now, go and unpack your things and I'll make some tea."

A quarter of an hour later they had settled in the sitting room, Hakim in his usual chair, Clare in hers and tea on the low table. Shopping in the morning while he was still asleep, she had bought a cake. Cakes reminded her of David, and of Ayesha who liked them, but she would never have bought one just for herself.

"Tell me about the stones", she said.

His face creased with anguish. He put down his mug.

"It is bad. It is not Palmyra. No one has blown up a building, a temple, a church, a theatre. But there is much harm, damage, careless damage which shows a scorn or a hate for the stones. This kind of damage is worst, or the worst that I saw, in Cyrene."

"O no. Beautiful Cyrene."

"I could not find that there had been looting. I was not sure. I was not there for long enough to be sure. But the stupid people who have done the damage are too ignorant to steal antiquities, I think. There are graffiti—words in Arabic spray-painted on stones, on columns, in temples and churches and the walls of Greek and Roman houses in Cyrene. Red and black words. I have never seen graffiti on any ruins in Libya until now. The paint can be taken off, yes, but it needs skill and time and therefore money, and there is no government in Haftar's Libya so there is no protection, no work happening at the sites. There are graffiti also at Apollonia, and terrible litter because of the beach. But at Cyrene worse than graffiti is building."

"Building?"

"On the edges of the city people have taken stones to build houses. They say the land is theirs. They have no history, no love—My professor in Benghazi has done everything possible," with his colleagues, to appeal to Marshal Haftar himself and what pretends to be a government in Tobruk, but they are not interested in stones. The priority is fighting the government in Tripoli. If Haftar loses this war, which he will soon I think, the fighting will not stop. There are tribes who have fought each other always. Gaddafi was strong enough to prevent this fighting. But now—The peace and law and policemen, not fighters, which are necessary to rescue the stones will not come back soon."

"And Sabratha?'

She saw the theatre, the blue of the Mediterranean behind its arches and the carving of the frieze, as she asked the question.

He drank a little of his tea.

"Sabratha is different. The Tripoli government has tried to protect Leptis. I saw nothing so bad there. But in Sabratha there are two things. There has been real fighting, as I told last night, and before I was there the stones have been damaged by shots and mortars, some damage is serious, but, again, there could be repairs by skilled restorers, if any are left and could be paid. But also there is the sea. The sea has moved further to the stones, to the baths, and specially to the two churches. The sea has always moved. The port of Sabratha has been lost to the sea for a long time. But if care and money and real archaeologists do not come soon to save Sabratha more and more of it will disappear. This is—"

He stopped, his head dropped as it had last night, but not because he was nearly asleep.

"Hakim?" she said, after a moment or two.

He raised his head and looked at her, his back straight, his one eye bright and direct.

"This is what I shall do. When there is peace in Libya, which will one day come, I shall raise the money somehow, the people, the skills, to save Sabratha. It is too valuable to be lost. I have decided. For Samira, for Ayesha, who are dead, I shall save Sabratha which is only stones."

She saw him relax.

He picked up his mug, drank some more tea, put down the mug, and took a bite out of his slice of cake.

"Yes", she said. "You will. I'm sure you will."

The next day was Saturday. After breakfast she sent Hakim out to do a little shopping and get her paper. It was good for him to go out, before he settled down at Simon's desk to sort out his notes and begin to plan his report. "My report. My first step."

A little after nine, Penny telephoned.

"Hello Mum. Good news. We're coming back to London this afternoon."

"I thought you were enjoying the lockdown?"

"Well, I did enjoy it, yes, to start with. The spring was lovely up here. But it gets a bit boring in the end and Charles is really keen to get back to the House, though how it's all going to work with the social distancing God knows. It looks as if they're going to have to take turns actually to be there. Charles says it's very important for the party to get the House going again. He says everyone's forgotten about Brexit because of the pandemic and the party's got to remind Boris to get on with it. How are you anyway, Mum?"

"O, I'm fine, darling, much the same as usual."

"Still sticking to the rules, I hope?"

"O yes. I do go for a walk in the Park sometimes, which is allowed now, even for the ancient. And I'm writing a book."

"Really? What about?"

"O, this and that. My life, I suppose."

"Goodness, Mum. Will anyone be—Well, don't put us in it, will you? Charles would have a fit. But I'm sure it's good for you to have something to do. I tell you what, Mum. I'll come and see you sometime next week if the weather stays fine. We could sit in the square with two yards of fresh air between us, and have a catch-up. You can't come to Barnes yet, obviously. There's no way of getting you there without you being too close to somebody. That'd be nice wouldn't it? A proper chat in the square, I mean. We haven't seen you for ages and there's something I want to talk to you about."

"All right, darling. That should work. Just let me know when you want to come."

"OK, Mum. See you very soon then. Lots of love. 'Bye."

"Something I want to talk to you about": that was going to be David's house and the flat. Penny was very persistent. The answer was going to be no. They would have to wait until she died—they had no idea that she might very easily have already died—and they could then decide what they wanted to do with both the flat and David's house. And Barnes. Penny and Charles, Carrie. and Daisy. Three places to live, all worth lots of money. Plenty to go round.

One day, one way or another, Penny and Charles were bound to discover that Hakim was living and working in the flat. They wouldn't like it. Well, tough.

She put the telephone back in its place and walked round the kitchen table to where her laptop waited for her to do some work on the book. She didn't open it but put her hand on its grey top with the apple upside down.

Penny was right to ask. She'd almost said, "Will anyone be interested?" In your not very interesting life, she meant. Well, that was the question.

She had asked it of herself often enough, and was profoundly uncertain of the answer. Probably not, she usually felt, but then, sometimes she thought, her own life, in these Brexit times when too many people didn't care any more about even the recent past, might mean a little, and not only to those as old as she was or even older? And the lives of David and Hakim and Ayesha were, at least, the lives of people one by one, each of them, as every life is, also the whole world.

Anyway, there was always the narrow line, on which we all have to get through each day, between the hill of beans and eternal memory. "On, on", as the two old men in *Waiting for Godot* say to each other.

She smiled to herself, as she went to look out of the sitting room window, and heard Hakim's key in the lock as he came back from the shops.